Into the Mist

A NOVEL

Sharon Mikeworth

River Nation Publishing

Into the Mist

River Nation Publishing
111 N 3rd Street #1021
Smithfield, NC 27577

The library of Congress has cataloged the hardcover edition as follows:
Publisher's Cataloging-in-Publication Data

provided by Five Rainbows Cataloging Services

Names: Mikeworth, Sharon, author.

Title: Into the mist / Sharon Mikeworth.

Description: Smithfield, NC : River Nation Publishing, 2025.

Identifiers: LCCN 2024926385 (print) | ISBN 978-1-7349365-6-8 (hardcover) | ISBN 978-1-7349365-5-1 (paperback) | ISBN 978-1-7349365-4-4 (ebook)

Subjects: LCSH: Time travel--Fiction. | Grief--Fiction. | Disasters--Fiction. | Historical fiction. | Suspense fiction. | Romance fiction. | BISAC: FICTION / Romance / Time Travel. | FICTION / Romance / Suspense. | FICTION / Romance / Historical / Victorian. | GSAFD: Love stories. | Suspense fiction. | Historical fiction.

Classification: LCC PS3613.I I465 I58 2025 (print) | LCC PS3613.I I465 (ebook) | DDC 813/.6--dc23.

Cover image by Shutterstock
Design by Lighthouse24

To Dawn

Into the Mist

One

Barely pausing, Cheyenne grabbed her phone off the kitchen counter where she'd left it, marched back through the house, and walked out the door.

It would seem amazing to her later how quickly it happened. No more than three seconds of frozen silence at the sight that greeted her as, like Eve, her eyes were opened and she was given the knowledge, followed by maybe seven more before she was leaving again. Ten seconds, and her life was over.

Rounding the front of the car, she registered a blur of movement off to the side and heard her neighbor Susan call out, "Hey stranger!"

But she wasn't having it. *Not today.*

A high-pitched buzzing intruded upon her shock as she flung open the door and climbed inside. "Dammit," she croaked as bright spots danced before her eyes. Sucking in a breath, she jammed the key in to start the engine.

The sordid scene she'd walked in on played through her mind again—undeniable, irrevocable. *This is it*, she thought, face creasing in anguish. *This is really it.*

"Just go," she whispered, shifting into reverse.

Not even glancing at the front of the house to see if he was coming out—it didn't matter if he was; she wouldn't be talking to him—she took her foot off the brake and, blinking away tears, backed down the driveway.

SHE DROVE AIMLESSLY, making huge roundabout circles, trying to figure out what to do.

One thing was certain, she was never sleeping under that roof again. Not after everything and not with the image of Brent and Serena now burned indelibly into her brain.

Her best friend Jill's was no longer an option since she'd moved two states away to Virginia. And her brother Caleb's place wouldn't work either with his spare bedroom being taken up by the guy he roomed with.

Which left her mother's one-bedroom apartment that was so tiny it contained only a loveseat and a chair in the cramped living room. A memory of her father seated on the couch at his house before he passed away flickered through her mind. She wouldn't have been able to stand staying there anyway, not with the girlfriend, who'd been the cause of her parents' divorce, also living there.

Focus, she told herself, noticing she'd drifted over the center line. Easing the car back over, she looked up and spotted another road not far ahead. *Good, I can let this guy get around me.*

She turned onto the road and thought she'd succeeded in losing the truck that had been following close behind her, but then she saw it turn as well.

A hotel was what she needed. Somewhere to go until she could decide what to do. And tomorrow would be soon enough for that. For now she just wanted to get some sleep and stop thinking about what she'd walked in on, a sleazy tableau that kept popping into her head over and over.

With a start she realized she'd zoned out again and been momentarily oblivious to the fact that she was now being seriously tailgated by the man scowling at her in the rearview.

She increased her speed as far as she felt comfortable with on the narrow, twisting road and held it there. The guy matched it for a while as if he could will her to go faster, or was contemplating pushing her out of the way, and then finally backed off.

He was no longer on her bumper, but she could see him back there trailing at a steady distance. And to make matters worse, now that the sun had begun to go down, a slight mist had formed, reducing the visibility.

As she came around a curve and started into a dip, the car was suddenly enveloped in a white haze so thick it nearly obscured the pavement ahead of her. She hit the brakes, then afraid the guy would rear-end her, let back off again.

She thought when the road leveled out it would clear up, but if anything, it only seemed to worsen. She peered through the windows, trying to see past the fog she was moving through, but only caught glimpses of bare dormant trees.

Her nerves were so taut she was ready to pull the car over and let the man go around her, but there was nowhere safe to do it there on the narrow, winding road.

All thoughts of Brent and what she'd seen had left her head and all she could think about was how badly she wanted that truck, which had reappeared behind her, off her ass. As if it were some physical manifestation of the monstrous knowledge she now had, it seemed to be looming back there, following her, and just as inescapable.

There! An opening in the trees.

She slapped on the blinker, stomped down on the brake, and whipped it in. She bounced in her seat as the wheels jolted over what she saw was scarcely more than a buckled strip of asphalt in the process of being covered by weeds. Clearly it hadn't been used in a long time.

Lights reflected off the side mirror, and she glanced up and got a quick look at the truck—black with huge tires—as it accelerated past. Lowering the window, she listened to the decreasing sound of it as it moved away.

And then it was gone.

She slumped in her seat, exhaling in relief. After a second, she straightened up and clicked her beams to bright and then back to dim again in an effort to see. The mist rising from the ground seemed to be heavier here off the main road surrounded by the trees.

Pressing down on the gas, she crept forward to find a place to turn around in. A decent room with a soft bed. That's all she wanted. She could have a nice hot shower and maybe a glass of wine.

Bumping slowly along, she was beginning to think she might have to attempt to back her way out, when she came upon a track leading off what was left of the old pavement, which had been steadily narrowing and becoming more eroded the farther she went. She veered to the right and found herself in an area so overgrown with vegetation it had climbed overhead into a sort of canopy.

This might have been a mistake, she thought as the longer branches scraped their way down the sides of the car.

Then she was out of it and moving along a gently curving section that had fared better than the previous part. It looked like the remains of a driveway, one that would hopefully loop back around.

THE HOUSE THE drive led to was old and obviously abandoned but still magnificent. It was fairly large and encompassed so many elements it was hard to take it all in. She brought the car to a stop and studied the complicated structure. The Victorian façade featured an eclectic array of windows—rectangular, arched, oval, and bay—a steeply pitched roofline with actual turrets, inset balconies, and a long verandah that ran the length of the home. Slender, round posts resting on rough brick bases seemed to be holding up the gabled roof of it fairly well except for one section that was leaning a bit. It had lengths of gingerbread woodwork, mostly intact, hanging from the top of it that matched the trim of the verandah railing. And below it, latticework covered the dark space underneath. She raised her eyes. In the center of each octagonal turret, wrought-iron embellishments pointed at the sky. *Lightning rods?*

All in all, including the basement, which she could see the windows of in the brick foundation, she counted four levels. The basement, two stories, and probably some attic space.

Just sitting there empty, left to fall into disrepair and be forgotten.

What a waste. She turned her head, shifting in her seat, and gazed around her at the overgrown land surrounding the home. The areas between the larger maples, elms, oaks, and hedges had nearly filled in with undergrowth, but the bones of what must have once been a beautifully landscaped property were still apparent.

Through the trees, she could see something pale, a fountain or some sort of statue. There was a muddy circle of water over by the house amongst decaying benches and tangled rose bushes that had probably been a fishpond at one point. And some of the less overrun spots, loosely bordered by rocks and containing a few plants tenaciously clinging to life, spoke of gone-to-weed flower beds.

Twisting back around, she shifted the car into gear and got going again.

Just past a large stone block she thought might have been to mount horses, she rolled to a stop across from the front steps and switched off the headlights.

All was still. And silent, she noticed, listening. No animals rustled through the undergrowth; no birds chirped in the trees. It seemed odd. But possibly her arrival had temporarily silenced them. She sat there a minute longer and then tentatively cracked open the door and climbed out.

Set back away from the road like it was and practically hidden by the gnarly trees, sprawling vines, and other woody invaders, the place was completely isolated. And although it was on its way down, the late afternoon sun remained bright enough to pierce the pines on the other side and cast dappled light onto the verandah floor.

Had she missed a No Trespassing sign? Possibly. But wouldn't there be another one here? Clicking the car door shut, she peered up at the weathered exterior of the house, expecting to see at least a faded "condemned" notice, but there didn't appear to be anything posted on or by the double doors.

Who would know if she looked around a bit?

It *was* abandoned, wasn't it? She had seen other houses she had thought were empty over the years that upon closer inspection had proven to be inhabited. She went to walk around the back to see if a vehicle was parked there and then didn't bother. It wasn't merely that the place was so obviously of a different era on an untended property with leaning posts, peeling paint, and rotting latticework—it was that the windows were completely dark and ... so *lifeless*. The place absolutely radiated barrenness and neglect.

The windows above her were too far away to see in, though the curtains had been left partially open, and most of the ones on the lower level were drawn.

But nothing appeared to be covering the panes in the two doors.

She turned around and inspected the front of the property again. Unless someone came down the old road and then drove up the drive, no one would ever know she was there. And there weren't any signs warning people away. How much trouble could she possibly get in?

For that matter, I can say I was looking to buy and restore it. They couldn't fault her for that, could they?

Feeling marginally more at ease, she followed the weedy leaf-covered walkway to the verandah and climbed the worn steps.

At the top she paused and surveyed the floor. It was covered in square tiles that were faded but mostly undamaged and looked sound enough. But to be sure, she moved one foot forward and gradually rested her weight on it until she knew it would hold her and then proceeded carefully across.

Though she knew it was irrational, before looking in she steeled herself and grasped one of the iron rings and used it to give three quick knocks.

Shifting around, she waited, idly staring at a cracked flowerpot parked on the end by a corroding metal swing, and then stood on her tiptoes to peer through the glass.

She could see the shadowy outline of a chair and a table against the wall on one side and across from them a staircase rising up into the darkness. Her eyes traveled upwards and then widened at the huge chandelier hanging from the high ceiling—a massive, opulent fixture that seemed to float over the foyer like a cluster of ornate balloons. It was made up of three layers of frosted glass globes that matched the tops of the banister posts and seemed to glow in the fading light.

She straightened up and walked over to the nearest window. Leaning in, she peered through a slit in the drapes, but it was too dim to make out much.

Glancing back at the car, she moved over to the rusting swing, motionless now in the momentary stillness.

Who were the people that once upon a time sat down and gently set it to swaying on sultry summer days or brisk autumn evenings like this one in the last rays of the setting sun? Who had ventured out onto this verandah in the coldest months to gaze at the winter wonderland it must have become when the land iced over and the snow fell?

She would have loved to have grown up here. What a different world it would have been.

She reached out to give the swing a gentle push and then froze at the sound of a click behind her followed by a slow *creeeaak.*

Lowering her hand, she turned her head and looked over at the double doors. One of them now stood ajar.

Fear traced its way down her spine at the same time she noticed that the mist shrouding the property had deepened and was creeping up through the railings from the overgrown lawn. And the sunbeams that had stretched across in yellow stripes had faded, leaving the surrounding forest dim and full of shadows.

It was time to go.

She strode across the verandah, but then couldn't help herself and paused by the doors. Something attracted her to the home even as it repelled her.

Stepping forward, she reached out and gently pushed on the one that stood ajar, feeling a tiny zap of static as she touched the metal knob, and it fell open soundlessly.

Sparing only a brief glance behind her, she stepped over the threshold.

The stained-glass window above her had been set aglow by the sinking sun, lending everything a warm amber hue.

Why, it isn't some decaying ruin from the past at all, she thought, moving on in. It seemed to have held up pretty well and still contained some furnishings and things in the rooms on either side of her. And were those portraits on the staircase wall?

She looked through the archway to her right at the desolate, dust-covered space and imagined how it could have been back in the day with other furnishings arranged around the single chaise lounge remaining atop the dull rug in the center—a crushed velvet loveseat, maybe, with a gracefully curved back, and two matching balloon chairs and other carved side chairs, doily-covered mahogany tables, softly burning candles, and hand-painted porcelain lamps.

Suddenly she wanted nothing more than to lie down in that sepia-tinged vignette of the past and let the real world recede. She was so weary, from the pain of the past year, from the shock and trauma of what she'd walked in on, and from everything she would have to face now.

If only she could go back to before everything happened and exist there for a time in those bygone days.

Had any of the people who had once resided there so long ago—those ghostly previous inhabitants who had truly existed and been made of flesh and blood exactly like her—ever wondered about the future dwellers that might come after they were gone? Had they wished they could meet them?

A cool gust of wind blew through the open front door, sweeping into her briefly, eliciting a shiver, and she became aware again of how gloomy it had become around her. While she had been lingering mesmerized, the sun had sunk even lower, leaving only the merest glimmer above the horizon. Full-on dark was approaching fast.

She swiveled around and walked back out, grabbing the knob to close the door. She yanked it shut and hurried down the steps and across the crackling leaves littering the walkway.

Once inside the car, she locked the doors and immediately started it up, switched on the headlights, and took off down the weed-infested drive, which did indeed circle around to the old back road. At least the weather seemed to be clearing, she observed as she turned the wheel to pull out.

In no time she had made it to the highway and was on her way to Greenville, where she hoped to secure a room for the night at the Holiday Inn, where no questions would be asked and no one would care if she had any luggage.

Two

She had forgotten they were having "Ice on Main" that week, so of course the less expensive hotels, including the Holiday Inn, were full. The event, featuring an outdoor ice-skating rink in the heart of Downtown, brought people in from all the surrounding areas.

Finally she managed to snatch a no-show room for three nights at the Hilton (she almost hadn't bothered checking) but she had to work hard to hide her dismay as she paid.

Help with her luggage was offered, but she smoothly declined, saying she didn't have much and she'd get it herself in a bit.

Nearly snatching the keycard when it was finally handed over, she thanked the woman, adjusted her handbag, and walked with as much dignity as she could muster to the elevators.

A half hour later after inspecting the room on the fourth floor she had been given, which was quite nice with a moonlit view of the river below, and brushing her hair and touching up her makeup, she was on her way back down to hit the nearby Target that was luckily only a few minutes away.

She had already decided to grab the bare minimum and then tomorrow or the next day break down and go home—*no, not "home," never "home" again*—to get some of her things. And then hopefully she could keep the room for another night or two, or find another one, while she figured out what to do. Obviously Brent was going to have to help her. He couldn't leave her *destitute*. She would talk to him and work something out about how much she'd take out of the checking account until she found a job and began bringing in her own funds. He owed her that much.

Abruptly she found herself before the car. She had been so lost in thought she hadn't registered crossing the lobby and parking lot.

She climbed in, cranked the engine, switched on the headlights, and quickly pulled out into the street to hop on the interstate.

LIKE A WOMAN on a mission, she grabbed a cart and started through the store. Festive décor and holiday decorations were in evidence everywhere. As usual they had gone all out. The section next to her alone had three different Christmas trees. She looked away and kept going. *Just get what you need and get out.*

Partway down the main aisle, she paused in the women's section, picked two shirts and a pair of jeans she thought might fit—she could wear the same pair for one more day if she had to—moved over and selected some undergarments and things to sleep in, and then veered back up and across the front.

On the way to find the toothpaste, she stopped at a cooler, took out a bottle of peach tea, and taking a drink of the blessedly cool liquid, continued on.

Two aisles down she tossed in a tube of toothpaste and a toothbrush, and stepped over for some deodorant. And then it was on to the food section.

Ignoring the fresh and frozen for the moment, she made her way down to the wine. After surveying the offerings, she settled on a dark, blood-red vintage. It seemed to fit her mood somehow.

She grabbed a few more things, including a gray duffel bag, a paperback novel, some waters and sodas, cranberry scones, and a ready-made salad, and then turned to start for the registers. *Wait, I can't get the wine open without a corkscrew.* Swinging the buggy around, she rolled down to the correct aisle, found one, and once more headed to check out.

Twenty minutes later she was back at the hotel. She took the foodstuff up, put the wine, salad, and some of the drinks into the fridge, and then went back for the duffel, which she filled with the clothes and other items.

Finally, she was ensconced in her room with everything she needed and the door secured with the "Do not disturb" sign on the knob.

She pulled out her phone and swiped the screen to check it. Still no texts, no calls, no messages of any kind. What the hell? She felt a ripple of uneasiness. Brent should have been worried about her and apologizing and begging her forgiveness by now. Could it be that what she'd witnessed was more serious than she had thought? No, surely not. Not with *her*.

She went into the bathroom and turned on the shower as she tried to process this unnatural silence of his and what it might mean. While she waited for it to warm up, she uncorked the wine, a relatively inexpensive blend, poured herself a cup from the stack by the coffee pot, and took a sip.

It was kind of spicy, but jammy too without being too sweet. She took another sip. Not bad. She turned it up, killed most of it off, and poured herself some more.

She adjusted the water a little, took a last gulp, parked the cup by the sink, and stripped off her clothes.

She stepped into the steaming shower. Warmth flowed over her and she closed her eyes. The hot water felt marvelous, soothing and relaxing, not only taking away her achy chilliness but also some of the anxiousness she was feeling.

There is nothing to worry about, she told herself. He'd cheated with Serena, who had probably thrown herself at him, the little hussy, but he'd do right by her. They'd agree on something moneywise.

Taking her time, she finished washing and then climbed unsteadily out, her head swimming. She'd drunk the wine too fast without eating. She quickly dried off and threw on one of the new pajama sets, ripping the tags off and tossing them into the wastebasket.

Settling on the bed, she took a few bites of the salad. But she'd waited too long and soon had to put it away and lie down.

I should have drunk some water, she thought, and then she was up and running for the bathroom.

Afterwards she flushed and stared down at the dark red of the wine swirling around the bowl. *Like blood.*

She closed the lid with a bang, stepped over and washed her hands and then her face. Grabbing the new toothbrush, she scrubbed at her teeth as she inspected herself in the mirror. Her face appeared wan between her messy, blond-streaked locks. She looked tired and unkempt—but not unattractive. Yet. But in just a few years she would turn forty, and fifty was right past it and then what would be left for her? Having children would be out of the question. And a decade or so after that she would be even older and she truly would become invisible to most of the male population. Who would want her then?

She had believed Brent would save her from that—that their love and memories together would keep them by each other's side throughout the years.

But she had been wrong.

She suspected she had been right about what she'd always secretly feared, though. She grabbed a water and crawled beneath the covers. He had probably only married her for security.

Boy had that backfired on him. She had become pregnant three years into their marriage and because there had been complications—what her obstetrician called "placenta previa," a condition where the placenta sits too low—they had made the decision that she would put in for a leave of absence and he would work overtime if that was what it took. So, she had left the job that paid significantly more than his and he had taken on more hours. It was supposed to have been temporary.

Shifting over onto her other side, she bunched the pillow under her head and stared through a gap in the drapes at the slice of moon she could see. She wanted to be out there somewhere, lying in a field or a meadow, gazing up at it. *Or at that old house,* the thought came unbidden. *With things as they used to be and a fire roaring away to keep out the cold.*

She had lost the baby. At six months. They had already decorated the nursery, and her baby boy and all the promise that went with him—before he ever had the chance to grow into a cute kid and then a good-looking man (she imagined)—had been taken away.

Brent had grimly made arrangements and then had driven her home from the hospital—not with a newborn son, but with a "certificate of life."

That was all she kept seeing afterwards. What could have been. What had been lost. A person, a human being, their son, who would have had a whole life ahead of him. Gone before he had ever gotten started.

Brent was visibly distraught at first but then seemed to recover quickly and would act frustrated with her when she couldn't stop crying, when she mourned excessively, he seemed to think. And when she couldn't bring herself to be intimate with him ... that was when the distance between them really began.

But it hadn't only been about losing the baby. It had also been about Brent's attitude toward her afterwards. His withdrawal, his inability to understand, his inability to *share* in her grief, and then his unwillingness to try and shake her out of it. He could have whisked her away on some romantic getaway and attempted to take her mind off of it. But he had done nothing, just more or less gone back to the way things had been before and ignored her and her pain.

And no, he hadn't finally understood like she'd thought and been merely giving her space, and he wasn't right that very minute planning something to help bring them close again. Oh no; instead he had decided to screw Serena, their other next-door neighbors' daughter, as soon as she left the house. Except this time she had forgotten her phone. She pictured it again: her husband, a forty-one-year-old man, banging the nineteen-year-old girl he'd draped over the armrests of the recliner.

I mean, for shit's sake. She flipped back over and punched at the pillow. She couldn't even accuse him of taking advantage. From what she'd observed, the girl had been around the block a few times and had been enjoying herself well enough.

Dammit, she thought. If only she hadn't waited to go back to work. If she had at least done that she wouldn't be in such a precarious position now.

IT WAS A GOOD thing she had put out the "Do not disturb" sign on the second night as well because the next morning she slept later than she had in a while. It was past eleven before she managed to drag herself out of bed, and after one before she was heading out the door to go get some of her things.

Maybe she imagined it, but it seemed like one of the housekeepers smirked at her as she passed. Whatever. She'd removed the sign from the door. They would either clean the room and replace the towels or not.

She had spent the previous day watching television, reading, and trying to rest, but had ended up brooding mostly, before kicking back to watch a movie with the rest of the wine and a pizza she ordered from room service.

She still hadn't heard a word from Brent.

As expected, he was gone when she got to the house. She let herself in with her key and made her way up the stairs. She didn't have much time if he came straight home from work, and she wanted to gather the things she was worried about the most before then.

She got a surprise in the bedroom—what was supposed to be their bedroom but had basically become only her bedroom when he had begun sleeping in the guest room across the hall.

A peach-colored tote bag sat between the bed and the closet, along with a pair of matching sandals. Her head whipped around to the tall bookshelf on her left where she kept many of her pictures and mementos from over the years, including the early ultrasound photo of their lost little boy.

She saw nothing seemed disturbed and turned to the dresser. Some of her polish and perfume had been shifted around. Had Serena *used* them?

It looked like Brent had retaken the room for himself as well. Serena hadn't slept in there alone. One of Brent's T-shirts lay draped over the end of the bed, which had been sloppily made—possibly by Brent; she doubted housework was a priority for Serena at her age—and a pair of socks had been left on the floor.

She knew they had been having problems for a while, but damn this was *fast*. The girl had certainly wasted no time. And Brent ... Did the man have no shame?

It seemed so out of character even for Brent. But she could also see it, too: him being complacent, just along for the ride. And blaming her the whole while.

Things were worse than she'd thought. But Serena stepping right in didn't completely surprise her. The girl had always been a little wild. Her parents were no doubt driving her crazy trying to keep her in line, and she was definitely driving them nuts. She had heard about it a few times out at the fence between their properties. They would be glad to let someone take Serena off their hands, despite him being old enough to be her father.

She pulled the string to lower the attic stairs and climbed up. She threw down a couple of empty boxes she had kept over the years, then decided she needed to focus on what really mattered first. She descended the stairs, walked outside, and raised the hatchback of her eight-year-old Chevy Cruze. If she packed it right, she might be able to fit a good bit.

Leaving it open, she went back inside and up the stairs to the other bedroom they used as a sort of study and began pulling out all the storage containers and crates of photos and albums kept in the closet there in order to get to the large black trunk underneath. The trunk held the pictures and keepsakes given to her after her father died and when her mother downsized to her apartment. The rest was hers, from before and after she met Brent and made Ian. That had been what she'd named the baby in the end. Because little Ian had been very real to her and not just some miscarriage as Brent wanted to believe.

Pushing away the painful memories, she tackled the biggest item first and nearly took her back out getting the trunk down the stairs and into the car.

But she managed it. And then she got everything else, all the photographs and videos, digital and otherwise, and various sentimental things stored in the closet, along with a cardboard box she filled with the framed photos around the house she wanted.

She could have probably told Brent she would come get them later, but she wasn't sure she trusted him now. And she definitely didn't trust Serena.

Knowing she had limited room left, at least for this load, she asked herself: What would I take if the house were on fire?

She already had her purse, but there was also her laptop and her tablet, among other things. She grabbed an empty box and placed what she thought was important into it.

Then she went for her jewelry, which seemed all there, left the perfume and polish, and started grabbing clothes. She stuffed them into the few good bags she had, and put jackets, purses, and shoes into large trash bags. She couldn't get it all. There was way, way too much. She would have to hope that they would give her time to come back and get the rest of it. Because she didn't want a fight. She didn't want to go at it in court. She only wanted what was rightfully hers and what he owed her for putting her in this position.

With the cargo space to the roof and all the seats and floorboards full, she slammed the back shut, climbed in, and took off for the new storage facility they had opened up not far from their subdivision. If she was lucky, it would be climate controlled. *And if I hurry, I might be able to get a few more things before Brent shows up.* She wasn't afraid of him really. She was the one with grounds; he had been the one to break the marriage vows. She simply didn't want to set eyes on him if she could help it.

The storage place did not have climate control, as it turned out, but the price was cheaper.

"And ya' gotta remember," the guy working the counter told her. He was slightly younger than her with tattoos crawling up his arms and would have been handsome if not for a missing front tooth. "We're well into autumn now. It's not gonna get hot in them buildings again for a while. That gives you time to get anything you're concerned about out before then."

He was right. She had months before she'd have to worry about it. "All right, I'll take it."

She handed over her card, and presently she was unloading everything into the largish space she had rented and planned to secure with the heavy-duty padlock she had also procured from the counter guy, whose name, she'd found out, was Donny.

Then it was back to the house, where the driveway remained blessedly empty, to see what else she didn't trust to leave there even for a short while.

This time she got more practical. Wherever she eventually ended up at, she would need certain things that she might not necessarily have the money to buy. So along with more boxes from the garage, she began collecting a few things: a pot or two, a few dishes, some silverware, a handheld can opener. And there was no way she was leaving the beautiful green glass bowl that had belonged to her grandmother, nor the wooden tray her father had made for her one year, or the decorative plate Jill had given her before she'd left for Richmond.

She placed them gently into one of the larger boxes, and gazed around the kitchen and dining room area, more to remember it than anything. There had been some good times there. And maybe she *had* been wallowing in self-pity and it was long past time she got on with her life.

There were so many things she would have to leave behind, at least for now. Her better glassware and dishes in the hutch, her cookbooks on the rack by the window. Her holiday decorations packed away, not to mention her favorite pieces of furniture and other knickknacks she had collected over the years.

She would have to return with a truck and some help to get the rest. And it needed to be soon. But she wouldn't take much. Only what was hers from before she met Brent and what she thought she needed in order to get on her feet.

But for now, she took what she could: her degree off the bookshelf in the study; the sextant in the handsome box given to her by Caleb one Christmas; the nice pen set, also from him; and her favorite books and movies, especially the ones once owned or given to her by her parents.

She had everything loaded up in the car, including a small cardboard box with a few food items, and was lugging out a laundry basket with a sleeping bag she'd had for years, her favorite pillow and blanket piled on top, when Serena's pearly green Prius pulled into the driveway.

Cheyenne watched as she expertly parked to one side under the Bradford pear trees. Clearly she had parked there before and this had become her spot.

She narrowed her eyes as Serena wasted no time getting out and striding down the driveway. The wind had begun to pick up and was blowing against her, sending her long blond hair streaming behind her.

"What are you doing?" Serena demanded when she was close enough, her face and tone decidedly hostile.

"Getting some of my things, obviously," she snapped back, cramming the basket in. "What are *you* doing?" You home-wrecking floozy, she wanted to say, but Serena was so young and when you got right down to it, it was Brent who was to blame. And maybe herself, too. A little.

She went to shut the back of the car and paused.

Serena had stepped closer and was now peering in at the contents. "You can't just come and get whatever you want when no one's here," she said. "This is Brent's house. And mine, too, now."

The gall of the girl! What little ill will Cheyenne had been feeling toward Serena went up a notch as fresh anger coursed through her. "It's Brent's house and *my* house," she retorted hotly. "I've just been gone for a few nights for reasons that are no one's concern and now I'm getting some of my things until I decide what to do. It's *you* who's the interloper here, sweetheart. Who do you think they'll throw off the property if I call the cops?"

Serena gasped. "You lie. You and Brent broke up and you left."

Cheyenne wasn't exactly sure what everyone's rights were technically, but up until that point she had not moved any of her stuff out and she was pretty sure until she removed *all* of her belongings and completely vacated the premises for a period of time, it was still considered her residence, especially with her name on the deed as well. "Tell me, have you paid one lousy cent toward living in this house? Is *your* name the one on everything with Brent's, or *mine*?"

She was practically yelling at this point, and when she viciously slammed the back of the car shut, Serena jumped back like she'd nearly been guillotined.

"So you see," she continued coldly. "I will be returning, probably tomorrow, with a truck and some help to get some more of my things. And you're lucky I'm leaving and not throwing you and your precious Brent out on the streets. So stay out of it and maybe you'll have your happily ever after.

"Or not," she threw in with a derisive snort.

"Yeah, well, we'll see about that," Serena muttered as Cheyenne moved down the side of the car.

On the way back to the hotel, she kept hearing Serena's parting shot like a warning echo in the back of her brain.

At the last second before passing it, she whipped into a branch for their bank, drove around to the ATM lane, and pulled out four hundred dollars, the most it would let her have.

Three

She got up early the next morning to drive to the nearest U-Haul center with a vague plan to get a truck and then cajole someone, maybe her brother, maybe their cousin who lived not far from there, into meeting her at the house. Worst-case scenario, *Brent* could help. She only wanted a few pieces.

She was thinking about what size truck she would need when she moved up to the hotel counter.

"Yes?" said the lady behind the computer screen. "Can I help you?"

"I'd like to keep the room for a couple of more nights, please." After that she was seriously going to have to find a less expensive place, one of those weekly ones, or better yet, get on into something more permanent so she could start searching for a job. Either way, she needed to talk to Brent right away.

"Let me check." The woman, a slightly older one she hadn't seen before, began tapping away. "Um ... yes, we can do two more. But then that particular room has been reserved and will no longer be available. Should you require a different one, though ...?"

"We'll see."

"All right." The woman quoted the price for the next two nights, and Cheyenne handed over her card.

She knew there was a problem when it didn't go through and had to be run again.

"It keeps being declined," the woman finally said. "Would you like to pay a different way?"

Cheyenne thought furiously. Was it a problem with the card, or was something else going on? Should she pay with cash for just one more night? No, that would take too much of what little she had. And though she did have one credit card in her name with a few hundred left on it, she hated to use what could be her only reserve.

The lady behind the desk gazed at her, still waiting for a reply.

"Uh … no …. that's okay."

"You don't want the room for two more nights?"

"No. Sorry." Swallowing, she turned away, then turned back. "Check-out's at eleven, right?" she asked inanely.

The woman nodded. Cheyenne thought she wasn't going to say anything else, but then she added kindly, "If you're a little past that it's fine, though."

Cheyenne thanked her again and headed back up to her room to call Brent.

"CAN YOU BLAME me, Cheyenne? You paid for three nights at the fucking Hilton, rented a storage building, and pulled out four hundred dollars! *And*, Serena said you were taking all kinds of stuff and planned on getting a truck to take more today!"

"Don't you cuss at me, Brent Tanner! I'm not the one who waited until you left the house and then banged the teenager next door."

"She's almost twenty!" he shouted back at her.

"Nineteen, eighteen, whatever. Maybe sixteen next time, huh?"

"Oh, don't even go there, Cheyenne. It's not like how you're trying to make it sound."

"Oh, well, how is it?" She lowered her voice, making it deadly soft. "Why don't you tell me, Brent?"

There was silence on the line for a moment and then he spoke again in a more reasonable tone. "Listen, we didn't know what you were going to do and we couldn't let you wipe us out."

We—he'd said *we* and *us*. "Well, listen. I have to have a roof over my head. And I need to rent a truck for a day and get the rest of my things. And then I can get straight to work. So, what do you want to do? Do you want to go with me today and help find something for me? Because that's where I'm at here, Brent. I need somewhere to stay. And after what you've done … We need to get me a place for at least a few weeks at—"

"Hold on," he said.

She heard the murmur of them talking. Then their voices got louder, there was the sound of the phone being jostled, and Serena's voice entered her ear. "Listen, Cheyenne, you guys are not together anymore. I'm with him now. And he doesn't owe you anything. If you think he does, take it up with the courts. Don't call back and don't try coming back in. We're changing the locks today." With a click, the line went dead.

Cheyenne looked down at the phone in disbelief.

He'd cut her off financially, and because of Serena, probably wouldn't feel inclined to rectify the situation.

She was homeless. And jobless. A crazed laugh burst from her lips. And not far from being moneyless.

IT WAS INSANE. Cheyenne stared at the aging Victorian house, bright and almost idyllic in the evening light.

But like she'd told Brent, she had to have a roof over her head.

Could she possibly stay there, for a night or two, even?

If no one caught her. And if need be, she could take her laptop to places that had free Wi-Fi or hunt for jobs on her phone. She could use the fireplaces and bring in water. She could get a post office box for her mail.

Was she actually considering this? But what other choice did she have? What could her mother, or Caleb, actually do? Her mom lived off a tiny pension and social security, and her brother was working his butt off trying to finish his degree while holding down a fulltime job and had no significant money to lend. And her cousin Larry, now living in her grandmother's old house, had let the property go so badly she feared what the inside of the house looked like now. And from what Caleb had told her, Larry was quite a fan of Miller Lite beer. Lite or not, living with a serious drinker would never do and the prospect of staying there nearly made her shudder.

Brent knew her father was dead and her mother or brother couldn't help. What did he think she was going to do?

How could this be happening?

Because she hadn't bounced back quick enough. Because the cash cow hadn't produced lately. Serena probably thought she would be wife number two, but she'd probably end up being only a temporary balm until Brent found another upwardly mobile female who would allow him the lifestyle he wanted and a child that stayed alive.

Her gut clenched at the thought of their little guy, never having a chance, and in a flash the relentless grief that still surprised her on occasion was on her again. Leaning her head on the steering wheel, she breathed in and out slowly and tried to push away the memories.

A soft tinkling noise in the distance brought her head up.

She pressed the button to lower the window and heard it again: a light tinkling in the breeze. It was windchimes, hanging on the verandah. Funny, she hadn't noticed them before.

She cracked open the door and stepped out. She'd just take a quick peek. After all, once she went to work and got straight, maybe she *could* buy the place and fix it up. Or at least that's what she could tell anyone who questioned her presence there. Probably someone died without an heir and there it sat on the county books with no buyers and not a cent coming in for taxes. The possibility that someone might actually purchase it could keep them from prosecuting her. *I'm actually thinking about doing this. I really am.*

Oh, just go and take a look, she told herself, and marched purposefully toward the front steps.

It didn't appear very menacing now, but she knew that would likely change come nightfall.

You could light candles and a fire, her mind whispered. *And you've got a sleeping bag and a blanket. You could hide your car around the back.*

For a night or two it might be okay, until she could think more clearly and come up with a plan.

She mounted the steps and crossed the verandah to stand before the double doors. They were still closed the way she had left them.

What if they had locked somehow when she'd yanked them shut and she had been standing out here worrying herself silly for no reason? Entering an open house was one thing; breaking and entering was another. That she would not do.

"There's no time like the present," she said aloud, and reached for the knob. "Or the past," she added when the door opened easily. How long had it been since someone checked to make sure it was secure?

Probably they'll get you for trespassing, the rational side of her brain tried to insert, but she was already stepping inside.

A bright shaft of amber shone down on her like a spotlight from the stained-glass window, and she stood there for a moment, bathed in color and soaking up the warmth, before walking on in.

She stopped to touch the elaborately carved post at the foot of the staircase, then crossed over to run a hand over the smooth surface of a table. A layer of dust came away, revealing a streak of still gleaming varnished wood. Craning her neck, she gazed up at the opal globes of the chandelier, faintly glowing in the dwindling sunlight streaming in, and imagined what it must have been like to enter this house as guests for some party or event.

Farther in, past a dusty library with tall bookcases containing disintegrating volumes to her left and the large, mostly empty parlor across from it, she turned right into a side hall and found it led to a long space that had probably been a ballroom. Retracing her steps past a smaller archway to the front parlor, she moved back out and turned into a narrow passageway, and there across from a second entrance to the library, she found a cozy space with two chairs still grouped in front of a fireplace. She continued on down the dim passageway and at the end, stepped into a wider hallway that ran along this half of the house.

Partway down it, she turned into another narrow passageway, and past another doorway on this side of the snug little room in the center, she veered left toward the back of the house and discovered what was probably the laundry room. Continuing on, she came upon the kitchen, the dining room across from it, and then a gorgeous sunroom at the rear.

Through the windows across the back, she could see traces of the old drive curving around the side.

I could park the car right there.

She turned away from the wild wintry landscape and went back to the little center parlor.

She ran her fingers along the marble mantel and lightly touched a small glass bird, coated in decades of grime. She picked it up gingerly and rubbed the top of it until she could see the deep ruby red of it. Like the wine she had drunk. Like blood.

She placed the bird back on the mantel and scrubbed her hands across her jeans.

The furniture in there didn't look too bad. It just needed cleaning up a bit. And the fireplace was fairly large and would put out a good bit of warmth. She should be able to find plenty of firewood in the surrounding forest. And it wasn't even below freezing at night yet. If nothing else, she could load her car up a few times with those small stacks of pre-cut firewood you see everywhere in the winter or else buy artificial logs. They sold those by the boxful.

She sat down in the nearest chair, a mustard-yellow wingback, ignoring the cloud of dust that puffed out, and trailed her hand across the faded fabric.

How had no one bothered this home during all of these years? Even if some obscure relative or county official routinely inspected the place, it still seemed likely that someone would have availed themselves of it, exactly as she was. But in spite of much of the furnishings being gone, the place had a strangely untouched feel and look to it.

She got up and walked to the larger parlor at the front of the house. There she took note of a few grimy lamps and a candelabra holding the nubs of burnt candles from long ago sitting atop a dingy upright piano.

She stepped over to finger an arrangement of dried flowers, but the old petals crumbled at her touch.

Finally she went back outside. Halfway across the verandah, she came to a stop. Everything seemed to have a haziness to it. She squinted her eyes and realized it was merely a mistiness emerging from the woods again, creeping across the grounds.

If she was going to do this she needed to go now. Darkness would be falling soon.

AT THE WALMART one town over, she grabbed two boxes of the least expensive logs and as many cheap gallons of water she could cram along the bottom and one side of the cart. Then, pushing it ahead of her, she started throwing in other essentials. *Just what you need for now*, she reminded herself. *You can regroup and come back later.*

She tossed in toilet paper (Lord knows how that situation was going to turn out), paper towels, trash bags, soap and cleaning products, and on impulse some bug killer as she passed a display, imagining all the spiders probably loose in the home. She took the largest can that promised "no unpleasant smell," then threw in a pile of candles and a lighter, and moved on to the deli section, where she grabbed a couple of sandwiches and a few other things.

That should do it. She got the cart turned around and headed for the front.

After finding and maneuvering her way into the emptiest lane, she pulled a cold Dr Pepper out of the nearby cooler, selected a magazine off the rack beside her, and began piling her items onto the conveyor.

Soon she was wheeling her way out to the car, dazed over how much everything had cost. She would have to be even more careful from then on.

Back at the old house—after all the money she had just spent, she was committed now—she drove straight down the side and parked in the back.

Before going all the way around to the front, she walked over to check the door to the sunroom. Stepping up, she twisted the knob, and the door came open easily. She fiddled with the little switch on the inside, but time or debris had frozen the bolt in place, keeping it from locking properly.

Filled with a sense of mystery again coupled with a feeling of relief at having found this place, this sanctuary in the storm her life had become, she carried her purchases in along with the other things she had chosen to bring with her. Most of the belongings she'd managed to get were in the storage building, safely locked away. The payment for that would come due in a month, but she would worry about that when the time came.

She knew in the back of her mind that what she was doing was a bit crazy, but the house, sitting there vacant and going to waste, called to her in her dire circumstances.

The food, she moved into a sectioned-off stone wine cellar she found tucked into one corner of the basement, candelabra (with fresh candles) lighting the way, down a set of stairs at the end of the rear passageway, where it was significantly cooler. She brushed the cobwebs away and stashed the remaining sodas and waters, sandwiches, and other food items away in the cabinets and drawers under a counter to one side, and then turned to inspect the rest of the cold, damp space.

Ceiling-high shelves covered the side walls completely and still held a few antique bottles of various spirits. There were also several dusty bottles of wine poking out of a built-in rack by a rectangular table and two chairs beneath a large ornate mirror, now cloudy with age.

Beginning to shiver, she walked over and grabbed a wine bottle at random and carried it with her out of the cellar and back up the stairs.

In the kitchen she parked it on the round, scarred table across the room from a white enamel sink and an ancient-looking stove, and got out the bug killer.

First she used a wad of paper towels and the broom she'd purchased with the cleaning supplies to knock down as many spider webs as she could, paying particular attention to the inner parlor, and then sprayed the perimeter of the front parlor, the library across from it, the kitchen, and finally the smaller, cozier room she preferred. That was enough for now. She was too damn tired and the place was too damn big. Tomorrow would be soon enough for that. And then she'd give it a thorough inspection.

But she was no fool. Strapped to her jeans was a pocketknife she had grabbed when she dug out her sleeping bag and she had a large stick she'd picked up outside. She hadn't had it in her to do more than a quick walkthrough of the house, and these measures would have to suffice. And it didn't appear to matter. Inexplicably, she felt safe. And at home, insane as it seemed.

She placed the candelabra on a low marble-topped table between the chairs and a smallish gold-colored sofa against the wall of the inner parlor, and then went outside before it got too dark, leaving the doors wide open to air the place out.

She gathered twigs and sticks and thicker branches to go with the logs and carried them by the armful into her inner sanctuary, as she was beginning to think of the little room, until the wire basket by the hearth was overflowing and more were stacked on the floor beside it.

After making sure the flue was open, which took some doing (the original recess for the fireplace had been filled with a cast-iron insert and she had to yank hard to get the damper to budge), she stacked twigs and sticks under and on top of one of the packaged logs, and lit the paper around it.

It took a few minutes to get it burning, but soon with a few bigger pieces of wood added, she had a crackling blaze going. There was a black cloud of smoke at first, and she was glad she had left the doors open. But eventually it died down and the fireplace began to draw properly. After a bit she was able to close up the house again. The only fear she had was that someone would see or smell the smoke. But hopefully the house was isolated enough that it wouldn't be detected.

She dusted off the mustard chair she liked, producing little sparks of static, then went into the kitchen. She rinsed out a small glass, retrieved the corkscrew and bottle of wine, and returned to the little parlor. She placed everything on the table beside the wingback, started to sit down, then spying the blanket she'd brought, lifted up to grab it. Pulling it across her legs, she dropped back down wearily and propped her feet on a footstool she'd dragged over.

With hands that shook, she went to work on the wine.

The cork popped out with a *thook*, and she filled the glass. After giving it a sniff—it didn't smell vinegary—she tentatively tasted it and was thrilled to find it smooth instead of bitter and tasting of fruit with only a slight earthiness. She took a larger sip and savored the plummy sweetness.

Sitting back, she sipped at it as she gazed at the flickering flames and the dancing shadows of the candles behind her.

Her mind wandered as she relaxed, content to sit and do nothing, not even think about her predicament.

The wine and her fatigue, though, soon had her moving over to the sofa. She swiped at it to remove some of the dust, spread the sleeping bag across it, and lay down with her blanket and pillow.

She knew if this was going to work, even for a short while, she was going to have to do a lot more cleaning, but right then she was too tired and emotionally spent to deal with it.

Four

Eventually she dreamed—of the house as it once must have been, pristine and gleaming with plush furnishings and richly colored drapes and rugs and golden lamplight, imbued with the scent of freshly baked cake and spiced apples.

There were people there, too, glimpsed dimly in the periphery of her vision, some walking arm in arm, some dancing to faint music she could barely pick up. Although they were smiling and conversing, she couldn't make out what they were saying. But as she approached the entrance to a long, open space, the occasional burst of laughter rang out loud enough to reach her.

It was the ballroom. And they were having a party. Folding her arms, she rubbed at the goosebumps that had formed on them. The air felt strange, like it was filled with electricity. She tucked a strand of hair behind her ear, and it crackled with static.

People swirled by her, oblivious as they danced past.

Lingering unnoticed by the sea of people gliding and twirling about, she marveled at their dazzling attire and the grandeur of the room as she turned to glance into a mirror on this side of the doorway.

Her image looked back at her, hair tousled from sleep and still wearing the nightshirt she'd put on for bed. But it didn't matter, for not one person was paying the least bit of attention to her.

She shifted her gaze over and flinched as in the reflection, she saw a man standing behind her against the far wall, his eyes boring into hers with full awareness. She whirled around.

His eyes traveled the length of her, then flew back up to meet her startled gaze.

They stared at each other as if mesmerized. Black-haired and tallish, he was dressed in a dark jacket and matching close-fitting trousers and was easily the best-looking man she had ever laid eyes on. And he seemed just as taken with her, although how that could be with the disheveled state of her hair and the way she was dressed, she couldn't imagine.

He started in her direction, his brow knitting like he was trying to place her.

Rooted in place, she could only stare back as he made his way across the floor and stopped before her.

"I believe I know you," he said in a smooth, masculine voice. "Although I can't quite recall how." He stood about six two, several inches above her five-foot-six frame. "Nevertheless, I'm happy you came. But I must say, you are a bit underdressed."

Cheyenne peered past him at all the people. "Yes, well ... I didn't realize I was ..." Her voice trailed away as her confusion mounted.

He gave a quick glance over his shoulder, then moved closer and grasped her upper arm to urge her into the shadows. "Explain to me," he said. "How my mother, whom I'm assuming you must somehow be acquainted with, has failed to mention knowing such a delightful creature as you?" He raked his eyes down the length of her again. "You must tell me who you are."

She wet her lips and swallowed. "I'm ... My name is Cheyenne. And I'm not ... I don't ..." She looked around. *Why was ...? This wasn't ...*

As though from a distance, she felt his fingers tighten around her arm. *Where ...?* Panic welled within her and she twisted away, pulling her arm free.

She hurried away from him, back through the house, heedless of his voice calling out behind her, moving in and out of shadow past softly glowing lamps and fluttering candles, along the narrower passageway and through the doorway into the smaller inner room.

And there she found herself in darkness that smelled of dust and smoke. My God, what had just happened? She turned in a half circle. She was in the old house—in the present, not a century in the past.

I must have been dreaming. And apparently she'd taken to wandering about in her sleep.

She had never sleepwalked in her entire life. And she didn't think she had ever had such a detailed dream before, either. Such an *exact* dream. It had felt so real.

Wincing at the stiffness in her muscles—the fire had died out and the room had grown cold—she shuffled over, lay back down, and tried to get into a comfortable position. She briefly contemplated getting up and throwing another log on, but then with her mind full of splendor and finery, and of *him*, the one who'd seemed so vivid, she fell back asleep.

THE NEXT TIME she awoke, it was daylight and there was a vehicle idling in the driveway out front.

She shot up into a sitting position and looked around wildly. There was stuff out everywhere and there she was snuggled up on the sofa. Throwing back the blanket, she jumped up and dashed out of the room. Quickly traversing the smaller passageway, she flattened herself to the wall, stuck her head around the corner to look down the hall and make sure no one was standing in front of the glass panes of the front doors, then rushed down the length of it and slipped into the library.

Staying to the side, she moved over and peeked out the nearest window and instantly jerked back, her heart bouncing in her chest.

A sheriff's patrol car sat directly across from the verandah steps.

Were they calling for backup? Should she shove her things out of sight and run out the back door and down through the woods? But what about her car!

Before racing through the house to conceal everything in a last-ditch effort to stay hidden, she took a deep breath and peeked out the window again.

Ever so slowly, she eased the curtain over a fraction more and saw it was only one officer and he was peering down at something he seemed engrossed in.

As she continued to watch, wondering if she was wasting precious minutes, he reached over, picked something up, and took a bite of it.

Oh, okay. She sagged in relief. Probably he rolled through the place occasionally to check things out and have lunch while he worked on his reports. As long as he didn't get an urge to take a look, she might be fine. *And if he doesn't lower his window and smell the previous night's smoke.*

Get finished and go, she willed him as she waited, alternating pacing back and forth with peeking out the window.

At last, she heard the sound of the engine change and the crunch of his tires as he started down the drive.

Hurrying out of the room, she crossed over to the front doors and stood there and listened to the diminishing sound of him turning out and heading back the way he'd come.

That was close, she thought.

She moved over to an armless chair by the parlor and collapsed into it.

But he hadn't caught her. With a little planning, organization, and preparation, this might actually be doable.

If she could figure out somewhere better to hide the car.

SHE STORED THE rest of what she'd brought with her in out of the way places like the dining room—still containing a dark, hulking hutch, a large, well-worn table, and four of what must have been eight chairs originally—so they wouldn't easily be found if someone came in. Then she tidied the fireplace enough to make it look like some homeless person merely spent the night and then moved on.

Next, she put her laptop, tablet, and handbag in the car in case she had to make a quick getaway. If anyone ran up on her once she was outside, she could always say she was merely looking around and then drive off to return later.

Sliding her phone into her back pocket, she pressed the button to lock the car and then walked over to a small brick building with a rusty lantern hanging above the doorway. She tugged the door open and stuck her head inside. It had been fashioned into a rough bathroom. There was an old pull-chain toilet similar to the one upstairs, an iron faucet poised over a bucket, and a small tub.

For the outside hands or ...? she wondered as she moved away and headed across the overgrown yard to inspect the various nooks and crannies of the property.

Over to the left, she found the remains of an old track cutting through the weeds and grass. Stepping onto it, she followed it down to a two-story, graying structure. The undergrowth had taken hold of it and thick vines had twined all the way up to the second story.

Judging by the set of huge double doors, it had to have been some kind of shed or garage.

Shooting a glance back at the house, she veered off the sandy track onto the slightly less overgrown area where countless others had once trod, and walked down the side.

She cupped her hand over her eyes to scan the area behind the building.

It looked like there was another structure, not quite as big, a little farther down.

Dropping her hand, she turned and moved past a half-buried pail and an old hand pump to work her way back around.

The weathered door at the front hung slightly ajar. Using her foot, she pushed against it, and it fell open with a groan.

She tentatively stepped inside. After giving her eyes time to adjust, she started forward in the dim light and felt something crunch underneath her shoe. She looked down and saw the floor was littered with broken glass.

She tilted her head back and found the source of it. The row of windows along the top of the high-ceilinged space she was in had cracked and then shattered with age.

Stepping around the shards, she walked toward the only thing in the room—a rusty wood-burning stove squatting beneath a black pipe extending upwards—then wandered over and passed through a doorway across from it. Except for a discolored sink, this space was as empty as the previous one.

She went back into the main room and crossed over to enter the hallway beyond.

At one end of the dim passage, she found a room still containing a sagging bed and a rickety wooden table.

This part of the building appeared to have been the outside staff's quarters.

She exited the room and walked to the other end, pulled open a door, and saw it led to a cavernous space that made up the rest of the building.

"*Oh.*" Across from her, highlighted by the light shining in through the windows on either side of it, sat an honest to goodness carriage—a horse-drawn carriage.

Stepping through, she approached the corner where it sat, staring in wonder.

Despite being stored away from the elements, there had been no stopping the march of time. The wheels had begun to split, the once-gleaming hardware had rusted in spots, and a layer of grime coated the windows.

She leaned in and tried to see past the dust and spider webs. Using the tip of one finger, she scrubbed a small spot clean, and peered in again.

The extravagant interior had probably been luxurious at one point, but now the velvet seats were faded and marred by mold and the drapes tattered and moth-eaten.

She pulled back, marveling at the old thing.

Even with it so deteriorated and covered in grime and cobwebs, she could tell it had once been classy.

It looked like it hadn't been moved in years ... decades. Just maneuvered into the corner and then left. All this time.

She moved up to the coachman's seat where two tarnished brass lamps perched on each side, still thinking about it sitting there undisturbed as the seasons changed and the years marched past.

She gazed at it a little longer, and then walked back across to go out the way she'd entered.

Not too far down the dirt track, she found the second building. Even more grown over, the definitely barnlike structure had not fared as well as the carriage house.

She picked her way over and nervously moved inside. It was as though the barn had dried up and shrunk to a skeleton as it aged, leaving cracks and gaps between the planks and boards, allowing the sun's rays to stream through.

She went far enough to see a line of empty stalls, doors hanging open, where horses had once been kept, and then came back to what must have been the tack room. Old rotting saddles and other equipment still hung from the walls across from a crude desk and stool so old and covered in dust they were nearly white. She cast an uneasy glance at the splintering rafters above her and decided she had seen enough. She quickly retraced her steps to the front entrance and walked out into the sunlight.

Suddenly conscious of how long she'd been gone, she hurried over to follow the track back up to the house.

She was panting a little by the time she crossed the backyard. She started along the side of the house, then eased away from it, not liking the way it loomed over her, casting her in shadow.

Before rounding the corner, she ran her eyes over the driveway and beyond, making sure no one was approaching, and then turned around to confirm what she'd suspected.

Behind the carriage house, especially with it overrun and crowded by trees and vegetation like it was, the car would be completely hidden.

But what about from the other side? What if someone stopped short and walked down to take a look over there?

Resolutely, she marched along the front as if she had every right to be there, and turned the corner.

It wasn't until she hit the end of the house and set off across the wild back lawn again that she was able to see the carriage house.

If she pulled up as far as possible it might do, for a cursory inspection, at least.

But she had a few things she wanted to take care of first. She climbed into the car and quickly backed out and drove around the house and down the drive to head into town.

Relying solely on candles wasn't really practical, and she needed a few other things as well, along with access to Wi-Fi. And she needed to charge her devices.

As comforting as it was to have found a place to stay, such as it was, she was also feeling a bit disconnected from the world.

She knew she should search the job postings, too, but she didn't feel ready to take that on that yet. Her resume needed to be updated first, anyway. *I'll take care of that tonight*, she thought. *It'll give me something to do.*

SHE KILLED SOME time at the McDonald's, where she ate a grilled chicken sandwich and sipped on a diet soda.

Then after the lunch crowd had mostly passed, she left and drove over to the nearest Panera, settled into a spot with an outlet, and plugged up her laptop and tablet. She had a car charger she'd been using for her phone.

The sandwich had mostly killed her appetite, so she merely nibbled on a lemon cookie and nursed a coffee while she waited. For something to do, she tweaked her LinkedIn profile, and then went ahead and did a desultory perusal of the local job listings. But she saw none that thrilled her.

On Facebook she found nothing but the same old, same old and not one message from Brent, who might have tried to reach her there if he hadn't been able to get her on her phone. Had she been getting a signal last night? She hadn't thought to check.

That wine must have hit me good.

Before signing off, she did a little digging and with very little effort found Serena's page, her public page, probably just so Cheyenne could see her status was listed as "Engaged."

En-fucking-gaged. Well she could have his cheating, coldhearted ass! His cheating, coldhearted, *opportunistic* ass!

Teeth clenched and breathing hard through her nose, she looked away from the screen and glanced around, trying to calm down. Since it was during the afternoon lull, there were only two other groups of patrons. She was about to refocus on the screen, when one of the guys at the nearest table cut his eyes at her.

God, she must look a fright.

Her tablet was only a little over half charged, but that was good enough. She yanked the cord out and stowed it away in her bag, checked the level of the laptop battery, saw it was at about seventy percent, and pulled the plug on it too.

Back outside, the cooler air felt good on her heated cheeks, and she took her time crossing over to the car.

Then it was on to Walmart, or "Wally World" as Brent would have called it.

Stop thinking about him, she told herself as she pulled out into the street. *He certainly isn't thinking about you.*

A few minutes later she was wedging her car into a slot. Her dream from the night before floated across her mind, and she remembered the dark-haired man who'd gazed at her so intently and seemed so taken with her. What would it be like to be loved by someone like that? To have someone *she* could love like that?

She looked around her at all the cars lined up beside her in the dreary lot and wished she had been born in a different era, with a different life.

But it wasn't to be. This was her reality, and it was nothing like her dream.

Inside the store, she soberly gathered an LED lantern, batteries, more candles and water, and a few food items. She was starting to become seriously concerned about the money situation. She needed to quit screwing around and get to work. And break down and tell her mother and brother what was going on and beg one of them to get a loan for her if they had to. Or they could appeal to Brent on her behalf. She couldn't keep staying in an abandoned house, for Christ's sake.

But that was a problem for another day.

IN CASE SHE ran into the deputy again, she had mentally concocted a story to explain her presence: she had lived nearby until recently and had become fascinated with the home and had been debating whether or not it would be possible to buy it and fix it up, not to flip it but to live in it. If pressed further, she was prepared to throw herself on his mercy and admit she was newly separated from her husband and needing a place.

But the driveway in front of the home remained empty, and without slowing she veered off onto the faint remnants of the smaller part that led around the back. This time, though, instead of stopping where it ended, she turned, praying she didn't hit a broken bottle or a nail, and began bumping her way across, tall brown grass sweeping the sides of the car.

Cranking the wheel, she swung in beside the old carriage house and pushed through the vegetation. She was probably scratching the shit out of the paint, but unless someone came out and searched, they'd never find it.

Later after she'd carried everything in and stowed it away out of sight down in the stone wine room and various other places, she made sure the curtains and drapes were drawn—all except for the front set in the larger parlor she was afraid to mess with in case it was noticed—and headed around to better inspect the rest of the house.

She decided to start with the large rectangular space that ran front to back, encompassing a large portion of the right side. She took the shorter hall past the other entrance to the front parlor, and stopped in the doorway.

Though devoid of furniture except for a few frail chairs against the wall, the high, open space still managed to convey a stunning and so-far unrivaled opulence with its lavish gilding and embellishments. Gilt reined heavily, in the brackets and other accents, along the trim and borders and the tops of the windows, and in the frames of the large, elaborate mirrors and paintings.

She crossed the hardwood floor to stand before the tall windows on the end, still framed by faded drapes, that looked out onto the front lawn. She stayed there, soaking up the heat and light streaming in for a moment, and then moved away where she wouldn't be seen as easily.

She tilted her head to gaze up at the vaulted ceiling. It had been spared none of the accompanying detail. If anything, it was even more richly decorated. In the middle, a huge chandelier, outfitted with what looked like a dozen thin candles and dripping with crystals, hung from a center petal-like rosette.

If it was this magnificent now, she could only imagine how grand it must have been years ago with the room lit up and men in fine dress coats swinging women wearing brilliant ball gowns around the polished floor.

Not for the first time, she wished she had been born earlier. Some would accuse her of glamorizing this "Gilded Age" that included abject poverty and hardship as well as glamour and grace. But, oh, the splendor and the style, if you were one of the lucky ones. She would give it all up—the computers and cell phones and associated social media and easy access to information—to live in such a time. Instead of sitting hunched before a screen or in front of a television set, slowly dying of atrophy and loneliness, she would be out playing croquet and listening to brass bands, attending evening soirées and balls and plays, going on exciting ocean voyages, making astounding discoveries, visiting wellness spas, and holding extravagant teas and dinner parties.

She gazed around her for another minute, imagining it all, and then turned, sighing, to go explore the rest of the house.

Back in the foyer, she gingerly grasped the banister and started up the staircase, bringing each foot down carefully. As they had the first time she'd gone up, the old wooden risers groaned and popped with the weight of her but seemed sturdy enough.

The gentle patina of time had turned the wallpaper behind the portraits to a soft pinkish beige interspersed with faded roses, whispering of days long gone. She wondered what those walls would say if they could talk.

It must have been dazzling—the house aglow with the soft luminescence of the lamps and the flames of a hundred candles, ringing with the sounds of chatter and laughter; servants bearing platters and bowls, the intoxicating aromas of rich and decadent food following in their wake, and in the background, the soft tinkling of a piano.

At the top, she moved out onto the upstairs landing and paused. Except for a settee with an oddly curved back by the railing, the hallway stretching out in each direction stood empty. Only dark sconces and intermittent wall hangings accompanied the dull burgundy rug running down the center.

When she had done her initial quick inspection, she hadn't gone all the way into any of these rooms—she'd merely stuck her head in to verify no one was holed up inside—and she now found herself eager to see what remained and what it might tell her about the previous inhabitants.

She glanced down the hallway reaching out to her right, then turned and headed in the other direction.

Many rooms were completely barren, leaving her to only guess at what they had once contained, while others still held some furnishings, allowing intriguing glimpses of the past.

She wandered back down the hall. The place was a historical treasure trove of Victorian excess. The chandeliers, gilded mirrors, and hanging lamps like the one above her alone had to be worth something, not to mention the rugs, marble mantelpieces and tabletops, and artwork on the walls. She found herself wondering again how so many valuable things could have just been left and forgotten. And surely she wasn't the first to discover the property. Yet no one had taken these things.

Unlike the other rooms she'd passed, the two she was standing between allowed access through paneled French doors. That and the intricate fixture above her clearly set these apart.

Had some married couple once slept across from each other in these "master" bedrooms?

One of the doors on her right was slightly ajar. She stepped over and pushed it open.

The room was devoid of anything except a bed with a high headboard, a single chair, an ornate metal floor lamp in the corner, and a few small tables.

She moved on in to glance through the tall glass panes at the wintry landscape beyond, then exited the room and crossed over to the other one.

Though the items it contained had obviously been there for a while, they appeared somewhat newer than the other things she had found. A man's suit jacket, dated but slightly more recent, hung over the back of a wooden chair next to a dresser with motheaten clothing spilling out of the drawers. A wicker laundry basket sat between it and a pile of yellowing newspapers. There was also a crate containing a few brown bottles next to a dingy floral-patterned armchair parked against the wall under a portrait of some other somber ancestor.

Curious, she walked over, lifted one of the bottles out, and wiped the label off. "*Howel's* ROOT BEER," it read in red script, "*with that Good Old Fashioned Flavor.*" She'd never heard of it. She gazed down at it, wondering how old it was, then placed it back in the crate.

She stepped over to stand before the windows. She pushed the drapes to the side, producing another spark of static, and looked out across the back at the dilapidated buildings and uncultivated field beyond.

How long until this house and everything with it fell completely into ruin, collapsed, and was reclaimed by nature?

After a moment, she turned away and walked back to the pile of newspapers. Choosing one at random, she carefully unfolded the creased, brittle paper and checked the date. August 27, 1937. She set it back down and picked up another. This one was also dated 1937. There didn't appear to be any particular significance to the front-page articles, and she could only surmise that they had been tossed in a pile and not kept for any specific reason.

On the next one she picked up, the headline read COAST GUARD AND NAVY HUNT AMELIA IN PACIFIC OCEAN, with *Believe Adrift in Shark*

Infested Waters beneath it. The date was July 3, 1937 and there was an accompanying photo of Amelia and her navigator standing before the Lockheed Electra she'd flown that last day.

She skimmed over the first part of the article. The prevailing theory seemed to be that Amelia had overshot her target destination, a tiny island in the Pacific, and ran out of fuel. Also mentioned were possible distress signals picked up in the midst of the feverish sea and sky hunt.

She carefully folded the newspaper and returned it to the pile. Little did they know that today, nearly ninety years later, they were still trying to solve the mystery of exactly what happened to Amelia, her navigator Fred Noonan, and the doomed plane.

Moving back out into the hall, she continued her inspection of the second floor.

A good bit of furniture, a surprising amount actually, remained, like in the last room on the left, which still contained an iron bed with a rotting mattress and a simple chest of drawers. But plenty had been removed. The things in the larger bedroom she'd found, though, spoke of someone inhabiting the home after the Victorian period. Possibilities ran through her mind. An impoverished descendant of the original owners who had remained, selling off certain pieces as necessary, until the upkeep and expenses became too much and they'd finally moved out? Or a distant relative from overseas who'd inherited and visited the place a few times before it fell into disuse, taxes being paid from an estate, until it was eventually abandoned?

The two turret rooms—half octagons built into the upper corners of the home—were surprisingly spacious.

The one on the other end had held only a sun-bleached green sofa comprised of three wide sections that curved around below a smaller version of the chandelier with the frosted globes on the ground floor. But the turret room on this side contained chairs, tables—one holding a phonograph with a darkening silver horn—stained-glass lamps, free-standing bookcases still displaying a few decaying books and ledgers, and a writing desk. It appeared this space had been much-used and, miraculously, left nearly intact throughout the years. Over near the windows, past a few grubby odds and ends arranged on a set of shelves, there was also an old fashioned, boxy camera on a wooden tripod with a faded black cloth hanging from the back of it.

Leaving faint footprints trailing across the floor, she walked over and looked out. The mistiness that seemed to plague the surrounding terrain had returned and was now creeping across the untended lawn.

"Cheyenne!" a voice suddenly echoed distantly through the house.

Gasping, she spun around, apprehension surging through her.

Eyes wide, she stared over at the doorway, alarm filling her even as her brow wrinkled in confusion. *Who? How?*

It hadn't been Brent's voice, or anyone else's she was acquainted with, though it had sounded vaguely familiar. And how would they know she was there anyhow? Was it the deputy she'd seen out front? But how would he know her name? A disturbing possibility occurred to her as she waited in fearful anticipation for whoever it was to appear. Had Brent reported her missing? But even as it crossed her mind, she was dismissing it. If he or anyone else needed to reach her all they had to do was call or message her.

She stood there for a long moment, listening for the footsteps of whoever was about to discover her. But the only sounds that met her ears were the faint sighing of the wind outside and the thud of her heartbeat.

As the minutes stretched and she continued to hear nothing, doubt began creeping in. *Had* she heard someone? Or had the atmosphere of the home somehow made its way into her subconscious and manifested itself into a man's voice calling her name?

Walking softy, she crossed over and peeked around to look into the hall. Seeing no one, she stepped on out.

She stood there and listened for someone moving through the home, and once more heard nothing.

Tiptoeing, she moved along the hallway, checking each room she passed, and started down the staircase. It had sounded so real. So real and so unexpected that she'd jumped and spun around. She *couldn't* have imagined it.

Five

The house was empty. And no vehicle sat in the driveway. If someone had been there, they were gone now.

She turned away from the front windows with the parted drapes she'd been staring out.

As she moved back out of sight, she remembered the raised section of the roof she had noticed the day she discovered the place.

She had completely forgotten about the attic.

It made no sense that someone looking for her would be lurking up there. But she knew she wouldn't rest until she checked it.

But how to get up there? She hadn't seen any obvious way to access it. But she hadn't really been looking; it was possible she had missed a door or a hatch with a ladder leading to it.

Letting out a sigh, she walked around to head upstairs.

She found the stairs leading to the attic behind a door on the second floor she had previously thought to be a closet, possibly for linens.

She was only halfway up the narrow, steep steps, which had only a flimsy handrail, when it became apparent that she could go no farther without some type of light source. Even if she could force herself to continue climbing into the inky blackness, she wouldn't be able to make out a thing.

She climbed back down, went and retrieved the battery-powered lantern, returned to the attic stairs, switched it on, and once more began carefully climbing upwards.

There was another balky door at the top, and she had to put her shoulder into it to get it open. Practically falling in, she jerked the lantern up, blinding herself in the process, quickly lowered it, and blinked at the spots filling her vision.

Raising the lantern again, she slowly began to make out the space around her. The ceiling was lower here, but not so low that she couldn't straighten up. There were a couple of high, triangular-shaped windows on each end, but they were too small and grimy to illuminate much beyond their immediate area.

Shadows leapt, fleeing from the light, as she moved it over the trunks, cartons, and unused furnishings—including a bed frame with no mattress under the sloping eaves. She walked over to the bureau beside it.

All the drawers were empty except the top one which had a tattered flyer lying in the bottom. Gently she lifted it up and flipped it over. It was an advertisement for someone named Clara Smith appearing in the Golden Ballroom at a hotel called The Palmetto. There was no accompanying photo, just the name in big bold letters.

She placed the flyer back in the drawer and moved back out to where she had more headroom.

Dust and cobwebs coated and hung from nearly every surface. Snatching an old walking stick propped against a washstand missing the basin, she forced her feet to move toward the far wall.

As she swept the stick back and forth to knock down the webs, she found herself pondering what treasures could be contained in this dank repository of history.

Vowing to come back another day, she stepped around to check the final corner. Satisfied no one was there, she hurried back across to get out of there.

Down on the second floor, she closed the door to the attic stairs and quickly walked away, trying to put the dark space out of her mind.

She'd had enough of the old house for the moment. For the first time since coming there, she found herself wanting nothing more than to step out of it into the bright sun—

Something thumped against the wall beside her.

Flinching, she came to a halt.

Silently chiding herself for being so jumpy, she marched over, flung the door of the room open, and strode inside.

A black mass of beating wings and feathers exploded out from behind the wardrobe against the wall. Crying out, she flung her arms up, nearly bashing herself in the face with the lantern, and stumbled back as a large black crow swooped across and shot through the gap in one of the open balcony windows.

Somehow she'd failed to notice it wasn't completely closed. Breathing hard, she moved over and hastily closed it.

More determined than ever to leave the house at least for a while, she started across the room, then came to a halt as a glint of red in the wardrobe caught her eye.

She walked over and opened it.

A long crimson evening gown was hanging on a wire hanger inside.

Gently, she lifted it off the rod and drew it out.

Her breath caught. Fitted to the waist and flaring out gradually to the hem, with gauzy off-the-shoulder sleeves and studded with sequins that sparkled in the shaft of light hitting it, the gown was one of the most beautiful she'd ever seen.

Women's lib had made female clothing more practical and comfortable, but she couldn't help feeling something had been lost in it all as she gazed at the breathtaking creation. She held the dress up to her, careful to keep the ends from dragging the floor, and imagined wearing it—the sensation of the delicate material against her skin, flowing down in a soft, glittering line.

The sun's rays dimmed as a cloud slid in front of it—and abruptly the spell was broken. She hung the dress back up. Where would she even wear something like that?

She shut the wardrobe firmly, and left the room.

THE HOUSE WAS dark but she could see by the illumination of the lantern and the moonlight shining in. She had heard a sound, coming from above. Her skin tingled, the hair on her head and arms bristling. She'd felt something similar once before years ago when she was a kid out hiking with a neighborhood girl and they'd walked under a row of high-voltage transmission towers.

Silently she climbed the grand staircase, and emerged onto the second-floor landing. On the other end of the hall stretching out from her, a glow from within spilled out from one of the rooms.

Following it like a beacon, she moved through the shadows, and halted just outside.

Quietly, she switched the lantern off, set it on the floor, and slipped through the doorway. She paused as the light hit her eyes, seemed to grow more brilliant, and then dimmed to the normal flame of a glass hurricane lamp. *You're dreaming again*, she thought distantly.

"Hello again." She turned. It was him, the man from before. She stared across at him, once more taking in the dark shock of hair, the chiseled cheekbones, and full lips.

His deep-set, nearly black eyes traveled the length of her, and a faint hint of appreciation lifted the corner of his mouth. Seeing her startled expression, the faint grin deepened into a wide smile that instantly made her knees go weak. She marveled at her body's reaction, which was very real and not merely something out of a romance novel.

"I was hoping you would come back," he said, his voice a low, masculine caress. *The voice I heard calling my name*, she realized.

She closed her eyes—can you close your eyes when you're already asleep?—then opened them and retreated a step. *This can't be real.*

"No, please don't go! I have something for you." He hurried over to a wardrobe against the wall, reached inside, and brought out a long red dress. *It's the crimson gown*, she thought.

"Do you like it?" he asked, holding it out for her inspection.

"I do," she breathed.

Beaming, he walked over and gently laid it across the end of the bed. "It's yours," he said, gesturing at it. "Try it on."

Hesitantly she moved past him and stopped at the foot of the four-poster bed. She looked down at the sparkling gown. She'd never had anything like it. Conscious of his dark presence hovering beside her, she touched the edge of one delicate sleeve, and then lifted the gown up and carried it behind a silk screen in the corner.

Emerging a couple of minutes later wearing the gorgeous creation, she felt like a different person. She never wanted to take it off.

Catching sight of her, the man drew in a breath and went still.

"Do you like it?" she asked, echoing his words and doing a little twirl.

Slowly, almost imperceptibly, he nodded, no trace of a smile on his face now, his dark eyes staring deep into hers.

Holding back a shiver, she ripped her gaze away and moved back behind the screen. She slipped the dress off and draped it over the top, then quickly pulled her clothes on, turned around—and there he was, standing only inches away.

Their fingers connected, sending a jolt throughout her body. As if in slow motion, he pulled her up against him, and she could feel the heat of his hand on the small of her back.

He bent his head, and she waited for the sensation of his lips on hers—but then a faint noise reached her ears, intruding upon her anticipation.

The distant buzzing came again. She turned her head in annoyance. The sound didn't belong here in this cozy room standing by this handsome man. The faraway vibration continued—relentless—and though she strained against it, she could feel herself being drawn away.

The warmth of his body and the gentle radiance surrounding them began to fade, growing distant until she slowly became aware of the dark room around her, lit only by the moonbeams shining in. Jerking her head right and then left, she strained to pierce the darkness where the bed and the silk screen beside her had been and found only bare space.

She looked around in disbelief. *You've been walking in your sleep again. You're on the second floor of a deserted house. One that hasn't been lived in for over a century.*

Shivering, she turned to head back downstairs—and froze at an unexpected rustle and feel of something at her feet. Mouth falling open, she peered down in surprise.

It was the red dress, lying in a pool of fabric on the floor. She stared down at it, and something like horror filled her.

On unsteady legs she walked over to the wardrobe. One of the doors hung ajar. She pulled it open and peered inside. Even in the faint light coming in, she could see that in the place where the red dress, now lying on the floor, had once hung, there was only an empty hanger.

For the first time, she felt the coldness of the room and shivered. Where was the lantern? Looking around, she remembered she'd placed it by the door in her dream. She moved through the dimness and found it just outside. She lifted it up and switched it on. She went to leave and paused. Heaving a sigh, she turned around and went back in, picked the dress up off the floor, hung it up, and closed the wardrobe.

Then with the comforting glow of the lantern to light the way, she made her way out of the room across the cold floor, along the hall, and down the staircase.

The fire in the inner parlor had gone almost completely out, leaving only glowing orange embers and a bone-deep chill.

She banked it back up and added some wood to get it going again and then tried to read for a few minutes to get her mind off the disconcerting vividness of her most recent dream. But her thoughts kept coming back to it over and over. She finally gave it up and just lay there, thinking of him and how he'd looked at her until she finally fell back into a deep, and this time dreamless, sleep.

IT WASN'T UNTIL lunchtime the next day that she remembered the vibration she'd heard the night before. She pulled her phone out and checked it. Jill had called—at 3:03 AM.

She immediately tapped her phone to call her back. Something had to be up for her to try and reach her at that time of night.

Jill, who used to be a dental assistant, was now a stay-at-home mom since the birth of her son, Joshua, and as Cheyenne was hoping, picked right up.

"Whatup, girl?" Jill said, using her fake homegirl accent.

"Hey. What are you doing? Is this a good time?"

"Yeah, I'm not doing anything right now. Josh just went down for an early nap."

Cheyenne frowned. This was probably the only time of the day Jill would get a break and there she was calling and bugging her. "I won't keep you long. I saw you called last night. Is everything all right?"

Jill gave a low laugh. "Everything's fine. I feel ridiculous now. I woke up and couldn't sleep and I was ... I was worried about you. Sorry about that."

"Don't apologize. You can call me anytime."

"I haven't talked to you in a while and I was thinking about it and it was the dead of night, you know how it is, and I had this uneasy feeling, like you might be in some kind of danger."

The only danger she was facing was falling in love with a man who didn't exist if she didn't get the heck out of this old house. "Well, I'm fine," she said as bits and pieces of her dream from the night before came back to her again.

Jill breathed into the phone in relief. "That's good. I'm glad to hear it."

She walked over to a chair away from the windows and dropped into it. "I was wanting to talk to you anyway."

"Oh, what about? What's going on?"

"I don't want to keep you on the phone too long, we can talk more another time, but I did want to tell you, tell someone .... Brent and I aren't together anymore."

Jill was quiet for a beat. "What do you mean? Are you still there at the house with him?"

"No. I left. After I walked in on him."

Jill sucked in a breath on the other end. "You don't mean he was ...?"

"*In flagrante*, yes. With the teenager from next door."

"*WHAT?*" Jill's shriek nearly split her eardrum.

"Technically she's nineteen, but she's almost twenty, as Brent put it."

"Still," Jill spat, but at least she'd lowered her volume.

"Yeah ... still. I walked in on him banging her over the goddam arm of the recliner."

Jill let out a sputter of laughter she quickly silenced. "I'm sorry. I know it's not funny."

"No. No, it's not." Cheyenne sighed. "Anyway. I'm fine. I found a place. It's just temporary, but—"

"Where are you staying?"

Stick to the truth as much as you can. She tried to be vague without arousing suspicion. "I'm staying down the road a bit, in this older house. The mailbox is shot, though, so I'll probably be getting a post office box." Even though only part of what she was saying was actually untrue, she felt terrible at having to lie to her best friend.

"Where are you working?"

"Um ... I'm not yet. But I hope to be interviewing soon."

"With your experience, as smart and capable as you are, you shouldn't have any trouble. Anyone who doesn't want to hire you is a fool."

Cheyenne felt a wave of affection for her longtime friend. Jill's unflinching support of her was just another example of the many reasons she valued her friendship.

"And about Brent," Jill added, "I'm sorry. I'm sorry about everything."

Cheyenne knew she wasn't merely talking about Brent; she was also talking about Ian, who she always referred to as the "baby" and not the "miscarriage." Something else she loved about her. "I guess it just wasn't meant to be."

There was a small silence, and then they both tried to talk at the same time. "Anyway, we can talk more another time." "You know you can call me anytime too."

"I know," Cheyenne said. "We'll talk again soon. Right now I've got to get on some of this cleaning. This place wasn't exactly left spotless."

Jill laughed. "Really? Okay, I better let you get to it then."

After reassuring Jill she would keep her informed, Cheyenne ended the call.

If absolutely necessary, Jill would probably take her in for a month or two. But she really hoped it didn't come to that. For one, it would mean relocating away from what little family she had, where nothing would be familiar.

Why had Jill been so worried about her? She'd heard of people being able to sense something wrong with their friends or family—and she and Jill had always been close. Was it possible Jill had sensed something of the situation she was in?

A frisson of foreboding swept through her.

But she was just being silly. There was nothing *dangerous* about the house, and nothing odd about Jill's concern. She had merely been stressing about how they hadn't talked lately and how unusual that was even now that they lived hundreds of miles apart, and she'd let her imagination run away with her.

Cheyenne was thinking so hard she suddenly found herself upstairs and halfway down the hall with no memory of having walked there.

The door to the room with the red dress squeaked loudly as she pushed against it and moved inside. She crossed the floor to stand in front of the wardrobe.

In her dream she had felt like a new person wearing the beaded crimson gown. She pulled open the door to look at it.

Again, she found it amazing how real it had all seemed and how easily she recalled the details even now, which had not faded and remained clear in her mind.

Am I losing my grip on reality? she wondered after standing there for nearly a full minute giving serious consideration to the possibility that it might have all been real. That somehow, she had slipped through a fissure in time.

Impossible. She closed the wardrobe with a bang, and left the room.

THAT EVENING, SHE waited as long as she could and then built a smaller fire (waking up to a patrol car out front had shaken her) and used only the lantern while she worked on the laptop revamping her resumé.

After a while, she was still feeling uneasy and decided to step outside.

She slipped out the front doors and stood there, scanning and listening for any vehicles, and then moved down the steps and into the moonlight.

She gazed up at the night sky. The moon hung there, a bright, nearly full circle of white beaming down onto the house and the tips of the surrounding trees.

Lowering her eyes, she waited for them to adjust, and then looked back at the house. She couldn't see any hint of light from where she was standing. Not from the glow of her screen, the fire, or the lantern.

To be sure, she turned and walked farther down the driveway, shoes crunching, to check from another angle.

She ascertained there was no light or obvious smoke showing and, giving a quick glance behind her, started back the way she'd come.

She had just passed the house and looked over to check once more, when a stray cloud slid in front of the moon, casting a shadow over the property.

She slowed and came to a stop in the near-perfect darkness. *What the hell are you doing here at this abandoned old place?* She needed to gather her stuff, put most of it into storage, and go sleep on her mother's floor, if that's what it took. Because this was crazy!

But then as fast as it had appeared, the cloud slid away, and the moon came back out, bathing the surrounding countryside in brightness. Along with it came a haziness, creeping out of the forest and encompassing the house, veiling the ravages of time and lending an elegant beauty to it.

She shot a look over her shoulder and headed for the front doors. The gauzy whiteness seemed to be emerging from the trees on all sides.

She found herself curious about what was out there again. Wilderness, or something more ... a hidden garden, a maze of hedges ... a hunting cabin?

Picking up her pace, she hurried up and into the house, closed the doors, and turned the lock.

Pausing there in the foyer, lit only by moonlight and, as always, the faint glow from the stained glass above, she took in a deep breath and reminded herself once more that it was only temporary. First sign of trouble, she would hightail it out of there, hopefully without anyone getting a good look at her or her tag number. She would call her mother, and Caleb, and they could have a talk with Brent. He couldn't just leave her in this kind of situation, after all. *Homeless*, her mind intoned. *You are homeless*.

But dammit, the humiliation of having to ask Brent for *anything*! She couldn't bring herself to do it. Not yet.

She was fine here for now. It would be fine for a short while.

Six

The next morning dawned sunny but cold. If she had dreamed anything the night before, she didn't remember it. She considered skipping a full bath and just washing up the best she could, but in the end her need to start the day completely fresh, along with her need to warm up, won out. She quickly got a fire going and put on some water to warm in a large black kettle she'd found under a table by the sink in the kitchen.

She'd already scrubbed out the clawfoot bathtub in the bathroom at the top of the stairs on the second floor, and by some miracle, she'd managed to get the toilet working. There was no water running in, but once she'd lifted the lid on the strangely high tank and filled it, she could see it was trying to flush. With the help of an old-fashioned brass-handled plunger, she'd soon had it *wooshing* down.

With the third batch—it took three mixed with more unheated water to make enough for a small bath—she also mixed up a cup of coffee.

In between sips of the scalding brew, she shed her clothes, then parked the mug beside the curved powder-pink tub that was so pale it was nearly white, and lowered herself into the steaming water. *Enjoy it while you can,* she thought. This little bath of hers had taken way too much of her supply. From here on out unless she had to wash her hair, she would have to heat a smaller amount and wash without soaking completely.

It could be hotter, but it was good enough. She slid down as far as she could and luxuriated in the warmth for a minute, raised up for a gulp of coffee, and then set to work on her hair.

Once she was clean, she climbed out, dried off with one of the towels she'd thought to bring, and donned the fresh undies, socks, sweater, and jeans she'd dug out. Scooping up her dirty clothes and damp towel, she hurried back to the gold sofa, dropped the clothes into a pile where she had been stashing some of her things, and draped the towel over the bags sitting there so it could dry.

She retrieved her moccasins, her go-to casual shoes, slipped them on, and began going over the rooms she'd been inhabiting. She moved the kettle back to where she had found it and tucked things away, trying to hide all signs of her presence.

She left the fireplace for last. It was obvious it had been used recently. Grabbing the broom, she used it to sweep most of the ashes into a dented metal bucket to be thrown out, but there was nothing she could do about the scent of smoldering wood still lingering in the air.

The entire time she was doing all this, waking up and getting ready for the day and setting things right, she was listening and sneaking peeks out the front. The drapes were mostly drawn, but what if a patrolman or anyone else got out and caught a whiff of lingering smoke or approached the door and heard her inside? Or took a look around back and found her car?

Then she would just have to deal with it. Explain and hope the consequences weren't too harsh.

She was still feeling somewhat isolated and decided to go out and upload her resumé on a few sites before checking out some more of the old belongings left in the house. She couldn't get Brent off her mind, either, which inevitably brought up memories of their almost family, and she needed something to distract her.

She went a little farther up the street to the Starbucks this time, and holding steady to her spot, munched on a grilled cheese sandwich and sipped a sparkling water with grapefruit while she determinedly set up accounts and uploaded her resumé on two different employment sites. She left the address the same for now, but she planned on changing it later after she acquired a post office box or better yet, rented a place. And anyone trying to reach her would most likely be doing it by email or phone.

Knowing she couldn't afford to keep sitting at restaurants and coffeehouses to job hunt, she took the time to attach and send a copy of her resumé to one of her other email accounts so she could later pull it down onto her phone and use it to apply for jobs. That way, as long as her phone was charged, which could be done in the car, she could do a lot of stuff at the house. She was able to get a signal there; she'd made a point of checking. Not in certain spots, but thankfully, it seemed to get a fairly decent one in the inner room she'd made hers.

SHE DRIFTED THROUGH the next several days, occasionally using her phone to search the job listings again or scroll disconsolately down her Facebook and other social media feeds. But mainly she just hung out, doing her daily chores—washing and dressing for the day, keeping her things tidy and hidden, gathering kindling and firewood—exploring the house, and sometimes reading a bit.

For the moment, making a serious effort to resolve her situation seemed to be more than she could handle, and she'd mostly shied away from such worries and allowed herself to coast along. Whenever Brent and their lost little boy entered her thoughts, she pushed them away firmly and turned her mind to the handsome man who had invaded her dreams.

In the evenings as she lay on her sleeping bag in the center room, she let herself imagine him again as a real person on some other level of existence who'd been yearning for someone just as she had, especially now that things with Brent were so irrevocably over.

But, inevitably, as the days passed, she grew bored with her own company and decided to venture out. She was fighting a sense of isolation and craving real human contact, even if it would only be with strangers. She also needed to replenish her water and firelog supply.

She left out the back through the sunroom. In the clear light of day, the reality of her circumstances struck her anew as she proceeded across to the carriage house and climbed into the car.

She started it and let it warm for a moment before backing out.

She would have to buckle down and choose a position soon, any position with a halfway decent salary so she'd have a paycheck and could at least rent a small apartment.

Because she couldn't keep on living here like this.

NOT FAR FROM her old place, she pulled into her usual convenience store to get gas, wondering if she'd see Brent. He was allowed an hour for lunch each day and sometimes chose to come home to eat and destress, which for him generally involved grabbing a bite while watching some news program, followed by a few minutes of loud music before going out the door. Would that still be his routine or would it now involve a quickie with Serena?

Holding back a shiver of distaste, she walked across the parking lot to pay with cash—another inconvenience of this new pared-down existence she was now living that didn't involve such luxuries as paying at the pump.

After gassing up, she waited for a break in traffic and then pulled out into the road to head for Target.

SHE HAD JUST taken a sip of the caramel Frappuccino she had been unable to resist on her way out, when she noticed the truck in the rearview behind her. Many men drove Ford trucks, but only one of them that she knew drove a yellow, custom-lifted F-250 and had messy swept-back hair with shaved sides and a phone cradle attached to the rearview. It was Brent. And judging by the way he was riding up behind her, he had spotted her as well. It was a little late for lunch, but maybe he had been held up at work.

She took another sip though the straw while she kept an eye on him.

For a couple of miles, he did nothing, then when she turned onto a different road that would take her to the house in a more roundabout way (she wasn't about to lead him straight there), he turned with her and flashed his lights.

She pulled over in front of the next place she came to, a junked-up tire shop that had seen better days. He turned in behind her and came around so their windows were side by side. He lowered his and she did the same.

"Long time no see," he said, as if they were merely friends who hadn't run into each other in a while.

"So ... where are you staying?" he asked when she didn't respond.

She rolled her eyes, ignoring the question. "What do you want, Brent?"

"Don't be like that."

Oh, for Pete's sake. If she had a dollar for every time he'd said that to her. Had he always been so passively aggressive? Coldly she stared at him, waiting him out.

He gazed back at her. "I've missed you," he said.

She didn't know what she had expected, but it hadn't been that.

"I have, I've missed you."

What about Serena? she wanted to ask, but she'd be damned if she'd give him the satisfaction.

"Look," he said. "I'm sorry. I am. I never meant for things to progress this far, this fast."

What was that supposed to mean? That he'd meant to take it slower, to let her down gently when he found someone more suitable? Was he finding life with Serena less than ideal? Served him right. She allowed herself a small smile. "Things not going well with Serena?"

He turned his head and stared out the windshield. What was going on in that mind of his? Did he actually want back with her? Or was he dumb enough to think he could turn to her for emotional support while keeping Serena by his side? A fuck-bunny in his bed and an ex-wife just a phone call away?

"No, they're not," he finally said, turning back to her. "Not really."

"Well that's what happens with girls that young." A small part of her was definitely enjoying this.

"That's enough," he snapped. "She's almost twenty and I'm no pedophile!"

She let out a sigh. And there it was. He had a charming side when it suited his purpose, but his true nature inevitably came out when you pushed him too far or things weren't going his way. But what did he expect? That she would melt at his renewed attention and count the days until she could have him back? Fat chance of that. But then he spoke and threw her again.

"I've been thinking about the baby."

"The miscarriage, you mean?"

He winced. "For God's sake, Serena. He was more than that."

"Serena!"

His eyes widened as he registered his error. *"Cheyenne.* I'm sorry. I can't believe I did that."

Fury coursed through her. "You can't even get my name right when you're talking about our *baby?* Our baby who also had a name!"

"I know! I'm sorry. Ian, our baby Ian."

Abruptly her anger faded, leaving behind only the familiar grief and despair.

"I do think about him all the time, Cheyenne. And you. I think of us and how it was at first."

Were those real tears in his eyes? Possibly. He wasn't a monster, after all. And he had lost a child too. A son. She felt herself softening toward him. The breakup of their marriage hadn't been all his fault, to be fair.

He scrubbed a hand across his eyes. "I guess things have gone too far, but I wish ..." He looked away, swallowing.

She had to blink back tears of her own. "I do t—"

His phone went off, interrupting her. She watched, incredulous, as he held up a finger at her and fished his phone out of his pocket.

He swiped to answer and shifted so he was facing partially away. She closed her eyes tight for a second. Then she put the car in gear.

She caught one last glimpse of him jerking his head around and then she was pulling away.

SHE SLOWED DOWN a little to let a car coming toward her go past—she didn't want to be seen heading for the old house—then cut the wheel and bumped onto the uneven pavement. She kept her eyes on the rearview, watching for other vehicles, but the road behind her remained empty.

Relaxing, she continued on and was soon following the driveway around.

She let off the gas, taking in the house again—the sun hanging above the tree line, sending shafts of light across it, bathing it in yellow—and then she was rolling past.

For a while she had been pretty successful in keeping the painful memories at bay, but now her encounter with Brent had brought it all back—the crushing sense of loss and the unfulfilled potential of the child that had never been.

"Don't think about it," she whispered to herself as she climbed out and walked over to the back entrance. Quickly mounting the steps, she yanked the door open, moved inside, and pulled it shut behind her.

Seven

Her pants and shoes were damp with dew by the time she pushed her way through the undergrowth and stepped onto the path she could still discern through the trees.

She had been up since dawn. Initially she had slept deeply, only to be jarred awake by her phone. Seeing it was Brent, she had ignored it and tried to get back to sleep. But blissful unconsciousness had remained elusive after that and she'd spent the rest of the night tossing and turning.

Figuring now was as good a time as any, she had finally dressed, hidden her things, and left the house to explore the other side of the property.

Something was definitely over here. Enough of the path remained to tell it had once been more than a game trail for the wildlife.

The trees ahead of her began to thin out and soon the way opened up and she found herself at the edge of an old cemetery. It was heavily overrun with vegetation, but the wrought-iron fence surrounding it had held some of it off.

There was no gate, just an opening in the pickets. Dead leaves crunched underneath her shoes as she passed between the two posts to enter the old burial ground.

She skirted the edge, then moved inward.

At roughly the center, she came to a stop. The more prominent graves were in the rear with taller, more intricately carved memorials and matching obelisks rising up on either side. In front of those were two meandering rows of headstones. The passage of time had been kind to the markers, and though some of them leaned a few degrees off center, none appeared in danger of toppling.

Turning, she began wandering amongst the timeworn, discolored stones, keeping to the narrow open strips between the plots. Many of them displayed the name Moore. The surname of the family that had once lived there?

One of the headstones farther back toward the older ones was particularly disquieting. Across the top, a skull with wings sprouting from it had been carved into the granite. It was a woman named Florence Moore's grave, and according to the weathered writing, she had died in 1860 at the age of fifty.

Cheyenne straightened up, stepped back, and read the inscription.

As I Once Was
So You Are Now.
As I Am Now
Soon You Will Be.
Prepare For Death
And Follow Me.

She pondered the disturbing words as she moved away to head up to where the newer plots were. *It's like she's speaking to me from the grave.*

Just past a memorial with writing so eroded it was difficult to read, her eye was caught by a thinner arched tablet. She walked over for a look.

The name AUGUSTUS MOORE had been chiseled into the stone in precise, elaborate letters. The dates were underneath. BORN MARCH. 3, 1854 and DIED JUNE 18, 1901. There was also an inscription across the bottom, but it had been covered by grass and weeds.

Squatting, she grabbed hold of the thickest part and yanked down on it to expose the worn writing. Below the name and dates was a single sentence: BORNE BACK INTO THE RIVER OF TIME.

It was a strange epitaph. And he'd been relatively young, only forty-seven, when he passed. What could have happened to him?

She turned her thoughts away from the ill-fated Augustus and slowly became aware of the absolute silence around her. When she'd set out, she had been cheered by the dappled sun shining through the leaves and the chirps and warbles of the birds in the nearby trees. But now the surrounding woods had gone silent and thick gray clouds had spread across the sky, dimming the light. It looked like she was in for a thunderstorm. The air felt strange, too. Her skin tingled and the hair was stirring on the back of her neck, as if a strike were building.

A sharp wind suddenly swept across, blowing her hair sideways and bending the tops of the trees. She pushed into it a few steps then had to stop as a strange feeling came over her. Time seemed to stand still and, stumbling, she fought to keep her legs under her.

Then as quickly as it came, the sensation passed and she regained her equilibrium.

Pushing the hair out of her face, she looked over and jumped, her heart giving a kick. There was a dark figure standing just inside the entrance. Good God. The woman, who had appeared as if conjured, stood utterly still, her dress the same deep gray as the sky, her eyes unnaturally wide and zeroed in on Cheyenne with unnerving intensity.

Another strong gust blew across, sending the hem of the woman's dress rippling. The surrounding countryside remained strangely hushed, and the only sound was the flapping of it in the wind.

"Don't be afraid," the woman's voice floated up.

But there was something *wrong* with the voice—the thin, reedy reverberation of it—and as the woman drew closer, the outline of her seemed to fade in and out, growing fuzzy and then sharpening.

"Please. You have to stay," the woman said, gliding slowly across.

Time to go.

Cheyenne lurched forward, cutting to the right to keep some distance between them. It was all she could do to not run in an effort to get around the woman and make it to the opening in the fence.

She had almost reached it, escape mere feet away, when she heard her speak again.

"*He needs you.*"

She stumbled to a stop and looked over her shoulder.

The woman was gone.

She darted her eyes about, searching for her, but the cemetery and the surrounding forest stood empty.

No way. There was no way she could have gotten completely out of sight that fast. Could she?

Had she been sleepwalking again? She looked down at her dew-dampened shoes, her brow wrinkling. No. No, she had not. She had most definitely been awake when she rose, dressed, and walked out there.

She took in a deep breath, let it out slowly, and then pivoted around to get moving again.

"THERE HAVE BEEN others," the handsome man murmured.

"Others?"

They were in the front parlor. She had entered through the smaller archway in the back hall that ran to the ballroom and found him standing there.

He continued staring at her, his body a silhouette against the brightness, and then stepped away from the windows and moved closer.

"Yes," he said, his face becoming more defined. "But they didn't remain long. And none of them returned."

The strange woman in the cemetery, what had she said? She'd asked her to stay. *He needs you*, she'd said.

"I-I don't ... I don't understand," she stammered.

"Neither do I." He smiled and tentatively took her hand. "But I'm glad you're here. I've thought about you ever since I first laid eyes on you." For a second there was only the cool touch of his fingers, and then warmth suffused her own as he tightened his grasp.

He pulling her against him. "I've waited so long." He leaned his head down and pressed his forehead against hers. His beautiful deep-set eyes closed, and then opened to stare into hers.

She'd never had anyone look at her that way, so intensely, as if their very life, their very soul depended on her. She let herself melt into him, and his arms went around her. All along this was what she had needed, what she had subconsciously yearned for.

"You could be happy here," he said, his breath gentle against her ear.

Happy? Could she ...? No, she thought, sadness filling her. Not after losing Ian, her little guy that never was.

"Look," he said, pulling away and throwing his arm out.

The mist that had shrouded the landscape had lifted and the clouds covering the sky were receding, filling the room with bright sunshine.

"There you are, Mr. Gus," said a voice behind them, and Cheyenne turned to see the woman from the cemetery entering, holding out a tray. "My homemade apple tarts," she said, smiling. She appeared plumper than she had and there were a few less strands of gray in her wiry dark hair, but it was unmistakably her.

"You can put them here, Myrna." He indicated a small table with two chairs, slightly to the side but still in the light from the sun.

"She's here," he said as she set the tray down.

The woman, Myrna, straightened up, an expression of wariness appearing on her brown face.

"This is her," he said, holding out an arm to indicate Cheyenne across from him.

Myrna's gaze shifted toward the space Cheyenne stood in, shifted back to Gus, then flew back to Cheyenne. Her eyes widened as if she hadn't noticed her until now as she went still and focused in on her. The woman looked like she'd seen a ghost. Blinking her eyes rapidly, she gave a quick nod and averted her gaze.

"Come," he told Cheyenne, paying the clearly disconcerted woman no mind.

Cheyenne followed him over and sat down. He stood behind her to help scoot her chair closer, then moved around and sat down across from her. Smiling, he reached for her hand, held it for a moment, then released it to pick up one of the tarts. "My favorite boyhood treat." He turned his attention to Myrna before taking a bite.

"No one makes them like Myrna," he said, and she beamed at the compliment.

Cheyenne chose one at random and bit into it. Buttery, flaky pastry along with tart, cinnamony apples enveloped her taste buds, and she nearly groaned aloud.

Laughing softly, Gus reached a finger across to brush a crumb from the corner of her mouth.

Instead of wiping it on one of the cloth napkins, he stuck it into his mouth to suck the crumb off, and Cheyenne felt a thump of desire low in her belly. Something she hadn't felt in a long time.

She was about to take another bite when something swooped toward the closest window and rammed into it.

She dropped the tart and shoved her chair back to stand. "I think a bird hit the window!"

The bird rose shakily up, darted away, then arrowed forward and slammed into it again.

"Oh, no ... do something!" The bird thumped hard into it again, this time leaving a smear of blood on the pane.

"What's wrong with it?" she cried, swinging around.

But he was gone.

He was gone; the tray of pastry was gone; the bright sunshine was gone.

"No!" she yelled—and looked back at the window.

She thought she was still dreaming as once more something crashed into it. And then the light seemed to seep back in and she became aware that she had risen not from a small table but from the chaise lounge there in the front parlor, where she'd only reclined momentarily to rest her eyes.

She staggered the rest of the way over and looked down. A glossy black crow lay on the verandah tiles, unmoving. Had it knocked itself out, or was it dead?

Still trying to shake off the incredibly vivid dream, she left the room and crossed the foyer. She had never had such realistic ones. It had seemed so real.

If only.

She pulled the front doors open and stepped out. She had forgotten to make sure no one was lurking outside, but thankfully the driveway remained free of vehicles. She closed the doors behind her and hurried over to the fallen bird.

It appeared dead; it lay completely still, the one eye she could see wide open and unblinking.

She prodded it with her shoe, and it came alive, floundered around, beating its wings. Taking a couple of steps back, she watched as it thrashed around some more and finally took to the air and made its way unsteadily across and around the side of the house.

She remembered the smear of blood on the window after the bird in her dream had collided with it. That bird had obviously been incorporated into it from the real one she must have heard in her sleep. And the woman, Myrna—she'd even given her a name—had originated from her encounter with the old woman in the cemetery, which had been strange but certainly real enough.

She turned and descended the steps, followed the walkway over, and started down the driveway, rocks and leaves crunching under her shoes. Snapping a quick glance up at the old road to make sure no one was coming, she stepped onto the path in the trees and headed for the old cemetery.

CHEYENNE STARED DOWN at the mossy, uneven marker. Instead of tall and arched, this one was low and wide and had begun to sink into the ground on one side. It had almost been hidden by the dead leaves where she finally located it to the side by the fence.

It held only one name.

MYRNA IRENE HALL.

She *must* have seen the woman's name when she was there before. She must have. But how? She had only walked around in the middle. She'd barely glanced over here.

If Myrna, the Myrna in her dream, the one *she had seen in the cemetery*, was a real person, then did that mean the man was—

She halted the direction her thoughts were taking. That was insane. Whoever she had seen during her previous visit, it couldn't have been this woman, because her death had also been recorded as well as her birth. According to the dates, she had passed away back in 1905.

But the name. It was the same name. It seemed too much of a coincidence. She *must* have seen it earlier and just didn't remember it. And it had woven itself into her subconsciousness. She had glanced over and read the woman's name without really registering it, then had seen the strange older lady, who was probably a neighbor, possibly suffering from dementia, who'd wandered by, and all of it had come together while she slept.

It was the only explanation, but she still couldn't rid herself of the feeling that there was more to it, that something *uncanny* was at play here.

What if there was? She gazed around at the graves closest to her. For a minute she let herself imagine again the handsome man as a real person existing on some other level, yearning for her as she now yearned for him. Someone whose love for her was real and not merely wishful thinking.

But it wasn't to be. Staying there at the abandoned home was doing a number on her head, was all, causing her imagination to work overtime.

65

Eight

The next day she received an email about a job. She found it that morning. She was a little surprised her phone was still on. But Brent had either missed it, or he'd left it alone on purpose. But for what reason? Out of decency to cut her some slack while she got on her feet? Or for some other ulterior motive?

She was betting on the latter, if how he'd acted the last time she saw him was any indication. No doubt with Serena he was no longer the center of attention. No longer just along for the ride. Now he had to act like a grown up and be responsible for things and cater to Serena's wants and needs. He had to play second fiddle, in other words.

Of course he would gravitate back to her, the one who had made him the center of her universe, the one who had always been there for him, who had cared and comforted him through thick and thin. Even when he had stopped being a comfort to her after he'd decided her mourning had gone on long enough.

Tough, she thought. *You made your bed now lie in it.* Which of course immediately brought forth an image of he and Serena writhing on twisted sheets. She hastily pushed it away, but it was enough to earn her a rush of pain at the thought of them together. *But* ... the pain was not as sharp as it had been. What she felt now was merely a glimmer of the agony she'd experienced initially.

The job opening was for an administrative assistant at a large corporation boasting a portfolio of award-winning projects that provided professional design and construction services. The pay was lower than what she had received before and the list of duties long, but it would do until she found something better. She quickly fired off a response and then went out the back through the sunroom to extricate her car so she could drive over to her mother's.

THE DOOR TO the apartment was closed even though it was the middle of the day when her mother usually kept it open for the added light.

But maybe she'd stepped over to the neighbor's. Her mother—Tabitha to the rest of the world but always "Tabby" to her father when he was alive—was getting on in years and as a result no longer worked, which had reduced her contact with other people. Finding herself still lonely after joining a nearby church, she had befriended Velma, the lady in the next-door apartment soon after she'd moved in.

She rapped on the glass then stood back to wait. She expected to have to rap again and then walk to Velma's, but almost immediately her mother appeared on the other side, looking nice as usual in a white button-up shirt and beige slacks with her hair recently styled.

"Hey. Did you try to call?" She moved back to let Cheyenne enter.

"No. I hope that's okay."

"It's fine. You know you're welcome to stop by any time."

"Why did you have the door shut?"

"I had to or the lady that moved in back here"—she gestured toward the apartment behind her—"would be banging to be let in. She won't knock if she sees the door closed, but if I open it up, here she comes."

"Do you not like her?"

"She's all right. But she comes over too often. And she's too old for me." She moved past the dining room table to enter the living room area, and Cheyenne followed behind her.

"She's nearly eighty," her mother added, plopping down in her favorite seat, an armchair facing the television.

That's not much older than you, Cheyenne thought in amusement as she lowered herself onto the loveseat, the only other place to sit.

There really wasn't adequate space for a coffee table, but her mother had one anyway. It would have to be moved for her to even put down a sleeping bag. But the bedroom was even tinier with hardly any space on either side of the bed her mother slept in.

"So, I've got some news," she began.

Her mother picked up the remote and pressed the button to turn the television down.

"We ..." She had been going to say *had a fight*, but that wasn't strictly true. "We're having some trouble," she amended.

"You and Brent?" A slight wrinkle appeared between her mother's brows, but she didn't look exactly surprised.

"Yeah." She decided to just come right out and say it. "I caught him cheating on me."

"Oh, Cheyenne. Are you sure?"

Was she *sure*? She squelched the ripple of irritation that ran through her. Did her mother believe she was merely jumping to conclusions, being overly dramatic?

But really, she couldn't blame her. There had been several times in the past when she had claimed to be through with Brent forever for some supposedly unforgivable reason or another.

"Yes, I'm sure. I *saw* him. In the living room. With the girl next door."

Her mother's expression darkened. "The girl next door!"

"She's almost twenty."

"But ... And you're positive?"

"*Yes*. They were *half naked*. He had her—"

Her mother threw a hand up. "That's enough. I get the picture."

"It wasn't pretty." Cheyenne sat back and ran a hand through her hair.

"What is wrong with him? Right there in the house!"

She shook her head in shared disgust. "He's a goddam man, that's what."

"That's right, he's a *goddam man*."

Cheyenne looked over at her in astonishment. Normally her mother would gently admonish her for her unladylike language and general disparagement of men, not contribute her own. She rubbed her eyes. She hadn't rested well the night before, though she must have slept because she'd dreamed of the handsome man again.

"They're not all bad," she said, thinking about him, the one so persistently appearing in her nocturnal imaginings.

"I mean, look at Caleb," she continued. "He was ridiculously faithful to Kaitlyn even when she was cheating on him left and right." Kaitlyn was the particularly slutty girl her brother had stubbornly dated for an unforgettable six-month period. "But Brent, he's something else entirely."

"What are you going to do? Did you make him leave?"

"No ..."

Her mother waited expectantly. Still thin-lipped but now concerned, as well.

"I don't suppose I can stay here, can I?" she asked jokingly. There was barely any room, but they could make it—

But her mother was shaking her head. "They won't allow it."

This was the first she'd heard about any such rule. But it made sense. Nearly all the units were filled with senior citizens subsisting mainly on social security checks.

"There's a stipulation in the agreement that says visitors can only stay up to three days."

"I didn't know that."

Her mother nodded. "And you know I would let you otherwise, but I can't risk being evicted."

"No, of course not."

"You can stay the three days if you need to, but I'm not sure where you'd sleep. And what would you do after that? It might be best if you remained at the house and tried to get him to leave."

Cheyenne wasn't about to tell her she'd already moved out, and God forbid, taken up residence in an abandoned house. She settled for nodding noncommittally.

They talked a little more. She made it clear there was no chance of her forgiving Brent even if he agreed to dump Serena, which he had not. Then when a decent enough time had passed, she stood up to leave.

"I did get a job offer, though," she told her before going out the door.

"You did? That's great!"

"So fingers crossed. I'm hoping they've already set up my interview."

Her mother followed her out onto the concrete square above the parking area. "Good luck. I hope you get it."

"Me too."

Cheyenne descended the slope to where she'd left the car, climbed in, and started it up. As was her custom, her mother remained outside, watching. She backed out, returned her mother's wave, and pulled away.

She wasn't quite ready to head to the house yet, so she drove over to the Hot Spot, her old familiar convenience store.

There were only a few vehicles out front, none of them Brent or Serena's. She turned in and parked in an empty spot on the side.

Her staying at the abandoned house had been a knee-jerk response when she'd been at her worst and not thinking clearly. But now what she'd seen as a choice, at most a temporary shelter in the storm while she caught her breath, was fast on its way to becoming a necessity, making her, in essence, truly homeless.

Shuddering, she got out her phone and stabbed at it to call her brother. He'd have to let her stay there. It was that or move two states away to Jill's, where nothing was familiar, and risk straining their already tenuous friendship.

She didn't think he was going to answer, but then he did. "Hello?"

"Hey, bro, whatcha doing?"

She heard the sound of the phone being jostled around, then his voice again. "*Ahhh*, I'm working on the damn car."

Talk about bad timing.

"What's up?" He now sounded like he was at a distance. "Everything okay? How's Mom?"

"She's fine. I just came from there."

"That's good." From the noise he was making, she could tell he was trying to work as he talked.

"I can call you back later. You sound busy."

"Wait." The sounds on the other end ceased and his voice grew louder. "I think it's just the battery. No big deal. Did you need something?"

Cheyenne thought about how to answer that. Yes, she needed something. But now was not the best time. "I was just wondering ..." She decided to go ahead and inquire at least. "Is Terrence still sleeping in the other bedroom?"

"Uh, yeah. Why?"

Dang it. Well, there was always the couch. But even as she thought it, she knew it wouldn't work. The first thing that would happen would be that one of them, most likely her brother, would insist she take his room and he'd end up on the couch. She couldn't do that to him. He worked too hard on his job and at his coursework to not get his rest.

"Oh ... Brent and I are having problems."

After a small silence he asked, "Is it that bad?"

"Yes, I'm afraid so."

She had to give him credit; he took her words at face value and didn't question her resolve. "I'm sorry, sis. What's the prick done?"

Cheyenne sputtered a laugh. Her brother was pretty easy going in a non-judgmental kind of way and she knew this was his way of supporting her. She felt a rush of affection for him. No, he was not like Brent. He was one of the good ones. *Like your dream man. If only he were real.*

"He cheated on me with the bimbo next door."

"No way."

"Yes way. Over the arm of the recliner."

He barked a laugh. "Over the arm of the … I'm sorry. I know it's not funny."

"No, it's okay. I'm okay. I've had some time to come to terms with it."

"Is he still staying there?"

"Unfortunately."

"What are you going to do? You're not going to let him get away with that, are you?"

"Hell no. Things are kind of up in the air right now but he will most definitely not be getting away with it. We're done. I'm done."

"Good. I'm glad to hear it."

"You are?" Was he just trying to make her feel better again?

"I've never really cared for the guy. Especially after … after you lost …"

"I know." Cheyenne squeezed her eyes shut. Would this grief ever leave her? Did she want it to? She never wanted to forget her baby boy—he'd existed, if only for a brief time; he deserved to be remembered. But it was so hard.

Nine

The house wasn't that bad. So what if it didn't have electricity or running water? She had the lantern she'd bought and candles and bottled water and the fireplaces. Set out there like it was, just abandoned and going to waste—nobody knew or cared the house was even there, or if she was in it.

You're just trying to make yourself feel better about the situation, she thought.

But still, she wasn't completely destitute without even a roof over her head; she was technically a squatter. Like one of those people you hear about that take possession of some empty place then refuse to move out, all the while baying about their rights.

You're doing it again. She looked around the larger parlor where she stood. *Don't kid yourself. You are homeless taking shelter in an old abandoned mansion.*

But luckily for her, it was an old, abandoned, *forgotten* mansion.

And why *hadn't* anyone else discovered the place and made use of it? Surely kids out playing or other homeless people had wandered upon it? There was the slightly newer stuff—the coat and newspapers and things upstairs—but that could have been left by a relative or descendant. Her eyes traveled across the room, flicking over the mantel, lamps, and remaining pieces of furniture scattered around the spacious area—the few delicate chairs and tables in the periphery, the chaise lounge, the stately grandfather clock, now silent. None of their dusty surfaces were marred by fingerprints other than her own, none of the walls marked by graffiti. No detritus had been left behind by a transient or a group of young people out partying. It seemed odd.

She turned slightly, facing more toward the entryway into the late afternoon sunshine coming through the small opening in the drapes she'd left alone. She let herself enjoy it for a moment, and then moved away. With it shining in like that, it would be easy for a cop or anyone else to spot her. She had to keep out of sight, stay quiet, and remain vigilant if this was going to work at all, even for a short while.

And a short while was all she planned on staying. Thank heavens she had the interview. And it wasn't until the day after the next, so she had time to visit the storage building and get a decent outfit and prepare.

The woman from the company's human resources department had called her late that morning. She had stepped out the back door in the sunroom—something she liked to do occasionally if she needed some fresh air but didn't want to risk being seen if someone came down the driveway—and the sound of her phone had shattered the silence that seemed to linger around the home, causing her to nearly drop it fumbling to answer. Managing to keep hold of it while accepting the call at the same time, she had dashed back up the steps into the house and down center hall to the cozy interior room where she'd left her laptop and things, to take down the details.

If she got the job right away, she could have her first paycheck in a couple of weeks. And a couple of weeks after that, she would have enough to get in a place, a small apartment if nothing else. One month. If she could make it one month. Or better yet, she could wait until she was on the job and then have Caleb or her mother get a loan for her if she couldn't get one herself. If she was very careful, she could probably just manage a small payment. That way she could get on in somewhere. And leave this place.

But she had to admit, she didn't hate it there. There was something peaceful and inviting about its spacious rooms, high ceilings, and many windows allowing in the warmth and light. Once upon a time it must have been a beautiful home full of joy and laughter, and hopefully of love. Generations must have lived in and visited this home nestled in the woods, this sturdy rampart against an ever-changing tumultuous world. There must have been the sound of feet scurrying about and servants bustling to and fro. And Myrna, she imagined, moving from the kitchen to the dining room, bearing some delicious delicacy. Treats to bestow upon Gus, who sat there waiting with a smile on his face.

There must have been others over the years who had braved the old back road shrouded in mist. Possibly the house had simply remained undisturbed throughout the many years excerpt for those wandering few after it was no longer maintained and fell into disuse. After it fell into the cracks of time. She could see it: a couple, or someone alone, taking the road on impulse or by accident, making their way along the buckled asphalt to turn in. And behold, there was the house. But for whatever reason, they had chosen to not go in or stay long enough to become beguiled as she had. She thought this abstractedly, knowing on some level she had become enamored of the home and its previous resident.

Stop it. He's not real. As if coming to, she discovered she'd drifted over to the windows again. *Vigilant*, she reminded herself.

She moved over to the side where she wouldn't be seen and sat down on a chair with a needlepoint seat that had fared better than some of the others.

She had instinctively called him Gus, too, in her dream, short for Augustus, the name on the headstone.

She was not only so troubled and lonely that she'd incorporated someone who had been dead for decades into her increasingly persistent dreams of a man who didn't exist, she was also assigning him the shortened version of his name.

SHE VENTURED OUT right before sundown to charge her phone and grab a few things. Not wanting to go all the way into a bigger store just for what she needed that night, she turned the car to head back to her old stomping grounds. She'd settle for what she could find at the Hot Spot.

She had fixed herself up a little, but she definitely wasn't at her best and prayed that Brent, or worse, Serena wouldn't come in.

Moving swiftly up and down the aisles and shooting nervous glances at the entrance, she selected a yogurt, a container of cut-up fresh fruit (a surprising find), two Lunchables, a bear claw, and a tea.

She paid for everything, along with a slice of pizza, took them out to the car, then went back in for the hot drink she'd wanted but had talked herself out of. If she was going to ride around while her phone charged then she wanted something while she did it.

She definitely wasn't up to dragging her laptop or tablet into Panera or anywhere else and had already decided to use her phone to find out what she wanted to know.

She felt faintly ridiculous as she walked back across in front of the youngish man working the register, but he didn't seem to think anything of it and took no notice.

After paying the man for the chocolate cinnamon cappuccino she'd chosen, which had sounded interesting and required minimal effort on her part, she left the store to hit the road.

She could have let the car run behind the house while her phone charged, but she hated to risk it. The way noise travelled in the country, especially at night, she was afraid someone might pick up the sound of it.

Once she was out and about, sipping her cappuccino while she drove some of the less travelled roads, she found herself glad she'd left the house. She had needed to get out of there for a while.

She felt even better after she parked at the Walgreens on the other side of town, picked up her phone, and learned what she did about squatter's rights.

Then seemingly out of nowhere, a slight sprinkle started that quickly turned into a deluge, pounding onto the rooftop, and the temperature seemed to drop about ten degrees.

She waited it out for a while, and then at the first sign of slackening, pulled out and hurriedly headed for the house, ready to get out of the elements.

SHE LEANED FORWARD and picked up one of the crackers topped with slices of turkey and cheddar from the plate on the table in front of her where she sat in the inner room. She'd already eaten the piece of pizza. She bit into the cracker and chewed contentedly. It was beginning to get cold at night, but the evening chill had been easily dispelled by the small stack of logs she had burning in the fireplace. She had been doing some cleaning, too, and with the room gleaming and the gloom dispelled by the fire and the soft candlelight, it was easy to imagine it a normal house and her a normal occupant.

This was further reinforced by what she had found out. The laws varied from state to state but basically, she had been surprised to learn, someone could inhabit a property and even claim ownership of it as long as the owner didn't evict or take action against them. She ticked off the basic requirements in her head. You had to take exclusive possession of the place. In other words, you couldn't share the property with any other squatters or trespassers. Check. You had to live there openly. Well, there was no one to see her, so ... You had to occupy a home that was abandoned or foreclosed upon. Check. You must live there exclusively. Check. She definitely fulfilled that one; she had nowhere to go even for a night without driving two states away to Jill's house. And finally, you usually needed to live in the place uninterrupted for seven years. But that was to gain the title, which didn't really apply to her.

Or did it? She uncurled herself from the sofa, walked over to the log rack, and bent down for one of the larger pieces she'd picked up out in the yard under a pecan tree. It made good firewood, she'd discovered. It burned well and barely smoked. She had also found an apple tree back beyond the dilapidated barn. Many of the ones hanging low or lying on the ground had been unblemished, and she had brought some of those in with her, too.

Of course she had no intention of staying there that long and trying to petition the county for the property. It probably wouldn't work, anyhow. Best-case scenario, she would be served an eviction notice and given a few weeks to vacate. But it was nice to know that there was a precedence for it. She wasn't necessarily a *criminal*. Just doing what it took to survive. And if she did take ownership, she would then be paying taxes on it, which would only benefit the county. A win, win for everybody.

AS SOON AS she opened her eyes the next morning, she knew she should be more worried about the flip side of her situation. The night before it had been easy to fool herself into believing that what she was doing was perfectly reasonable, but in the cold light of day now that she was rested, she thought it more likely that the worst-case scenario might occur and she would be hauled in for trespassing.

With that cheery thought to galvanize her, she quickly set about bathing, getting dressed, scraping her hair back into a ponytail, and hiding her things. Then it was on to the storage building for an outfit to wear to the interview.

At the end of the old road, she stayed back like she always did before inching up to make sure no one was coming. She didn't want to be seen pulling out too many times. If the locals were aware of the house, they might report suspicious comings and goings.

Fifteen minutes later, she passed through the open gates of the storage facility. She waved at Donny behind the counter, then nosed the car around to head to her unit.

Ten minutes after that, she had the door rolled up on her space and had let herself become distracted by a photo album she'd plucked out of a plastic crate. She had started it when she was still working at Cracker Barrel, back when people still occasionally printed their photos, before she had even entered college.

She flipped the page and gazed at a shot of her and Jill standing in the shop wearing their brown, yellow-starred aprons in front of a shelf of jarred preserves. That was where they had met. Cheyenne had been a cashier and Jill had been the giftshop manager. Jill had worked there while in a long relationship with a guy who did road construction that didn't end well before her so-far successful marriage to Ben, the man she was with now. Cheyenne adored Ben. He never cared how much time Jill and she spent together (unlike Brent who could barely conceal his resentment of her best friend), and always seemed to genuinely welcome her whenever she came around.

A wave of sadness swept over her at the thought of those days now gone forever, when they were young and fresh and still had their lives ahead of them.

They had both taken a few hits since then. Her father's death. Losing the baby. Jill's bad break-up after a lengthy engagement. Jill and Cheyenne's joy when Jill finally met and married Ben and then their anguish when his job necessitated their move to Virginia. And now Cheyenne's impending divorce from Brent.

She turned to the next page and smiled at the snapshot at the bottom. It had been taken by Cheyenne's then sort-of boyfriend Bryan, the backup cook that played the drums in his spare time. He had liked to carry his sticks with him and beat them on anything handy, she remembered. He'd had her and Jill shift to the right to get out of the glare and then clicked the photo just as Cheyenne raised two fingers in the classic "bunny ears" or "devil's horns" sign behind Jill's head (more like devil's horns in Jill's case; she had been pretty wild then). Cheyenne had been in the habit of playfully doing that. Jill, having no idea, was smiling broadly. She hadn't even cared when she saw it later because she had loved the fact that she looked skinny in the jeans she had on in the picture. Jill had still been fighting to keep off the weight she'd lost after what she claimed was a notoriously chubby phase of her adolescence.

Reluctantly, Cheyenne closed the album and placed it back in the crate. She could look through it again later, wherever she ended up. Right now she needed to find something decent to wear.

The position she was trying for, along with the pay, was significantly lower than the one she'd held before. Her most recent employer had been a medical group where she had become the office manager one memorable month when not one but three of their key people were out—one (the residing manager) for health reasons, one because of a bad wreck that required a long recovery, and one who took a sudden leave of absence to help her daughter after a difficult birth. When it became clear that someone needed to step in, they'd nominated Cheyenne, who had worked the closest with their last manager. And she'd performed the role so well for so long that when it became clear none of the three would be coming back at all, at least not in the foreseeable future, they'd allowed her to keep it. In time her previous position had been filled, she'd stayed where she was, and that had been that.

At this new company she would be the equivalent of a glorified assistant. And the list of duties provided with the job description had been extensive, especially for what was basically a junior position. But it wasn't anything she hadn't done or overseen before, and at least it was a foot in the door. She could negotiate a few months down the line.

She found the set of clothes she had in mind draped across the trunk with the other garments still on hangers she'd grabbed out of the closet. She had bought the light-gray trousers and matching jacket not long before she'd found out she was pregnant.

She studied them critically. A little wrinkled but not too bad. She laid them back down. Now a shirt. She dug through the various bags, boxes, and trash bags, and finally came up with two possible choices. A maroon blouse that was fairly nice but was, well … *maroon*. And a simple white button-up that had been her go-to top at one point.

She'd take them both. And her dark gray heels if she could find them.

She searched around until she located the shoes and added them and a pair of knee-high leather boots she occasionally wore in the winter to the small pile. *Oops*, she'd almost forgotten.

She stepped over and lifted up the mesh beach bag she'd packed some of her hair products and a few other things in and extracted the small bottle of wrinkle release spray she'd bought the one and only time she had flown to Richmond to see Jill's new place.

Then she stuffed everything inside the largish charcoal-colored handbag she usually carried with the outfit, grabbed her other blanket while she was there, and toted everything out to the car.

Ten

She was given a visitor's badge by a young lady that didn't look old enough to work there and told to wait and someone would be down to fetch her.

Cheyenne moved away from the reception desk and walked over to stand near the elevator alcove. The modern, sophisticated décor of the place was a world apart from the barely pleasant, serviceable areas and halls of her previous job.

She smoothed down the front of her jacket, wishing she had gone with a different outfit, maybe splurged for something new. Her mother might have been able to help with that. What had seemed like a classic, chic pantsuit, that she'd been complimented on by her previous co-workers, now appeared a little worn and rather dated in such shiny surroundings. Her hair was good, at least. She had gotten up early to wash it and then had let it dry by itself with a bit of gel, and it had behaved itself for once and settled into gentle waves.

The elevator nearest to her opened, and a second later out stepped a smartly dressed fortyish woman with brown hair twisted expertly into a bun.

"You must be Ms. Tanner," she said as she reached Cheyenne. "I'm Marcia. We spoke on the phone."

"Yes. Thank you for seeing me."

Marcia turned back toward the elevator, and Cheyenne fell into step beside her. "You'll actually be meeting with Dafne. She'll be doing the interview." The woman was a trifle older than everyone else she'd seen so far, but well put together in her slim, ankle-length pants above high, strappy heels, chiffon blouse, and three-quarters-sleeve jacket.

Cheyenne followed her into the elevator and moved to the back as the only other occupant, a young man nicely dressed in a casual suit, pressed the button on the panel for them.

Cheyenne was starting to get a feel for the place. Nice, dressy, but trendy seemed to be the pervading fashion. She was definitely going to have to pick up some new clothes.

Halfway down a corridor with natural slate flooring, Marcia slowed at a closed door then led the way through without knocking, past a group of four desks in open workstations, to a closed door of a private office on their right. Marcia tapped on it, and then stuck her head inside.

"You can go on in," she said, stepping back.

"Wish me luck," Cheyenne murmured. But if Marcia heard she gave no indication.

"Come in ... sit down," said a thin woman with dark red hair who was all of twenty-five, half standing behind the desk that dominated the space. This Dafne Keller, as her nameplate stated, didn't seem to feel a handshake was in order and sat right back down, so Cheyenne didn't offer one either. She did, however, introduce herself.

"Hello, I'm Cheyenne Tanner." She lowered herself onto the wooden chair across from her. "Thank you for meeting with me."

The other woman unpeeled a sticky from a folder in front of her. "You're applying for the Administrative Assistant position?"

"Yes—I am." Should she have said "ma'am"? No, that didn't feel right. She cleared her throat and shifted slightly. The chair was uncomfortably hard and set a little too far away from the desk, given the proceedings an interrogative quality.

Dafne—somehow Cheyenne couldn't think of her as Ms. Keller—raised her eyes and regarded her.

Finally she dropped her gaze. "Although this is one of our more junior positions, it *does* require someone who has had extensive experience performing a wide range of advanced administrative duties."

Had the woman not read her resumé?

"You would be providing support for our teams in the project development department. For example, managing calendars and travel to expedite work results, maintaining contact lists, scheduling meetings and preparing agendas, creating some reports, as well as monitoring and contributing to our social media presence. You would also oversee company hospitality for any visitors and for corporate functions including food and entertainment." She stopped to look at Cheyenne briefly, then picked up a pen and scrawled something on a small pad.

What could she be writing at this point?

"You will also be expected to help coordinate the board of director meetings, as well as provide assistance and hospitality to the tradespersons." Her gaze shifted down, and Cheyenne could see her taking in her faintly creased, slightly worn clothing. Well, let her, she thought. Her clothes were less than new, but they were of good quality and hadn't been cheap. And her shoes were well made and had held up fine. She crossed her legs defiantly.

"And then there's the invoice management. And you may be expected to field incoming phone calls."

Cheyenne decided to speak up. "All that's fine. I've done a lot of that before, or saw to it. On my former job."

Dafne continued relentlessly on. "At times you may even be asked to monitor deliveries and help organize workspace. Ultimately, Miss ..."

"Tanner," Cheyenne supplied, not bothering to correct the honorific. For Pete's sake.

"Ultimately, Miss Tanner, you would be expected to provide support to the engineers and project managers in almost all areas."

Cheyenne moved her head up and down. The woman seemed to be trying to scare her off with the long list of tasks, especially for a position not that far above entry level. Or maybe they just expected a lot more nowadays. For a lot less money. "That all seems fine. As I said, I do have experience with most of that."

Dafne opened up the folder in front of her. A slight frown appeared between her brows. Cheyenne knew that if she was finally looking over her resumé, she was seeing the gap in the dates from the last time she worked and now. And the fact that she was a bit overqualified for this job. *Some personal issue*, Dafne would be reading into it ... *some kind of drama or even a disfunction, possibly*. Because she had never returned to work after losing the baby.

Saying nothing, Dafne read on, flipping to the second page, and then looked up at her. "Frankly, you seem a little *too* qualified for this position."

"I suppose I am," she responded carefully. "But it's fine. I think it will be a nice transition for me."

Dafne picked up the pen again and began tapping it on the desk. Cheyenne found her eyes riveted to it as she struggled think of something else to say. She had been out of work too long. She had forgotten how to play the game.

She tried to rally herself. "I would like a chance at this. I know I can do a good job for you. I'm fully capable, as you can see, and I'm—"

Dafne sat back in her chair. "I'm not sure you would be satisfied here."

"Oh no, I assure you, it will be fine." Was the woman kidding? Clearly she would have enough to do. But she could be worried Cheyenne would only stay for a short while before moving on. "And I promise I won't up and leave you in the lurch or—" she stopped talking as Dafne's phone went off. She hadn't bothered to silence it for the interview. Why was she begging this woman, anyhow? She wasn't even sure she wanted the job now. The pay wasn't that great. She could probably do better somewhere else if she put some effort into searching.

"I'm just not sure you would be a good fit," Dafne said, apparently rejecting the call, no longer looking at her. Clearly her mind was already on other things.

And that's when she knew it was lost.

She got to her feet and held out her hand. "Thank you for your time, Ms. Keller." She gave Dafne's reluctant hand a brief shake, smiled grimly, and walked out.

SHE SHOULD HAVE shown up looking sharp, exuding confidence, and acting positively thrilled with the idea of everything she could do for Eastern Designs. She should have led right off with how she'd had a health issue a while back—she wouldn't have had to go into detail about losing the baby—but had since recovered and felt that their company would be a perfect chance to rehone her skills and gain a new family that she hoped to be working with for a long time ... yadda yadda yadda.

Instead, she had made minimal effort with her appearance and then had gone in there and basically sat there mute.

She flipped on the blinker, started moving into the lane she needed, and was nearly sideswiped by a silver Lexus, unconcerned with her signal, whipping around her.

"Dammit!" she cried, veering away. The son of a bitch! Now she was in danger of missing her turn. She looked over her shoulder again, saw that mercifully the guy who'd been coming up behind the jerk had stayed back, and she was able to get over.

Blinking back tears, she tried to calm down. She was positively shaking. From the near miss, and from the morning she'd had. Not to mention the fact that she still had no job. A week or two more of this and she would have to break down, swallow her pride, and beg her mother, brother, Brent, and her cousin, if that's what it took, to fix her situation. She could end up in *jail*. She was going to have to take some sort of job, any job, that she could get fast. Enough was enough. She could keep looking after she was hired on. She could do interviews on her lunch break.

Vowing to start fresh the next morning and really make a concerted effort to find some type of employment to at least get the ball rolling, she switched on the radio and tried to put it out of her mind for the time being.

ON THE LONG stretch before the old back road to the house, her phone began to vibrate down in her bag where she'd stuck it.

She waited until no one was coming and then dug it out while keeping her eyes on the road, and risked a quick glance. It was Brent. Again.

She put the phone down. Why did he keep calling? What did he want from her? Did he imagine she'd already landed some high-end job she might be willing to help support him with if he deigned to devote himself to her again? It was possible he thought just that. He didn't make that much at the bait and tackle shop he worked at. The pay reflected the number of actual tasks he performed, she suspected, which was probably why he had never looked for anything better. He had it made there. Just like he'd had it made with her when she'd brought in a substantial amount of their income, took care of the shopping, the cooking if any cooking was done, and most of the housework, all the while basically catering to his every want and need—his moods, his fears, his insecurities. He had to be aware of this, if only in the back of his mind.

And yet she could see him thinking she might still take him on again despite all of this, and despite his affair with Serena. He probably saw it as merely an indiscretion that was not entirely unjustified. And maybe he was right. He wasn't solely at fault for what happened. And there was a part of her that still leaned in his direction, that felt the connection between them, solidified when they'd created a child. Even now, something deep inside her didn't want to give that up. Her tiny unborn son, possibly the only child she would ever have for all she knew, had been made from their love. From Brent. To give that completely up, to give up Brent, was like destroying the last vestige of their life together, leaving her with not even the man who'd help make her little Ian.

But, she reminded herself a second later as the image of he and Serena rose in her mind, eclipsing her thoughts of the baby and that period—he didn't have to do it that way. He could have had the restraint and decency to not have done it right there behind her back in the home they'd made together, in the home they'd made tiny Ian in. She had deserved better than that. They had made a sacred commitment to each other and they had begun a family together, and it had deserved more than to be sullied in such a way.

He'd made his recliner, now let him lie in it. She chuckled humorlessly to herself, slowing, and checked the rearview. No one in sight. She turned the wheel and bumped onto the old pavement. She got on the gas a little to get all the way out of sight, bouncing in the seat, and then slowed to maneuver around a pothole.

The heater, which she had blasting in an effort to combat the chill that had fallen over the car while she had been squandering her chance at Eastern Designs, was beginning to get to her. She reached down and turned it off, then pressed the button to lower the window.

Cold air along with the smell of earth, damp bark, and pine needles rushed through the opening, and she quickly raised it back up a little. *Hold on.* She hit the brake, bringing the car to a stop, and lowered the window all the way. She wanted to see if she could smell the lingering scent of smoke from the fireplace.

She leaned her head out the window and then went still, eyes going wide, at what she heard. Somewhere up ahead, a vehicle sat with the engine running.

She tried to shove the gearshift into reverse, missed, and landed it in park instead. "Shit!" The sound of the other vehicle changed, and she heard the horrifying crunch of rocks as whoever it was began moving.

She ripped it back out of park, managed to get it into reverse, and started backwards, immediately hitting a raised part of the asphalt, jarring her sideways.

There wasn't much space left between the invading trees and brush and she had to try and stick to the middle where there was still pavement, but in her haste, she kept swerving. Frantically, she looked for somewhere to hide the car—she doubted she had time to turn around, even if she had room—fearing she would be overtaken by the other vehicle any second. And then what would she say if it was the law? *I took this road by mistake and was trying to find somewhere to turn around?* Which considering the state of the old road and the fact that it was damn near impossible to spot, was pretty unbelievable. And if they had already discovered someone had been staying there, they would then logically conclude it was her. And she had left plenty of things in the home that would identify her. She'd grown lax in her precautions and had failed to bring her laptop or tablet with her this time.

Even if they hadn't already figured out someone had been staying there, her being seen might cause them to become suspicious. They might start watching the house or search it better. She would be discovered.

There! Down in a lower area off the side, between two larger trees, there was a slightly less overgrown stretch leading back into the shadows of the denser terrain.

Speeding up while trying not to wreck, she hoped they had their windows up and didn't hear her as she accelerated backwards, cut the wheel, and bounced up and over a small log she hadn't seen, and crashed through the trees and mostly dormant vegetation, branches sweeping the sides of the car. As soon as she could, she swung around, still backwards, stopped so she could put it into drive, and took off forward again.

It being nearly winter, there was less coverage than there would have been. *But if I …* She cut the wheel viscously to the left, away from what she thought might have once been a dirt road. It was still too visible for it to have merely been a trail, but she'd seen no sign of a blacktop. She careened down and over some tree roots, sliding a bit, then straightened up and made for a higher, flatter spot and a clump of cedar trees. If she just didn't get stuck, with the angle of the road and the sun, and with it being in shadow, she might not be spotted. He would actually have to look *back* once he came around the bend in order to see her. If she could just … get … up there. With one final burst of speed, she hit the slope, car tilting upwards, and shot to the top.

Cresting, the car leveled out, and she rolled to a stop and cut the engine.

Where were they? They should have come around by now.

A second later there it was, flickering sunlight hitting the windshield as a sheriff's cruiser rounded the bend and came into sight.

She watched as it rolled toward her. There was only one figure inside. She thought it might be the same deputy from before, but his face was in darkness and she couldn't make out his features or even which direction he was looking.

The cruiser crept along, rocks crunching underneath the tires. Any second she expected him to lurch to a stop and jerk the door open.

As he was coming up on the part where she was most likely to be seen, the sun went behind a cloud and the old road and surrounding woods fell into shadow. In the dimmer light, she finally became aware of the mist creeping up from the ground. She twisted in her seat. It was in the forest all around her, a white haze floating up, growing thicker as she watched. She twisted back around. The deputy was still coming, but he had slowed and was barely moving now. He might have noticed what she had, that the mist which was now more of a fog had thickened in the woods around them, shrouding the forest in opaque whiteness.

The cruiser came to a complete stop and sat there motionless, the sound of its engine oddly muffled.

What was he doing? Up on higher ground like she was, she was able to see him easily. But hopefully the mist and the angle had hidden her from him.

Afraid to move, she waited for him to drive away. If any part of her car *were* visible, he only had to look over and slightly back to see her.

Finally, the cruiser started forward, first slowly, and then quicker, and soon it had moved out of sight.

She listened to the muted sound of it as it continued on down to the end, turned, and accelerated onto the main road. She could still hear it even then, until finally, the sound of it faded and was gone.

Exhaling, she let her head fall back onto the headrest and closed her eyes.

Eleven

Extricating the car from the top of the slope was both easier and harder than she had anticipated. She couldn't go back the way she'd come, so hoping for the best, she edged the car over to the more gradual side and started down it. The car handled the descent and the path she took well enough, but when she headed up the slight rise of the shoulder, it quickly bogged down. She had to back up twice onto a dryer section and then take off forward again to finally make it up onto the old pavement.

Back behind the carriage house, she hesitated before shutting the car off. She no longer felt good about hiding it there. If the cops or anyone else found her, she could explain that she'd had nowhere to go and was thinking of trying to take possession of the home, all through the proper channels of course, or some such shit. I mean why not? What was the worst they could do to her? Arrest her, haul her in, and make her go to court? She might have to hire an attorney. And pay a fine. She couldn't imagine them doing much else. But it would be a pain, and expensive, and ridiculously embarrassing. She wanted to avoid that if she could.

She backed the car out and then cautiously bumped and pushed her way through the tall grass to the faint ruts still visible that led past the stable and barn to the rear of the property. The grass on each side was high but the ground was reasonably level and free of debris.

The area that had once been a lawn stretched on down a little farther, past the pecan and the apple tree, and then expanded on the other side of a magnificent magnolia. It was a huge specimen, untrimmed, with drooping lower branches that rested nearly on the ground. The car would be essentially out in the open back there, but with the magnolia where it was you couldn't tell the partially clear area extended over on that side until you got past it. It might work if no one went all the way out.

Feeling a shade more at ease, she parked the car close to the tree to hide it the best she could, got out, and started for the house.

She felt sure the deputy would come back. He'd sensed something that had given him pause. Not to mention he'd witnessed the strange mist. Unless she was just being paranoid and all he had been doing was something like talking on the phone or radio and hadn't thought anything of it. But somehow she didn't think that was it. She hadn't seen the last of him. She felt it in her gut.

Inside, she walked around gathering her things and sneaking looks out the windows. Anything she didn't think she'd use in the next day or two, she put in one of the bags she had with her and ran it out to the car, and the rest she took up into the attic, where it might blend in if anyone bothered to check.

When the light began to go, she took a last look around for anything she might have missed. She had tried to erase all signs of her presence, but now it seemed too clean. There was a noticeable difference in the amount of dust and grime in the rooms she'd tidied up.

She walked back to the fireplace in the inner room, scooped up a handful of the ashes, and carried them to the front parlor. As a test, she scattered some on a small table. The effect wasn't ideal. But it might do for a cursory inspection. She leaned over and lightly blew on them to disperse them more. Good enough.

She shook ashes all over the tables and floor, basically flinging them around and up in the air so they would lightly settle on everything and mimic the appearance of dust. Then she went and cleaned most of the remaining ashes out of the fireplace and sprinkled on a little water. She'd almost missed that. There had been some in it when she got there but not many and they'd looked like they had been there a while, in contrast to the fluffy white, clearly recent ashes she'd accumulated.

Once she finished with that, after a quick peek out the window, she stepped out onto the verandah to listen for a moment, then went back in and began searching for somewhere to put herself for the night. There was no way she was going to sleep on the sofa. Nor was she going to risk a candle or a fire.

She thought about it. There was what she assumed was a cloak room adjacent to the ballroom at the end of the back hallway, but it was basically wide open with nothing to hide behind. And there was the space through a small door on the far end of the ballroom that was more promising that had a settee with forest-green cushions against the wall under a faded mural of some tropical place. The space had probably been used for ladies to retire to whenever balls were being held. But if anyone walked all the way across, spotted the door, and looked in, she'd be found.

The best place for her would probably be in the attic. But it had been bad enough to go back up there to hide her things; she couldn't imagine having to *sleep* there. The spiders would be dormant from the cold and not likely to be moving around much, but the thought of them there, lurking all around her, staring out with their glowing, iridescent eyes ... She shuddered, imagining one of them scuttling over, attracted by the warmth, and then running across her body.

She really needed to spray up there if she was going to explore the things left behind. Which immediately made her think of the bug killer she'd already used on the first floor. Would he *smell* it? She could no longer detect it, but she might be used to it.

She would just have to hope he, or anyone else, didn't come all the way into the house.

But still, there was that lingering suspicion in the back of her mind that he might come back for more than a quick look, and soon. And so, with reluctance, she took her pillow and temporary bedclothes, her tablet, the LED lantern, and two gallons of water down to the wine cellar in the basement. What little food she had was already shoved into the back of the inset cabinets there, so that was convenient. The only problem was the lack of a toilet, and there was no remedy for that she was willing to entertain. The only recourse was to carry water with her each time to put in the back of the tank upstairs—water she was nearly out of again—and do her business quickly.

The stone cellar was even colder than the house, which was good as far as creepy-crawlies went, but it was going to be a frigid night. And there wasn't anywhere decent to sleep. She looked down at the rough wooden floor. *I do not want to sleep on that,* she thought, envisioning huge rats roaming around. Did rats mind the cold? She didn't want to find out.

She ended up making a bed on the rectangular table set against the wall. After testing it to be sure it would hold her weight, she brushed all the cobwebs away, pulled it out some, and fashioned a nest on top of it with her sleeping bag and blankets.

It wasn't the best hiding spot, but it would have to do. She wasn't directly in view. You would have to turn at the bottom of the basement stairs to go around and enter the wine cellar and then move on in and follow it around to see her, and with any luck he wouldn't go that far.

Dinner was the other Lunchable she'd bought, washed down with the last of the tea. Then she dashed back up into the house to visit the bathroom one last time, and came back down and snuggled up with her tablet to read until she grew sleepy.

CHEYENNE, UNSEEN AND unnoticed, stood back in the dimness behind the drapery hanging from the archway leading in. A woman with graying blond hair sat on a raspberry velvet sofa flipping the page on an elaborately decorated photo album. She tapped a larger portrait with her fingernail. "Look, Helena. This is Gus." She lifted the album, still open, and placed it on the table in front of her. She turned it slightly for the younger lady perched on the matching chair to see. "He was ten," she told her, smiling. "I thought he was going to be my only child, but then years later along came Celia."

But the beautiful, chestnut-haired Helena didn't appear interested and merely raised her eyebrows and stretched her neck out for the barest of glances.

The more mature woman's smile faded as she gazed over at the haughty thing sitting across from her.

With a deliberate air, she gave a sniff, carefully closed the album—and said not another word.

The seconds ticked by. She obviously had chosen to not respond at all to such blatant rudeness. Though her eyes occasionally strayed to the offending photo album, Helena completely avoided it by shifting away.

The other woman's nostrils flared at this new affront and she seemed on the verge of speaking, when Myrna entered the room carrying a tray.

Face stony, the older woman picked up the album and moved it to the smaller table beside her so Myrna could set down the tray of sweets and coffee. "Thank you, dear."

Myrna beamed at her and then switched her attention to Helena, who must have found the proffered refreshments just as boring as the curtailed walk down memory lane and had just stifled a yawn. "I hope it's to your liking, Miss Helena," she said, and then stood there and waited. Faced with the combined scrutiny of the two women, Helena managed to rouse herself enough to reach over and pick up her cup.

Myrna turned and retreated to the other end of the room, where she lingered in the doorway.

The other woman, now that Helena had finally decided to take part, also lifted her cup. She brought it to her lips as Helena took a sip.

Helena's eyes immediately went wide and she drew herself up, clanking the cup down into its saucer. "Why, it's ice cold!" she sputtered. By the shocked expression on her face, it was evident her very sensibilities had been assaulted.

The older lady, unperturbed, took a most unladylike slurp, eyeing her over the rim, then gave a little lift of the cup in Myrna's direction. "I think it's perfect. Thank you, Myrna."

Helena's face flushed and her mouth closed up into a mean little bow. She stared hard at her and then looked across at Myrna.

"Won't you have something to eat, at least, Helena?" the woman asked, reaching toward the plate of sweets.

"No! I don't think so." Helena abruptly deposited her cup and saucer onto the table and stood up. "I do believe I'll be going."

The other woman made no reply and proceeded to take two delicate star-shaped cookies.

Helena stood there a second longer, then as she understood no acknowledgement would be forthcoming, gave an angry huff and spun around.

In the midst of taking a bite, the other woman gave no reaction as Helena walked out of the room, her heels clacking on the parquet floor.

Cheyenne moved across and into the shadows on the other side.

The sound of the doors banging shut came a moment later.

Drifting back over, Cheyenne looked in and saw the woman drop her cookie onto the saucer in front of her and sag back on the velvet sofa. "Myrna?"

Myrna hesitantly went to her, as if she feared a scolding. "Yes, ma'am?"

She gestured at the tray. "You can take this." She didn't say a word about the inexplicable temperature of Helena's coffee.

After Myrna had gone back to the kitchen, the woman picked up the photo album and opened it again to the picture of Gus.

From where Cheyenne stood, feeling that weird prickly sensation again, knowing she had to be dreaming though it felt so real, she could see the photo from over the woman's shoulder. Gus lay on a chaise lounge, a smaller, shorter version of the one in the front parlor, his head leaning against the taller side of it. Only his eyes were turned toward the camera. His hair was a mass of dark waves and he wore a naked, vulnerable took on his face as if he'd been sleeping.

The woman began to flip through the album.

One by one the pages turned, photos of Gus and other unknown people sliding into and then out of view to be replaced by others.

And there were cards and bits of ribbon and more photographs, all of it shuffling first slowly and then faster and faster—until it was nothing but a blur, and then not even that when Cheyenne turned, nearly swooning, and moved away.

The rooms and spaces she passed, previously full of light, were now filled with shadows. The first passageway led away like a dark tunnel to her left before the black hole of the laundry, and the basement door was barely an outline at the end of the second expanse.

Before long she found herself in almost complete darkness.

Where? What ...? The dim shape on the wall directly across from her solidified into the dusty, nearly empty wine rack, and everything came back in a rush. She staggered over to feel around for the tablet she'd fallen asleep reading. She found it and pressed then held down the button to turn it on, but the screen stayed black. It had completely died.

It was freezing. She could feel the coldness of the floorboards seeping through her socks. She hurriedly stepped over to the shelf she knew was nearby and groped for her phone.

Her fingers closed around it, and she pressed the button to wake it. The screen came on and light sprang out in a reassuring circle around her.

She checked the time. Not quite seven. A little early to get up. Taking the phone with her, she padded over to her makeshift bed, climbed back onto it, and got herself arranged again.

She checked the phone's battery, saw it still had a little charge left, and pulled up her Facebook.

There was a message from Brent: "Hey girl. Call me." That was all it said, and he had left it the evening before.

"Please," she muttered. It would serve him right if she called him right then and got him in trouble with Serena.

Unless Serena wasn't there anymore. She decided to find out.

"Why?" she typed. "What's going on? Did you and Serena break up?" Then she checked a few notifications and went ahead and logged off.

She stuck the phone under the edge of her pillow and turned over.

The next time she awoke it was 8:15 and the faint gray light seeping through the high basement windows had brightened.

I need coffee, she thought—and the dream that hadn't felt like a dream popped into her head. She sat up, blinking sleepily, and rubbed at her eyes as she pondered the detailed sequences her slumbering mind had come up with. She had never had such graphic dreams before. Not before coming to this house. The older woman had been trying to show a younger lady—Helena her name had been—a photo. Helena's dress had been mint green trimmed in darker green with a tighter fit and a V-neck bodice and all sorts of long vertical tucks and darts to accentuate her slim figure. And there'd been no bustle; instead all the volume had spilled out below her hips. The other woman's gown had been a lighter apricot color and had been looser and more informal, with a long matching jacket, almost like a robe, trimmed in lace.

She had even created a boy's—Gus's—vaguely forlorn face gazing out from the photo.

The house was doing a number on her. She stared blearily around her at the pale stone walls. *I definitely need to get out of here for a while.*

Coming back through the house a few minutes later, she had just tightened the blanket she'd wrapped around herself, thinking about everything she needed to do, when a noise from the front of the house reached her ears.

She sucked in a breath and fell back against the wall of the side hall she was in that ran parallel to the center one.

It sounded like someone had just entered through the front doors.

Holy shit, had she left them unlocked? A sick feeling came over her as she tried to remember. She couldn't recall locking up. She had no memory of it at all. Which meant she must not have. *You idiot!*

She whipped her head from side to side, frantically trying to figure out where to hide. In one of the nearby rooms? Back in the basement? Only if she could get past whoever it was. *It has to be the deputy*, she thought.

A floorboard creaked, somewhere off the main hall it sounded like. To get to the basement door, she would have to enter the connecting passage that ran between her inner sanctum and the kitchen and other rooms at the back of the house. If he was on the other side, she would be caught.

Picking up the occasional sound, she could tell he was moving through the center of the home, checking things out. When she picked up footsteps approaching the first passage that ran on this side of the inner room, she was forced to move, knowing when he reached the end and turned, he would be greeted with the sight of her cringing against the wall.

Grabbing up the blanket so she wouldn't trip on it, she tiptoed ahead as fast as she could and turned the corner into the second passageway.

And not a moment too soon. Back on the other end of the hallway she'd just vacated, a police radio blared to life before the volume was rapidly lowered. Biting back a scream, she gathered up the blanket again and sprinted as quietly as she could, instinctively turned left, and then froze again, unsure of her next move. She couldn't just leave without her purse, which was in the basement. And her *phone*, she remembered, was still lying by her pillow where she'd left it and liable to go off any second!

She spun around and sped back down the passageway to the basement door on her left.

She tried to quiet her breathing.

Grasping the knob, she went to pull it open then caught herself. What if he heard? She didn't remember the door being particularly loud, but she didn't think it had been completely silent, either.

She stood that way for an eternity it seemed, afraid to risk peeking around the corner for fear he was standing right there.

Finally she got her chance when his radio, at a lower volume now but mercifully loud enough, blared to life again. She turned the knob and pulled, and the door came open with a *crack* that seemed loud as a gunshot. She quickly slipped though, pulled it mostly shut behind her, and took off down the stairs, wondering if he was coming after her right then.

Rounding the bottom, she sprinted over to the wine cellar, passed through the arched doorway, and skidded around to the table, ripping the blanket from around herself. She snatched up the phone, silenced it, and stuffed it into her pocket. Then she crammed her feet into her shoes, hung her purse around her neck, yanked the blankets and sleeping bag off the table, ran over, and shoved them into a cabinet under the inset counter.

That left the lantern, her tablet, and the half-empty water jugs. She retrieved the tablet from the shelf it was on, grabbed the lantern, and managed to stuff them into a lower cabinet as well. But there was no room for the water.

Picking the jugs up by their handles, she ran out of the wine cellar and rapidly scanned the larger space, searching for a spot.

Somewhere along the line someone must have cleaned the basement out, because it was virtually bare now, and there was nowhere, *nowhere,* to put the plastic jugs.

Even the area below the chute set high in the wall where coal had once been dropped and stored in one corner was wide open with only a shaky partition separating it from some sagging shelves and disintegrating baskets where produce and canned preserves had once been kept.

The only possible place was behind the huge cast-iron hulk of a furnace and its squat companion she suspected might be an early water heater, which were both set slightly out from the wall. But it was too obvious. He was sure to check the other side.

She had no recourse but to take the water with her. Trying not to fall to her death, she clambered up the stairs, a jug in each hand, and paused at the top to listen.

All was silent. He could already be gone. Or he could be on the second floor, or in the attic, or moving back down, straight for the door she was standing behind.

Skin prickling, she sensed he was headed her way. He had checked the ground floor, then probably gone to the upper one, and now he was coming back down to finally inspect the basement, which he had left for last.

Leaning away so she wasn't directly in front of it, she used her foot to nudge the door open farther. When nothing happened, she stuck her head out.

The passageway on either side of her stood empty. She eased her body through, trying not to bang the jugs into the doorjamb. She had already decided to make for the car. He'd stop her and arrest her, or not. She might even be able to say she was only taking a look around, though it would be hard to explain the water she was carrying or why she had hidden her car behind the magnolia.

Turning, she tensed herself to run—and picked up a faint creak from the direction of the staircase. He *was* coming back down. She took off in a wide-legged gait, arms out to the side to accommodate the water jugs.

Without slowing, she flew around the corner and ran for the back of the house, the closest way out, expecting a shout behind her any second.

She made it into the sunroom, and once again there was nowhere good to put the blasted water. She set one jug down, eased the door open, grabbed the jug back up, and squeezed through.

Down in the yard, she cut to the left rather than go straight through the middle, thinking she might blend in better and be harder to spot if he looked out.

When she'd gone far enough, she ditched the water behind the trunk of a thick tree and took off down the old dirt track, daring to hope.

As she came around the magnolia, she slowed to a walk, chest heaving and shaking with adrenalin.

She'd made it to the car. Now what?

She didn't dare crank it and try to leave. All she could do was wait and pray he didn't come all the way out to where she was.

She wouldn't put it past him. Taking the purse out from around her neck, she pulled the door open, slid inside, and clicked it shut.

Sinking down in the seat, she stretched her legs out as much as she could and took in a shaky breath.

SOMETIME LATER, ANXIOUS and tired of just sitting there, she pushed the door open and climbed out.

In the distance, a semi truck rumbled down the highway. She walked over to the edge of the woods. A bird somewhere above her in the top of the magnolia made a high, sharp noise that was promptly echoed by another one across from her. She wrapped her arms around herself as the cool breeze that had been blowing picked up, rattling the dead leaves stubbornly clinging to the nearby oaks.

She double-checked she had the keys, then started forward, angling to the left to cut through the trees.

It proved harder than she had anticipated. Though it was basically wintertime, there were plenty of branches and thorny vines to get caught on and snag her clothing.

Determinedly she kept on, plowing her way through it, and soon she was stepping onto the ruts again.

She followed them up and crossed over to hug the exterior wall all the way to the front of the house.

She peeked around the corner.

The driveway stood empty. *Good.* He was gone. Pulling back, she let herself relax into the old boards for a second.

Then she straightened up, turned, and headed back around to go in through the rear.

After she was dressed properly, she was getting out of there for a while. And no later than tomorrow she was going to buckle down and look through the jobs again, maybe even ride over to cousin Larry's.

SHE RETURNED TO the house right before sunset. Too tired to really care anymore after two beers and Chinese takeout at her brother's, as well as the use of his shower (she'd told him she had left home before she was able to take one, implying she and Brent had been arguing), she drove down the side and parked behind the carriage house.

She entered through the sunroom. Did the deputy realize the lock was useless? *Oh whatever. If he finds me here, he finds me here.*

She set the two gallons of distilled water she'd bought while she was out down on the floor, tossed her purse onto the sofa in the inner room, and ran outside before it got dark to retrieve the other two water jugs.

Then she headed to the basement to get the things she'd hidden there.

Once she had everything she wanted back in the little parlor, she changed into something more comfortable, clicked on the LED lantern, and settled on the sofa with a book she'd borrowed from Caleb. It should be fine. The light wouldn't show from the outside. The deputy would have to come inside to see it. That reminded her. Uncurling her legs, she got up and walked around to the front entryway to check the doors.

She found them closed firmly and locked. *He must have gone out the back*, she thought, studying the ancient mechanism. Any keys to it would have been lost long ago and the only way to secure it was to turn the thumb-sized knob on the inside. She supposed that meant he knew the lock on the sunroom door was useless.

Still thinking about the unlocked back door, she returned to the inner room and rooted around until she found her pocketknife, then stretched out on the sofa in her sleeping bag, placed the knife within easy reach, and picked up the book again.

She hadn't made it five pages before she was nodding off. Closing it, she placed it on the marble table, switched off the lantern, and was fast asleep in minutes.

SOMETIME AFTER DAYBREAK in the early morning hours while the world remained still and quiet, the vague flashes and disjointed, drifting thoughts of her slumbering mind coalesced, and she slipped into a dream.

Soundlessly, she padded through the house, grateful for the socks she'd slipped on before bed.

As she rubbed her hands against the goosebumps on her arms, she heard a sound through an open door on her right and turned to go inside.

A young boy lay sprawled on a sleigh-shaped bed with a high headboard. He looked over and sat up as she entered. She tried to see his face but the light shining in didn't reach his features.

Swinging his legs over the side, he dropped down onto the floor and scampered over to her.

Oh, it was Gus, younger but still recognizable. "Hello," she said.

Gus, who had paused, his expression intense, as if he were trying to place her in his mind, became animated again at her words. Smiling, he threw himself into her. His strong little arms squeezed her tight and then released her.

"I'm Gus," he said.

"Oh, I know," she replied, smiling.

He giggled. "You're dressed funny."

Cheyenne looked down at the pajama pants and shirt she had on and laughed. She guessed it would seem strange to him, here in this place, in this time. As the significance of that registered, the smile faded from her lips.

Confusion crept in, and she turned away from him, thinking hard. Where was ...? What ...? It wouldn't come, though, and after a moment she drifted back out into the hall.

For a while she knew nothing, and then sometime later she came awake and opened her eyes, instantly recalling her dream encounter with the young Gus. But she had no time to dwell on it, for once again she could hear the sound of an engine idling.

Oh, for the love of ... It had probably been inevitable, though, that she'd get caught. Holding back a groan, she pulled her stiff body into a sitting position, stood up, and looked around for her shoes. It was broad daylight and she had no idea what time it was. And where was her phone? She listened for the car to cut off or for another one to join it as she found her mocs, slipped them on, and grabbed the phone off the curio cabinet in the corner. Then, tucking her hair behind her ears, she walked to the front of the house.

She could probably get Caleb to bail her out if it came to that, if he could get a bondsman and it wasn't too much. But then what? Would she be allowed to go and stay with Jill in another state?

Instead of going into the parlor with its open drapes, she turned and moved into the library. *Might as well get the lay of the land before walking out to face the music.*

Staying to the side, she shifted the edge of the fragile, once white curtain, now frayed and yellowing, and peeked out.

It was him, the same deputy in the gray cruiser. As usual he had stopped directly across from the verandah steps. She switched to the other side and peeked out again.

What was he doing?

She let the curtain drop and moved away. Should she go out, or not?

She moved back over to the window and looked out again. The deputy was gazing down, reading something if she wasn't mistaken.

Stepping back, she pondered what this meant as she quickly crossed in front of the window and sat down in a chair to the side.

She stayed there listening to the sound of his car out front, nerves taut, for at least a half hour it felt like, expecting any minute to hear another vehicle or two pull in for backup then the slam of doors as they all climbed out to handcuff her and drag her away.

She was just envisioning her walk of shame through the local detention center and subsequent exile into a dirty cell full of tough, jeering women, when she finally took note of what she had heard but not fully registered. The sound of the engine had changed and was now growing fainter.

She leapt up and dashed to the window and caught the back end of the patrol car as it followed the curve of the driveway around.

Taking in shallow breaths, she stood there and listened to the sound of it as he continued down the old back road. Could she be that lucky? Had he ascertained (incorrectly, luckily) that no one had been there and then went right back to his normal routine of stopping there occasionally?

She wondered if he had walked around the outside of the house while she slept. Thank goodness she hadn't built a fire and had at least parked the car behind the carriage house.

She still couldn't quite believe it though and decided to get out of there for a bit while she could.

After dressing, she took everything she was worried about out to the car, then climbed inside, started it up, and bounced her way across the overgrown yard. He could be coming down as she was going up, but as long as she made it off the property, she didn't think he could do much. Anything important that could be traced back to her easily was now in the car with her.

But she wouldn't be able to come back if that happened. *That might be for the best*, her mind whispered. But what was the alternative?

Coming almost to a stop at the end of the driveway, she lowered her window, mercifully heard nothing, and kept going. Soon she had made it up to the highway and pulled out unseen, by the cops anyway. A man in a work truck was approaching as she turned out, but that was it. And then she was on her way.

Twelve

With no makeup on and her hair sticking out in unruly waves, she didn't want to go to her mother's or her brother's, so finally, reluctantly, she drove over to the small brick house that once belonged to her grandparents on her father's side before they passed away.

It looked like Larry was home—unless he was out in some other vehicle; the GMC pickup he'd been driving for years was parked in its usual spot.

She tried to smooth her hair down again, got out, and headed for the front door, then heard a clank from the garage he did work out of and changed direction.

A tall discolored barrel slouched against the side, empty beer cans overflowing onto the ground. How long had it been since he'd emptied it? How much did you have to drink to warrant having a barrel just for that?

"Hell-o-oh." she called out as she came through the first roll-up door.

Larry's familiar lanky form popped up from behind a car near the back.

"Oh, hey, Cheyenne." Wiping his hands on a rag, he came around the car, which appeared to have been recently painted.

She walked on in to meet him. "How's it going?" she said, smiling. He looked about the same, though his salt-and-pepper hair was more salt than pepper now, and he had the beginning of a slight potbelly. *Or a beer belly.*

"I can't complain. What's up?" He seemed happy enough to see her but faintly curious. They had spent plenty of time together when they were kids, but he had been closer to her brother. She only saw him now at the odd holiday dinner or on the rare occasion when they needed his services for some issue with one of their vehicles.

"Oh, I was just out and about and thought I'd stop and speak." Larry lived there alone and would most likely let her stay, but she wasn't ready to bring it up yet, not until she scoped the situation out.

He nodded, wiping his hands again.

"So, what are you working on?"

He glanced back at the gleaming silver and black car he'd been over by. "I'm working on that Chevelle for a buddy of mine."

"Sharp," she said, nodding appreciatively. "Do you get a lot of business?" The garage, as usual, as well as the space directly around it, was crowded with vehicles. But that didn't mean anything; some of them had been there for years.

"Not as much as Dad had going on. But I get a fair amount."

"We spent a lot of time here when we were kids." She gazed around the place with him. "Do you remember going down the back trail? And getting in the boat?"

The trail behind the house had been amazing to them when they were growing up. The first part had been lined on both sides with junked automobiles, weeds and vines growing up around them and supposedly infested with all manner of snakes, spiders, and who knew what other dangers, according to the grownups who'd forbidden them to go there. Of course they had gone anyway. And the boat had been parked over to the side of a corn field. The patch of land the corn had grown on wasn't actually very large, but back then it had seemed a veritable maze as they ran through its rustling stalks. She hadn't thought of it in years.

"Yeah, I remember," he said, chuckling. "Dad always told us not to go down there *or* get in the boat."

"But we did it anyway." They both laughed.

"You still with that Brent guy?"

No. She tilted her head from side to side. "Sort of."

His eyebrows rose a little but he didn't question her about it. "How's your mom?"

"She's fine. Still over at the apartments."

"That's good." He shuffled his feet, refocusing in on her with his slightly bloodshot eyes, probably thinking it was great to remanence but he had things to do. Cheyenne racked her brain. She needed to get into the house before she left. And then she could make her decision about whether or not to hit him up for a place to stay.

"I hate to ask," she finally said, unable to come up with anything better, "but I have a long drive ahead of me—I thought I'd ride over to Walmart—do you mind if I use the bathroom right quick?"

"Uh ... sure." No doubt anticipating her imminent departure, he turned and led the way over to the house at a brisk pace.

She had her first inkling the place wouldn't be suitable when a shaggy mutt came around the house, shoved between them, and followed Larry in without him batting an eye.

"It's down the hall. You know where."

She started for the bathroom on this side, giving the dog a wide berth.

"Stay off the furniture!" Larry roared behind her, and for a second she thought he meant her. Then she saw the dog had jumped into a chair.

At least it doesn't bark mu—

The dog let out a series of loud, gruff barks, which Larry responded to by yelling even louder, "Shut *up!*"

Wincing, she kept moving down the hall as he grabbed the dog's collar and dragged it down.

The state of the bathroom left something to be desired as well. The toilet in particular. This tub didn't appear to be used much, but the commode was so bad it made her grateful she didn't actually have to go.

With the tips of two fingers, she put the seat down—which was up, of course—to make it look good, and waited. The entire house had been spotless when her grandmother had still been alive. But from what she'd seen so far, that was no longer the case. And that *dog*. Would its barking keep her awake?

She gave a small start as Larry's voice came through the door. *"I'll be outside, Cheyenne."*

"Okay," she answered back, and presently heard the muffled thump of the front door.

She waited a few seconds for good measure, and then walked out of the bathroom.

The dog, back in the same chair, immediately started up again at the sight of her.

"Hush!" she told it.

It paid her no mind and continued its gruff barking. If it kept it up, Larry was bound to hear and come investigate.

"Shut *up!*" she finally yelled, and amazingly the dog immediately stopped and settled back down. Good grief, she'd lose her voice if she had to do that all the time.

She continued on through the living room into the dining area instead of going out the front door. She figured she could say she had wanted a drink of water if he caught her.

She came to a halt halfway past the same scarred table and chairs that had been there for as long as she could remember and stared over at the floor by the far wall. On top of the worn linoleum below the two windows there, the dog had left two large deposits, which she could now smell, as if it had gotten as close to the outside as it could.

If it had been just one accident, she might have thought Larry merely hadn't had time to clean it up yet. But there were *two* piles. And she hadn't even looked around much. There could be more hiding in the other rooms.

She wouldn't be able to take it. She'd be cleaning up after the dog all the time.

And I'll end up washing all the dishes too, she thought, looking into the kitchen and seeing the stack in the sink and on the counter. The stove was covered in pots and pans too, some of which still held crusted food.

Again, if it had been just a few recent dishes she wouldn't have thought anything about it.

Over by the back door, a fly lazily lifted up off the trash can, which also needed emptying, and she spun around to get out of there before he found out she'd seen how bad it was and it became awkward for both of them.

She had been through this before. For a brief, very brief, period after leaving home, she had roomed with a girl named Deena from high school. Deena's mother had never made her clean and Deena hadn't seen any reason to break tradition after moving out. Although Denna herself had never been a mess— she'd showered each day and was usually well put together—her room, and any other space she spent a significant amount of time in, had always been a wreck. When she'd confronted her, Denna had told her that if it bothered her that much then she could clean it. The entire time they'd stayed together Cheyenne had done the bulk of the housework. The morning she'd woken up to a trail of ants and began having visions of collecting Deena's dirty dishes and piling them into the front seat of her car, she had known it was time to go.

Larry was coming out of the garage as she walked up. "Everything all right?"

"Yep." She pulled out her phone and made a show of checking the time, then slid it back into her pocket. "I guess I better get going. But it was good to see you."

"You too. Stop by again some time. We'll have a beer."

"Cool. Sounds good." She tried to keep her eyes from straying to the barrel of overflowing cans. "Take it easy," she told him and turned to make her escape.

IT WASN'T THAT she minded having to clean up after him. It would be in return for room and board, after all. It was that she minded having to clean up after the *dog*. It would be that or learn to love the smell of dogshit. And she couldn't get the sight of all those beer cans spilling onto the ground out of her head. No matter how pleasant he seemed now, that might change come evening after a six-pack or two.

After a quick run through a drive-thru for a small cheeseburger and a soda, she headed back to the house.

At the last traffic light before her turn, a truck pulled up beside her as she waited for it to change.

She glanced over. Crap; it was *Brent*, and he was looking directly at her. Giving a half-wave, she went to turn away and saw him gesture something.

What? she mouthed. He made a circular motion with his hand for her to lower her window. She pressed the button, glancing up to make sure the light was still red.

"*Pull over*," he called out as soon as it was far enough down.

At her baffled expression, he said it again. "*Pull over. So we can talk.*"

Out of the corner of her eye she saw the light change, and hit the gas. She looked in the rearview as she raised the window back up and mulled over this turn of events. Behind her, Brent was switching lanes, getting over so he could follow her.

Having no choice—she couldn't lead him to the house—she waited for an SUV to pass and then turned into the self-service car wash that had been closed for years. Passing through one of the far lanes, she pulled the car around so it was facing out, and came to a stop.

A second later, Brent did the same. Expecting him to lower his passenger window—he was also facing the road—she was a little thrown when he shoved the truck into park, shut it off, and climbed out.

Her eyes widened as he continued on around both vehicles without pausing.

Mama always said keep your doors locked, she thought wryly as he yanked the passenger door open and slid in beside her.

"What do you want, Brent?"

At her admittedly rude brusqueness, he recoiled slightly and fixed his attention on something out the window.

"I'm sorry," she said after a moment, eyeing him warily.

"I got your message," he finally said. He shifted around to face her. "And so did Serena."

Shit. Yet, despite, or possibly because of his obvious distress at this, she couldn't help but feel a tiny thrill of satisfaction.

But now was not the time. "You did message me first, you know."

"I know. You hadn't been answering my calls, or my texts."

Damn, she thought. He still looked handsome to her, even after everything. Not like the man of her dreams, but still appealing on some level. The chemistry was definitely there. She ripped her eyes away from his dark good looks—the shadow of beard she'd always thought so sexy, the green eyes so startling against his nearly black hair. It's just chemistry, she told herself firmly as her gaze strayed over and caught sight of the tattoo peeking out from under his sleeve. She'd always been attracted to masculine men ... to "bad boys." And look how that had turned out.

The ethereal presence of their lost child hovered in the periphery of her mind for a second before swirling away to be replaced by the sordid image of him and Serena together.

"I don't know why I was always so against having children," he said suddenly.

Had he been against having kids *ever*? They certainly hadn't planned on creating a child when they did; she had been just as surprised as he when the two birth control pills she'd missed on a weekend away in Charleston (when she'd accidently left them behind) had actually resulted in a pregnancy. But this was the first she'd heard that he had been against procreating in general.

Pain squeezed her heart and she had to look away. Did he see now what he had lost, what they both had lost? What their *child* had lost?

The warm feel of his hand wrapping around hers brought her attention back around.

"It was hard for me too," he said, gazing at her with moist eyes. "Still is, sometimes."

Wordless, she nodded. Why couldn't he have been this way before?

Releasing her hand, he shifted back over. "I don't know, maybe I'm just better able to handle it now. I don't think I fully appreciated what it meant when you got pregnant. And then when you lost it—*him*—sorry ... I pushed it away. But now ... I think I c—" He stopped talking abruptly.

She waited for him to continue, then finally finished for him. "You think you could have been a good dad?"

A ripple of emotion crossed his features before he looked over to meet her gaze again. She thought she could see something there, something unspoken, before he dropped his eyes.

She tried to think of what to say as the silence lengthened. What was he thinking? That he wanted to try again? For a fleeting second, she felt her heart lift a little at the thought. Then reality intruded and she knew it was what could have been that she wanted. And that was forever out of reach.

She wrenched her mind out of the past and tried to focus. "So, what, Serena got mad because you messaged me?"

He leaned his head back against the seat. "Yeah, your reply popped up on my phone and she saw it."

"So why have you been trying to reach me?"

"That was be—" Once again he bit off whatever he had been going to say. Both of them stayed silent for a moment, waiting for a particularly loud truck to make its way through the intersection.

"Things are so different," he said. "I miss the way it was with us."

Cheyenne felt herself bristling at that. *You miss how I made good money and made it easy for you.* But then he added, "I miss how you loved me. Just the way I was. Before ... you know."

Her anger drained away. It must have been difficult, having her turn so completely off, so completely away from him, after losing the baby.

But what she'd walked in on ... It had been more than him seeking comfort in his time of need. There had been a need, all right. She saw again the sleazy tableau of he and Serena together. A need for a young nubile female. A *teenager*, basically, and him over forty. Some of her previous anger and disgust rose up in her anew.

"Look I'm not proud of what I did," he said, as if reading her thoughts.

As quickly as they had surfaced, the turbulent emotions ebbed, leaving behind only the familiar sense of loss.

His phone went off in his pocket. She watched as he grabbed at it and then visibly restrained himself from answering. "Listen, we need to talk again soon, but right now I have to go."

Talk about what, *divorce* or them trying again?

"I need to grab something to eat and get back to work." He glanced down at the small sack with the single cheeseburger she'd bought. "What's that? Is that supposed to be lunch?" He paused in the act of pushing his door open, and once again she thought she could read something hovering behind his eyes.

"I'm not exactly flush with funds right now," she said, since he seemed to be waiting for an answer.

His face immediately cleared and he finished getting out and began reaching into his back pocket.

What was he doing? Jesus, he was pulling his wallet out right there beside the road in view of everyone. "What the hell are you doing?" she hissed. "Get in the damn car!"

He fumbled his way back in, still trying to extricate a few bills. "I want to help you out. I should have already, but things have been ... Anyway, here." He shoved all but one of the bills at her.

She made no move to take them. Then common sense reared its head as he thrust the money at her again. "Here, just take it."

"Fine." Without looking, she folded it and shoved it in her pocket. "Thank you."

"Okay, well ... I better go."

Before shutting the door and walking away, he leaned his head back in. "Be careful," he told her, as he had countless times before in their years together.

To which, as always, she replied, "You too."

ON IMPULSE SHE stopped at Coker's, the slightly shabby supermarket she'd passed a few times on her way to the old house.

Before going inside, she pulled the money out and counted it. A hundred and forty dollars. More than she had expected. Shoving it back into her pocket, she got out and headed for the entrance door, picking up her pace as the brisk wind sweeping across cut through the hoodie she wore.

A bell tinkled overhead as she entered, and from off to her right an older gentleman by a drink cooler called out a greeting. Absently returning it, she grabbed one of the small carts provided and started through the store.

It wasn't a very large place, but it had a pretty decent selection, considering. The prices weren't on par with some of the larger grocery stores, but all in all they weren't too bad. She tossed things in as she went. A carton of orange juice, some instant coffee, canned milk, and sugar. Then on to the basic stuff. A few gallons of water, a pack of bathroom tissue, and a small container of clothes detergent (she'd been washing things by hand until she could get to the washerette across town).

Shoving into the cart to get it going, she swerved over to the butcher counter for a look at the cuts of meat and seafood on display. "*Serving You For Over Seventy Years*" boasted the sign across the back. Waving away the somewhat younger gentleman who made to approach, she looked over the steaks and chops and fillets of fish nestled in ice for another minute, and then moved on.

Seventy years. She did some calculations in her head. It would have still been way after Gus's time. He had lived in the late Victorian era. The real Augustus, that is.

As she selected whatever food she thought she could easily store and eat, she imagined what she might have been doing that evening had she been lucky enough to live back then with a man like Gus. Instead of soup or box macaroni and cheese followed by store-bought cookies or snack cakes, she might be dining on roast duck or oysters Rockefeller, followed by cherries jubilee, or better yet, a warm, cinnamony bread pudding. With Gus and his family across from her.

But—it was not to be.

She looked around some more, catching sight of the older gentleman a few times as he moved around the front near the three checkout lanes.

Then she threw in some batteries and headed to the one open register, where the man now waited.

He seemed friendly enough and smiled as she approached. "Has it warmed up any?" he asked as she began piling her items onto the conveyor.

"Some," she said, lifting the gallons of water out of the cart. "But it's still breezy."

"I don't know how often you get over this way," he said as he ran her items across the scanner, "but we've got a sale starting on Wednesday. And it runs through next Tuesday." He paused to punch in the quantity so he could slide the water down. "There's going to be a lot of buy one get one free products."

"I'm actually only staying over this way temporarily. I don't know how long I'll be around."

He nodded and turned to start bagging some of the items. "Well, I try to have one about once a month."

"Okay, good to know." She pulled out the money Brent had given her. She hoped it was enough. She hadn't exactly kept track as she went.

It was enough, with change left over. Happy, she rolled the cart out into the gusting wind.

Thirteen

She drifted through the house, occasionally reaching out to touch a knob or a chairback or trail her hand along a mantelpiece or a tabletop. The sun had sunk low in the sky, sending shafts of light into the stained-glass window, bathing the foyer in yellowish orange. It was the time of day she liked the most. When all was winding down and the world was preparing to sleep. When all your cares could be set aside until the morrow.

Tinges of salmon and indigo crept across the sky as the sun dropped below the horizon. And then not long after, like a comforting cloak, darkness settled over the landscape. All day the temperature had been dropping steadily. She would be in for another frosty evening.

She walked over to the windows that looked out onto the circular drive and gazed up at the bright stars flickering over the treetops. A sense of longing stole over her as she gazed out into the clear, cold night. How alone we all were, riding through space on our great dewy sphere. Like rare, undiscovered flowers deep in the rainforest that bloom once and then die, unknown and unseen.

After a moment she turned away from the night sky and moved into the shadows, groping for the lantern she'd placed on a table.

Switching it on, she left the room and padded down the hall, through the lefthand passageway, to her inner sanctum.

She parked the lantern on the marble coffee table in front of the sofa, dug out her lighter, and lit each of the candles on the candelabra. She took it over and placed it in the center of the mantel over the fireplace, then squatted down and used the lighter again to start the fire she'd already built with one of the store-bought logs, some branches from outside, and for extra kindling, a pile of twigs.

As the fire took hold and grew, she held her hands out to the flames licking upwards and thought about the strange direction her life had taken. One day she had been a happy (well, a relatively happy) woman with a good job and a husband she loved and a baby on the way—and the next, she had been a grief-stricken wreck with a stalled career, a baby she had lost, and a husband who'd discarded her.

And now she was here in this decaying relic of the past, all alone except for the fading echoes of a time long gone.

Gus and the accompanying individuals of his world that her slumbering mind had created, born out of grief and loneliness, drifted into her thoughts, and she let herself exist there for a minute in a warm, hazy room full of smiling people with Gus somewhere close.

A piece of wood popped in the fireplace, sending a burning ember flying out onto the hearth where she knelt. Ripping her shoe off, she slapped at it until the reddish glow went out.

Dammit. There was now a crack running through one of the leaf-motif tiles. She exhaled in disgust.

Rising, she stuck her foot back in her shoe, moved back over, and sat down facing the flames in the chair she preferred. She needed to rest. She had a big day ahead of her tomorrow. She'd already done a load of clothes at the washerette that morning, but she still needed to ride over to the storage unit again and then go sit somewhere for a while to charge her tablet and laptop and search the job listings. Her resumé was ready to go. If she ran across anything promising, she might have time to put in for it right then. And the following day she could apply for a few more. Anything at this point would be good until she could find something better. She needed to work on her clothes more, too. And after that—

Enough. She called a halt to the relentless list running through her brain of everything she needed to do. She'd taken care of all that she could for now; there was no sense in going over and over it, stressing about it.

But after a few minutes the worrisome thoughts began to creep back in. She stood up. She was never going to sleep like this. A glass of wine would help, if any decent bottles remained.

Carrying her trusty lantern, burning brightly with fresh batteries, she walked through the chilly house to the basement door, descended the stairs, and went around to enter the wine cellar.

There were several bottles left in the old rack on the wall. She pulled one of the grimy bottles out, brushed some of the dust off, and inspected the label. It was a Madeira, according to it, which featured a faded illustration of purple grapes. The bottle, similar to the one she'd opened when she first got there, looked more or less the same as the wine bottles she was used to, only thicker looking toward the neck. *Let's hope it's stood the test of time.*

After locating the corkscrew, she took it and the bottle back up into the house with her.

In the kitchen she paused to retrieve a glass from an old cupboard where she'd stored a couple she'd found after rinsing them, then continued on to the inner room.

Grateful for the warmth, she moved over to the fireplace and set the bottle and glass on the hearth. Kneeling, she positioned the opener over the cork, twisted until the corkscrew was fully inserted—who knew how tight the thing was—and pushed down on the wings. Slowly, the cork came out with a muted *thook*. She gave it a minute to breathe, and then poured a small amount into the clear, tulip-shaped glass.

The color was unexpected, not red or white, but sort of a pale copper hue. It was quite pretty, actually. She picked up the glass and swirled it around.

After giving a sniff and detecting nothing odd, she took an experimental taste, and the lightly sweet, nutty flavor of something like burnt sugar filled her taste buds, followed by the slightly pungent notes of some unidentifiable fruit. She took a larger sip. She didn't think she'd ever had anything exactly like it. She tossed back what was left. The closest she could compare it to would be the drops of nectar she'd pulled out of honeysuckle flowers as a kid, only with a bite.

How much of a bite she found out later three quarters of the way through her second glass when she got up to move over to the sofa and lost her balance and nearly fell rounding the side of the chair. "*Whoa*, Nelly." She caught herself and swayed in place for a second, then continued on across.

Reaching the sofa, she sank down onto it and collapsed back. Maybe she'd be able to sleep now. Maybe she would dream of him. *That would be nice*, she thought, and let her eyes drift closed.

SHE AWOKE SOMETIME later to near darkness. The fire had died down and the room had grown cold. Her tongue felt like a dried-up slug in her mouth. She lurched up from the sofa and moved over to the small curio cabinet she had been keeping things on. *Where was the water jug?* There was a partial one in the bathroom, but she thought she'd left a nearly full one here.

Giving up on finding it, she staggered out of the room and down the passageway, sliding a hand along the wall as she went.

The only illumination was from the moon, and the house seemed pregnant with previously unseen shapes and shadows. Veering right, she groggily made her way down the center of the house, mostly by feel, to the entryway where the rays shining in had set the stained-glass window alight. She walked through the ambient amber glow and started up the wide staircase. She still felt slightly buzzed. She hadn't really drunk that much, but she had done it on a mostly empty stomach and with little sleep.

She reached the landing at the top and passed by the dark shape of the settee with the curved back to cross over to the bathroom.

The silvery moonlight illuminated the floor where she thought she'd put the jug well enough for her to see it wasn't there.

Turning, she dragged her eyelids open wider and then faltered at what she caught in a moonbeam coming across. As she watched, another drop of something pooled at the mouth of the faucet and then fell with a *plop* into the pedestal sink below.

Stepping over, she moved her face closer and watched as another drop fell. She reached out a finger for the next one, brought it to her mouth, and touched it to her tongue. Expecting it to be foul, she was surprised to find it tased of nothing. Frowning, she reached out a hand and tried the righthand knob. It turned easily, releasing a stream of water.

Cupping her hands, she filled them and, at first tentatively and then more eagerly, drank it down.

When she'd had enough, she wiped her hands on the fuzzy sleepshirt she was wearing and left the bathroom to head for the stairs.

On the landing, she thought she heard something and paused.

It almost sounded like the tinkle of music. Wishing she had brought the lantern, she turned around and moved on down the hall. She was beginning to feel a little more awake and no longer sick to her stomach. The delightful nectar she had chosen to imbibe had delivered a hell of a punch.

Her mind, though clearer, still felt somewhat muddled, while her nerves and senses seemed particularly sensitive. The pattern in the wallpaper appeared sharper, the rug softer on her socked feet, the creak of the house more audible. In the silence, she could hear the rush of the wind outside as well as the heavy thump of her heart. And on her body, her skin and hair felt tight and prickly.

She came to a halt, freezing in place. Ahead of her, faint light spilled out from the turret on the end, illuminating the floor ahead of her.

There was no way the turret should have been lit up. Which could only mean one thing: someone was in the house. While she'd lain there in a decades-old wine-induced stupor, someone had entered the home and climbed the staircase. Fear coursed through her, ramping up to new heights as she began to notice other things as well—things that didn't make sense. At regular intervals along the hallway, the wall sconces, previously dark, were now burning softly, giving off a warm glow.

Shaking, she forced her feet to move through the pockets of darkness toward the doorway leading in to the turret.

Music, something haunting and sad, drifted out to her.

Trembling and barely breathing, she walked on, turned—

—and stepped into a warm space lit by golden lamplight with velvet drapes and rugs no longer dull with age but bright with shades of burgundy and emerald. And Gus ... my God, Gus right there standing by the old-fashioned camera.

This ... this was not a dream. She knew this as well as anyone who'd awakened to the undeniable concreteness of reality after being lost in one. Her legs trembled at the undeniable truth, threatening to give way beneath her. She sagged against the doorframe. *This is not a dream*, she had time to think again, and then she was collapsing as Gus's shout rang out.

SHE JERKED AWAKE, then lay there blinking, trying to remember who and where she was. Adding to her confusion, the ceiling above her looked completely unfamiliar and she could tell by the light that it was morning.

She turned her head and nearly shrieked at the sight of her dream man, undeniably solid and real, seated beside her.

"Shh, it's all right," he said. "I'm afraid you fainted and may have hit your head. You've been out for some time." He rose and turned toward the doorway. "Myrna!"

"This can't be happening," she mumbled, trying to sit up as everything came back to her, but the room revolved sickeningly and she had to lie back again. She felt ill and off, but she was undeniably awake. She was awake and this couldn't be happening. Gus and Myrna and the rest had been created by her mind while she slept. She had to be hallucinating. That must be what was happening. From the wine. Gus and his family and all the trappings weren't really there. Her mind had superimposed them over this old house.

She squinted up at him, hovering over her worriedly, looking so concerned. "If only," she murmured. If only there was someone special who cared that much about her. She closed her eyes, then ripped them back open at a fresh surge of nausea.

She shifted away from the specter of him and his concerned scrutiny, and after a minute, began to feel better. Her stomach was settling and the room had stopped its slow spin and stabilized around her. Absently she rubbed a hand down one arm, remembering the strange staticky feeling.

"Are you cold? I can get you a quilt." He made as if to move away.

"No." She managed to heave herself all the way to a sitting position. Everything wavered around her, but only for a second, and there was no accompanying tingling sensation. "I have to go."

Who was she talking to? This wasn't real ... was it? And go where? Where was she going? And *when* exactly was it?

"Please don't leave," he said. "Try. Try to stay."

"I ... I don't ..." What was she attempting to say, that she didn't know what was truly happening anymore?

If she could get to the little inner room then she could lie down and wait whatever this was out.

Blearily she got to her feet, stood there swaying for a second, then started out of the turret on shaky legs.

He immediately rushed forward to get ahead of her. Cringing, she veered away.

"Wait, please."

Close on her heels, he followed her around the larger front section, to stop her or talk to her, she didn't know and didn't care. None of this was actually happening. It couldn't be. She just wanted to get somewhere familiar and lie down. She pivoted again to leave, and once more he blocked her way.

She'd lie down there, then. And soon this would all be over. Or she would remain here in this dreamworld her mind had invented until they came to take her away. For if she wasn't having some delayed psychosis from the century-old wine, then clearly she had gone crazy.

But were you supposed to know it if you were insane?

He hovered beside her, hanging back as if unsure what to do. *You and me both, dude.*

There wasn't anywhere to lie down there in Gus's domain with all of his things. But there was an armchair by itself in front of a cloud-specked blue backdrop. She walked unsteadily over and sank down into it.

The chair sat slightly to one side by the windows across from the boxy camera on its tripod.

But it wasn't real. It couldn't be. Still struggling to comprehend what was happening, she couldn't make herself believe she had traveled back in time. She was hallucinating. And feeling faint again, though thankfully not queasy.

"Yes. Stay right there," he said, moving over to the camera. He almost seemed to be talking to himself. He fiddled with knobs and levers, dividing his attention between the camera and her as she tried to slow her breathing and combat her lightheadedness.

She kept her focus on the framed photographs on the wall opposite of her to give herself an external reference. It seemed to be working, but she was starting to feel that prickly sensation again.

What was he doing? He attached something to the back of the camera, fastened it down, stuck his head under the dark cloth, twisted a knob, then came out from under it.

"Please, let me capture you," he said, staring over at her. When she said nothing, he disappeared under the cloth again. "Now just turn your head slightly back," she heard his muffled voice say. "The way you had it. That's it." Again she almost had the impression he was talking to himself, as if he wasn't sure *she* was real.

Out of the corner of her eye, she saw him pull something on the front of the camera. "Just keep looking straight ahead," he murmured. And then after a few seconds, there came a click.

And it was over. And barely in time; her ears began to buzz loudly as goosebumps broke out on her skin and the outer strands of her hair lifted.

When her vision began to darken around the edges, she tried to stand—but her legs felt like jelly and she slid to the floor instead. "I'm going, I think," she said. And then the world went black.

SHE WOKE UP the next time with her check pressed against the floor in a puddle of drool. That's what it felt like—as if she had already woken up before this, when in fact she knew she must have still been asleep then, *or else awake and delirious.* She sat up and wiped her face. *I am never, ever drinking antique wine again.*

Slowly, she got to her feet and shuffled off to get some water.

THERE WAS SOMETHING niggling at the back of her mind. Every time she thought she had it, it would slip away again. She had felt so wretched after she'd awakened that she had built a fire once it got light and used all her water to take the world's smallest bath while drinking a scalding cup of coffee. Then she had dressed in a T-shirt and jeans and worked on straightening the place up and hiding her things while she waited for her hair to dry.

An hour and a half later, she was at the storage unit and still feeling out of sorts. She felt fine physically—she was currently in the process of hydrating with a large iced tea in between bites of a steak biscuit from Hardees—but she still had an uneasy feeling, like she was missing something, something crucial. She lifted the crate with the photo album to get behind it ... and she almost had it, but once again whatever was hovering in the back of her mind retreated.

She'd been avoiding thinking about her most recent experience, preferring to chalk it up to too much extremely potent, extremely aged wine, but as she sorted through her clothes and things and picked out what she wanted, her mind kept drifting back to it. Most likely the whole thing was the result of what she'd drunk and her feverish mind looking for an outlet for all the stress and pressure of the situation and the strangeness of the house she was now forced to live in. But still, it bothered her. The loss of the baby had been the worst thing she had ever been through, and yet she hadn't experienced any unusual dreams that had resulted in her walking around the house while she slept. And she'd never heard of anyone having such side effects from wine, even long-lived vintages. Something else was going on here. But what? Did she have a brain tumor? Was she having a mental breakdown? Or was there something about the house itself or even the land where the house sat ... some kind of natural phenomena she was feeling the effects of?

A vehicle door slamming brought her out of her troubled reverie, and she decided she had enough for now. She tossed down the plastic bag of things she'd been going through and grabbed up the tote with the clothes she had ready.

The sun felt warm after the chilliness of the storage unit. She put the tote bag in the car, turned and yanked on the rope to pull down the roll-up door, slid the latch over, and secured it again with the padlock.

Fourteen

It was right at lunchtime when she got to Walmart, and the store was already crowded with shoppers. Grabbing a cart, she took the main aisle on the grocery side all the way down to the rear wall where the beverages were and steered her way over to the bottled water.

Determined to get enough this time so she could stop worrying about it for a while and concentrate on getting a job, she filled the bottom and inside of the cart with gallons of distilled water, and then, as an afterthought, slid a case of Aquafina off the shelf and carefully positioned it on the top.

This was going to take a chunk of what money she had left, but it couldn't be helped. Anything to keep from having to go around with her hand out to everybody. Though before it was over, she might still end up having to ask her mother or Caleb, or Jill, for help even if she did get back to work soon.

She remembered firewood at the last minute and swung around to get a box of artificial logs, which she had to place on its side in the child seat. And since she was going to all the trouble, she stopped where the candles were on her way up to the front and stooped down to grab a few packages of the ones she needed.

As she straightened back up, she glanced over at all the different sizes and styles of picture frames on display beside them, and a bell rang in her head. She almost made the connection to whatever had been nagging at her, but then it was gone again.

Standing in line a few minutes later, she glanced over and then did a double-take at a couple standing two registers over. He was facing away so she couldn't be sure, but the build and hair matched Brent's and it looked like Serena standing beside him.

Something twisted in her gut. But then the guy turned to say something, and she saw he was too young, around the same age as his companion, unlike Brent who was twenty years older.

Releasing the breath she had been subconsciously holding, she pushed the cart forward as the woman ahead of her moved up.

On the way home, she found herself curious about why she hadn't heard from Brent. He'd acted almost like he wanted her back, at least in some capacity, and then nothing. Had he and Serena broken up completely? Considering he hadn't tried to reach her again, it seemed unlikely.

Back at the house, she left some of the water in the car to be fetched whenever needed and took the rest inside, along with two of the artificial logs, the tote, and the plastic bag holding the candles. She had to make two trips to get it all, but only from the carriage house. She hadn't bothered to park way out by the magnolia. She doubted the deputy would walk behind the house again any time soon, if he ever had. And if he did and caught her there? So be it. She'd deal with it. There were worse crimes. Surely she wouldn't do much, if any, actual jail time.

Later after she had pulled the curtains closed in the rooms she used, leaving the ones in the front parlor alone as usual, she was coming back through the sunroom after unsuccessfully attempting to free the deadbolt again, when a framed portrait to her right caught her eye.

She stepped over for a closer look. Unlike the frames she'd seen in the store, this one, displaying an older but still attractive dark-haired woman, was clearly nineteenth century in design, with an oval instead of a rectangular shape and a domed glass and raised ribbon of berries and leaves.

Her dream from the night before drifted into her thoughts and she remembered sitting in the armchair before Gus—and finally her brain made the connection to what had been lurking in the back of her mind. In the dream, she had been staring across at framed photos on the wall across from her.

And she'd seen them before. In the attic.

Over to one side there had been some framed portraits and landscapes propped where the roof sloped down and the ceiling was lower.

But of course you've seen them before, she chided herself. *That was how you were able to incorporate them into your dreams and delusions.*

She had given them no more than a passing glance when she'd gone up into the dark space, but she now had a sudden urge to go and inspect each one.

She laughed ruefully to herself. What did she think she was going to find?

Over the next couple of hours, she kept busy washing up some towels and smoothing the faint creases out of the dress pants and blouse she had picked to wear for her next interview. She was hoping they would suffice for now. But if she got called in for another "executive" position, she would have to do better. She draped the outfit across the end of the bed in the front-facing "master" bedroom, and opened the tall balcony windows to let in the breeze. She hadn't wanted to risk starting a fire during the day when the smoke might be noticed.

Then she checked her Facebook (nothing from Brent) and email, and briefly scrolled through some job listings.

But all the while, her mind kept coming back to the pictures above her, patiently waiting to be noticed after all these years, and she became acutely aware of the slow descent of the sun as the day wound down and the light began to fade.

Finally, when she'd almost let it go too long, she snatched up the lantern to go do what had been inevitable all along.

THE DOOR AT the top of the attic stairs scraped open part of the way and then stuck, and once more she had to put her shoulder into it to free it.

Holding the lantern out, she moved on in and ran her eyes over the things scattered and piled up in the center of the dim space. There was quite a bit of stuff. Again she found herself amazed that the home's remaining contents could have avoided being trashed or stolen. *Was* there something about the property and where it was situated that discouraged it? There was that strange mist she kept noticing.

She carefully navigated her way between a beat-up foot locker and a wooden chest. Amongst the trunks and reticules and cartons with curling papers and belongings spilling out, there were discarded bits of furniture, racks of moth-eaten garments, coats, and scarves, mildew-stained hat boxes, a hanging bird cage, and over in one corner, a dollhouse and a rocking horse. She could have spent a week in there happily examining all the tantalizing glimpses of the past these things would give her.

But first things first.

The pictures were on the far side, straight across from her. She squeezed between a dress form with a wire skirt mounted on an iron pedestal and what she thought might be a plant stand to get over to where a row of them leaned against the rough planks.

Before examining them, she squatted down and moved the lantern closer to inspect herself in a mirror propped alongside.

She didn't look unhinged. A trifle thinner, perhaps; her cheekbones seemed a little more pronounced. And her hair was a bit wild with the curls she'd let it dry into, but the hazel eyes gazing back at her were clear and steady.

She shifted over to the first stack of pictures.

The outermost one had an ornate metal frame. It was a gorgeous full-length shot of a woman wearing a long dress in some unknowable color with a plunging back and gathers at the hips that trailed behind her in a train.

Cheyenne gazed at the elegantly dressed lady, her brow wrinkling. The woman was standing sideways with mostly her back to the camera by a table holding a plant in a decorative pot. Behind her, a backdrop of stone pillars made it appear as if she were standing in some grand palace. There was something vaguely familiar about her, but it was hard to say what. Although she wore no hat and her hair had been artfully arranged on her head, only her profile was presented.

The next one, larger with a carved wooden frame, was a landscape of the house taken from the right front corner of the property. The lawn and bushes had been neatly trimmed then and the trees were smaller, leaving the home more open to the sun. The photo had been taken in full daylight, and although it was black and white, the contrast of light and dark, ranging from the brilliant white of the house gleaming in the bright sunshine to the nearly black shade of the nearby trees darkening the edge where the photographer had been standing, gave it a realistic depth as well as an aged quality that would have been hard to surpass.

The next photo also had a fancy metal frame and displayed a younger version of the same older lady in the sunroom portrait. The matriarch of the family, perhaps?

Mentally shrugging, Cheyenne stood up to get the feeling back into her legs, and moved over to the next group.

She cocked her head. The photo facing out was of a young woman with light brown skin. The photograph was backed by blue velvet and framed with a simpler, now tarnished frame. The woman was thin but not skinny, with a bohemian sort of style. The simple straw hat she wore, turned up above of her long black hair, only emphasized her beauty—the well-shaped eyebrows above wide dark eyes, high cheekbones, and full lips. She sat in a hanging chair suspended before a background with a southwestern pattern, her hands clasped together and resting atop the handle of an umbrella. Dressed in a fawn-colored shirt and snug black pants, with a fringed shawl across her shoulders and furry, calf-high boots, she looked beautiful and exotic and strong, despite her small size.

Cheyenne peered closer at the intriguing photo, sliding the lantern over. Down at the bottom where the image faded out, was the name *Clara*. Just that and nothing else. There could be something written on the back to indicate where and when it was taken, but she didn't want to try and pry it out, possibly damaging it.

She tipped it toward her, wondering vaguely if it could be the same Clara from the flyer she'd found in the drawer, and looked down at the photograph behind it. It had been placed in an oval frame similar to the one in the sunroom and was of a girl, around ten or so, wearing a frilly dress and a gentle, almost sad expression. She was pretty with blond ringlet curls that hung past her shoulders. Despite being sepia-toned, Cheyenne could tell where the sun had kissed the girl's skin and hair.

She moved on to the one stacked behind it—the last one—and let out a gasp.

Letting the other pictures fall flat, she stood up so fast her vision darkened for a second.

No, it couldn't be. How...?

It was Gus. Her Gus. Like an old friend seen years later, she instantly recognized him. The young man staring out at her had the exact same features of the man in her dreams. And it was more than just some family resemblance. It was *him.*

Only it couldn't be. Spinning on her heels, she looked around her in bewilderment. There was nothing, no other pictures anywhere, that could have planted his appearance in her brain.

She dropped into a squat again. They say everyone has a twin. *Could* it be that he only strongly resembled her Gus? In the portrait he sat on a hardback chair with his arms folded and a half smile on his face. Though a different age—he appeared around twenty-something here—she would have bet everything she owned, which admittedly wasn't much, that it was him. The resemblance was downright eerie.

Hold on. She straightened up and stepped over to the first group and examined the woman posing before the faux pillars again. Now she thought she knew why she seemed familiar. She could have been a double for *Helena,* the snooty woman from her dream. If that's what it had been.

Stop it! You're thinking crazy. She moved back and knelt down again, stood up the pictures she'd dropped, then shifted over and rapidly went through the ones to the right of them. There was an oil painting of the house from the same angle as the photo of it, a picture of a man, older and clean shaven, standing by the carriage house, and a portrait of an older girl in a lacy white gown, her pale, wavy hair hanging almost to her waist, gazing out with a faintly provocative look on her face. It was the girl with the ringlet curls, on the cusp of adulthood.

Taking the lantern with her, she walked over to the next stack.

Shaking her head, she grasped hold of a folding chair someone had carelessly left leaning against them, dragged it to the side, and squatted down to look at the image facing out.

It was of a young man and it stopped her cold.

Putting out a hand to steady herself, she stared at the photo before her in disbelief. *It's not real.* Only it was; it was just as tangible as the dirty boards beneath her fingertips. She lifted her hand and wiped it on her jeans.

Tearing her gaze away from the disconcerting image, she refocused her eyes on the slowly darkening space around her and tried to understand.

She had seen these people before—in what she'd thought were dreams or hallucinations.

She glanced across at the dark mouth of the narrow staircase leading down, and for a second the scene before her seemed to shifted almost imperceptibly and she felt the hair stir on the back of her neck.

Then as quickly as it came, the feeling was gone. Blinking, she checked the high window behind her—the light visible through it was almost totally gone now—and forced herself to look down at the unsettling photograph again.

It was a shot of Gus as a child, almost exactly like the one from the photo album Helena had disdained to examine. *All of it fantasy, made up by my mind.* Only here in front of her was proof that it was not. He half lay across a short chaise lounge, his head leaning against the tall side, his dark hair tousled and eyes half closed.

She took in a ragged breath and stepped over to the remaining pictures, which were slightly apart from the others, resting against the brick chimney running through the attic.

The outermost one was an even older photo, judging from the quality and faint blurriness, and featured a man with thick side whiskers sitting at a table with his hand wrapped around a bottle. She saw nothing familiar about where he sat but she was almost certain he was somehow related to Gus. There was a definite resemblance. Could this be his father?

Gingerly, she grasped the wooden frame, lifted it off the one it had been lying against, and set it to the side.

She looked over again in the direction of the window and saw it had gone completely dark. Night had fallen.

She had an almost irresistible urge to get up and run out of there, down the stairs and out the door, and just drive away.

She had never looked at these pictures. She'd merely glanced over and then dismissed them, vaguely thinking she might check them out later. And yet she had seen them in her "dreams." But what did any of this really mean? She still couldn't bring herself to believe that somehow she had actually ...

It suddenly hit her. Of course! She wanted to smack herself on the forehead. She must have walked up here in her sleep and looked at them then. And her slumbering mind had subconsciously filed them away. The answer had been so simple, and there she was thinking all kinds of ridiculous things.

She gave a low laugh that quickly turned into a strangled cry as she finally paid attention to the final picture in front of her.

Lurching up, she stumbled backwards, shocked nearly out of her wits at the face and figure she saw in the old photo, which was not of some stranger or person from her dreams—but of *herself*. Crashing into the table behind her, she fell backwards in a slide, and hit the floor hard on her hands and knees, narrowly missing an oil lamp.

She stayed that way, breathing hard, and thought about how real that had felt. Then, shaking and feeling faintly lightheaded, she slowly got to her feet and moved back over to the inexplicable photograph, lit by the glare of the lantern.

It was her all right. Any doubt she might have harbored was instantly removed by the sight of what she had on in the photo. Though it was blurred around the edges, she could still make out the lighter shapes of the tiny white sheep on the fuzzy sleepshirt she'd been wearing.

It was truly her. She had really been there, in the turret, and he had taken her picture. It had happened. He was real. They were all real. God in Heaven, it was all real.

Backing away, her foot hit the lantern and for a second it stuttered and winked out. When it flickered back on, she noticed how dim the bulb had become. The batteries were going and if she didn't hurry, she was going to find herself in complete darkness.

After only a small hesitation, she stepped forward and snatched up the picture of herself, grabbed the lantern, and hurried out.

SHE PACED BACK and forth in front of the photo. She'd propped it on the mantel and had the lantern burning, along with her usual candelabra and another one she'd brought up from the wine cellar. The house had grown so cold she expected to see her breath any minute, but she hadn't wanted to start a fire yet.

What she needed was a second opinion. Someone to look at it and tell her what they saw.

She pulled her phone out of her back pocket and checked the time. If she hurried she might barely make it, if the library still closed at nine. She reached behind the sofa to retrieve her purse, lifted the framed photo off the mantel, and blew out all the candles.

She would probably have better luck at the larger main branch for part of what she wanted, but it would take too long to drive that far.

In the sunroom, she left the lantern on a shelf after switching it off, and went out the door.

The moon had lit up the few ragged clouds drifting across, laying a soft radiance across the surrounding land. The temperature, made worse by the sharp wind, felt like it was near freezing.

She hurried across. The house was going to be ice cold when she got back. Reaching the car, she yanked the door open, slid inside, and jammed the key in.

It fired right up, thankfully—she'd been afraid it might not— and she switched on the heater.

She didn't wait long before backing out and bumping her way across to the driveway. She still didn't know exactly how far away her nearest neighbors were and she didn't want to risk letting it warm up too long.

On the way into town, she was tempted to stop for a hot drink, but she knew she was too pressed for time and continued on.

At least the car heater worked. If felt like the first time she'd been truly warm in days.

The photo sat on the passenger seat beside her. Her eyes kept straying to it as she drove. It looked like her, but how could that be? It was crazy. Impossible. Yet there it was.

Slowing, she flipped on the blinker at the road she needed, and made the turn. She kept going over and over it in her head as she traveled the five miles to the main strip where the library was located, trying to piece it all together and somehow make sense of it.

If at least part of the time she *hadn't* been dreaming, then ...?

There had been that staticky, charged feeling in the air, she remembered, as if lightning were eminent. In fact, she'd experienced some form of it each and every time.

Thinking hard, she barely noticed as she turned in and parked in a free slot near the covered walkway.

She switched off the engine, grabbed her purse and the framed photo, and climbed out. Pressing the key fob to lock the car, she headed for the entrance.

She'd let herself become enamored of the home and had basically enclosed herself in it. The house, and Augustus, had been on her mind much of the time. Had immersing herself in the past somehow made her susceptible to … To what? Traveling back in time?

In the vestibule she paused to silence her phone, and then passed between the automatic doors.

The warm, hushed atmosphere settled around her like a soothing blanket as she walked across to the circulation desk.

This time of night, not too long before closing, the place was nearly deserted. Besides a woman having her books checked out, there were only two men on computers in the corner and a young couple perusing the wall of available DVDs.

She stood back a little, clutching the picture to her chest, while she waited.

Finally the woman ahead of her gathered her books and moved away and she was able to approach the sixtyish lady with bobbed gray hair working the desk.

"Hi," she said, smiling, as she moved up. "I was hoping you could look at something for me?"

She held the photo out, turning it around for her to see. The woman, whose name was Barb according to the nametag on her cardigan, was already reaching for it, half rising, so she waited before saying more, curious to see what her reaction would be. After all, what she wanted was a completely unbiased opinion of what she had there.

Studying it, Barb held it in her hands, then looked up at Cheyenne again. She scrutinized her for a second before returning her attention to the old photo. "Where'd you have it taken?" she asked. "They did a good job making it look antique."

Well, that answers one question, she thought as Barb handed it back over. She wasn't imagining a resemblance that wasn't there. There seemed to be no question in Barb's mind that it was her.

As Cheyenne hesitated, Barb added, "My sister and her husband had their picture done like that up at Ghost Town in the Sky before it closed down, except they were dressed like a saloon girl and a gunslinger. But it didn't seem completely authentic like yours."

Ghost Town in the Sky had been an amusement park located in the mountains of North Carolina that had featured local Cherokee dancers and a staged shootout each day. She had gone there once with Brent and had loved it. They'd walked around with large cups of draft beer, thrilled to even be allowed such a thing. And of course Brent had drunk too much and then insisted on riding the Black Widow, a ride that spun you around while slinging you back and forth inside a dark building to the earsplitting sounds of Metallica. He had ridden it not once but *twice*. Cheyenne held back a smile at the memory of him leaning over the side of the chairlift on the way down the mountain, upchucking onto the slanted dirt and rocks in full view of everyone behind them and all the passengers on the train slowly chugging its way up the incline across from them.

"It was at a studio," she finally responded. "I know it's different, but I think I kind of like it." She said it as if she had been unsure and had merely wanted to show it to someone to get their opinion. She supposed there were people out there lonely enough to resort to seeking out the local librarian for something so personal.

"Also," she added. "I need to do some research while I'm here, maybe check some things out, and I know I don't have much time."

Barb twisted her arm to check the slim gold watch on her wrist. Cheyenne could see from the round clock on the wall behind her that she had exactly twenty-five minutes. "I'll be glad to help. If you'll give me an idea of what you're hunting for, I can see what we have while you look."

"I'm actually wanting information on mysterious places, areas with supposed strange properties."

"You mean like mystery spots?" Barb's left eyebrow rose, but she gave no other outwardly sign she thought it odd.

"Yes. And any other interesting anomalies, especially in this area of the county if possible."

The librarian's brow arched a little higher, but she made no comment and started jotting notes on a small pad.

"Also, time travel. And if you have anything on a family, a local family that lived not too far from here back in the late 1800s.

Their name was Moore. One of them was Augustus Moore. I'm sorry. I know that's a lot."

"We'll see what we can find. You can search online, too, if you want, while I try my luck."

Cheyenne thanked her and moved over to the tall workstation.

For the next ten minutes she and Barb tapped away, searching the vast catalogue, making note of anything promising, then seeking out and collecting the ones on the shelves there.

With a little more than ten minutes to spare, Barb walked over with one final selection. "You might like this one."

Cheyenne turned to read the proffered title. *Bizarre Cracks in the Continuum.* By somebody named Josh Rogers. "Nothing about the Moore family?"

"No, nothing in particular. But you may be able to find something at the South Carolina Department of Archives. I believe they have a decent collection of material they've scanned and digitized, too."

Cheyenne nodded. "Okay, thank you so much. You've been a great help." Gathering up the books she'd collected, she moved over to a table situated by the stacks to glance over them one last time before deciding.

The first one she had found was a smaller work titled *The Reality Concept*, shelved in the nonfiction section, by someone named Blair Tyson.

It had been published back in 1996 and did seem to include some of the elements she was interested in, specifically "interesting anomalies that can't be explained by traditional science." She set it to the side.

She picked up the hardback Barb had found for her, glancing over to check the time. Only a few minutes left.

This one mostly consisted of different individual's accounts of strange incidents out in the wild, compiled by the author, a retired math professor. But she thought it could provide some insight, so she placed it with the one she wanted to take.

The only other publication she'd found with anything even remotely close to what she was hunting for was a book on unexplained mysteries. Flipping through it now, she saw it mainly covered things like spontaneous human combustion, mass hysteria, and alien encounters. But it did have one small section on mysterious spots and various oddities in the back. She decided to take it too.

The other two were books on local history. The larger one was about the entirety of the Upstate, and the other was a small trade paperback specific to the towns in their county.

Glancing over, she saw Barb stand up and knew she was out of time. She'd take the paperback, she decided, and leave the other one.

She piled the books up, with the unwanted one on top to give back, and started for the desk.

SHE KEPT HER head down and pushed into the frigid wind blasting across the icy tundra the back of the property had become. Tall, frozen clumps of dead grass and dormant weeds brushed and slapped against her as, hunched over the books she'd checked out, she crunched and slid her way to the sunroom.

Shifting the books to the other arm, she carefully climbed the steps and wrestled the door open.

Temporarily parking the stack on the little round table between two fraying rattan chairs, she pulled hard to get the door to close properly, gathered the books back up, and moved into the house, grabbing the lantern as she went.

In the diffuse circle of light, her breath billowed out in front of her as she walked past the dark kitchen and dining room, and turned into the righthand passageway. The house, normally silent, creaked and groaned around her, and shadows danced in the moonlight from the trees being tossed about in the gusting wind.

In the smaller parlor, she paused at the curio cabinet to pull off her jacket and set down the lantern, books, and her purse, and then went straight to work on the fire.

Using a stick, she swept aside the ashes—she was too cold to worry about cleaning them out—stuffed some balled-up magazine pages under the blackened grate, tossed an armful of small branches and twigs on top, and threw on a store-bought log.

Now where was the darn lighter? She grabbed the lantern, swept it around, and spotted the dim shape of the plastic Bic on the floor to the right of her. She snatched it up and with a shaking hand, ignited it and held the tiny flame to the packaging on the bottom and top of the log.

Shivering, she watched until she was sure it wasn't going to go out, and then walked over to reach across the back of the sofa for the blanket she'd stashed there. Wrapping it around her shoulders, she left the room and went down to the kitchen.

She opened the lower cabinet of the cupboard she'd been using and collected the gallon of water and coffee things she had ready on a dark pewter platter. She'd found it jammed into the back of the dining room hutch. Taking it with her, she hurried back to the inner room, set it and the gallon jug on the hearth, and knelt before the fire, which had taken nicely and was crackling away.

She added a few more pieces of wood, waited until they began to catch, and then poured water into the small pot she had accidently left out. *Vigilant*, she reminded herself, balancing it over the flames.

She settled back in front of the fire and shifted first one way then another to warm her body while she waited. The wind, though still blowing, sounded as though it might be dying down.

When she judged it ready, she spooned instant coffee into the cup she used, poured the hot water over it, and doctored it up extra sweet with canned milk and sugar.

She was beginning to feel less like a popsicle now and more like a human. She got up to move over to where she could relax.

With the lantern on one side and the larger candelabra on the other, she settled on the sofa with her hot drink and the stack of books on the table in front of her.

Fifteen

She sat at the larger table in the dining room reading through each of the books—she had only managed a few pages the previous night, before beginning to nod off—and doing various searches online.

The information in the library books and website articles she was poring over didn't fit her experiences exactly, but there were enough eerie similarities in the various accounts and descriptions for her to find some of it compelling.

Of the three books on unusual phenomena, the smaller one was the most relatable, and she was able to put a name to the bizarre experiences she'd been having. "Time slips" such as hers, according to the author, a self-proclaimed ghost hunter who was also interested in this phenomenon, were sometimes brought on by close proximity to historical objects and places. He then went on to take that a step further and postulate that if the person was not in fact slipping backward or forward in this timeline, then they might be traveling to a parallel universe—one that was only slightly distant and mirrored our own.

But what caused the slips at these particular places, was what she wanted to know. Merely being surrounded by the relics of a bygone era couldn't completely account for it.

The larger hardback the librarian had recommended contained several accounts of supposedly "unexplainable cracks in reality" experienced by people in wilderness areas. Which didn't really apply to her. But one thing she did find interesting was that some of these people claimed to have witnessed someone either appearing (in strange clothing at times) or disappearing right before their eyes. And one even reported a strange fog in the air, which made her think of the odd mist she occasionally saw creeping across the ground.

She got her answer partly in the collection of unexplained mysteries she'd chosen, which included a section on time warps. There was the inevitable mention of the Bermuda Triangle and the Philadelphia Experiment, then a bit on mysterious oddities and locations that were purported to have peculiar properties.

And there she found it: the assertation that *certain places were sensitive to fluctuations in time.*

This belief was further expounded upon on a page she landed on about similar anomalies after fixing herself a fresh cup of coffee and switching to Google. The ability to unexpectedly find yourself walking down a street or into a shop from forty years before, the author hypothesized, came from entering what was referred to as a "time vortex."

She knew she'd hit on something and the rest of her coffee soon grew cold as she read on.

These vortexes, these especially sensitive places, were sometimes thought to interact with the earth's magnetic field, making them especially vulnerable to fluctuations.

There were other eerie similarities. Some witnesses spoke of a strange feeling in the air, and some claimed their hair had stood up *as if they were on the verge of being struck by lightning.*

Exactly like the strange staticky charge she'd noticed.

As to why these vortexes didn't always transport the unwary traveler to another era, it was theorized that these periods when the timelines overlapped could occur in phases or cycles when the barriers between them were particularly fluid. The author claimed that time was not linear, but rather, flowed like a river.

She stood up and rolled her head around to get the kinks out. She could feel the beginnings of a headache building behind her eyes. She decided to get out of the house for a while and charge her phone and get something decent to eat while she contemplated everything she'd learned.

IT WAS STARTING to get dark sooner now, and the sky was already awash in pink and violet as she pulled out onto the highway. What was Brent doing right then? Was he thinking about how different it was with Serena? Did he miss her?

She still hadn't heard from him, she realized. She'd been so caught up in Gus and the mind-boggling knowledge that *somehow* she had discovered a link to a bygone era—which she still had trouble accepting—that she'd barely thought of him in the past couple of days.

Her mind drifted to the astounding, precarious position she now found herself in as she turned onto the secondary road that led into town—if she *were* truly in danger of falling into the past again, that is, during some electromagnetic fluctuation and not merely batshit crazy imagining a similar-looking woman in an old photo as herself. The possibility had occurred to her.

Not being too keen on dining alone, she decided to ride over to her mother's and invite her along.

By definition, the term "fluctuate" meant to rise and fall. So if it did come in cycles, then ...

Then maybe it would stop.

But did she want it to?

Her phone went off, interrupting her musings, and she fumbled to answer it without swerving.

"Hello?"

Jill's voice filled her ear. "Hey girl. Whatcha doing?"

Cheyenne grinned. "Uh, right now I'm driving down the road." She'd been cooped up in that house too long with no one's company but her own (not counting the previous inhabitants), and she was glad to hear from her.

"I just thought I'd call and check on you. How's it going on the home front?"

How exactly to answer that? Keeping it vague seemed the best course of action. She could imagine how Jill would react if she told her she had stumbled upon a segue to a different time period in the abandoned Victorian mansion she'd been squatting in.

"About the same. He's still with Serena as far as I know."

Jill hesitated before speaking again. "Is ... is he helping you any?"

Not much, but Jill didn't have to know that. "Some."

"Listen, if you need me to—"

"No," she interrupted before Jill could go any further. "I'm good." *But*, she best not sugarcoat it too much. "For now." She might have to turn to her yet. "If it comes to that, I'll let you know."

"Okay, well, have—" A commotion in the background drowned out the rest of what Jill was saying.

"What was that?"

"Hang on, Cheyenne. My neighbor's here."

She waited patiently through the noise of their greetings and Josh's excited chatter, clamoring for attention, and then Jill was back on the line.

"Sorry about that. We're going out tonight and her daughter Katy's going to babysit."

"Oh, well I better let you go so you can do your thing. We can talk again soon."

"Definitely! I want to hear more."

Cheyenne raised her voice slightly over the racket in the background. "Have a good time!"

"I will! Love you!"

"Love you too!" And then Jill was gone.

Although she was glad Jill had found a new friend, she found herself saddened by it. How long would it be before they began speaking less often and then finally stopped altogether?

Turning into the apartment complex a few minutes later, she looked for her mother's car and found it in its usual space.

She parked directly beside it and got out, hit the lock button, and hiked up the hill.

The door was closed, the curtains drawn. It was too early even for her mother to be settling down for bed, which meant she was probably avoiding the pesky neighbor in the back.

She crossed the tiny patio and rapped briskly.

"Hang on," she heard from inside. A second later her mother's face appeared on the other side of the glass, and she pulled the door open.

"Hey! I didn't know you were coming by." She stepped back for her to enter, and Cheyenne saw she was dressed even nicer than usual.

"It was a spur of the moment thing. You going out?"

"I am. You just caught me. I was just about to leave. Me and Velma are going to a play." She said this as if it were the most amazing thing.

And in a way, it was. While married to her father, her mother had led a very conservative life that revolved around her husband and children and didn't involve going to plays or any other shows. And the fact that the tiny neighboring town of Pelzer actually boasted a pretty decent community theatre was another source of amazement to her and her mother ever since it had caught on and begun holding top musicals and plays that packed its historical auditorium.

"It's a little early," she said as her mother turned to grab her pocketbook. "When does it start?"

"Oh, we're going to get a bite to eat first. I'd invite you to join us but I don't know if you could get a seat near us. We bought our tickets ahead of time."

"That's okay."

"There she is."

Cheyenne turned to see a bespectacled face peering in. She opened the door, greeted Velma, and slipped out while her mother locked up.

"Bye, talk to you later," her mother called out as they descended the slope to where the two women's cars were parked.

"Bye, enjoy the show," she answered back, but her mother had already turned away to speak to Velma and didn't appear to hear.

Letting out a small sigh, Cheyenne trudged the rest of the way, trying not to feel disappointed at being left out. It was good her mother had a life, after all. She unlocked the car and climbed in.

She sat there for a minute before leaving. She really didn't want to eat in a restaurant alone, but she wasn't ready to go back to the house yet, either.

This connection she had to this man, this Augustus, was undeniable, as was her attraction to him. But underneath it lay depths and undercurrents, possibly dangerous ones, she wasn't sure she would ever understand. And that frightened her. The fundamental beliefs she'd held of the world around her and her place in it had been shattered and now her grip on reality felt shaky and tenuous.

The short sound of her phone receiving a text jarred her back to her surroundings. The streetlights were winking on now. Twilight had arrived.

It was Brent: *Can you talk?*

Could she talk? Of course she could. Could *he*?

Not bothering to reply to his text, she called him instead.

"Hey," he said, picking right up.

"Hey, what's up?"

"I just got off work earlier than I expected. I thought I was going to have to stay late and ... and well ... I was thinking about you."

She stayed silent, reading between the lines. He had gotten off early and now had some time to himself, which Serena would never be the wiser of.

"There's a new kayak launch by the river in Pelzer. Rodney showed it to me the other day." Rodney was his friend at work. "I was thinking I could show it to you and we could hang out and talk."

"In *Pelzer*?" First a community theatre and now this.

"Yeah, I didn't know about it either. I thought we could grab something to eat, get a drink, ya know, and check it out."

"Come on, Cheyenne," he said when she hesitated. "I just want to talk."

She guessed she owed him that much. They were together for over five years and had created and then lost a child together.

"All right," she said. *I hope I don't regret this.* "Where do you want to meet?"

SOMETHING TO EAT and a drink turned out to be three hotdogs, two for him and one for her, slathered in mustard, onions, and relish, the way both of them liked it, accompanied by a six-pack of Coors from the nearby Spinx station.

"I am *starving*," he said as drove into an otherwise empty lot after successfully navigating the narrow, interconnected maze of streets she couldn't possibly ever hope to easily find her way through again.

He pulled the truck all the way down to the far end, as close to the water as he could get, and switched off the headlights and engine. "I hope you don't mind," he said, reaching for the bag of food.

"No, that's fine. Give me mine, too." She needed to eat if she was going to drink, and with the way she was feeling, she was definitely going to drink. Not too much, though, she reminded herself; she had to drive.

She took her hotdog from him, unwrapped it, and took a big bite as he crammed his in and bit off nearly half of it.

She finished chewing and said, "Serena's not going to appreciate the onions."

He immediately replied, "I don't *care*," and both of them laughed.

It was hard to believe they could find humor in anything about this. But he'd always had that ability, when he actually made the effort. He could be plenty charming when he chose.

"So what did you want to talk about?" She reached down to grab two of the beers.

She handed him one and kept the other for herself.

She took another bite and watched as he twisted the top off of his bottle and took a long pull. He didn't seem in a hurry to get to whatever it was.

She carefully parked the rest of her hotdog on a napkin, and went to work on her beer. The store must have kept their cooler at a decent temperature because the brew was still cold and went down smoothly.

"You want to show it to me first?" she said, letting out a small burp.

He nodded, balled his wrapper up, and tossed it into the bag. He picked up his beer and took another drink, set it down, and opened his door.

She climbed out and walked to the front of the truck to meet him as he came around. He held his hand out as he had so many times before, and without thinking, she took it.

They strolled over, stepped up onto the dock, and followed it out over the river, where it joined a floating section with launches on each side.

"See there," he said, nudging her and pointing at the metal rollers running down a chutelike ramp. "That's where they launch the kayaks."

"Oh," she said. "Cool." She'd never actually seen anything like it. They had gone canoeing once early in their marriage, but they'd had to get in and out the hard way.

She looked out across the water. Now that the sun had gone down, the temperature had dropped and a cool breeze had sprung up, creating ripples and peaks across the surface in the glow of the tall lights illuminating the area.

"Are you cold?" he asked as she tightened her jacket, giving a little shiver.

"A bit."

"Come on. Let's get out of the wind."

He led the way over to the side where a wooden bench sat back against the trees, facing the river flowing past.

"Looks like a good place to fish," she said, gingerly sitting down.

"You wouldn't want to fish out of here." He remained standing with his back to her, gazing out at the dark ribbon of water.

"Why not?" Although she could guess why.

"It's too polluted."

"Figures."

He turned and walked over to where she was and sat down on the other end, leaving a good three feet of space between them.

"What is it, Brent?" she asked him quietly.

He gave a slight shake of his head, his eyes fixed on the shadowy tangle of trees and vegetation on the other side. Finally he shifted around to face her. "We could have been something, don't you think?"

She nodded. "Yes, we could have, I believe." And then because he seemed so miserable, so sad as if he were about to *cry,* she slid over and leaned into him.

"I had hoped," he murmured, "up until … that you and I might try …" His voice trailed away.

That they might try again? Might try to have another child? A sister or a brother for their little Ian, though the two would never meet on this earth?

"Serena's pregnant," he blurted.

She froze for one long terrible moment, feeling as if she had been sucker punched, and then sprang away from him.

Her face contorted as she worked to hold back the sound of anguish that threatened to erupt from her throat as a roar began to grow in her ears, expanding until it eclipsed the sound of the wind and the river.

He couldn't be going to have a child with Serena. That couldn't be right! Her brain struggled to comprehend it, drifting from the child he and Serena were having to their little guy who never was.

"NO!" she cried, her voice echoing over the rush of the river.

"Take it easy," he said, sliding over to grip her arm.

She shrugged him off and stood up. He and Serena were going to have a baby. He and Serena were going to be a family. *Serena's* child would replace the one they had made. It wasn't fair!

Her little guy had never had a chance. The tears finally came then and she turned away in silent grief for the boy and the family that were now irretrievably lost.

How had they gotten here? How had *she* gotten here?

"I am so sorry, Cheyenne," he said in a thick voice.

She raised her head, his words cutting through the despair and grief she was feeling.

She looked over at him standing there, miserable and sad in the shadows under the trees.

He was apologizing to her. Because he was going to have a child.

But he shouldn't be sorry for having a child. He was going to have a *baby*. And there he was apologizing for it. Abruptly she felt ashamed of herself.

She wiped at her eyes. "No, don't apologize, ever, for that baby." She forced her lips into a smile. "You're going to have a kid. That's something to be happy about."

He kept his eyes on the ground for a moment, and then looked up and nodded.

Sixteen

The sound of lightning splitting the sky with a loud clap of thunder jerked Cheyenne awake. A storm had descended with a vengeance. The house howled with the winds sweeping into it, and deep, rolling thunder echoed across the landscape in the wake of the bolts popping all around.

Taking the blanket with her, she left the room and navigated her way through the darkness, lit by occasional flashes, to the larger front parlor.

Halfway across the floor, she felt the hair on her head and arms stir as a huge bolt struck the ground somewhere close by with a deafening crash, lighting up the sky outside the windows. But it wasn't the storm that stopped her in her tracks. It was what she saw in that brief, brilliant flash.

Moving slowly and keeping her eyes fixed, she peered ahead of her and caught it again in the next longer burst of light: a different, newer-looking version of the room from years past overlying this one.

She went still and looked down at the floorboards beneath her feet and watched them switch from dull to gleaming then back to dull again. Blinking, she jerked her head up.

The room as it had been slowly became more distinct around her and the sound of the storm lessened in her ears. Soon the light changed too, becoming brighter as the clouds slid away and the moon shone in unimpeded.

The grandfather clock ticked somewhere to her right, and she whipped her head around at the unfamiliar sound of it.

This can't be happening, she thought, her mind still resisting the reality of it. *I can't actually be in the past.*

She slowly turned in a circle and gazed at the irrefutable proof around her. She smelled the faint scent of flowers and the hint of something recently baked. Where was Gus? Upstairs asleep in his room?

It was going to be difficult to explain not only her presence but her appearance (she had on a pair of low-slung lounge pants and a thin cotton top, sans bra) if she ran into anyone. But she couldn't seem to stop herself and turned to head around to the staircase.

Soft amber shone down on her from the same stained-glass window as she slowly ascended to the second floor, fighting a feeling of strangeness the entire way. She veered right, entering the dimly lit hallway, and followed it to the last room before the turret.

The door creaked as she eased it open, but the dark form beneath the mound of covers remained motionless.

She could tell by the deep, even sound of his breathing that he was fast asleep. Dropping the blanket onto a chair, she walked toward him.

"Gus," she whispered when she got near enough.

His breath hitched in his throat and then resumed.

"Gus," she whispered a little louder, and his eyes flew open in the dimness.

He stared uncomprehendingly up at her for a second, and then lifted upright, shoving himself back against the headboard.

"It's me," she said.

"It's you," he parroted back. He stared wide-eyed at her for a beat, and then said, his voice barely audible, "I was beginning to think you weren't real."

"Are *you*?" she responded softly and on impulse, stuck out a finger and poked him.

He jerked as if she'd struck him, eyes going even wider in the moonlight shining in, then seeing her mischievous grin, he smiled back and responded by shifting closer, letting the sheet around him fall away. She got a glimpse of bare skin and dark hair, and then he was encircling the back of her neck with his hand and pulling her toward him.

His lips melded gently with hers and then clamped down harder, his tongue delving inside, and she felt herself go weak. He pulled her down onto the bed and covered her with his body. *Oh my*, she thought as he moved his mouth off of hers and slid it down her neck.

She no longer cared whether it was his world or hers; all she could think about was the very real response he was eliciting within her, a sensation she hadn't felt in a very long time.

"Gus ... Augustus ... how is this happening?"

"Stay and find out," he murmured, kissing her neck. "Just stay." He moved down to her collarbone, his mouth leaving a fiery trail across it. "Stay."

And then there was no more need for words.

SOMETIME IN THE early morning hours, still in Gus's bed, she felt the air around her begin to stir. Slipping out from under his warm arm, she got up and moved over to retrieve the blanket she'd dropped into the chair the night before. She picked it up and wrapped it around her shoulders. The fire Gus had lit to supplement the slight bit of warmth rising from the furnace had died down to nothing but embers.

She could feel it coming now that she knew the signs. She tried to ward it off by concentrating hard on the room around her. It seemed to work for a bit, but the more she tried not to think of her own world, the more it invaded her thoughts of this one.

She padded over to Gus's sleeping form. He had turned on his side, leaving his upper body exposed. She reached down and plucked at the cover to pull it up and felt a tiny zap of electricity.

Leaving it, she backed away. *Stay*, she willed herself as he had entreated her earlier. She moved over and touched the thick mahogany bedpost, feeling the reassuring solidness.

This is real and you are here. But not for much longer it didn't feel like. Suddenly she had a disturbing thought. What if she concentrated too hard and whatever this was, this slippage, stopped happening, and she ended up *stuck* here? She found the prospect wasn't completely abhorrent, but there was her mother and her brother, and Jill, to consider.

Abruptly the scene around her changed even further as thoughts of her family intruded upon the bygone era she had existed in for the past several hours. The room and the things in it seemed to go flat and lifeless with no effects of light and shade, like etchings in woodwork.

Afraid and unsure, she made no effort to resist as she began to be drawn away.

A moment later she found herself in a room now bare and cold.

SHE STARED INTO the murky bathroom mirror at the reddish bruise-like mark on her neck.

If she had needed any more proof, there it was. She sure as hell hadn't given herself a hickey.

She gripped the edge of the sink. She didn't know why or how, but as impossible as it seemed, it appeared she truly had existed somewhere else for a while. Augustus was real. And he wanted *her*. *Boy, had he*, she thought.

She turned away from her reflection and walked out of the bathroom.

The sky outside the windows looked gray and overcast, though it seemed to have warmed up some. The house was chilly, as always, but not frigid as it had been.

What she and Gus shared the previous night had been mostly wordless, but later when she had conveyed her bewilderment to him again, he had murmured, "I don't know. I don't know how you're here, but I am so glad." They hadn't talked much after that. Both of them seemed afraid to break the spell. But right before following him into sleep, not sure if she would still be there when she awoke, she'd interrupted the silence to ask about the other people he'd mentioned to her before.

He had whispered to her that when he was a boy he had seen a man, an unfamiliar man in funny clothes, out in the garden behind the house. He had been only six or so, he told her, when he'd run up and watched the man disappear right in front of him. And then not too long after, he had witnessed a woman crossing the ballroom, who was there one minute and then not there the next. He hadn't recognized the man, but the woman had looked like his great-aunt Florence who had recently passed away. (The woman with the disturbing tombstone in the cemetery, she'd realized.) Neither one had stayed more than a few moments. "And don't forget you," he had reminded her. "I saw you that first time when you came into my room. When I was around the same age."

When she had further inquired what everyone else thought about their land's odd properties, he'd murmured that there had always been rumors about the place.

It seemed no one, except Gus, had noticed anything unusual around that time. And for a while he had halfway believed what he'd seen were spirits. "You're not a ghost, are you?" he'd asked her. Cheyenne smiled as she remembered her reply: "Do I feel like a ghost?"

So, it wasn't just the house. It was the ground beneath it. And it reached at least as far out as the cemetery, where she'd seen the older version of Myrna. And it sounded to her like *Gus* might have been the one to travel that day in the ballroom to a time before that when his great-aunt Florence had still been alive.

Cheyenne thought back to that day in the family cemetery as she stepped off the staircase, walked across, and entered the front parlor.

What had Myrna said? She'd said ... *You have to stay* and *he needs you.* That meant Myrna already knew who she was before she ever went back and met her that first time. On this end anyway.

Moving into the center of the room, she put a hand to her head and sat down on the discolored chaise left abandoned in a sea of empty floor. Trying to figure it all out was about to give her a headache.

Inhaling deeply, she reclined back and attempted to fit the pieces together. There were rumors about odd occurrences, which meant it had happened before. But after that period when he was a boy, Gus hadn't noticed anything else until later when he was older. That meant it most likely did come and go, waxing and waning with years, *decades*, in between with no events.

Heaving herself up, she continued trying to fix the timeline in her mind as she left the parlor through the back hall that ran to the ballroom and walked to the kitchen to grab the large kettle and start the first batch of water heating for her bath.

She had shown up there when he was a kid, and then again sometime after that when the woman she was assuming was his mother had been perusing the photo album. And she had appeared at the party. Then in the turret when he'd taken her photo. *And later in his bed.*

Halfway to the fireplace in the inner room, she came to an abrupt halt as something amazing occurred to her.

Not once since she'd found herself with Gus the night before had she thought about Brent and the terrible news he had imparted.

IT TOOK MORE than an hour for her to heat enough water to wash her hair and take a decent bath, and even then it was lukewarm.

As she dressed in snug leggings and an oversized sweatshirt, she tried to imagine what it would be like to stay back then with him, something that, wonder of all wonders, might actually be possible. What would the day-to-day life be like?

But could she really leave this world? Could she leave her family, possibly for good? *Yes*, if meant another chance at some semblance of happiness. She would always miss her family and mourn her lost little boy—even now she could feel the sorrow pulling at her—but with Gus she'd felt lifted out of it, somehow. Augustus was someone she could love, someone to help bridge, if not fill, the hole left in her heart.

But how? She hadn't felt even a hint of the anomaly occurring again. No charged feeling, no static, no superimposed images.

As the day wore on, she found herself returning over and over to the bathroom mirror and the mark on her neck to reassure herself that it was all true, that she wasn't losing her mind and imagining what had happened.

That evening, Jill called, worried about how she had cut Cheyenne short the last time they'd talked and wanting to tell her how her night had gone.

Before it was over, Jill had her laughing and feeling better about the future state of their friendship. It seemed Jill's neighbor not only couldn't hold her liquor, but also couldn't abide by her marriage vows. She had admitted as much to Jill in between throwing herself at anything even remotely attractive in the bar. But the icing on the cake had been when, after disregarding Jill for so long that she'd forgotten she was there, she had *left without her*.

"There I was," Jill told her, "in a friggin' *honky-tonk*"—Cheyenne broke up at this; except for a few select, mostly older songs, neither of them enjoyed country music that much—"and my stupid cell phone is dead and of course there's no sign of a goddam *landline* and there is no on, absolutely no one, I want to ask to even borrow their phone, let alone for a ride. It was, like, nearly two o'clock so I didn't want to call Ben. I knew ..."

She had ended up accepting a ride from some guy she'd thought was leaving with his girlfriend, but as it turned out, had only been walking the lady out. Still, Jill had climbed on into his car—the bartender and other people seemed to know and like the man, after all. But she had grossly underestimated how inebriated he was. He had driven so badly she hadn't even minded when he abruptly vomited, splashing some on her, as they pulled up in front of her house and then had lingered out front, causing Ben to put her on the couch. "I was just so happy to make it home alive."

After hanging up with Jill, Cheyenne took the center hall, past the smaller passageways, the old laundry room, and then the dining room across from the kitchen, to the sunroom.

The view through the windows was particularly mesmerizing as the day came to a close. Soft, lingering light glowed through the trees and streamed in golden arrows across the barren, shadowy wildness of the backyard and field beyond. So beautiful in its own way. But so different than it must have been in Gus's time.

Jill's call had brought the modern world into focus again and reminded her of everything she would be leaving behind. And the very certainty she now felt of Jill's friendship only served to make her more uncertain about what to do about Gus. Although she might not necessarily have a choice in the matter. For all she knew, the phenomenon might not ever happen again in her lifetime.

This was her reality. This in front of her, this old house on this overgrown forgotten ground that she'd been inhabiting ever since her life had crashed and burned. This was her world.

Seventeen

It had been two days, and nothing. She was anxious and bored and hungry for human interaction and decent food, but she was afraid to leave. She had resigned herself to the possibility that she might not make it back to Gus again, that it wasn't meant to be, but she couldn't get what Myrna had said out of her mind. *He needs you.* The image of him as a child kept popping into her head as she imagined all the disasters that might have befallen him. What had Myrna meant?

Before it got too late in the morning, while there was less chance of anyone being around, she left out the back and walked down to the pecan tree.

She examined the ground underneath it and was pleased to see there were still some nuts the squirrels hadn't run off with yet. Stooping, she began collecting them, dropping them into the bowl she'd brought.

When she judged she had enough, she moved over to the apple tree, grabbed a few of the lower-hanging ones, and went back to the house.

She left the pecans in the sunroom and took the apples into the kitchen. She pulled out an empty drawer and dumped all but one of them into it. Then, using the gallon of water she'd stuck in the cupboard, she rinsed the apple, grabbed a steak knife from another drawer where she'd stashed a few pieces of silverware, and took it and the apple back to the sunroom.

Cutting off pieces, she ate the crisp, juicy fruit while she contemplated the pecans before her. They still had the outer husk surrounding them, but they had begun to split open, revealing the familiar brown shell inside. Hopefully that meant they were ripe.

After she'd eaten her fill of the apple, she opened up the door again and tossed the core out as far as she could, walked back to the kitchen to rinse her hands, and returned to the pecans.

She carefully lowered herself onto one of the rattan chairs, which gave a little in the seat but held, and pulled the bowl over.

Her thoughts drifted as she pushed her sleeves up and set about prying off the husks, moving from Brent and his new life to Augustus and the fleeting happiness she'd felt with him.

She didn't really know that much about him except for what she had read in the paperback from the library, which she'd been surprised to find, actually contained a brief mention of a family named Moore settling in the area and building first a grist mill and then later a textile mill in 1880. The accompanying photo of a house—black and white and grainy from underexposure—had come as a slight shock when she'd looked closely at it and realized it was the very same one she now inhabited. But there had been few accompanying details and nothing about what came later after the cotton mill's opening.

The last few times she had slipped back, he and the other members of the household had seemed to be doing fine. Could it be something to do with Helena? Instinctively she distrusted the woman, who hadn't even had the kindness to humor Gus's mother that day with the photo album.

She picked up the last pecan, pried the nut out, and added it to the pile in the center of the table.

After tossing out the husks and refilling the bowl with the unshelled nuts, she took it into the kitchen and parked herself at the small round table there. Next to the little inner room, this was her favorite place in the house because of the warm sun coming in on this side as it climbed across the sky.

She picked up the first two nuts, made a fist around them, and squeezed hard until one of them cracked. After pulling off the shell, which had split all the way around, she picked out a piece of the nut meat and popped it into her mouth.

It was softer than what she was accustomed to, but still tasty. They'd be excellent sprinkled with a little sugar or salt and roasted over the fire.

She got up and dug out another bowl, then sat down again and grabbed the next two pecans. She squeezed them together, and one of them cracked.

Something flickered in her peripheral vision. She turned her head to glance over at the windows, but saw nothing amiss. *Probably another bird.*

She pondered who else might have sat at that very same table shelling nuts from the same exact tree. She picked the pieces out and dropped them into the empty bowl.

The light coming into the kitchen brightened, and then dimmed. She stood up and moved over to look out, expecting to see the sun moving in and out from a cloud.

But the sky remained as clear and blue as it had been earlier.

Behind her came the sharp *crack* of another shell breaking.

She whirled around and caught a glimpse of Myrna's stoutish figure seated at the table. Rooted in place, she stared as Myrna faded, becoming more indistinct.

Trembling, she walked over and took hold of the chair she'd been sitting in. She flinched at a tiny jolt of static discharged at her touch, and dragged it back some. Concentrating hard on the barely there form of Myrna, obliviously working, she slowly sat down across from her.

On the outside edges of her vision, the room had become a haze of white. But as she kept her eyes pinned to Myrna, other things—a kettle on an ancient cookstove, pots and pans on hooks, and shelves of crockery began to take shape around her.

Myrna was growing more detailed as well, sharpening and becoming more animate before her eyes.

"Myrna," she said, and Myrna's head jerked up.

"Myrna," she said again, louder, and suddenly Myrna was right before her, or rather she was right before Myrna.

With a shriek, Myra leapt to her feet, clapping a hand to her chest—*Holy crap, I've killed her*, Cheyenne thought—and cried, "Sweet Jesus," shoving her chair back so hard it tipped over and banged to the floor behind her. Eyes comically wide, she staggered backwards, sending the pecans she'd been working on clattering across the floor.

Cheyenne threw out a hand as the woman made little wheezing cries of distress. "It's okay!"

"It's okay," she said again, then added stupidly, "It's me." This version of Myrna before her was younger than the one in the cemetery, but was she too young? What year had she landed in?

"They told me not to work here," Myrna moaned.

Why had they warned her not to work there? Because of the rumors about the place?

Myrna risked a glance at Cheyenne, as if confirming she was still there, then quickly averted her gaze. "This place gonna put me in an early grave."

You die in 1905, she thought but didn't say. She didn't imagine the woman would appreciate that little tidbit.

How long did she have? The room around her seemed solid enough, but that could quickly change. Even now she thought she could detect something, a tingling on her arms, a faint buzzing in her ears. *Stay*, she told herself. Don't think about the present at all, only of the past. Of where you are now, with this woman, in Gus's time.

"Where's Augustus?" she asked, trying to hold on.

Myrna, looking directly at her now, clutched at her apron. "He's not here."

Before either of them could say another word, there came the sound of quick footsteps and around the corner appeared a youngish girl around thirteen or fourteen. "He's with *Helena*," she said, apparently having heard some of their exchange. "Oh, hello."

"Hello," Cheyenne answered back as the buzzing in her ears decreased. The girl's undeniable entrance into the room had captured her attention and seemed to help anchor her a bit more firmly in this period. "Who are you?" *It's the sister*, she thought even as she asked. The sun-kissed child and then later the older almost provocative girl in the photos.

She cocked her head at Cheyenne. "I'm Celia. Who are *you*?"

"I'm Cheyenne."

"Go on, now," Myrna told the girl, making shooing motions at her. "Me and this ... lady need to talk."

At the mention of "lady," Celia's eyes traveled the length of Cheyenne, taking in her clothes, and then Myrna was urging her out into the hall.

"I don't know how long I can stay."

Myrna turned back to her, twisting worriedly at her apron again. "But what ... where ...?" she started to ask then paused when Cheyenne shook her head at her.

"We don't have time for that. Listen, I think something's going to happen."

"What?" Myrna's eyes had grown wide again. As well they should, considering she was basically a harbinger of doom from the future.

"Something to Gus, I think. You told me yourself in the cemetery."

Myrna gaped at her. "I ... told you?"

"Yes, when you were a little older. You said he needed me. I can only assume you were talking about Augustus."

Myrna moved her head back and forth, mouth open, as if in denial.

"Is there anything you can tell me now? Anything you've been worried about? Anything wrong in the family?"

With a quicker, bewildered shake of her head, Myrna's gaze turned inward as she gave it some thought.

"Hurry," Cheyenne said. She could see through some of the objects in the room now.

"I don't like the woman he's with today."

"Helena?"

She gave a curt nod. "She's up to something, that one, and whatever it is, it ain't nothing good."

Cheyenne narrowed her eyes. "Myrna, have you met me before now?"

Slowly, looking a little dazed, she nodded.

"When you made those delicious apple tarts?"

Myrna nodded again, smiling faintly.

"Has Gus mentioned me since?" Dammit, she could now see the scuffed-up boards of her time superimposed over the gleaming floor beneath her.

Abruptly, like being caught in a rip tide, there was no time to hear Myrna's reply before Cheyenne was yanked away.

And then her forehead was banging on the table as she pitched forward in her time and nearly knocked herself out.

She lifted her head and rubbed at it as she tried to get her bearings.

Though she hadn't been able to stay long, she was still cheered by the fact that the fluctuations hadn't stopped yet. All she had to do was keep trying, keep visualizing herself there, and maybe one day she would cross over and be able to remain long enough to see him once more, and maybe help him.

SHE HALFWAY EXPECTED to dream of him, and slip into his timeline, that night—she'd had him on her mind so much—which lent an air of expectation to her evening ritual of making her nest in the inner room. But her anticipation at possibly seeing him again was also tinged by uneasiness. Gus needed her, but there were forces at work here she didn't understand, and as she flipped back and forth on the sofa, trying to get comfortable, her disquiet grew into a sense of foreboding at what hidden dangers she might be subjecting herself to.

Visions of all the catastrophes, illnesses, downfalls, betrayals, and other calamities that Gus, and by extension she, might be facing, played through her thoughts like a film reel until at last her breathing slowed and she drifted off to sleep.

She awoke sometime later, surprised to find her surroundings unchanged. She groggily got up and visited the bathroom by the bluish glow of the lantern, then returned to the inner room, lay down, and instantly fell back asleep.

She came awake briefly once more after that, drifted off again, and then she was waking up to the morning light. The inner room had no windows of its own, but through the archways on each side of her there was some coming in from the library across from her and from the righthand passageway's ceiling-high windows on the end.

Vertebras popping, she stretched as she came fully to, and dragged herself into a sitting position. She hadn't slept that well in a long time. She picked up the nearly empty bottle of water on the marble-topped table and drank down what was left.

"You're still here," she said aloud. *And if I dreamed, I don't remember it.*

She pushed herself off the sofa and shuffled over to rekindle the previous night's fire.

Using the poker from the curly wrought-iron set she'd found shoved behind a chipped statue of a bulldog, she turned the coals over to get at the hot embers, then dropped some twigs and small branches on top and blew on them until flames appeared.

A few more sticks and branches and she was ready to start the water for her coffee—her ultimate goal.

Without the cloak of darkness to lend a flattering ambience, all the dust and stains and ravages of time seemed to jump out at her as she made her way down the narrower passageway to fetch what she needed.

She paused before heading for the kitchen, gazing toward the front of the house at the luminous glow of the colored glass, and then turned right instead.

The foyer with its grand wooden staircase rising up and the parlor on the other side were as empty as always, dust motes swirling in the sunrays shining in. As was the driveway out front, she was thankful to note, peeking through the gap in the curtains.

Was Gus thinking of her, wherever he was? Or had she never returned and in time become a distant memory to him?

The image of his gravestone floated across her mind, and she rubbed her arms against a sudden chill. He had only lived until he was forty-seven. What could have happened to him?

As she moved away from the windows she'd been gazing through for too long, she thought she felt something.

Going still, she stared across the open space where the chaise lounge sat. Were the fluctuations coming quicker now?

Even as part of her welcomed it, if only for a chance to be with Gus again, the other part instinctively shied away from the increasingly strange uncertainty of it.

Turning, she steeled herself and strode forward, crossing the dull wooden floor, and passed beneath the unlit globes of the chandelier to move into the hallway beyond.

She was halfway down it, heading for the brighter rooms ahead of her, when her ears picked up a noise. Increasing her pace, she strained to identify it and then jerked to a stop at the unmistakable sound of someone or something running back and forth up ahead.

That's not shoes, she thought, the blood freezing in her veins. *That's bare feet or ...*

The rising and then falling, blood-curdling sound of someone or something racing back and forth, like a bird or an animal trapped inside trying to get out, continued, dying away for a second and then growing louder.

Cheyenne felt a scream building as whoever or whatever it was ran for the doorway leading in—

—and burst out into the hall and flew across, appearing and then disappearing into the dining room beyond. It happened so fast she was left with only the impression of something pale and dirty with wild, snarled hair. And then Cheyenne was running herself, trying to make it to the sunroom.

As she passed the dining room, she caught a blur of movement inside and skidded to a stop.

Breathing as quietly as she could, she backtracked, stretched her neck out, and peeked around the doorjamb.

It was a girl, and she was older than she'd first appeared judging by her size. Dressed in nothing but a nightgown that might have once been white, she was splattered with dried mud, her hair was a matted, tangled mess, and she was alarmingly thin.

Cheyenne hadn't been noticed yet and watched as the girl frantically moved over to another window, recoiled at what she saw, whirled around, and ran to the table in the middle of the room. She staggered around it, then catching sight of the hutch that remained, dashed over, bare feet slapping on the old boards. Cheyenne saw with horror that she was leaving little smears of blood.

Falling on the hutch, the girl yanked the cabinet doors open and began ripping drawers out until, with a little cry, she spun around.

And that's when she spotted Cheyenne.

The girl flinched in surprise and froze. Then her face changed, clearing and filling with intense relief. "*Cheyenne*," she croaked in a hoarse voice—from disuse or from *screaming?*—and rushed toward her.

As Cheyenne stepped forward to meet her, her brain finally recognized the dirt-smudged features before her. She stumbled in shock. "Celia!"

Eyes bright in a dirty face, Celia was nearly to her, arms thrown wide, when from out of nowhere a shockwave slammed into them, sending Cheyenne stumbling. It felt like all the hair on her body was standing straight up. And indeed Celia's longer strands were rising into the air above a mouth wide open in terror.

She heard her wail—and then the room around her abruptly winked out and Cheyenne was flipping from one period to the next:

In the dining room at another time, possibly before Gus's, with heavier, more elaborate furniture and a large palm plant she'd never seen before.

In a later, less cluttered but not yet abandoned version of the home.

In an even later time—Cheyenne gagged, almost passing out—when the house had begun to collapse around her.

"Celia!" she tried to shout, but she seemed to have lost her voice. *Think!* she shrieked to herself. *Think of where you want to be!* Squeezing her eyes closed, she desperately tried to picture the place as it was in her time, empty and abandoned, and then, remembering Celia, as it had been in Gus's time

Concentrating hard, Cheyenne brought up some of her recent memories of the home when she'd gone back. In Gus's bedroom, the kitchen, Celia's entrance into it when she met her.

Ripping her eyes open, she saw an environment had begun to form around them.

No, she cried soundlessly, not recognizing any of it. But Celia was still across from her, mouth stretched wide in a silent scream. Cheyenne tried to concentrate on Celia's years in the home again. But it was no use; she hadn't been there enough to properly visualize it.

Straining hard, she dug deep, forcing up images and memories of her life and the house as it had been for her. The first time she'd mounted the pitted steps out front and tentatively crossed the old tiles to peer in. The creak of the door coming open behind her. The feel of flopping down into the wing chair before the fireplace and dust flying up. Then she moved on to the world outside. Brent, her family, and Jill. Their time together at Cracker Barrel.

It wasn't working! The strange, unknown vegetation had sharpened around them, as had the terrifying forms standing silently back in the shadows. There was something *wrong* with them. Cheyenne struggled frantically to make them go away.

Your life! she screamed to herself. *Keep thinking of your life, your time.* Brent, and their wedding, and ... and Ian, their tiny little guy.

That did it. As the happy months she'd carried him filled her mind—*undeniable* and *precious*—the thick, steaming atmosphere began to dissipate, and the alien jungle around them to fade. She'd only had little Ian in her life for such a short while, but he had existed and he had meant everything to her.

Her hearing was returning now and she fought back tears, remembering the grief and sorrow later, as Celia's scream gained in strength, sounding like it was rushing at her from far away.

Abruptly everything snapped to and Celia broke off and swayed before her.

Trembling, Cheyenne moved her eyes over the space around them. The wood floor under her feet was scarred and darkened by age. The little bit of furniture dull and decaying. The walls stained, and the drapes motheaten. All of it the same as it had been in her time.

But was that exactly when it was? "Stay here," she said, and left Celia to unsteadily make her way around and into the inner room.

There she found her purse and bag with her laptop on top of it behind the sofa where she'd left them. Where was her phone?

She located it sitting on the curio cabinet. She picked it up and checked the date and time. The date was right, and according to the time, she'd returned to roughly when she had left, counting the added minutes she'd been away.

She slumped in relief.

Okay, now what? Straightening, she turned and went back to the dining room where Celia stood, eyes wide and staring, exactly where she'd left her.

She called out her name sharply, and Celia jerked then rolled her eyes toward her. The girl was in worse shape than she'd thought, in a state of shock at the very least.

That galvanized her into action. "I'll be right back," she said, and darted out again to get the blanket she should have already thought of. She took the time to dash down the basement stairs and snatch a bottle of water, some crackers, and a candy bar from her stash in the wine cellar first, and then clambered back up and grabbed the other blanket she'd been using.

Celia had moved over to the windows and was now staring out at the desolate, overgrown property beyond.

"Come away from there," she told her. "We don't want to be seen if somebody shows up."

Celia jerked her head around, eyes widening, and quickly moved away and crossed over to where Cheyenne waited.

"Let's go in here," Cheyenne said, and started out of the room.

Celia silently followed behind her as she walked down the hall and into the library. Other than Gus's domain upstairs, this was the room with the most furniture left in it.

Celia immediately went over to the rolltop desk and began searching through it.

"There's nothing there," Cheyenne said, continuing on to a table by a faded pinkish armchair. "There are a few things upstairs, but nothing much here, except for the books."

Dropping the snacks and water on the grimy table, she walked over to Celia, who had turned away from the desk. She unfolded the blanket and swept it around her shoulders.

Celia, giving a small shiver, tightened it around herself gratefully.

Cheyenne gestured at the chair. "Come sit down. We don't appear to be going anywhere for the moment." At Celia's fresh look of alarm, she quickly added, "No, don't even think about that. Just focus on right now with me."

Celia obediently accompanied her over, sat down, and settled back into the chair.

"Now," Cheyenne said, picking up the water bottle and holding it out to her. "Here."

Drawing back and lowering her brows, Celia made no move to take it.

"It's only water." She unscrewed the lid for her and held it out again. This time Celia accepted it, turned it up, and drank greedily.

"And I have some snacks to hold you until I can do better." She tore open the crackers, pried one out, and handed it to her. "It's peanut butter."

Celia took it and bit down on it, chewed a few times, and then crammed the rest in. "Good," she mumbled, and held out a hand for more.

Cheyenne gave her another one, took one for herself, and handed her the pack with the last three.

She looked around for something to sit on. The only other option was a creased leather sofa across the room. But there was an old step stool pushed up against the tall bookcases and floor-to-ceiling shelves still holding deteriorating hardcover books.

Shoving the cracker she'd taken into her mouth, she walked over and grabbed it, toted it back to Celia, and gingerly seated herself on it.

Celia had nearly finished her crackers. Cheyenne wondered how long it had been since she'd last eaten. She ripped the KitKat open, broke off a section, and held it out to her. "I assume you like chocolate?"

Nodding, Celia took it and bit off a piece. Obviously enjoying it, she quickly devoured the rest, and Cheyenne handed her the remainder.

She waited patiently, perched on the step stool, while Celia finished eating and took a final drink to wash everything down.

"Where are we?" Celia eventually asked, wiping her mouth with her hand. "This looks like my house but ..." Her voice trailed away as her eyes roamed the dusty library.

"It is your house," Cheyenne answered quietly. "Just not when you lived in it. From what I've been able to gather, it's about a hundred and thirty years later, give or take."

Celia's face lost all expression as her young mind tried to comprehend such a thing. "What happened to everyone?" she asked in a small voice.

"I don't know. I haven't been able to find out much."

"But why are you here? Who are you hiding from?"

Cheyenne shifted around on the stool. "It's not like that. Not exactly. It's just that no one's allowed in here. But I had nowhere else to stay. And we can't let them find out we're here or they'll make us leave, possibly even arrest us."

Celia's face went white. Cheyenne tried to recall what little she knew about nineteenth-century jails and immediately pictured squalid, cramped cells riddled with disease. "I mean, it wouldn't be like it is in your time," she hastily reassured her. "And we wouldn't be there for long." She gave her head a shake. *Focus.* "But it would be better if we avoided that."

Celia nodded and settled back again. She gazed off to the side, blinking slowly.

Leaning forward, Cheyenne snapped her fingers. "Hey, don't go to sleep yet. We need to get you cleaned up first."

Celia allowed herself to be pulled out of the chair and helped across the foyer and then up the stairs to the bathroom. Cheyenne had her sit on the closed toilet lid while she gathered a towel and washcloth, soap, and water.

"Let me check your feet," she said, coming back in a couple of minutes later. Celia obediently stretched her legs out for her to stoop down and inspect the soles. "It's just superficial cuts it looks like. Should be fine. The bleeding has stopped."

Straightening, she glanced out the dingy windows by the tub. Situated up high on the back of the house like they were, she could easily see where the old track ran through the weeds, vines, and brambles to the carriage house and barn beyond.

She turned back to Celia. "There's no running water of course. But you can get in and wash. Sometimes I heat some for a bath, but I have to build a fire first, which is risky in itself because someone might see or smell the smoke, and I have to warm like six potfuls, or more, and that takes a looong time. Not to mention how much water it uses up. And that right there is also a problem …" She realized she was babbling and forced herself to stop.

Celia stood up, wincing, and pulled the blanket off.

"Do you need help doing your hair?"

"I believe I can manage."

"Oh, hang on," she said, remembering shampoo. "I've got something you can wash it with."

She clomped back down the stairs, went around to the smaller room again, and dug out her shampoo and conditioner along with a brush and one of the pairs of pajamas she'd bought what felt like a lifetime ago, the best she could do for the moment.

She found Celia propped against the edge of the bathtub, looking wretched.

"Here's some clothes. Sorry, I don't have anything better. But these"—she held up the shampoo and conditioner—"will make things easier. And while you're washing up, I'll build a fire, and you can come get warm by it as soon as you're out."

Celia made no response, her eyes merely flicking over to the bottles Cheyenne placed by the tub.

Did they have conditioner back then? For that matter, did they have *shampoo*?

"You have used these before, haven't you?" When Celia hesitated before answering, she continued. "You wash your hair with the shampoo, rinse it out, and then work just a smidge of the conditioner in, and then rinse it out. It will help remove the tangles. And I think you're going to need it."

Cheyenne left her to it, pulling the door closed behind her.

One thing was clear. Celia slipping forward into her time would now change things, and she had no idea what that meant for Celia or for her, or if it mattered at all. The whole thing, trying to figure out all the possible outcomes and paradoxes, was enough to make her head swim.

Eighteen

Cheyenne headed out the sunroom door, with Celia, scrubbed clean and damp hair freshly brushed, right on her heels. "You are not leaving me alone," she'd exclaimed, and Cheyenne, not knowing what horrors she had gone through, hadn't argued.

They trudged through the dead grass, Cheyenne in her mocs and Celia in a pair of faux-fur slides Cheyenne had grabbed the last time she'd visited the storage unit.

"Wait," Celia said, stopping beside her and tilting her head back. "What is that?"

Cheyenne was so used to the sound she hadn't registered it. It was a plane—an airliner—carrying dozens, if not hundreds, of passengers, slowly crossing the sky, the distant rumble of its engines trailing behind it. "It's a jet."

"A what?" Celia asked, holding a hand up to shade her eyes.

"A jet plane. An airplane." When exactly had planes been invented? "Carrying people."

Celia dropped her hand and gazed at her. "An air ship?"

Cheyenne racked her brain. Did she mean like the *Hindenburg*? "Uhhh ... sort of. But *not* using hydrogen and with much faster engines."

"Oh,' she said, blinking. "A flying machine." She craned her neck to look up again.

"Come on," Cheyenne said. "We don't need to linger out here."

Silently Celia followed along behind her as she angled over in the direction of the old carriage house.

Best not to hit her with too much, she thought, contemplating the questions Celia would inevitably ask. This world in the twenty-first century with all its inventions and marvels was sure to be amazing to a Victorian, considering their own rapid advancements and love of knowledge and exploration. She smiled to herself as she pictured inappropriately dressed men in bowler hats and women holding parasols riding gangly camels bound for Giza.

But when Celia found out exactly what had been lost ... Cheyenne's smile faded. Everything and everyone Celia had ever known was gone. Her home as it had been. Her family, every one of her contemporaries—her very society. That way of life with all its optimism and its extravagance—and its romance—had come, and gone, never to return. The girl wouldn't be able to handle it. She had to get her back. *With or without me.*

The car was where she'd left it, shoved hoodfirst into the dormant weeds and vines.

Celia had stopped on the other side of a blackberry bush, now died back from the cold, that had grown up beside the decaying structure. Instead of the wide-eyed amazement she'd halfway expected, Celia was gazing with a blank expression at the vehicle in front of her.

It was too much, especially in the shape the girl was in. She needed to get her back in the house so she could rest, and then ... And then what? Sit there and wait for the next slip to drop them back into that hellish jungle where the unnatural, eerie creatures waited?

What else could they do? She had to try and get Celia back before any more of the timeline was disrupted. She could only imagine what kind of consequences might be brought about by Celia never returning.

She unlocked the door, pulled it open, and slid into the driver's seat. She had no intention of leaving; that would surely have a detrimental effect on Celia's psyche, although part of her wanted to do exactly that—just start the car and get the hell out of there. But she couldn't do that to Celia. To Gus. For now she merely wanted what she'd found in the storage unit and stuck down in the console. Rifling through the packs of Kleenex, old masks, and hard candies, she retrieved the black canister of pepper spray and climbed back out.

She hit the lock button, shut the door as quietly as she could, and pushed through the grass over to Celia, who was now gazing across the overgrown backyard at the rear of the house. How different it must look to her with its dark, desolate windows, slowly in the process of being taken over by the encroaching vegetation.

"Come on," she said, moving past her. "Let's get inside."

She listened for the sound of a vehicle as she pushed through the sea of brown grass. But blessedly she heard nothing but the sigh of the wind rushing through the trees. As far as she knew, the deputy hadn't been by again, at least not while she was there. Which meant any minute he was liable to come rolling up. Glancing back to make sure Celia was still with her, she climbed the steps and went inside.

Her mind was so intent on what she needed to do to keep them hidden—put the rest of her things away, maybe have them hole up in the basement, or better yet, stay in the inner room so they could hear better, with everything out in the car so they could run out the back at the first sign of anyone—that at first she didn't notice that Celia had not accompanied her to the front parlor.

She crossed over to look out and confirm the drive out front was empty, then retraced her steps.

"Do you feel it?" Celia asked as she entered the kitchen where she stood.

Now that she'd mentioned it, Cheyenne did feel something. But only faintly. Her arms had broken out in goosebumps, though that could be from the cold, and under her feet she thought she could sense a subtle vibration. Or maybe it was the very air around her, humming, shimmering ever so slightly. What was really happening here? Were the two time periods being propelled or drawn into each other, colliding and overlapping or merging like giant cosmic streams? Or was it completely different versions of their world, as the multiverse proponents believed?

"Cheyenne!"

Celia's cry brought her out of her musings and with horror she saw the alien jungle had drifted in, overlapping the space where they stood.

"I want to go *home!*" Celia shrieked, which only seemed to bring it on more.

With a rushing sort of *woosh*, Cheyenne felt the now familiar wave of something charged, like a current, flow into her, and static crackled in her hair.

It's getting stronger, she thought, and just had time to wonder if this was a good or a bad thing, when suddenly it was too late and the feeling was intensifying.

Abruptly they were there.

Cheyenne choked back a scream. They stood beneath a sick, yellowish sky. A hot wind smelling of something acrid, like sulfur, swept against them. Mercifully Celia had fallen silent beside her.

"Don't move," she whispered hoarsely, her voice barely audible. Holding back a cough, she slowly unclipped the pepper spray from her pocket and thumbed the safety over.

It wasn't much, but it was all they had. She would go down trying at least. And thinking of her little Ian. As he crossed her mind, she felt a tiny frisson of electricity in the air.

The creatures back in the shadows around them must have felt it too, and known what it heralded, because one of them surged forward. Cheyenne, panic coursing through her, pressed the button on the pepper spray and ejected a stream into the horrific thing's weirdly large eyes as Celia collided with her in terror.

Making a hissing scream, the thing fell back, and she whirled to the right as another one shot out. She barely caught it in time, and then she was holding her finger down, with Celia clutching onto her, spraying a steady arc as she whipped it back and forth. She let off the button, and one more made a halfhearted try, to further take their measure it seemed, which was all the more frightening, but she lunged forward, narrowly missing a direct shot to its narrow, reddish face, and it also retreated.

The mutated, feral creatures' humanity might have been a distant memory, but they had retained at least some of their intelligence. She wouldn't be able to hold them off for long.

Cheyenne's mind worked furiously as she and Celia stood there shaking and breathing shallowly. Celia wouldn't be any help getting them back to the twenty-first century. She'd barely been exposed to it at all.

They needed to think about something they'd both experienced, something they both remembered.

"Concentrate," she told her. "On going home."

Up until that point, the aftershocks of the latest fluctuation had been minimal, something she heard and felt like a distant buzzing on her skin and in her ears. But as she turned her mind to the moments she'd spent in the house during that earlier time, the sensation amped up, becoming almost painful.

"Think of home!" she cried as she sensed the creatures stirring. "When you walked in that day and I was there! When Myrna was shelling pecans!"

Celia joined in. "When you were asking about Gus!"

"And you said he was with *that Helena*!" Cheyenne turned her mind inward and tried to call up everything she remembered from that day as the ground seemed to buck beneath her. The way Myrna had looked. The dress Celia had been wearing.

Pressing closer to Celia, she sifted desperately through her memories and found the one that stood out the most: her night with Gus. She'd been destroyed by what Brent had told her, when she'd had to face the final dissolution of their family. But Gus had pulled her out of that. For a few hours she had been able to move away from it all and just enjoy the incredible gift of being there with him. For one peaceful night, she hadn't felt so alone and forlorn. That sense of contentment was something she hadn't believed she was capable of experiencing again.

And Gus and Celia's mother ... how adoring and proud she had seemed gazing down at the photo of Gus as a child.

Maybe this was what finally tipped the scales—Celia might have been thinking of her mother at that very moment as well—because right then the air around them brightened and Cheyenne had to close her eyes as everything went blindingly white at the edges.

A moment later the surface under her feet felt different, and she cracked her eyes open.

Celia was still beside her and the floorboards she stood on gleamed. She lifted her head as Celia shifted away.

"Are we really here?" Celia asked in a disbelieving yet hopeful voice.

From what she saw around her, if it wasn't the exact right time, it was close enough. *Oh, thank heavens.* They had made it.

Celia grabbed her arm in excitement. "We're home."

Home, she echoed in her mind. Celia turned her head and shouted, "I'm here!" and dashed across the room and through the doorway .

She took in a deep breath. She had gotten Celia back before it was too late. But as a result, she might have sentenced herself to a lifetime away from her own world. *Careful what you wish for*, she thought as it suddenly struck her, compounding her faint dismay at the reality of her situation, that she was no longer experiencing any of the telltale signs of a slippage. The low background buzzing and slight shakiness had totally ceased. And for all she knew, it wouldn't begin again until decades or centuries had passed.

Maybe that was a good thing. Maybe it was all over and no other hapless individuals would be swept through. And maybe her getting Celia back would somehow prevent whatever had been going to happen. Besides, she was probably worried for nothing. Most likely she would be dragged back to her world at any minute.

And if not? Well, then she would deal with it.

She went to leave the kitchen to follow Celia, then paused as she heard someone enter the sunroom from outside and start in her direction.

Gus walked in and jerked to a halt at the sight of her. He sucked in a surprised breath and then rushed forward. "Where is she?" he cried, taking hold of her upper arms. "I said, where is she?" His eyes were wild and he looked ready to shake her. A second later he did, his face creasing with emotion. "What have you done?"

This Gus was worlds away from the gentle soul she had spent the night with, and for an instant she was frightened.

Abruptly, seeing the fear on her face, Gus seemed to get ahold of himself and loosened his fingers around her arms. She would look later and find matching bruises encircling each one.

"Do you know where she is?" he asked in a softer tone, his expression now almost pleading. "We can't find her."

Cheyenne opened her mouth to set his mind at ease, then didn't have to as Celia and then Myrna came hurrying into the kitchen.

"I'm right here!" Celia cried, seeing Gus. "She brought me home!" She ran over and threw herself against them, enveloping them in an awkward three-person hug.

Gus released Cheyenne to return his sister's embrace with one arm and dropped the other one to his side.

Cheyenne, perplexed, stepped away when she was able. She could feel the chill coming off of him as he pointedly ignored her. Celia, oblivious, chattered away about how she'd been so hungry, and so scared. Her voice broke at this point, revealing the depth of what she had gone through, before she hurriedly continued on, possibly trying to gloss over the more horrible parts for his and Myrna's sake, and related how they had ...

Cheyenne met Gus's eyes over Celia's head. He *knew* the place was rumored to hold strange properties. How could he be blaming her?

She dropped her gaze as Myrna, sniffling, set about heating a kettle and preparing something to eat for Celia, who she declared was nothing but skin and bones.

Gus blamed her. He thought she'd brought it on them again, somehow. And maybe she had. Maybe her interest in the home, in their family, and her subsequent intrusion into their lives had somehow compounded the effect. She'd already seen what her thoughts and perspective could do when the anomaly did occur. So maybe it was partly her fault.

Abruptly she realized she was close to tears. Everything she'd gone through ... everything she'd already lost ... And now this.

Quietly, she turned and left the room.

She moved down the long center hallway, gazing sightlessly ahead, ignoring the shout from Gus behind her, the rich rugs and wallpaper and drapes and furniture lost on her.

Pausing for only a second at the base of the staircase, she glanced back at Gus hastening down the hall after her, then walked over and wrenched open the doors.

Bright daylight and a light breeze met her as she moved out onto the verandah. Though in brilliant technicolor now, the front lawn and grounds extending out appeared very much like they had in the large framed photograph she'd found in the attic. Everything was beautifully landscaped. And the driveway, where a horse-drawn carriage sat, was a clean white curve without dirt or weeds showing through.

She looked dazedly over at the carriage again and saw with dismay that it was occupied and the person now alighting from it was *Helena*. "Oh, for fuck's sake."

At a sound behind her, she looked over her shoulder as Gus joined her. From his slightly shocked expression, she knew he had heard. But as she stared stonily back at him, one side of his mouth quirked up in amusement before he shifted his gaze to Helena, now in the process of delicately making her way up the walkway to the steps.

Cheyenne didn't know much about her but imagined she came from an even grander home, an estate, or a plantation even. From the moue on her face as she made a show of trying not to ruin the pale peach ankle boots peeking out from her matching skirt, she more than likely saw coming here as akin to visiting a poor relation. What was the woman's involvement here? How was she connected to these people, and what did she want?

Cheyenne stared coldly down at Helena as the woman lifted her gaze and took in the strange and possibly scandalous leggings and long shirt she had on. Cheyenne lifted an eyebrow, refusing to be intimidated. She had faced down a barely human species evolved into monsters on some future Earth; this lady was nothing compared to that.

"Well!" Cheyenne heard her exclaim as she grasped the railing and started up.

"Perhaps you better come back inside," Gus murmured into her ear.

He took hold of her arm, gently this time, and she allowed him to lead her into the house. Helena, sounding as if she were struggling a bit—*I bet you are*, she thought, envisioning a tight corset underneath several layers—hurried to catch up to them.

"Someone needs to help see to my horses," Helena announced as she crossed the threshold, unnecessarily Cheyenne suspected, just so she could establish herself as the center of attention and place things on the proper footing.

"Of course, Helena," Gus responded a trifle wearily, and she saw Helena shoot him a glance.

"And who might you be?" Helena inquired, switching her attention to Cheyenne and away from Gus, who turned and disappeared, to go out the back, she assumed, and have some unknown hand—possibly the mustached man by the carriage house she'd seen in the photo—take care of Helena's team.

Helena, her chestnut hair twisted up into a loose chignon with fetching, wispy pieces curling at her temples, stared at her with honey brown eyes, one corner of her upper lip raised in a faint sneer.

Cheyenne smirked and gave a tiny derisive snort right back at her. She had known females like this before. *Mean girls.*

Helena's snarky grin dropped away and anger filled her perfect features. Even without the elaborate hair and the hat and the clothes, she would still be beautiful with her perfect skin, small, pert nose and button mouth. Was she wearing some kind of Victorian cosmetics?

Helena moved closer and began taking off her gloves. "I said, just who are you?"

From the hall came the sound of footsteps, and Helena smoothly moved away as Gus came back in. "Where is your mother, Augustus?" she asked, stepping in front of Cheyenne.

"I'm afraid she's not here." He walked across and made as if to open the front doors. "Perhaps we should postpone to another day when—"

Helena cut him off. "I'm not only here for your dear mama, darling, as you well know." Smiling prettily, she walked over and tucked her arm into his. "Let's go into the parlor." She glanced over at Cheyenne. "Perhaps she could see to some refreshments. I'm positively parched."

She attempted to guide him away, but Gus, flashing Cheyenne a look of alarm, planted his feet and pulled his arm out of her grasp. "In a minute. You go on in and I'll join you shortly."

Helena's pretty pink mouth twisted into a pout. She remained standing there until Gus swung back with a scowl, clearly irritated, and then she finally swept around and left them.

Again, this was a side of Gus she hadn't witnessed before. During their night together, he had been gentle and sweet. But there *had* been an intensity, a sense of reigned-in strength. And that steel and that heat, that nearly overwhelming desire he'd had for her, had fueled her own excitement.

This was a man of passion. But this was also a man not to be trifled with.

"I'm sorry if I appeared ungrateful," he said, not meeting her gaze. Though only a dozen steps separated them, the distance seemed much greater.

She listened for the sound of ringing in her ears and tried to gauge the air around her. If she walked over and touched the banister, would static spark at her fingertips?

The seconds ticked by. Cheyenne stared at the side table with the curved legs against the wall across from her. The same table she'd spied the first time she'd looked in and raised her eyes to the chandelier floating overhead.

"Cheyenne ... That is your name, correct?"

She snapped her head around so fast she nearly wrenched her neck. "*What?*"

"I ... I'm sorry ... Cheyenne." He took in a deep breath. "This is all just so ..." His voice trailed away.

"Tell me about it."

He tilted his head at her. "I would like for *you* to tell *me* about it. Are ... are you here to stay?"

"I don't know. It feels like it. I'm not picking up anything. But it's hard to say." She gave her head a shake and looked over at him. "What year is it?"

He stared back at her, looking discomfited. "It's eighteen ninety-five."

She nodded. She had figured it was somewhere around there.

"What, um ... When ...?" he said tentatively, like he was almost afraid to ask.

"What year am I from? I'm from twenty twenty-five. Two thousand twenty-five. About a hundred and thirty years from now."

He blinked at her slowly as he absorbed this.

She looked around for somewhere to sit. She was so tired she felt nearly sick. Was moving back and forth taking it out of her somehow?

"Forgive me," he said, stepping closer. "You must be exhausted. Let's find you somewhere to rest."

Not in your room? she thought. She knew this whole thing had been a shock—her showing up again and then Celia disappearing, and now both of them reappearing—but she didn't make it a habit of sleeping around and his aloof attitude was starting to irritate her. Now that it was broad daylight instead of the dark of night, he seemed to not know what to do with her. Did he regret their time together? Was he trying to *hide* that he'd been with her?

It must be Helena, she thought. There was some kind of relationship there, between her and Gus. *And now he doesn't know what to do about me.*

Gus headed up the stairs, then paused and came back down when she turned and started moving away instead. "Wait. Where are you going?"

She ignored him and continued on down the hallway. She could hear him following behind her as she walked to the kitchen at the other end.

Myrna was in the process of assembling a tray. "Miss Celia done gone up," she said as Cheyenne walked in. "I told her to get in that bed and I'm gonna bring this up to her."

"Thank you, Myrna," Gus replied, entering behind her. "And then maybe you could find something for ... ah ... Miss Cheyenne."

"Already working on it." Myrna pointed the knife she held in her hand at another tray to the side. "Just as soon as I get this one upstairs." She glanced over at Cheyenne. "You can go on up and I'll bring yours shortly."

Cheyenne nodded her head. "First, though"—she turned to Gus—"would you mind carrying the tray to Celia so I can speak with Myrna?"

His eyebrows rose nearly to his hairline. "You want me to take it up?"

"Yes," she said. "I do." She gazed back at him. Did he have a problem with that?

He looked away after a moment. "Of course." He moved over to Myrna and accepted the tray without further comment. Holding it stiffly in front of him, he carried it out of the room.

"I suppose that Helena gonna be needing something too," grumbled Myrna as soon as he'd moved out of earshot.

Cheyenne snickered. What would it be this time? Arsenic cookies? "Iced coffee, perhaps?" she suggested.

Myrna jerked around, her face comically surprised, then burst out laughing. "Oh, Miss Cheyenne, you wicked! How you know about that? Never mind, don't tell me."

Smiling, Cheyenne walked over and sat down in one of the chairs at the same round table. Now that things had settled down, for the moment anyhow, she could feel her exhaustion again and wanted nothing more than to go lie down somewhere and absorb everything. But she hadn't wanted to give him the satisfaction of meekly following him up the stairs so he could stash her somewhere and brush the whole thing under the rug. As if he regretted their night together.

But why? Was it just that she was something so exotic that he didn't know how to deal with her continued presence? Or *was* it to do with Helena? He hadn't seemed particularly enamored of the woman; if anything, he'd seemed downright ill-disposed toward her.

"So what's her hold over him?" she asked Myrna, who had gone back to assembling bread and cheese, slices of cake, and some kind of broth it looked like, on the tray before her.

"'Scuse me?" she said, glancing around at Cheyenne.

"Helena. What's his relationship with her?"

Myrna took the time to smooth out the napkin she'd just added before answering. "I suspect you'd have to ask him about that."

Cheyenne regarded her. "That serious?"

Myrna met her gaze, then glanced over at the still empty doorway and gave a shake of her head. "Not so much anymore these past few weeks."

"Really."

Myrna looked across at the open doorway again, and Cheyenne got the message and got up and moved closer to casually lean against the long table beside her.

Myrna grabbed a pitcher and began filling a glass with what appeared to be apple cider, judging from the color and sediment in the bottom. "I think he gave her money," she said in a low voice while keeping her eyes forward.

What would he have given her money for? A flurry of possibilities, both good and bad, rushed through her head. An illegitimate child? A charitable contribution? A business venture? Because she was blackmailing him for something?

"And I suspect she wanted more than that," Myrna added under her breath.

Ohhh. She closed her mouth, which had fallen open. "I see." So ... there was some kind of financial tie between them, but nothing romantic, at least nothing serious. But not for Helena's lack of trying, if she was reading the situation correctly. "And my being here ...?"

Myrna cut her eyes at Cheyenne. "You are a serious complication."

She had heard enough for now and moved back over to her chair.

Gus reentered the room a minute later.

"Celia's all settled," he told Myrna, then looked across at Cheyenne. There was wariness and curiosity in his gaze but also something more, too, something that gave her heart.

And now that she had discovered a little more about his situation, she could understand his attitude better and she found herself sympathizing with him.

She stood up. "I do believe I would like to rest for a bit."

"Oh. Of course." He remained where he was as if unsure how to proceed. He was obviously pleased she was ready to retreat upstairs out of sight but also worried about where to install her.

"If you would kindly show me to whichever room I'm to be ensconced in?" Why was she talking like this?

Gus spun around to lead the way out, then spun back around so fast to address Myrna that she nearly bumped into him. "Ah ... would you like for me to carry ... um ... Miss Cheyenne's tray?"

"Thank you, but I can ..."

"Get it," Cheyenne hissed in his ear and kicked the side of his shoe.

He lurched forward, and she held back a laugh as he made his way over and took the tray.

Biting her lip, Cheyenne turned and left the room, leaving him to trail behind her.

At the top of the stairs, she paused on the landing with the same oddly curved settee, then followed behind him as he turned left and moved down the hall (away from his room, she noted).

At the last door on the right, he stood back and silently waited for her to open it.

She complied and moved inside.

It looked nothing like it did in her time. A brass double bed and other furnishings were arranged around a gorgeous cranberry rug vibrant with newness, accentuated by blush-colored, ruffled bedclothes and pink, rose-appliqué curtains.

She paused to admire a glass hurricane lamp painted with roses on the bedside table, then stepped over to the window and pushed the muslin panels apart to let in more of the light.

"Cheyenne, listen," he began behind her.

She turned and held up her hand. "No, it's okay. I understand."

"No, I don't think you do. Helena … she …" He gave his head a shake, as if unable to put it into words or even know where to begin.

"You can explain it all to me later." She walked across to the bed, which had begun to seem more and more inviting the longer she stood there. Emotionally and physically, she felt spent, as if the whole thing had weakened her somehow. Tiredly she sat down on the side of it.

"Here, let me help you." He set the tray down and moved over to pull the spread back for her to climb in.

She pushed her mocs off, crawled across, and slid under the sheet. The bed was as soft as it looked, and she sighed with pleasure as she relaxed into it.

"What did you tell Helena?" she asked as he brought the tray over and placed it within reach on the bedside table.

"Ahhh … I told her …"

Cheyenne rolled her eyes. The man could not complete a sentence. "Out with it. What's the story?"

He retreated a few steps and raked a hand through his hair. "All right. You're an acquaintance. The sister of a former classmate … in town visiting friends."

"Your very close acquaintance?" she teased, grinning at him.

He frowned, his expression darkening.

"I know, it's okay," she said. "I'm not going to give it away. Now come here."

"What?"

"Come *here*."

Tentatively he shuffled closer, checking behind him to make sure no one lurked in the hallway.

When he was close enough, she took his hand and pulled him down over her. Before he knew what was happening, she had grabbed the back of his head and pressed her mouth to his.

His lips remained hard for a second then softened as he responded and allowed her to deepen the kiss.

After a moment, he pulled away from her, breathing raggedly. "We can't … not with …"

Cheyenne gave up on him finishing his thought and reached for the glass on the tray. "Isn't she waiting for you?"

He gave a start. "Yes, she is," he said. "Unfortunately," he added in an undertone.

Cheyenne took a sip of the cider and found it perfect, light and sweet and not too tart.

Gus paused in the doorway. "I'll check on you later."

"Okay. If I'm still here."

He looked ready to rush back in, and she quickly waved him away. "Go, I'm not going anywhere." *At least I don't think so,* she thought.

She expected him to hurry away so he could get back to Helena and whatever business he had with her, but he remained standing just outside.

"Should I get Celia out of the house?" he finally asked.

She hadn't even thought about that. She and Celia had been so glad to be back and since then things had felt so concrete, so steady. But that could quickly change, she knew, with hardly any warning. She recalled the terrifying humanoid creatures she'd fought off in that poisonous world and couldn't suppress a shiver.

"That settles it," he said. "She's going away until all of this stops."

Before she could make any kind of response, he was gone.

Nineteen

Cheyenne heard a click and opened her eyes to the gray light of dawn seeping in through the curtains. She turned her head as Celia's slight figure slipped into the room. "Are you asleep?" she whispered.

"No, I'm awake." *Barely.* Except for the first few hours, she had hardly slept at all. Once she had sampled a bit of everything on the tray, she had eventually fallen into a hard sleep only to awaken just before dark. After visiting the strange toilet with the high tank in the bathroom down the hall, she had eventually managed to get back to sleep. But sometime later she had woken up again and spent the rest of the night dozing off and then jerking awake in an agony of anticipation that she might suddenly find herself back in her time.

Celia moved over to sit on the end of the bed. "I wanted to tell you goodbye."

Cheyenne pushed herself up. "Where are you going?"

"To my Uncle Harvey's. That way I can see Mother before she returns."

Celia, with her hair now braided neatly down her back, tucked her hands underneath the long skirt she wore and swung her legs nervously. "Gus says the longer it goes without happening, the greater chance there is that it's over."

Cheyenne nodded. For the immediate future at least. "What about your mother?"

"Oh, she doesn't want to believe there's anything strange about this house. It's kind of a sore point Daddy says ... or said, that is. He's gone now."

So that was why she never saw Gus's father around. Was he the man with the wide sideburns in the older photograph? "I'm sorry. What happened?"

Celia hitched in a breath. "Doctor Carter said it was his heart." As if she didn't want to talk about it, she hurriedly continued. "So I'm to say that I was eager to start my visit and insisted on having Gus drop me off to begin it early."

"Sounds plausible."

Celia said nothing more for a few seconds, then, "Are you going to be staying here? Because I've never had a sister. I mean, I know you're not really my sister. You're a little old ..."

"Hey!"

"But so is Gus—Mama says I was a change of life baby— and if you were to marry him, then you would be my sister-in-law which is nearly the same thing."

Despite herself, Cheyenne felt her cheeks grow warm. Her and Gus. Married. Here, with Celia as her sister-in-law.

Ian. Her little guy who'd never had a chance drifted into her thoughts, as he always did. Her stomach tightened and she had to work hard to control her expression. *You can't change that,* she told herself as tears stung her eyes. *You can't. You couldn't help him when he needed you—but maybe you can help this girl and her family. Help Gus.*

"I don't know about all of that," she finally responded.

"You don't like him? Most women *love* him." She said this last part as if disgusted by it.

"No, I *do*." Cheyenne swallowed and tried to blink away the tears. "I just don't know how long I'll be able to stay." But what was waiting for her there?

"Well," Celia said, kicking her legs. "I hope you're still here when I get back." She hopped off the bed, stepped over to install a quick kiss on her check, and scampered across the room. "Bye," she said with a wave, and disappeared around the door.

"Bye," Cheyenne echoed to the sound of her footsteps moving away.

She waited as long as she could before sliding out of bed and padding over to look out.

The hallway stretching out before her in each direction stood empty, appearing both different and the same with its familiar burgundy rug, now vivid with newness, bright wallpaper and shiny sconces burning softly.

All was silent. Which was a good thing because she couldn't wait a minute longer. Moving on out, she shot a glance behind her and took off for the open door on this side of the landing.

She watched for someone ascending the staircase, but luckily no one appeared. She darted into the bathroom, swung the door shut, and slid the latch over.

AT LEAST SHE hadn't landed in a time when all they had were chamber pots. She moved over to the same pedestal sink, washed her hands with an oval chunk of nearly translucent soap stamped with PEARS from a blue-and-white dish, then splashed water on her face, and dried off with a hand-embroidered towel.

But she wished she had a toothbrush. Rinsing would have to do. Using her cupped hand, she swished several mouthfuls around, used the towel again, and peered into the mirror.

The little bit of mascara she'd had on had smeared and her hair, pushed up on one side where she'd slept, was a snarled mess. She wiped under her eyes and used her fingers to comb and smooth her hair the best she could, then gave it up as hopeless. Nothing but a washing was going to fix it.

She gazed longingly at the curved powder-pink tub. But what would she put on afterwards? She looked down at what she was wearing.

If she was going to inhabit this world—and from the feel of the air around her, or rather the absence of anything in the air around her, it appeared she would be, for the next foreseeable future at least—then she needed to acquire some better clothes, right away.

"*No*," CHEYENNE CRIED at the size of the sleeves puffing out from the dress Myrna held out. "I am not wearing that."

"I know it's not exactly the latest fashion, but—"

"No, it's just ... No."

"All right." Myrna returned the gown to the armoire, one of several in the room where Gus and Celia's mother—whose name was Lydia, she'd found out—stored some of her older garments and accessories. It was in the space adjacent to the "master" bedroom across the hall from what must have once been Gus's father's before he passed.

"Something a little plainer, please."

"Miz Lydia don't do plain."

"Well then something less poufy ... less ruffly."

Making a *humph* sound, Myrna dove into the clothes again, picked one, put it back after a second's consideration, and started to pull out a bright pink one. "No!" Cheyenne cried, and Myrna shoved it back in. She switched to the other side, sliding hangers back and forth, and finally selected a long dark purple skirt and from right behind it a fitted pale lavender blouse with a high neckline and only minimal poufiness at the elbows. She turned them around for Cheyenne to see and gazed at her expectantly.

"Okay, those might do." It was the best she'd seen so far, other than fancy creations like the red gown that were impractical and inappropriate for daytime.

Myrna produced another skirt, navy blue this time, and a simple but nice lighter blue shirt, and at Cheyenne's nod, also laid them to the side and then moved over to a trunk. "These day dresses old but maybe ..." She dug down into it, rummaged around, and pulled out a cinnamon brown dress. Unfolding it, she let the ends fall to the floor. "This plain enough for you?"

Except for some gold braided trim on the fitted bodice, the ankle-length, high-necked dress was completely unadorned. It was fairly simple, rather drab, actually. But not hideous. "Okay, it might work."

The next one Myrna got out had way too many bunches and gathers, and Cheyenne rejected it, but the following one Myrna reluctantly held out looked more promising. It was a little faded but still pretty nonetheless.

It had once been pale blue but now looked almost white and had red pinstripes and buttons and only a bit of lace at the cuffs and around the neckline.

"I like that one." She took it from her and laid it with the others across the chaise in there.

With that settled it was then only a matter of choosing the necessary underwear.

Myrna began looking on shelves and tugging open drawers and spreading out the undergarments for her to choose from.

There didn't seem to be anything even remotely resembling a bra—or panties, for that matter. Cheyenne stared in dismay at the myriad collection of "drawers," which looked more like pants than underwear, hung to the knees, and had no crotch to speak of. She could guess why, but still it was a shock.

And the closest thing to a brassiere was the corsets Myrna produced. There was also what Myrna referred to as a "combination" consisting of basically a camisole bodice attached to form-fitting drawers that sort of looked like a knee-length jumpsuit. It also had a split crotch, but this time there were buttons to hold it closed. And it looked fairly comfortable; it was thin, made of cotton, and had only a bit of lace for embellishment. Cheyenne set it to the side and picked up a shorter, strapless, royal-blue corset.

"That one laces up the front," Myrna said. "You can do it yourself as loose or as tight as you like." She shuffled around to pull open another drawer. "Ain't nothing wrong with giving a little support where it's needed." She glanced pointedly in the direction of Cheyenne's chest.

It *was* pretty. She held it up to herself. Laced up it would barely cover her nipples, but something was better than nothing. She set it to the side too.

"Here's another one," Myrna said, laying out a slightly longer-waisted pink satin corset with lace straps.

Cheyenne decided to take it as well, along with another short white one and two lightweight, almost sheer chemises—a small one that resembled a tube top with tiny ribbons, and a longer, sleeveless one with buttons down the front.

"You probably gonna be needing these, too," said Myrna, inspecting another pair of short white bottoms. "They got buttons too." She added them to the pile.

"Now," Myrna said, surveying everything. "We just need stockings and shoes."

Cheyenne's eyebrows rose. But she made no protest as Myrna moved over to a larger armoire, because what she had barely noticed when she'd first risen had slowly become more apparent as she stood in the barely heated room. It was *cold*. Something for her feet and legs sounded pretty good right about then.

"What about these?" Myrna asked, holding out a pair of gray stockings.

"That's fine. Whatever."

Myrna searched around some more and found a pair of dark gray shoes with small heels and bands across the top that fastened on the side. "These some good walking shoes, here." She set them down on the floor and reached in for a handsome pair of tan midcalf-length boots. "She don't wear these no more, either." She placed them on the floor beside the walking shoes, rummaged some more, and added a pair of black lace-up boots.

"And these a little dusty but I always liked them." She produced a pair of blue silk slippers that were mostly flat with only a tiny nub of a heel, brushed them off, and added them to the others. She peered over at Cheyenne's feet. "They should fit. May be a trifle big, is all."

"I think we have enough," Cheyenne said. What was Gus's mother going to think about her appropriating her things?

Myrna must have read the worry on her face. "Oh, don't you fret. Miz Lydia don't usually wear any of these anymore."

Cheyenne gathered up everything she'd selected while Myrna collected the footwear and stockings (including several more pairs in different colors). She grudgingly agreed to a pair of lacy garters out of necessity—it was that or wear a contraption that fit around the waist and had long straps with clips at the bottom— but she flat out refused to even consider any petticoats. You had to draw the line somewhere.

Now that a bath and fresh clothes were imminent, Cheyenne was eager to finish up and urged Myrna out of the room before the woman could try and outfit her for the next ball or fox hunt.

MYRNA FOLLOWED HER into the bathroom. She bustled around laying out towels and fresh soap and scent, started the tub to filling, and then left her to it.

A couple of minutes later Cheyenne was just relaxing into the floral-scented water when there was a tap at the door she'd failed to lock and Myrna walked back in.

She grabbed the cloth she'd been given and tried to cover herself, but Myrna merely stepped around to place a bundle on the hamper and went right back out again.

She relaxed back into the water. *This would be an unfortunate time for me to be sent back*, flitted across her mind before she could stop it, along with a vision of her landing naked in the pale pink tub in her time. She pushed the thought away and sank down into the water, trying to focus on how good it felt. Letting her head drop back, she submerged it to wet her hair, then jerked as a faint ripple traveled around her like a current. She sat up, water streaming off of her.

Blinking and wiping at her eyes, she looked around, examining each item: the inset shelves and drawers, the sink and mirror, the tall woven hamper.

She tried to calm her quaking nerves. If she ended up in the wrong timeline ... Those eerily human yet terrifyingly alien creatures under the acid yellow sky tried to insert themselves into her thoughts, and she quickly shoved the images away and snatched up a wide glass bottle with a cork stopper on the ledge by the tub.

Shampoo Cream the label read. So, they *did* have shampoo. She opened it, poured a large dollop into the palm of her hand, and went to work on her hair.

Despite her best efforts, her thoughts inevitably kept turning to certain aspects of her situation as she rinsed her hair and finished washing up. But there was no accompanying jolt this time and when she stepped out and began drying off, she detected no static. It appeared that despite everything on her mind, she was staying put for now.

This was good to know, confirming what she had already been suspecting: that she had no effect unless the conditions were right. Again she imagined flowing timelines in a giant cosmic river (or two cosmic bubbles if there *were* multiple universes) with her moving from one to the other, as if propelled by her very thoughts.

Shaking her head, she stepped over to the bundle Myrna had brought in.

It was a light-gray, blue-trimmed robe of sorts that wrapped around and tied with a cord. Atop it sat a strange wood-handled toothbrush with brownish bristles. She carefully set it to the side so it wouldn't get dirty (if it was even clean to start with) and slipped her arms into the robe and tied it around her waist.

Her clothes and possibly a comb or a hairbrush would be waiting in her room, but what about deodorant?

She checked the shelves and found a small lidded pot of "TOOTH PASTE FOR REMOVING TARTER AND WHITENING THE

TEETH," but nothing like antiperspirant or deodorant among the various pots and bottles and tins. What did people do?

What they did she found out during those first days in that sometimes fairytale, sometimes grim world, was wear dress shields and change clothes frequently, partly so they could sponge off their pits, which was sometimes still done at a washstand— there was a marble-topped one with a pitcher and basin in Cheyenne's room.

After thoroughly rinsing the rustic toothbrush with hot water, she scrubbed her teeth with the minty paste, left the bathroom, and padded down the hall to the pink room, as she was beginning to call it.

An hour later, she was fully dressed and no longer as cold with her hair haphazardly arranged into a sort of twist.

"Normally someone else does these kinds of things," Myrna told her around the pins in her mouth she was using to catch a few stray pieces in the front. "My sister's youngest daughter Clara supposed to be coming today, but she's late." She stuck a last pin in and then stood back. "I guess you'll do."

Clara, Cheyenne thought. Could it be? She moved over to look in the mirror above the washstand. She had to admit, the dark purple skirt and lavender shirt, both feminine and practical, looked well together with her new updo and, oddly, suited her. And the walking shoes she'd fastened on over the gray stockings accompanied them perfectly. She was still trying to get used to what was underneath, but at least she was fairly warm now even with only the shorter chemise, corset, and drawers.

There was nothing to be done about her face, though. With no makeup and not much sleep, she looked every bit a women approaching her fourth decade.

She wiped ineffectively under her eyes and rubbed at her cheeks, attempting to garner some color, then gave it up. There was no disguising the pallidness of her skin or the dark circles.

Downstairs, she expected to find the house virtually empty and silent with Gus and Celia gone and Lydia not there yet, but it was anything but.

As she lingered in the background, drifting from the dining room to the kitchen while Myrna conversed with someone in the library, a plump, fair-skinned, older woman in a long dress topped by an equally long apron—the cook, she presumed—answered a call on a boxy wooden wall phone that wasn't there in her time and then opened the side door off the kitchen to two different taps for tradesmen as she cleaned up the remains of breakfast, which Cheyenne must have missed.

A few minutes later, through the sunroom windows where she had retreated with a book from the library, she saw there was activity outside, as well. The man with the bushy mustache was heading for the carriage house as a redheaded boy, probably no more than fourteen or fifteen, led a horse toward the barn.

She leaned into the window to look the other direction.

Up closer to the house, a dark-skinned man with wiry black hair poking out from under a cap was adroitly splitting wood, pulling his hand away at the last second while bringing a sledgehammer down to drive in the wedge he was using.

Farther back, past the spot where over a hundred years from now she would hide her car behind a great magnolia tree, out stretched the back field, not fallow and partially grown over but containing the remnants of last year's fruit and vegetable plants in neat rows from one end to the other.

Above it, the sky was a clear blue without a cloud in sight. Excerpt for the coats on the men and the absence of leaves on the trees amid the evergreens in the surrounding forest, you would think it was a warm summer day and not the cool one it was.

She went over and sat down in a chair by the same oval portrait of the attractive older woman. Looking at it now, she thought she could see a faint resemblance to Gus with his darker hair and complexion. Celia's hair was light like Lydia's (if she was indeed the woman Cheyenne had seen perusing the photo album), so maybe this was Celia and Gus's father's mother?

Settling back onto the cushions, she opened the novel she'd picked—*The Picture of Dorian Gray*—and turned to the first page.

But it was no use. After rereading the same paragraph over and over, she closed it back and stood up.

If she wasn't going to be fed, then maybe she could at least get some coffee. Her stomach growled its agreement as she walked out and headed for the kitchen.

She could hear the murmur of voices within as she neared. The plump middle-aged woman and two others, it sounded like.

As she stepped through the doorway, all of the three inside fell silent where they stood around the rectangular table in the center.

"Hello," she said as they stared at her. "Would it be possible for me to get some coffee?" Where had Myrna gotten to?

"No ... sorry," Cook said after a pause. "There isn't any more coffee." Her voice had a slight British burr to it.

She waited for her to add something more, then finally said, "Okay then. Mayb—"

"Breakfast is always at eight," Cook said, talking over her. "Sharp."

Cheyenne gazed back at her steadily, and then slid her eyes over to the larger of the two younger women. There'd be no help there, she saw, taking in the taller, darker ones closed, almost hostile stare.

She switched her attention to the smaller woman beside her—and went still.

Was it really her? The gorgeous tawny complexion was the same. The delicate facial features, the full mouth, the midnight black hair that would hang long when unwound—they were all the same. But still, she wasn't sure until the woman first lowered then lifted her eyebrows at Cheyenne's scrutiny, giving her features the same slightly haughty cast she'd seen in the portrait.

It was her all right, the same intriguing beauty in the hanging chair. Unconsciously one side of Cheyenne's mouth lifted into a smile and for a second, uncertainty flickered across the young woman's features.

"You must be Clara."

The woman opened her mouth to say something and then abruptly closed it. "Yes, ma'am," she replied, shifting her gaze to the floor.

"It's nice to meet you, Clara," Cheyenne responded quietly.

She pondered what it must be like for her in this society—to be not entirely viewed as property anymore but still dependent to a degree on the master or mistress of the house for a place to sleep and food to eat. After a moment she turned back to the other two. "I'm Cheyenne, and I'm going to be staying here for a little bit."

It was the only way she could think to put it. She had no idea if she was there for a while or for only the next five minutes. Before, when she had first noticed that her nocturnal ramblings weren't merely dreams, the "episodes," for want of a better word, had been proceeded by signs and indications. But then later they had come on quicker and stronger with virtually no warning. There was simply no way to know.

"And you are?" she asked the older woman.

She looked back at Cheyenne with faded blue eyes, her cap a bit askew on her graying curls. "My name is Agnes, ma—" She stopped short, biting off the last part.

The woman was clearly unsure how to address her. They didn't know who the heck she was or what she was doing there.

"You must be the cook." *Oh, how daft.* Agnes seemed to agree and didn't bother to respond.

Cheyenne switched her attention back to the tallest woman, who immediately barked, "Ruth," before she could utter a word. *Okaaay.* She decided to leave it at that, still not liking the look on her face, which was definitely hostile.

"I'll just grab some water," she told Agnes, and walked around her to search for a glass.

She heard the rustle of fabric behind her and halfway expected one of them to offer to get it for her, or to suggest something else, maybe some of that fresh cider, but save for the sounds of them chopping and kneading there was only silence.

She started looking on the shelves and tabletops, and from behind her came the sound of a knife slamming down.

"For goodness' sake!" Agnes said behind her, and Cheyenne spun around as the woman flung out an arm and pointed at a glass-fronted hutch on the other side of the room. "Over there."

Pardon the hell out of me, Cheyenne wanted to say, but she held it back. What right did she have to be outraged by their behavior? She was the outsider here and she couldn't possibly know how it was for them or what kind of behavior was expected of her. *A stranger in a strange land*, she thought.

Silently she walked over and took a crystal drinking glass out of the hutch and carried it over to the sink. Would the water make her sick? So far the cider hadn't caused any issues.

With an exaggerated sigh, Agnes turned and walked over, snatched the glass out of her hand, and took it over to a large wooden cabinet against the far wall.

Cheeks reddening, Cheyenne watched while Agnes opened the right side of what she now knew was an icebox and filled the glass from a pitcher of water inside.

If this keeps up, she thought, *they're going to think I'm the worst sort of aristocrat. Or a complete imbecile.*

She figured laughter and whispers would follow in her wake, but either the women weren't that petty or else they were waiting for her to move out of earshot.

Back in her room, she set down the book she'd retrieved on her way up and stared at the glass of water dubiously. It might quite possibly make her sick. But she had to have something. Her stomach growled again, making the decision for her, and she raised the glass and drank most of its contents.

Twenty

In the front parlor across the foyer from her, the grandfather clock ticked. The house was so quiet she could hear the pendulum as it swung back and forth, marking the passing of another minute in another hour of a very long day.

Myrna, whom she already knew had her own room at the end of the upstairs hallway across from the righthand turret, was still mysteriously absent. And Agnes had gone home for the day. She'd heard the smallish buggy as it came around the drive with a clop of hooves and had looked out and watched as Agnes came into view below her, climbed up beside the driver, and it resumed with a slap of the driver's reins. Clara and Ruth were still in attendance as far as she knew but had disappeared, presumably to their own personal spaces. Ruth seemed to come and go from the basement quite a bit and she'd seen Clara climbing the narrow stairs to the attic, leaving her to conclude that this must be where they slept.

She had learned a few other things besides which of the servants called this place home. Before she had made the mistake of lying down for a bit (which had turned into a lot longer) instead of parking herself at the dining room table and insistently ringing for someone—if she could figure out how to ring for someone—which might have resulted in her actually being fed, she had gone outside via the sunroom door and taken a walk around the place.

After glancing inside the small brick lavatory, she'd ambled across the trim yard, speculating again on who used it, then continued on down past the white, two-story carriage house, appearing in much better shape than it did in her time, and behind it, the barn.

Where the magnolia tree would someday stand in splendor, she'd veered over and paused at the edge of the forest and thought about what she might find in the family cemetery on the other side of all those trees. Neither Myrna nor Gus's headstone would be there yet. Would he want to know when he was going to die? Even if he did, she wasn't going to tell him. It was possible that her being there could change things somehow and prevent his early demise.

She had just started back across to look out over the field that was currently a huge garden, or what remained of one from the last harvest, when she'd heard a distant bang and glanced up to see the mustached man walking away from the outside bathroom.

Then as she was nearing the rear of the house a few minutes later, Ruth had come around the side and, glowering at her, crossed over to the building, stepped inside, and slammed the door shut.

Evidently the outside bathroom was for all the employees, inside or out, regardless.

Standing in front of the library windows now, she was debating about whether or not to raid the kitchen for something now that the formidable Agnes had left—she'd long since lost her appetite, but she could feel her empty stomach gnawing at her— when her thoughts were interrupted by the faint crunch of gravel and clip-clop of hooves that quickly grew louder as a horse and buggy appeared out of the forest on the far end of the drive. It was moving toward the house at a steady clip, throwing up gravel and dust as it came.

She went to turn away, then paused as another carriage, smaller and completely open but moving even faster, came around the bend.

She left the library, hurried across the foyer, and heaved the double doors open.

Gus was stepping down from the first buggy as she walked out onto the verandah. He turned to face the other one as the driver shouted "Ho!" and brought his horse, snorting and tossing its head, to a halt.

The man, young and clean-shaven wearing a black bowler, jumped down, flinging the reins carelessly aside. "You can't run from this," he yelled.

"Go home, Daniel!" Gus bellowed back at him and turned on his heel to stride for the house.

Undeterred, the man—*Daniel*—shouted, "We're going to talk about this!" and marched after him.

Cheyenne, standing at the top of the steps, moved out of the way as Gus reached her and right behind him came Daniel.

Barely glancing at her, Gus entered the house through the doors she'd left open, with Daniel right on his heels.

She gave it a few seconds, listening to their footsteps moving away, and then followed them inside.

There was no sign of them in the foyer, but she could hear the rise and fall of their voices behind the closed library door—Daniel's, harsh and insistent, and Gus's, weary, impatient, and bordering on anger.

She walked over and hovered beside it, listening unabashedly.

"...should have known better!" she heard Daniel say. And then right after from Gus: "All of you were given the same information I was! No one forced you!"

Daniel said nothing she could make out for a few seconds, and then there came the sound of something banging down, one of the liquor decanters she thought, and she caught, "We went on your recommendation, Augustus."

"For crying out loud, Danny, we don't even know if it's true."

Daniel's voice rose to a shout. "I have told you time and time again not to call me that!"

Even through the heavy wood, she picked up Gus's sigh. "All right ... all right. I'm sorry."

With that the fight seemed to go out of them.

"Have a drink," Gus said. "Not that you need it."

"I'm telling you. I smell a rat." His voice had changed, becoming plaintive, and he sounded close to tears. "If it's true, what am I going to do?"

Cheyenne moved away from the door, having no wish to eavesdrop on something so intimate.

Gus's troubles had begun, it seemed. And from the sound of it, money was at the root of it.

She had just taken a chair in the parlor, when, incredibly, she picked up the sound of someone else coming up the drive.

Boy, this place is hopping, she thought, standing up.

She walked over to look out. This carriage, driven by an older gentleman in a tallish hat wearing a dark bluish-green coat that matched the interior she could see, was larger and completely closed off except for the windows on the side. Was the mustached man she'd seen the groom and this one the coachman who did the driving?

Leaning forward, she saw a somewhat disheveled lady she instantly recognized as the one with the photo album climbing out.

The driver, whose first name was Milton but who was always referred to as Mr. Gilbert by one and all she would soon find out, took some bags up into the house after helping the lady down, and then came back and climbed up, got the two horses going again, and steered them around the side of the house.

"Myrna?" the lady called out as she moved inside, and Cheyenne hurried around to greet her.

"Myrna!" she called out again and then turned, smiling weakly, when she spotted Cheyenne. "Hello, you must be Cheyenne."

The woman appeared exhausted, as if she could barely stand up. "Yes. And you must be—"

"Gus's mother, yes. You may call me Lydia." She attempted another smile. She either hadn't noticed Cheyenne was wearing her clothes, or was too polite to show it. "Augustus told me we had a houseguest. You met at William and Mary?"

Cheyenne blinked, momentarily stumped. William and Mary?

"Your brother, I believe, studied at the college?"

Oh. "Yes, that's right. He and Gus were classmates."

What exactly had Gus told his mother? He'd only briefly mentioned something about saying she was a fellow student's sister.

"And what brings you to our little hamlet?" Lydia asked, turning and shuffling into the parlor. "Augustus says your family's not from around here."

Cheyenne trailed behind her. "I'm visiting a few friends. When I ran into Gus"—*please don't ask me where*—"he invited me to come spend part of my time here. I hope I'm not imposing?"

"Oh no, dear. You're very welcome to stay as long as you like." Lydia came to a stop and put a hand to the slightly crooked hat crowning her wilting chignon. "You'll have to forgive me. I've been a bit under the weather. I had to cut my visit with my brother and his family short ... and I'm afraid I'm not at my best."

Cheyenne looked at her in concern. As well as being pale, a light sheen of perspiration had broken out across her forehead. "Maybe you should go and lie down."

"I do have a rather severe headache. That horrendously bumpy carriage ride ..." She turned fretfully back and looked across at the bags the coachman had deposited inside the foyer. "But where is Myrna?"

"I don't know. She's not here. And Gus is in the library with Daniel."

"Oh ... well," Lydia said, swaying ever so slightly, "we need Ruth."

"I'll get her," Cheyenne immediately offered, though she didn't relish having to be the one to summon her. But Lydia looked ready to drop and no one else was at hand. "Why don't you go ahead and head on upstairs and I'll get Ruth and we'll see to everything else."

Lydia let out a breath, blinking tiredly. "Oh, wonderful. Thank you. I believe I will."

Cheyenne waited as Lydia slowly shuffled out of the room and around to the staircase. She gave it a little longer, then went in search of Ruth.

Moving past the bags, she took the main hallway to the second passageway and followed it down.

The basement door at the end was closed as usual. Was she supposed to knock or go on in? She decided to err on the side of caution. Stepping forward, she knocked briskly. "Ruth! Are you down there?"

Nothing. Not a sound. She knocked again, harder this time. "Ruth!"

Pressing her ear close to the wood, she once again heard nothing.

"All right, I'm coming in." She twisted the knob, the metal cold in her hand, and yanked the door open.

Ruth was waiting for her at the bottom of the stairs, her features twisted into a scowl.

"Miz Lydia needs you," she told her, automatically referring to Gus and Celia's mother the way Myrna had. "Gus is in the library having an"—she almost said "argument" but caught herself—"a discussion with Mr. ... Daniel, and Myrna still isn't back."

Ruth remained where she was, a narrowing of her eyes the only indication she'd heard.

"There's luggage in the foyer that needs to be taken up and I could use some help, and Miz Lydia's not—"

"—feeling well," she finished as Ruth abruptly swept by her and started up the stairs.

Well, shit. Cheyenne grimly grabbed the handrail and started after her.

Ruth, who was at least thirty pounds heavier but also four inches taller, had already scooped up all three bags and begun ascending the staircase by the time she made it back to the foyer.

Now what? She tentatively took a few steps in the direction of the library. Gus would surely want to know his mother had arrived. Did he realize she was ill? He must have seen her that morning when he dropped Celia off. But the sound of a raised voice—possibly Daniel's—followed by a crash brought her to a halt. She turned and scurried through the parlor archway, stepped to the side, and shrank back until she was partially behind the wall as Gus, furious, roared back at him. And now she could hear scuffling as well as grunting and then a meaty thud, followed by a hard thump as something, or someone, hit the floor.

Knowing she might only have seconds, she dashed across the room, darted into the rear hall that led to the ballroom, and took it back the other way to the center hallway.

She heard the library door being yanked open at the same time she picked up the sound of Ruth clomping down the stairs.

Swinging around, she waited for Ruth or Gus to come into view.

He strode across without seeing her, and incredibly, Ruth only came as far as the second passageway before turning toward the basement.

It was possible that Lydia was fine and merely wanting to rest, but it was also possible that Ruth had merely dropped the bags and walked back out again.

"Dammit," she muttered, resuming her journey. Sleep was probably the best thing for Lydia right now, but did she even have so much as a glass of water by her bed?

And what do these people take for headaches?

In the kitchen, she opened the left-hand door of the icebox, found a huge chunk of melting ice, closed it, and opened the one on the right. She briefly considered the pitcher of cider on the lower shelf then decided against it and pulled out the one of water instead.

After filling a tall glass, she walked out, taking it with her, and made her way down to the now-silent library, doors closed firmly once again. Was Gus inside? And what had happened to Daniel? She imagined him lying on the floor, hurt or maybe—

Stop it, she told herself, moving on past to start up the stairs. *You're being melodramatic.*

At the top, as she turned to head for the master bedroom on the left, the bathroom door came open and out stepped Lydia.

If possible, Lydia looked even worse than she had. She was still wearing the rumpled clothes she'd traveled in—though she had managed to shed the hat, coat, and shoes—and now smelled faintly of vomit.

"I brought you some cold water," Cheyenne told her as Lydia fluttered a hand at her and headed for her room.

Cheyenne followed her down the hall and into the bedroom then stood back and waited while Lydia carefully padded across and seated herself on the bed.

"My goodness, I must look a mess," Lydia said, pushing ineffectively at her mussed hair.

"Feeling better, though?"

"A little."

"Here." Cheyenne walked over and held out the glass. "You need to stay hydrated."

Lydia appeared a little perplexed but took the water and dutifully downed part of it.

"Now," Cheyenne said, taking the glass from her and setting it on the table by the bed. "Would you like for me to run you a bath?"

"No ... not yet. I think I'll let my stomach settle a bit first."

"Do you need some help with your clothes?"

Lydia shifted, turning her upper body toward Cheyenne. "If you could just undo me."

"Of course." She went around the side of the bed to her.

Beginning at the top, she set about unfastening the long line of buttons that ran all the way down her back.

"There," she said when she'd finished.

At the door, she paused before going out. Her stomach had just rumbled loudly, reminding her how empty it was—it had been a long time since the tray the evening before. And Lydia probably needed something as well. "Would you like for me to try and find you something to eat?"

"Yes, I believe I could do with a little something. Thank you, dear. But where is Ruth ... or Myrna, has she still not returned?"

"I don't think so." She made no mention of how Ruth had already scooted back to the basement. And who knew what was going on with Gus. Or with Clara.

A wave of exhaustion swept over her, and she thought longingly of the soft pink bed waiting for her upstairs.

But first they needed sustenance. "All right, I'll leave you to rest while I see about getting something prepared."

CHEYENNE STARED DUBIOUSLY at the iron behemoth against the wall in the kitchen. The belly of the beast contained no less than four oven-like areas with various knobs and handles, a thermometer, and a large round control of some sort. Above that there were six plates she assumed were burners, two more regulator thingies, and a compartment over that with a black pipe running up into the ceiling.

This was not the same stove from her time, which she thought might have run off of gas. That one had been a compact, more modern-looking range and she was almost certain it had not been designed to burn wood like this one, as the brass holder full of cut pieces on the floor beside it seemed to indicate. Did it use coal, too, like the many-limbed furnace and its squat, water-heating companion in the basement?

She stepped closer and tentatively grasped the upper handle on the left and pulled down on it to look inside.

She could see a partially burnt piece of wood amidst a pile of ashes in the bottom.

"What are you doing?" Gus demanded behind her.

She jumped and spun around. Good grief, another shock like that and he was going to send her straight back to her time. A shiver of uneasiness ran through her at the thought, and it struck her again just how crazy this whole thing was. How impossible. Yet here she was.

Shakily, she walked over to the kitchen table she'd once shelled pecans on and pulled out a chair.

"Cheyenne? Are you all right?"

Lowering herself down, she leaned forward and rested her forehead on the table. After a moment, she attempted to gain control of herself and raised back up again. She felt profoundly weary and a bit lightheaded. She needed to eat and get some rest soon. Lord knows what would happen if she actually passed out. That cheery possibility sent another shiver through her.

"What is it? What's wrong?"

What's wrong was she was thirsty and hungry and she didn't really belong here but she didn't have anything waiting for her there, either. But before she could give voice to any of this, from the other end of the house came a muffled bang.

"That must be Myrna finally," Gus said. "She can help see to you."

She can help see to me? she thought incredulously. Like she was one of the horses. Like she was nothing but a problem to be pawned off on someone else. The nerve of the man. He had no idea. Some would have already gone stark raving mad at what she knew and had gone through. She thought she'd earned a bit of his precious time and attention.

"I don't need Myrna to see to me," she said, slightly emphasizing "Myrna." She stood up and, bracing herself against the table, turned to face him. "Your mother is here if you are unaware and I thought she"—*and I*—"might like some tea and toast." *At the very least, you thoughtless oaf.*

He opened his mouth to say something in return then didn't as a muffled but distinctly male voice echoed through the house.

"Who in the world?" he said, swinging around to stride for the door.

Before going out, he paused and looked back at her. "Listen, I need to take care of this. But first, where has everyone gotten to?"

"Ruth seems to prefer the basement," she replied evenly. "And I believe Clara might be in the attic. As for Myrna, I haven't seen her since early this morning."

"Good Lord." He pivoted back around and strode from the room.

None of this bode well for Ruth or Clara. But was that her fault? Should she have tried to procure their assistance more vehemently?

She drifted toward a large rectangular tin she thought might contain bread, but then her curiosity got the better of her and she reversed direction to follow Gus out and see what was going on.

Once again she could hear raised voices coming from the library. This time the door had been left cracked open and she could see a tallish young man with wavy, sun-streaked hair standing rigidly inside as she moved quietly past. There was no sign of Daniel, who must have already departed. Hopefully no worse for the wear.

"I want to know what you're going to do," the man snapped, "about that inept, mismanaging *jezebel* and that conniving miscreant"—his voice rose—"she was foolish enough to marry!"

"That's enough, Henry. Unless you want to take it outside."

Cheyenne, in the act of seating herself on a corner chair in the parlor, straightened in alarm. Then Henry responded, "No! Of course not!" sounding shocked, and she relaxed back down.

Henry continued in a more subdued tone. "But I'm tired of all these delays and someone has to get to the bottom of this!"

"All right, Henry. I'll ride out tomorrow and see for myself."

The volume of Henry's voice increased as the library door was pulled open. "Talk to that friend of yours, too. He has to know something. Or else I'm going to talk to mine."

The heels of his shoes thudded on the floor as he crossed the foyer, wrenched open the doors, and stalked out of the house.

Gus walked into the parlor a moment later. "He's gone," he said, seeing her.

"Good." She got up and went over to him. "Now if you could help me start the stove, I can get that tea and toast for your mother. And for me, too, if you don't mind. I haven't eaten all day."

His eyes widened. "Nothing at all? Why on earth not?"

"I missed breakfast. And then I rested for a bit too long and missed lunch, too, I guess. Anyhow, I'm starv—" she broke off as he abruptly pivoted on his heel and set off down the hall with long, angry strides.

She hurried after him. Ahead of her, he passed the first passageway, continued on, and turned into the next one.

At the end, he stopped at the basement door as she'd feared he would and rapped sharply on it.

He rapped again, then jerked it open. "Ruth!" He started down the stairs then stopped as Ruth apparently appeared. "In the kitchen," he barked at her, then came back up and joined Cheyenne where she stood.

"I can do it if you'll show me how," she offered, feeling bad about the big deal that was getting made about a few pieces of toast.

"No." He stopped and, surprising her, reached out and smoothed a lock of her hair back. "You go on into the library. There's a fire lit. And there's some brandy in the cabinet. Have a bit of that and I'll join you shortly."

There was indeed a bottle of brandy, along with a half-full box of macarons and a hunk of fudge on a crystal plate under a clear dome.

She poured a small amount of the brandy into one of the glasses on a tray and took it over to the same table, now shiny and new, she'd placed Celia's snacks on.

The room seemed to waver around the edges as she thought of that, and once again she felt almost lightheaded. She tried to keep her mind on the here and now—which was ludicrous if you thought about it. The *here* and the *now*.

But it seemed to work and she was able to go over and help herself to two of the macarons and a sizable chunk of the fudge.

A few minutes later she was beginning to get her second wind. The cookies and fudge had taken the edge off her appetite, and now all the sugar and the sips of brandy she'd consumed were hitting her system, reviving her and leaving her pleasantly relaxed as she stretched her legs toward the warm fire burning steadily in the fireplace.

She had no idea where Gus had gotten to. A second later, as if her thoughts had produced him, he appeared in the doorway and walked across the room to where the bottle of brandy sat.

He sloshed some into a glass and then brought it over with him to where she waited.

Before sitting in the other chair, he surprised her again by pausing and planting a kiss on her startled lips.

With a little thrill of pleasure, she brought her hand up to her mouth as he took the other chair and threw back most of the brandy he'd poured.

"We haven't been very hospitable, have we?" he said, shifting toward her and settling his deep, nearly black eyes on her.

Jesus, he was so handsome. She had a sudden urge to walk over and straddle him, and felt a blush building at the carnal direction her thoughts had taken. She tried to drag her eyes away from the sight of him sitting there in the firelight with his shirt partially unbuttoned and very white against his golden skin and silky—

Oh, for pity's sake.

"The ... ladies ... are preparing a late supper for us as we speak, and a tray of tea and toast, as you suggested, along with her favorite jams has already been taken up to Mother."

She nodded. "That's good."

"You look very beautiful in the firelight, Cheyenne."

The sound of him saying her name was like a soft warm caress. *Cheyyeenne.*

"Those clothes are very becoming on you."

"Thank you," she said, looking over at him again.

He was gazing at her intently, with just the tiniest hint of a smile. As she stared back at him, she caught something else in his expression ... something she didn't think she cared for. Was that ... arrogance ... or ... *smugness?*

He couldn't possibly think she was like some easily conquered Victorian cougar, for lack of a better description, now totally in his thrall, could he? Hospitable or not, she was more than a notch on his bedpost and he needed to get over himself. Had it been this way with Helena? Had he slept with her? Was he still sleeping with her? No, she thought, probably not. He'd no doubt taken advantage of her charms sometime in the past and now spent his days evading her while still trying to manage whatever business venture he'd gotten himself, and some of his associates, into with her.

And now she was another problem to be seen to, one already smitten and easily dealt with. She thought about letting him in on the fact that she was there to help him. That Myrna, looking years older, had told her he needed her. That she knew something was going to happen to him and she couldn't bear the thought of it.

That he was the only one who truly saw her and wanted her and might possibly grow to love her.

But it was too much, too soon. And for all she knew, she could be ripped back to her time at any moment. But she didn't think so. She had no way of knowing for sure but she suspected the longer she managed to stay, the greater the hold the place had on her.

Gus, hearing something she hadn't as she sat lost in thought, turned his head as Ruth's dark form filled the doorway. "I believe we can adjourn to the dining room now," he said, getting to his feet.

She stood up and followed him out of the library, down the hall, and into the large, high-ceilinged space.

Silently she sat down in the chair he pulled out at the table that would still be there a hundred and thirty years later, and he took the one at the head to her left.

There was a fire burning in here too. Later as the sun dropped below the horizon and the temperature fell it would become chilly even with the hot air rising through the few grates in the house. But for now it was warm and cozy with the flicker of the flames and the lamps and candles chasing away the growing shadows.

Neither of them spoke as first Ruth and then Clara brought in biscuits and half an apple pie and added them to the platter of chicken and bowl of potato salad already sitting there.

"Would you like some wine, Cheyenne? Or would you prefer something else?"

"I'll just have water, thank you," she said, picking up her glass and taking a sip.

"Are you sure? Coffee perhaps?"

Coffee did sound good. And it would help keep her awake long enough to eat. "I believe I will take some coffee. Thank you."

Gus turned and gave a sort of half-snap at Ruth. To her credit, she showed not one iota of resentment as she nodded and hurried out. The whole time the young women had been filing in and out, neither of them had made eye contact with Cheyenne. Which was probably for the best.

"So what did you say to them?" she asked when they'd finally retreated for good and he'd reached over and grabbed a chicken leg.

"Chicken?" he said, pushing the platter toward her.

"Yes, please." She selected a thigh as he plopped a large spoonful of potato salad onto his plate. She found how casual he was being even in such formal circumstances (to her anyway) comforting on some level.

"I simply asked them if they enjoyed living here."

"Nooo," she said as he took a biscuit. "You threatened their jobs?"

He held the basket of biscuits out for her to take one then dropped it back onto the table. "I explained to them that you are a guest in this house and are to be treated as such."

"And?" she prompted.

He gave a laugh and reached for his glass, already nearly empty of the dark red vintage he'd poured.

Dark ruby-red wine. Almost like blood, she remembered. Swirling in the water in the hotel after she'd caught Brent with Serena.

"I told them that if you or anyone else in this household was ever so grossly neglected again then their stay here would come to an end. And I plan to have a word with Agnes as well."

She winced. "Isn't that a bit harsh?"

"I don't believe so. Do you have any idea what it cost to keep a household like this going?"

"No, I truly don't." She took a bite of her chicken. *But I know what it would cost in my time, and it would be a pretty penny.*

"I pay them a salary unlike some people as well as their room and board." He filled his glass with wine again and thumped the bottle down. "They can live at home and go to work in town somewhere or even at the mill now if they wish. No one's forcing them to be here."

"What about days off?" she asked without thinking and regretted it as he dropped his fork onto his plate with a clatter.

"I do not neglect nor mistreat anyone in my service, neither here nor at the mill." His eyes, suddenly gone flinty, drilled into hers.

Geez, clearly this was a touchy issue with him.

He picked up his glass and took an angry swallow. "Of course they get time off. They get Sundays and every other Saturday, as well."

She had absolutely no idea how to reply to this—his world was so alien to her—and merely nodded.

After that they spent the next few minutes eating without speaking.

Everything was good even if it was cold leftovers. The biscuits were fresh and hot, though, as was the coffee Ruth brought in after a bit along with a dish of sugar and a small pitcher of cream.

Finally, she pushed her plate away, still containing the remains of the pie she'd been working on in between sips of the strong, sweet brew. "That was good. People don't do this enough anymore."

"Don't do what?" he asked, wiping his mouth.

"Oh, you know," she said, trying to make light of it, "sit at the table and eat like civilized folks."

He raised his brows, regarding her quizzically.

"Things are a lot different where I come from," she explained. Then because he was still waiting expectantly, she added, "I'll tell you what I can. But not tonight." How much should she reveal? Not much, she decided. The less he knew—the less she changed in other words—the better.

Excerpt for whatever danger Gus was facing. That, she had to avert somehow.

Twenty-one

The sky was beginning to lighten from black to gray outside the windows in the sunroom where she reclined on a settee in near darkness contemplating the relativeness of reality and what it meant for her in this strange world she now found herself in.

As soon as she'd heard someone up and about, which turned out to be Myrna, who must have come home after she'd gone to bed, she had made a dash for the bathroom when she saw it was open, then returned to the pink room a few minutes later still damp from the furtive bath she'd taken and gotten dressed in the navy skirt and light-blue blouse, determined to accompany Gus when he left.

The smell of coffee drifted in a few minutes later, and she roused herself from the pile of pillows she was propped against, stood up, and went around to the kitchen.

"Where's Agnes?" she asked, crossing over to where Myrna stood by the stove, humming to herself in the light of the two lamps she'd lit on the shelf above the table that served as counter space by the sink.

"She'll be in at her regular time. I'm just fixing a little something for Mr. Gus since he's leaving out extra early."

Not without me, he's not. "Did he say where he was going?"

Myrna, shaking off the manual hand mixer she'd been using, glanced around before answering. "He said he needed to check on something and meet with that lawyer friend of his, Mr. Wells." She grabbed a ladle and began using it to pour batter into the waffle pan sitting on one of the iron plates. "Said he'd be getting home late." She glanced around again. "I suspect it's about that hotel Helena's putting up."

Oh, so that was it. Helena had managed to siphon off some of Gus's money into her little business venture—money left to him and still being produced by the textile mill on the river somewhere outside town, she'd manage to glean, which had been built by his father with the help of the money left to him from *his* father. And now there was some problem.

"I'm going with him," she told Myrna, then turned and left the kitchen to cross over to the dining room.

She was seated at the table under the soft glow of the oil burning in the glass fixture above her nursing a cup of coffee in the same spot she'd been in the night before, when Gus walked in. He jerked to a stop at the sight of her, and then continued on to his chair at the head.

Dressed in a charcoal-colored vest and matching trousers with his hair brushed back, he looked handsome as always.

"You're up early," he remarked, reaching for the carafe.

"I didn't want you to leave without me." She shifted back in her chair. "I want to go with you. There's no sense in me sitting her doing nothing all day again."

He carefully spooned sugar into his coffee, gave it a stir, and took a sip. He liked his sweet, she noticed, but without cream. "Any other time, I would be more than glad for you to accompany me ... but unfortunately today I have to travel quite a distance and won't be home until late this evening."

"That's fine. I don't mind." *I won't learn anything sitting here* was on the tip of her tongue, but she didn't want to get into everything yet. Since she'd arrived, he'd had other things on his mind and hadn't pushed it, but she had a feeling she was going to have to give him something soon.

He picked up his cup, took another sip, and looked over the rim at her. "I don't think you understand. We will be traveling for *hours*—with no help. And I won't be stopping often."

The way he said "won't" so decisively and mentioned "no help" once again revealed to her how different their worlds were and how at odds they currently were with each other. He probably thought she was under the mistaken impression that they'd have a pleasant outing where they could take in the clean air and visit the shops while handling any business, with a nice lunch, maybe even on a blanket by a stream if they did it picnic style, thrown in before heading home at a decent hour.

"I understand," she said evenly. "And I'm still going."

"Really, I don't think you—" he began, but she overrode him.

"I don't think you realize how far I've already come. And what I've already gone through."

That stopped him cold and he stared at her silently for a moment before picking up his fork and cutting into his waffle.

"You don't have to worry. I won't be any trouble, I promise."

Finally, after she'd just about given up, he responded. "All right, Cheyenne."

THEY LEFT FORTY minutes later after Augustus enlisted Myrna's help in outfitting her with a midnight-blue coat trimmed in black fur—which looked rather dusty when Myrna produced it but after a good brushing off turned out to be gorgeous—pale blue gloves, and a felt hat adorned with minimal flowers just large enough to provide some protection from the elements.

She felt rather well put together as she took his hand, stepped up, and settled onto the stitched leather seat of the small buggy he referred to as his trap.

Augustus looked very much the man about town himself in his matching pants, vest, and jacket, darker outer coat, and black western-style hat he'd donned. He climbed up, switched the reins to his left hand, and grabbed a long whip.

"Hup!" he called out to get the horse he had hitched going, and with a lurch, they began rolling down the driveway.

They started around the curve heading into the trees, and she felt herself tensing up, halfway expecting something to happen as they moved away from the property.

But there was no buzzing in her ears, no staticky, charged feeling in the air around her, no change in her surroundings, and she soon found herself relaxing.

They rode in silence. Which was fine by her. She was busy marveling at how familiar it all seemed. Excerpt for the fact that they were traveling a dirt surface and moving slower than what she was used to, she could have been heading for town on some back road in her own time.

There was a lot less traffic, though. They only passed one man perched on a wagon full of hay and then a buggy with open sides and a raised top like Gus's during the ride into town.

On the bridge spanning the brownish water rushing over the rocks, he pointed the mill out to her. She looked over at it stretching upwards on the hill to their left as they entered a section of elegant, mostly two- and three-story homes followed by the stores, businesses, and government offices of Pelzer.

It looked completely different. And not just because there were no cars. The streets were wider and unpaved with higher-than-average sidewalks, and there wasn't nearly as many people. After crossing the bridge, they only had to ease the buggy over once to make room for a larger two-seat carriage, and only a few conveyances were pulled up along the main avenue, with their occupants strolling along the sidewalk or entering and exiting the various establishments.

But she took comfort in the fact that there *was* a town, with substantial buildings, many of them brick, as well as telephone and telegraph poles and lines.

On down past a two-story building she saw was a Post & Telegraph Office, Gus maneuvered them around and over to an impressive building on the corner by a bakery and a drugstore.

She eyed the brick pharmacy across the street from them uneasily for a moment, the limitations of nineteenth-century medicine floating across her mind like a dark cloud, then turned her attention to the larger structure Gus had lined them up before.

BANK OF PELZER read the carved lettering on the front. Above the double doors, one tall glass pane stretched the height of the second floor, flanked by pairs of arched windows under a decorative cornice running along the edge of the roof.

"I shouldn't be too long," he told her. "You can wait here." Not giving her time to respond, he turned and headed for the impressive entrance.

She shifted around. During the time it had taken them to make it into town, the wind had died back but the temperature felt like it had dropped and thick, low-level clouds had drifted in and covered the sky. They had already seen a few flakes as they climbed the hillside past the river, and she was seeing even more now as she tried not to feel on display there in Gus's trap. He had raised the folding roof, at least, but it didn't provide much privacy with the front and sides mostly open.

A man holding the hand of a little boy in a plaid coat and knee breeches looked up as she glanced over and gave a dip of his chin at her. She nodded in return and quickly averted her eyes.

She should have gone in too. That was the whole point of accompanying him. Shifting around again, she peered down the street at the other shops and stores close by.

It looked like there was a boutique of some sort right before a place that sold furnishings. That might be interesting to check out. She could kill a few minutes there until he was finished.

She waited until two older ladies turned the corner, then carefully climbed down. Now what to do about Gus's trap. Should she just leave it there? There was no way to lock it; someone could easily grab the reins and drive off with it. What did everyone do?

The solution to the problem came from an unexpected source. While she had been standing there uncertainly, a boy of about ten or eleven had sauntered around the corner and settled up against the wall of the bank's façade. "Hey lady," he called out now in a voice still a few years from changing, "you want me to watch your buggy?"

As she hesitated, he came forward, face eager. "I'll take good care of it, ma'am. You can count on me."

She understood he wanted more than her gratitude and groped in her pocket. Her fingers found the coin she had felt earlier, and she held it up for him to see. "This is all I have, I'm afraid."

Quickly stepping forward, he snatched it out of her hand. It must have been enough. Shoving it deep into his pocket, he dashed back over and took up his position against the wall again.

Eyeing the boy's somewhat dirty skin and ratty clothes, she wished she had more. It was a very real reminder that the "Gilded Age" veneer over this era masked a troubled society rife with poverty and hardship.

After checking to make sure Gus wasn't already coming out, she turned and walked along the front of the bank, underneath the awning of the bakery beside it, to the recessed entryway between the display windows of the dress shop.

The shop wasn't so little, she discovered as she stepped inside. The space, lit by chandeliers—*electric* chandeliers— hanging from the high partitioned ceiling on either side of a line of columns, went back farther than she expected.

Three hatless women wearing similar black dresses with white bows at their necks—a kind of uniform, she supposed— stood attending customers behind the longer of two glass cases situated to form an L on her left. Another saleswoman held out a length of material for a lady in a fur stole on the other side of a low cabinet with shelving behind it.

The lady appraising the fabric moved away, and the woman attending her, dressed differently than the other two in a light beige skirt, white shirt, and black bow, a sort of reverse of what the other two wore that served to clearly differentiate her, started across the carpeted floor. Cheyenne would bet two to one that this was the top dog.

And she was heading straight for her.

Well, let her, she thought, walking over to look at one of the gowns displayed on a headless dress form.

The gown was beautiful but not what she needed really. Not that she had a way to pay for anything.

"May I help you with something?" the saleslady asked, wasting no time as she reached her.

Shifting reluctantly around, Cheyenne studied the woman's face, but couldn't read her expression. She looked to be in her mid- to late thirties and was pretty enough even with the strangely high, sweeping, Frankenstein's-bride updo she wore as opposed to the other women's flatter, wider chignons.

"I'm just looking, thank you," she replied, trying to keep her eyes from straying up to her towering hair.

She had hoped the woman would move away, but she remained stubbornly at her side.

"This one would be stunning on you," the saleslady said, moving closer to touch one of the cap sleeves. "Are you looking for a gown specifically?"

"No, no gowns." She still hadn't gotten to wear the gorgeous red one yet, which Gus had unearthed when she'd asked about it. *Had he bought it here?* she wondered. Maybe she could wear it for the holidays, if she was still there. In her mind she visualized a white Christmas with her descending the staircase in the dazzling crimson gown, which seemed an actual possibility considering the snow she'd already seen, with Gus and his family and friends waiting below.

Belatedly she clued in to the fact that the woman was speaking again while trying to gently lead her across the store. "...something from one of these collections?"

Cheyenne let herself be gently coaxed over to the first of several long racks. It seemed easier than continuing to protest.

The woman drifted away but stayed close as Cheyenne began to walk up and down the rows of hanging garments.

She didn't really see anything inspiring other than an embroidered purse she picked up absently from a nearby display table—she actually did need one, to carry a handkerchief in if nothing else. She kept going past an arched partition and out of curiosity moved into the alcove beyond. She slid the dresses there over—and discovered a gorgeous turquoise skirt and jacket combo.

"Now I like this," she said, lifting the jacket and holding it out.

"What a marvelous choice," gushed the saleswoman, immediately rushing over and taking it from her. She held it up to Cheyenne and surveyed it critically. "I think it will fit with minimal alteration."

"Oh, no, I'm not—" Cheyenne began, but it was too late.

"Mimi!" the woman fairly shouted, and from around the glass case out shot one of the black-clad women.

"Really, no," Cheyenne protested. "I'm afraid I'm currently relying on the kindness of friends due ... due to unforeseen circumstances, and I can't ... In fact he'll be returning, looking for me, at any moment."

"And who is this delightful host you speak of?" The woman handed the outfit over to the other saleslady and then proceeded to lift a hat with a round flat top and a bluish green plume off a display stand. "Someone from this area?"

"Um ... yes, it's the Moore family."

The woman directed the other saleslady to a shelf of low-heeled shoes with multiple straps against the far wall. "Yes, those," she told her then turned back to Cheyenne, her eyes catching on something behind her before focusing in on her. "If you are speaking of Mr. Augustus Moore ... perhaps we should ask the man himself?"

Cheyenne looked over and there was Gus, just catching sight of her.

He does cut a fine figure, she thought as he started in their direction. She hadn't truly understood what that phrase meant until now. She wasn't the only one admiring him; both the other salesladies and the two customers in the near vicinity had also swiveled their heads around to follow his lithe, well-dressed figure.

"There you are," he said, reaching her. "I thought I might find you here." He glanced briefly at the saleswoman, touching the brim of his hat. "Good to see you, Mrs. Davenport."

"I was just killing time," Cheyenne began, annoyed at his assumption that she would head straight for the dress shop, then broke off as Mrs. Davenport, seeing her chance, dove in.

"I was just about to tell your charming houseguest that you and your family are some of our oldest, best customers and that your patronage is always greatly appreciated."

He squinted at her, then glanced down at the embroidered purse Cheyenne had forgotten she was still clutching. "Oh, of course. Whatever you need."

Mrs. Davenport's face lit up. "Excellent. I also have some exquisite peignoir sets just in that you must see." With a twinkle in her eye, she scurried off to join one of the other women heading for the back.

"I don't think you realize what you may have gotten yourself into," Cheyenne said.

"It's fine. As long as it doesn't take too long." He stepped over to glance out the windows, and she moved over with him. "The snow's really coming down out there. We need to get going. But first there's one other person I have to speak with."

"Your lawyer friend?"

"How do you know about that?" He lifted his hand. "Never mind. Yes, my lawyer friend. He has an office down the side street here. So finish up, and I'll meet you back at the trap in, say, half an hour."

She nodded. "All right, sounds good."

She thought he was going to simply turn and leave, but he surprised her again by leaning in and giving her a quick kiss on the corner of her mouth before walking away.

She continued facing forward, deliberately avoiding the eyes of the others, who had converged by a wooden counter across from her where they were carefully arranging items.

He pulled the door open, sending the bell overhead jingling, and she caught a glimpse of fat snowflakes coming down. *Boy, he wasn't kidding*. It was snowing like crazy out there.

Acutely conscious of each minute ticking by, she marched over to see what the women had collected. She needed to finish up and get her butt around the corner and down to that law office.

They parted to make room for her, all of them beaming. It would serve him right if she made these women's day even better and went hog wild and ran up a huge bill. But there was no *time*.

She looked down at what they had assembled. They seemed to have made it their personal mission to come up with the most complete, perfectly accessorized ensembles ever created in the history of the store. Gus must not have been hurting for money too much, or if he was, these ladies had no knowledge of it, because they seemed to feel it was appropriate, expected even, for them to go all out. *They're living vicariously through me*, she thought, gazing at their thrilled expressions.

"I love this one," the slightly younger brunette said—Cheyenne was starting to be able to tell them apart—holding out a shining creation in silverish gray with a silk-buttoned black velvet jacket. "You have to take it."

"That is pretty. But I'm afraid I need to get going."

"But we must take your measurements! Then we can make any alterations, if necessary, and deliver everything to you in a couple of days."

"All right," she reluctantly agreed. "But you'll have to hurry."

As the brunette rushed off for a tape measure, Cheyenne walked back up to a stack of boxed bon bons she'd seen on a display table, took three of them, then moved over to some baskets of scented soaps, and selected one in rose, one in jasmine, and one in lavender.

"I'll be taking these with me," she told Mrs. Davenport, who had joined the saleslady hurrying back over to measure her.

Again she felt the press of time as she forced herself to stand still long enough for them to get what they needed. At last they were done and she was able to snatch up the bag holding the candy and soap, now thoughtfully wrapped in tissue paper, give them her thanks, and hurry out of the store.

Outside, the wind had picked up and a smattering of snowflakes blew into her as she moved out onto the sidewalk and headed for the trap. The snow was beginning to stick and accumulate in places where there was no traffic.

She didn't want to carry the bag with her and was hoping if she stuck it under the lap robe Gus had brought with them it might not get stolen. For all she knew, the boy had already taken off.

But when she reached the trap, she saw he had remained at his post. She wasn't sure how warm his coat was, but at least the buildings and the slight overhang above him protected him somewhat.

There was still no sign of Gus. She went to stash the bag inside, then paused.

On second thought. Changing direction, she moved away from the patiently waiting horse, head lowered against the onslaught of flurries, and started down the side of the bank to enter the street beside it.

There were even less people out now that it was snowing in earnest. Would he still want to drive in this weather all the way to wherever Helena's hotel was being built?

The wind suddenly gusted, sweeping with a howl between the buildings and billowing her skirt. Through slitted eyes, she snatched looks at the buildings she came upon.

There! Across the street there was one with "Harwood, Pittman & Wells Law Office" above the entrance. She angled across the street, wind whipping into her, and stepped up to approach the arched recess.

She paused before entering, took in a deep breath, steeled herself, and pulled the door open.

Inside, the atmosphere was hushed, with only gentle murmurings and the distant sounds of doors being opened and closed.

She moved past a set of matching chairs to approach the reception desk.

A somewhat stoutish lady, who was probably referred to as handsome in this time, waited expectantly. In front of her sat a tall skeletal-looking telephone with a crank on one side. *To ring the operator?*

Now came the hard part.

Trying to appear unconcerned, Cheyenne flashed a smile at her as she got close then deliberately veered away toward the door to her right. "I just have a delivery." She held up the bag with the candy and soap and then quickly dropped it to her side.

The receptionist instantly stood up. "I'll take that," she said, and started around the desk.

Not pausing, Cheyenne made it to the door, grasped the knob and, relieved to find it unlocked, yanked it open. "No, sorry," she said, trying to radiate *I've got this and you are just a formality.* "I was told specifically to give it *directly to him.*"

Undeterred, the woman, who was proving just as relentless as Mrs. Davenport, kept coming. "Well, you are not allowed back there. You'll have to give it to me."

In a last-ditch effort, Cheyenne glanced to the side as if her attention had been caught by someone at the end of the hall stretching to her left and lifted her chin, smiled brilliantly, and raised a hand like she was acknowledging them. Then with only a last tight smile in the woman's direction, she continued on, letting the door fall shut behind her.

She listened for the sound of it being opened followed by a shout, but it appeared her little ruse had worked and it never came. Now if she could just figure out which office it was.

Part of the way down, following the murmur of voices, she took a connecting corridor and soon found herself before one of those doors with a window at the top you could open and close for ventilation. There was nothing written across the frosted glass, but there was a metal plate with the name Perry Wells attached to the wall beside it. Not that she needed it. As soon as she'd gotten close enough she had recognized Gus's voice.

Now what, just stand there and listen?

Casually glancing both ways, she stepped over and nonchalantly arranged herself against the wall. She cocked an ear toward the somewhat heated conversation going on inside. If anyone questioned her, she could tell them she'd been hesitant to interrupt, considering.

"...telling you, as far as I know," a man said, "except for a few miniscule details everything is proceeding as planned." Probably this lawyer friend, unless there were other people present.

"I would hardly call it *as planned*, Perry," Gus scoffed.

"These things move slowly sometimes. You know this."

"I don't know what I know," snarled Gus.

Cheyenne picked up the sound of footsteps inside and jerked to attention—but it was only one of them pacing back and forth. Gus, she thought, listening to the rise and fall of his voice.

"I have it on good authority that ... Henry went to the address given and found only an empty ... I also received a visit from Daniel, who made his own accusations concerning this ..." His voice faded again to where she couldn't make it out.

"But it's not true," Perry replied, his voice low but steady. Probably parked behind a desk. "You were at the meetings the same as everyone else. You saw the plans, and we rode to the proposed sight together!"

"Be that as it may," Gus said.

"You know the bids were put in and we accepted—"

"We—and I say *we* loosely because I was against that particular decision—accepted the lowest one, is what we did. One that was maybe too low!" He seemed to have stopped pacing.

"Really, Augustus." There was the sound of a chair being scraped back. "You shouldn't let Daniel and Henry get to you like this. I'm sure these rumors are all unfounded."

Gus's voice dropped, making her have to strain to make it out. "Do you take me for a fool?"

A period of silence followed before Perry finally responded.

"Gus ... Listen, I've been out there myself and they *have* broken ground."

If that was the case then why hadn't he mentioned it before? Unless he had and she had missed it. Still, the way he blurted it, almost desperately, made her suspicious.

Maybe it had resonated the same with Gus, because he chose to abruptly end the meeting right then.

She barely had time to straighten up and move away from the wall as his footsteps sounded on the floor and he jerked the door open.

He pulled up short at the sight of her, opened his mouth as if to say something, then snapped it shut and banged the door closed.

Stepping over, he clamped his hand around her upper arm, yanked her over, and began forcing her down the hall with him.

"Hey, let go of me!" she exclaimed. Planting her feet, she wrenched her arm back, and jerked free. "I can walk of my own volition!" *You damn manhandling brute*, she thought, glaring at him.

His glowered back at her for a second, then turned and resumed making his way down the hall without her.

She hurried after him, trying to keep up, but she wasn't going to *run*.

With his longer legs and the fact that he was making no effort to walk *with* her, he had soon left her behind.

Gentleman, my ass, she thought, trailing in his wake past the startled receptionist. So much for Victorian manners.

When she reached the trap, he was standing beside it. At least he was going to help her up.

But no, wrong again; he had other plans.

"I thought you could accompany me to pick up some lunch to carry with us," he said as she reached him. "Since you seem to enjoy being out so much."

She actually would have rather gotten under the roof of the trap and covered her legs with the robe. *But you won't learn anything that way*, she reminded herself. "Fine." She reached in and stuffed the bag out of sight.

"Which direction?" she asked him, glancing over at the boy leaning against the wall watching them.

Instead of pointing the way, he stuck an elbow out and waited for her to take it.

She looked from his face to the proffered elbow then back up to his face again.

As he waited patiently, one side of his mouth quirked up in amusement.

Rolling her eyes, she stepped over, slipped her arm through his, and began walking with him down the sidewalk into the swirling snow.

The few people out and about or in the storefronts gazing through the windows at the growing accumulation nodded or smiled as they passed. Augustus was apparently well liked—or else everyone was just friendlier in 1895.

Of course, his family's roots in the community and their ownership and operation of the mill—which provided jobs to many of the locals—had to lend a certain respect. But she didn't think that accounted for all of it. People seemed genuinely happy to see him.

She was beginning to think he planned on walking clear to the other end of town, when he slowed and grabbed her hand. "It's just over here," he said, and pulled her around a gleaming rosewood carriage to cross the street.

Though the heavy gusts and snow had died down, there was still a light breeze blowing, and she was happy to get out of it as she entered through the door he held.

Instead of being divided into private boxes or alcoves, the dining area was wide open with a line of rectangular tables and chairs against the wall on the right and smaller round tables on the left, with the inevitable row of white columns running down the center.

Electric chandeliers had been installed here as well, producing a glittery light over the few patrons—mostly men on their own seated by themselves at otherwise empty tables.

With his hand lightly on the small of her back, Gus steered her over to a table near a high wooden counter.

"We can wait here while it's being prepared," he said, giving her a gentle nudge.

Obediently she sat down as he moved over to speak to the young lady behind the counter. Despite the assurances from Perry, especially now that the snow had stopped, he seemed intent on continuing on to the site for Helena's hotel.

She tried to ignore the frank appraisal of the nearby men and curious glances from the women workers milling between the tables. She glanced over her shoulder, wishing Gus would hurry up, and saw a woman sitting with what might have been her grown daughter—they both had the same thickish eyebrows below piled-up curly hair—quickly avert her eyes.

The woman had been staring! Why? Casually she glanced around at the few others present. She seemed to be dressed more or less the same as they were. Not quite on the same level as the two women with the large hair (probably to support their large hats) but close enough.

Then one of the women servers glanced down at her hands resting on her leg as she walked past, and Cheyenne figured it out.

No one still had their gloves on but her. Even Gus had removed his and stuck them in his coat pocket as they entered.

Shifting around slightly, she moved her hands farther under the table and began peeling them off. *Crap.* What about her coat?

I don't care, I'm not taking it off, she decided. They weren't there to dine; they were there for takeout.

Not knowing what else to do, she left her gloves in her lap once she had them off and sat back again to wait for Gus, who had been waylaid by a balding, heavyset gentleman at one of the smaller tables.

Eventually he managed to extricate himself and came back over to her. "It should be ready any minute," he said, seating himself in the opposite chair. "I ordered us two lunch boxes and a jug of lemonade. I hope that's adequate."

"That sounds lovely," she replied.

Sitting forward, he rested his arms on the table and regarded her silently, his look probing.

She gazed back at him. His eyes had tiny flecks of gold in them, she saw. She hadn't noticed that before.

After a long moment, he sat back and looked away, and she released the breath she'd subconsciously been holding.

After another ten minutes of tense silence in which neither one of them spoke—he was clearly brooding, unhappy about things, and she hadn't a clue what to say—one of the women workers came out and deposited a larger box with their lunches and lemonade onto the table.

Cheyenne remained seated, cramming her hands into the gloves as fast as she could while Gus gathered up the box. Then she stood up and followed him out, where she saw it was snowing again.

Twenty-two

"Wait here," Gus said, and turned to head down the sidewalk the other way. She watched as he walked up to a middle-aged woman carrying a basket who'd just exited a store that sold groceries.

After a minute, he left the woman and made his way back to her.

"What was that all about?" she asked.

He shrugged, falling into step beside her. "That was one of Myrna's sisters. Her daughter just had a baby."

"Oh, so that was where she was."

"Yes." He grabbed her hand with his free one and tugged her out into the street to cross back over.

She hurried to keep up then slowed with him as they stepped up on the other side. The flurries which had been falling intermittently since they'd exited the restaurant had grown to fat clumps of snowflakes falling continuously from the gray sky.

What was Brent doing right that moment? Was it snowing there too? And her mother ... Had she tried to call? *I should have left some kind of message for her to ease her mind,* she thought, *just in case.* She had been a good mother. And she'd stayed with her father for longer than she'd wanted to, just for her children's sake. And what about Caleb? They had always been close. What would he do without her in the years to come? She was his only sibling and with their dad already gone and their mother getting on in years ...

And Jill, her best friend. Really her only friend. Would she be okay? Would she find another BFF who wouldn't strand her at a bar? If not, at least she had Ben. He was a good guy and he loved her.

And Brent ... he would be fine. People like him always were.

Other than her mother, brother, and Jill there was no one that would miss her all that much.

Ian would have, she thought. He would have been her son and he would have loved her and needed her.

Had he lived.

Her face twisted, the back of her neck tightening and eyes filling with tears. She tried to smooth out her expression and blink away the moisture, but something of the endless supply of grief she held must have been apparent as they reached the trap.

"Are you all right?" he asked, stopping beside it.

The look of concern on his face nearly caused her to break down, and she worked to hold in her emotions. Lifting her foot to the iron step, she hauled herself up onto the seat and slid over, still unable to speak, so he could have the right side, which she'd noticed all the men seemed to prefer for some reason.

After a long moment while he waited in vain for her to speak, he went around to stow the box.

By the time he came back, she had gained enough control of herself to request that he hand the boy, who had determinedly remained, another coin. Glancing over at the child, he gave no argument, merely dug into his pocket, drew out a fistful of change, and held it out to the boy, who darted forward to receive it. Pleased with his downfall, the boy stashed it away, grinning from ear to ear, and scampered over to the corner of the building and around the side.

The horse seemed just as eager to be on its way and jolted forward when Gus climbed up beside her and gave the signal.

"So what do people do, anyway?" she asked him. "To keep their horse and buggies from being stolen?"

He shot a glance at her. "They do what you just did. They pay someone to watch it, or if they are going to be a while, they use a stable."

"But surely," she said, raising her voice to be heard over another carriage and two horses moving by them. "There must be times when there is no one and nothing available."

"Yah!" he called out to speed up their horse, who had slowed as they came abreast of the other two. "In a small town like this most people know and recognize their neighbors' carriages. And most of the horses are branded."

As Gus's was; she'd seen the little circle with an M on its flank.

"And woe be to you if you steal a man's horse," he added as they reached the end of the retail strip and started past the graceful homes sitting back along the street.

The town appeared virtually empty now with the snow and the wind blowing hard again and hardly anyone in sight. She wondered again if he truly intended to try and drive them out to the site in such conditions.

Her answer came a few minutes later when he extended the whip—which she'd only seen him use on the horse once when he'd tapped it gently on the rear—to alert the sole buggy behind them and then steered them not across the bridge but onto a dirt and gravel road to the right.

"Where are we going?" she asked as they dipped and angled toward the flowing river below. "I thought we were going to the hotel."

"*Easy*," he called out, slowing the horse a little. "We better not chance it. I was hoping the snow would taper off, but it seems to be getting heavier."

That was a relief. The coat she was wearing along with the plush robe across their laps and metal warmer full of hot coal briquettes at their feet had worked well enough until now, but with the wind cutting into her, she was starting to feel the cold.

But if they weren't going to the hotel, then where was he headed? She raised her voice again to be heard over the rushing water. "Where are we going then?"

"We can stop for a few minutes here."

She stole a look at him, taking in his determined jaw, and knew he wasn't merely stopping for lunch.

Gradually the way opened up, and he steered them into a wide parking area by the mill's cluster of buildings. Well, she had known she would have to come clean at some point. She was surprised he'd lasted this long, even with other things on his mind. If she'd known beyond a shadow of doubt that she was in the presence of someone from the future, she would have been bombarding them with questions.

He brought them to a stop on the lower end, and assisted her down. After he saw to the horse, he grabbed the box and headed for a set of stone steps.

At the bottom he stopped to wait for her, then continued alongside a waist-high rock wall separating them from the river below.

She was becoming seriously chilled but there was no way she was saying a word, not after agreeing to accompany him without complaint.

Where the wall ended, he climbed another set of steps and veered over to a sort of patio built into the corner of the jutting wings of the structure.

Thanks to the two exterior walls, the balcony above them, and a smaller building on the other side of a stone bridge across from them, it felt almost cozy with the sun shining in from the front and the breeze blocked for the most part.

She looked up before joining Gus, who had deposited the box onto one of the trestle tables under the overhang.

Even this place had a gothic quality to it. In addition to the many additions, pipes, wires, and chimneys sprouting from the complex of buildings, there was also a cupola perched atop the ridge of this building's roof.

"I thought we'd go in to my office," he said, picking up the box again. "If that's agreeable."

Hell yes, it was agreeable. And thank God they weren't going to be riding in a half-open trap all the way to who knew where. "Yes, that would be lovely."

Again with the "lovely"? She didn't even know how to speak here. *Because you don't belong*, her mind whispered as she pulled the door open so he could enter with the carton first.

She tried to mentally compose what she wanted to say to him as they moved through an indoor area with more tables, many of which were occupied by men and women eating, smoking, or drinking coffee who spoke or lifted their hands at Gus. Evidently they were not at all surprised, or tactful enough to hide it, to see him coming in the back with a strange lady.

At the far side, Gus led the way into a long space with cubbies and lockers on either side of a wooden bench, empty for the moment. He set the box down on the bench and opened up a mounted cabinet by a metal door with a square window at the top.

"It's loud in there," he warned, taking out a small greenish tin. He lifted the lid and held it out to her. "It's wax, to protect your ears. A friend of mine brought some of these back from Germany.

I've been encouraging the workers to use it, but most of them are resistant. Some of them even believe they can build up a tolerance to the noise."

"Is it that bad?" she asked, loath to cram blobs of wax into her ears.

In lieu of an answer, he pulled the metal door beside him open a fraction, and through the gap came such an onslaught of ear-splitting, thunderous noise that filled her head and seemed to pierce her very eardrums, that she immediately grabbed for the tin.

Grimacing, she took two of the wax blobs as he mercifully let the door fall shut.

He selected two for himself. "Here, I'll show you how."

"I think I can figure it out."

When she was as ready as she was going to be, he opened the door once more, took the box of food from her, and they stepped through it into the hellishly loud, deadly, dusty atmosphere of the 1895 textile mill. She was instantly grateful for the blobs filling her canals. It was still loud—human speech would be impossible over the piercing, pounding, thudding, clanking voices of the machines—but the cacophony was not quite so staggering now.

Looms ran all the way down to the right and left of them, with workers bent over the big rolls, weaving their magic. Between each aisle, clumps of excess cotton fluff lay piled on the floor, some of it thicker in the places where a young man pushing a broom hadn't reached yet. And in the air everywhere, tiny particles floated.

In the peculiar, roaring silence, they moved between the mechanized looms and the workers walking along occasionally reaching out to gently touch the fabric.

Rounding the last one on this side, she had to hold back a cough as they passed two men holding a silent, exaggerated conversation based solely on lip reading and hand gestures.

Then they were moving out of the cavernous space and into a hallway and the deafening noise was fading.

The noise dropped even further when they entered the office on the end and Gus shut the door behind him.

She reached up and pried the wax out of both ears, then didn't know what to do with it until she needed it again.

"You can throw it away," Gus said, holding out a wastebasket. "I have more."

She dropped the wax in and looked around curiously.

There was a fireplace, bookcases holding similarly bound volumes, a few plaques and degrees. An umbrella stand, exactly one extra chair, sitting to the side as if to discourage visitors, a walnut cabinet, and a large desk, ornate with intricately carved legs but dull and worn from heavy use. And on the wall across from her, a series of black-and-white photos.

She walked over for a closer look.

"Did you take these?" she asked, leaning in to peer at the bottom one of the mill in its initial stages of construction.

"Oh ... yes, I took those, and a few others you may see hanging in various places."

She turned back to him. It was all so reassuringly normal. It could have been any office, anywhere. Only instead of a computer on the desk, a typewriter held center stage amidst the folders, periodicals, pens, and paperweights.

She moved around the desk to check it out.

The typewriter sat on a wooden base with a matching cover, now lifted back. Oddly, it had only two rows of ebony keys and they were arranged in a curved pattern. "Huh."

He stepped over to join her. "Are they different in your time?"

"Uh, y— Um ... you could say that."

He stared at her, and then shook his head and began unpacking their lunch.

He was going to let it go for now, but she had a feeling she wouldn't be getting out of there without giving him some answers.

The food was delicious. Neither of them had eaten more than a few bites that morning, and they fell on it like a pair of starved wolves. Gus ate his thick sandwich of sliced chicken and bacon on toasted bread, boiled egg (sprinkled with salt from a shaker he produced from a drawer), and slice of cake behind the desk while she sat on the chair she'd dragged over in front of it, alternating bites with drinks of the lemonade he'd poured into two crystal tumblers fetched from the cabinet.

Gus seemed to find the whole thing amusing and watched avidly as she stuffed her face and gulped lemonade.

"That was good," she said, stifling a belch. "Thank you."

"You're very welcome." He stood up, the faint smile on his face fading, and began cramming the remains of their lunch into the cardboard box.

"Now," he said, tossing it over by the wastebasket. He took his seat again. "Don't you think it's time we talked about this?"

She didn't need to ask him what he wanted to talk about. It was the elephant in the room. There they were going about their business as if it was just another day, when he had clearly seen her disappear on more than one occasion. It was one thing to witness something when you were a child and speculate about it years later; it was another to experience it as an adult and know without a doubt.

Where to begin. "What do you want to know?"

"Anything you can tell me."

She gave it some thought. There was so much. Things he would find amazing, things he'd have a hard time believing. Things he would be horrified by. As she sat there faintly shaking her head though unaware of it, his demeanor changed and became alarmed.

"Cheyenne, what is it? What can't you tell me?"

Blinking slowly, she tried to concentrate. What could she tell him that wouldn't scar him or change something pivotal, possibly to his detriment?

He leaned forward. "I need to know if my family is in danger."

"I ... I'm not sure." She took in a breath, thinking back to the day she'd seen Myrna in the cemetery.

Suddenly his fist banged down on the desk, causing her to jump. "You must tell me whatever it is! Why else are you here? Dammit, I have a right to know!"

He had a point. And if there was some underlying purpose to her being there ... "Okay." She sat up straighter. "Fair enough. But you may not like what you hear."

"Fair enough," he repeated back to her.

"Seriously, Gus, we have to be very careful. Do you understand how high the stakes could be?"

He took a moment to consider this before replying. "Yes." He leaned back in his chair. "I believe I do."

"I'm still not sure where to begin."

"How about you begin by telling me what had you so upset earlier."

She looked off to the side at the abrupt change of subject and thought about when she'd held tiny Ian in her body, a time full of hope and joy ... and then later, a time of indescribable sorrow and despair, and as always she felt the pull of her grief. Quickly she stood up and moved over to a different set of pictures by the fireplace. "Did you do these as well?" she asked in a thick voice, blinking back tears.

"Cheyenne, I'm sorry. I can see this is very hard for—"

"This first time I knew it was all real," she interrupted, turning away from the two older men's portraits she'd barely looked at, "was when I saw the photo you took of me."

She walked over, sat back down across from him, and raised her eyes to his. "I found it in the attic. The other pictures, the ones of you and your family and the house, I thought I must have seen during one of my little sleepwalking episodes and then subconsciously incorporated them into my dreams—what I thought were dreams. But then I found the one of me."

"The one I took."

"Yes, that's right. And I couldn't deny it any longer."

"But I don't understand. Why were you there? Did you ...? What ...?" His brow wrinkled. "Who ...?" Words seemed to fail him completely as he pondered what might have come of everything in a time he could barely imagine.

"The house was empty when I began staying in it."

"It was empty?"

She nodded. "Clearly no one had stayed there for a long time." She told him about the items she'd found on the second floor with the newspapers.

"So you think that was the last time anyone lived there?"

"As far as I know. I just came up on it when I had to leave my house. And it was weird. There was this mist and everything seemed strangely untouched—"

"Wait a minute. What do you mean, when you had to leave your house?"

Ah, hell. "Uh ... there was an issue with my husband and I had to leave. I didn't have anywhere to go and not much money, so—"

"You're *married*?"

"Technically, yes. But we're separated, as you see. And we were well on our way to a divorce."

"That's why you were crying, because he wishes to divorce you?"

Now why would he assume Brent wanted to end things with her and not the other way around?

Because he was a man of his time. And really, he barely knew her. "No," she said. "It was because I lost my baby and then I found him with my next-door neighbor, a girl young enough to be his daughter. And she moved right in and he cut me off financially and I haven't worked since I got out of the hospital." She came to an abrupt halt as she noticed the stricken look on his face.

"Oh, honey." He stood up, chair scraping against the floor, and swiftly rounded the desk.

"You lost a child. I'm so sorry." He pulled her up and put his arms around her, hugging her tight against him.

"It was a miscarriage," she told him when he'd loosened his grip. "But I was six months along."

He winced. "I'm so sorry that happened to you. Here, sit back down and I'll get us a drink."

She smiled at him gratefully and just managed to keep from saying *that would be lovely*.

Through the bottom half of the one barred window in there, she could see snow still drifting down. They would have a cold, though thankfully short ride ahead of them.

He was back after a moment with a decanter holding a caramel liquid.

"Brandy?" she asked, and threw back the last of her lemonade so he could pour some into her glass.

"Yes. I didn't take you for a sherry person."

"You guessed right. I've never had sherry in my life."

"You're kidding. Are you normally some kind of teetotaler?"

Before she could answer, there came a hard knock at the door. A second later it came again, loud and insistent.

"Excuse me," Gus said.

Twisting around, she watched as he opened the door to reveal a youngish black man in a suit jacket over work clothes.

"What is it, Samuel?"

"There's a problem in the picking room," he said, his dark eyes darting over to Cheyenne. "You better come."

Gus turned back to her. "I shouldn't be long."

She nodded.

"What's happening?" she heard him ask, and then the door closed behind him.

He was gone a good fifteen minutes, during which she filled the time by flipping through a leatherbound volume on polar exploration she found stuck near the bottom of one of the bookshelves.

She was checking out a chart of the Arctic region when he finally returned.

"Sorry about that," he said, coming around and sitting down across from her.

She closed the book. "Is everything all right?"

"Yes, everything's fine now. It was just an issue with a fan. I had some installed to try and carry off the cotton dust and help with the heat." He gave a wave of his hand. "But I'll deal with it later."

"I noticed earlier that you do have electricity here in town."

"That's right. And I hope to talk Mama into getting it for the house soon."

"She doesn't want it?"

"She's undecided so far about electricity, but she is *dead set* against gas. She is deathly afraid of it and will never abide it. So, it's electricity or nothing."

Someone after Lydia must not have been afraid of gas, she thought, remembering the different stove in her time. She was almost positive it as well as some of the lights had been run off of gas that had been added, at least in some capacity, at a later date— possibly when whoever it was stayed there in the 1930s.

"Our upper mill was the first in the state to have hydroelectric power transmitted from a distance through cable lines. That way they were able to build up on the hill and keep things from flooding."

"Wow. Really?"

He took a sip of his drink, and sat back. "One day in the not too distant future, I hope to build another one employing the same progressive methods and practices we have here."

What else did he consider progressive? "Such as?"

"Such as using large windows and electric lights to reduce dependance on candles and oil lamps, and taking measures to reduce static electricity. To lessen the chance of fire."

"Do you use child labor?"

"Of course not," he snapped.

Of course he didn't. Stupid question. She hadn't seen any children. "What other methods do you employ?" she asked, steering him back on track.

"For one, we, unlike some others, apply an oil emulsion to the raw cotton to prevent it from releasing as much dust."

"Oh ... well, that's good."

"We should get going," he said, standing up. He tossed back the remains of his brandy and wiped his mouth. "But we will be finishing this discussion at home."

Home. There was that word again.

She tipped her own glass back for a last swallow, set it down, and followed him out.

Twenty-three

As they halted in front of the house, the mustached groom came over and took control of the horse. "I was hoping you'd see fit to turn around," he said over the animal's shuffling and snorting. "Looks like we're in for a real blizzard."

"That it does," Gus replied grimly, reaching up a hand to help her down.

She followed on his heels as he climbed the steps, crossed the verandah, and entered the foyer. It was warmer inside, but only slightly. The coal-eating octopus below didn't seem to do much unless you happened to be near one of the grates emitting the rising hot air.

"Good, you're back!" called out Myrna, gliding down the hall. "I was worried you'd gotten stuck in the snow. Isn't it something? I'll have the girls fix you a nice lunch. With the weather the way it is, I told Agnes it would probably be best if she went on—"

"Thank you but we've already eaten," Gus broke in, stemming the tide of words. "Just coffee, please." He cast a meaningful look at Cheyenne. "We'll take it in the library."

"Of course," Myrna replied. "Right away." She lifted her brows at Cheyenne and pivoted on her heel.

Ruth was already inside lighting a fire when they entered, and Gus waited until she left before speaking. "Sit down," he said, gesturing at the chairs grouped by the hearth.

She remained where she was as he walked over and seated himself before the growing flames.

When he saw she hadn't automatically done as instructed, he looked around with a frown.

She stared stonily back at him. Did he think he was going to interrogate her? "I'd like to give these to the girls," she said, indicating the bag she still held, "if you don't mind." Or *even if you do*, she thought. "And then we can talk."

She turned around and walked out of the room. It would do him good to realize she didn't take orders from him. She was not one of his servants or employees at the mill and she was not one bit intimidated by him. How could she be? The things she'd faced ... Who did he think he was?

All of the women, except for Agnes, were in the kitchen when she entered. Myrna barely looked up, intent on the tray she was assembling with coffee things. But Clara, placing what looked like scones on a small plate, glanced over and froze at the black expression that must have been on her face. Catching this, Ruth, who was rinsing a dish in the sink, looked around and went still as well.

Cheyenne tried to put a clamp on her emotions. *Of course he wants answers. And it's just his way because of the time he lives in.* But she couldn't help feeling anxious and ill at ease being there basically at his mercy, dependent on his kindness, as she'd told Mrs. Davenport. How did the women stand it there with the men calling all the shots and, unconsciously or not, abusing their power over them?

She looked from one face to another. Even Myrna was giving Cheyenne her complete attention now.

Inhaling deeply through her nose and closing her eyes tight for a second, she tried to shake it off.

"I have something for you," she told them. She reached into the bag, withdrew one of the boxes of candy, and held it out to Myrna, who took it with a tentative smile. Then she held one out to Ruth—who looked at it like it was a snake but took it anyway— and one out to Clara, who accepted it without expression.

"And I picked up some scented soaps for you." She shrugged apologetically. "I wasn't sure what to get."

"Why ... that's very sweet of you," ventured Myrna.

Cheyenne reached into the bag again. "I have rose scented, jasmine, and ... lavender."

Clara said nothing, but Ruth unexpectedly spoke up. "I like rose."

Cheyenne held back a smile as a tiny spark ignited within her. "Okay." She handed it to her and turned to Clara. "What about you? You seem like a jasmine kind of girl."

That got a slight reaction out of her, and she favored Cheyenne with a look that clearly said: What would you know about me? Because, of course, she had no idea that Cheyenne had seen a portrait of her that wouldn't be taken for several years yet, judging from the age she'd appeared in it.

"Or would you rather have the lavender?" Which seemed like an old-lady scent to her, but what did she know?

Without answering, as if reluctant to prove her right, Clara reached out and took the jasmine one.

Cheyenne held the remaining bar out to Myrna. "I hope lavender is all right."

"Oh, I love lavender." She took it, raised it to her nose, and breathed in deeply. "I like it best of all."

"Good, that worked out then." Cheyenne turned to include the others. "Well ... enjoy," she said, and exited the room.

Only Myrna called out, "*Thank you,*" behind her. Not that she had expected anything different. She knew it would take time to win their trust. Time she could only hope she had.

IT WAS RUTH who came into the library a few minutes later carrying the tray with the coffee and scones. She deposited it on the small oval table in front of them where they sat by the fire, then instead of moving away, reached into the front pocket of her apron and brought out a small square of something wrapped in wax paper. With a shy smile that was so pretty and almost childlike it had her gaping, she handed it to Cheyenne.

She was gone before Cheyenne could respond, leaving her wondering as she unwrapped the little gift.

It was two of the chocolate bon bons. Oh, how thoughtful; she'd wanted her to have some too.

"I think you have a new friend," Gus remarked.

"I hope so." She wrapped the candy back up, tucked it away, and leaned forward to pour them a cup of the dark, heavenly scented brew.

After she'd handed him his and fixed hers to her liking with plenty of sugar and cream, she took a few sips and then sat back, holding it in her hands for the warmth.

"Before I knew for sure I was actually travelling into the past," she began, "I saw Myrna in the cemetery."

"Our cemetery? Was she …?"

"Dead? No." *Yes*, she thought. *Her headstone, and yours, was right there.* "At first I thought she was some sort of apparition."

He nodded matter-of-factly, reminding her how much the Victorians were into their occult.

"But then I figured out it had been Myrna at a later date."

"And," he prompted.

There was absolutely no way she was telling him she saw his grave and knew when he was going to die. But she could tell him the rest of it. "And she spoke to me before I took off. She told me you needed me and she asked me not to go. And that was it. That was all she said."

He frowned and waited for more.

"I think something bad is going to happen, Gus. To you or to someone close to you. And I think it has to do with Helena."

"What …? With *Helena*?"

"Yes." She leaned forward to set her cup down. "What exactly is your relationship with her? Do you have a history?"

"Helena and I are just—"

"Save it," she said. "We don't have time for evasions."

He sat back and gazed at her with wide eyes, then scrubbed a hand across his face. He looked tired and more than a little disturbed.

"Okay," he said. "A few years ago we were … We had an … We had a …"

"You had a thing," she supplied. "Then what?"

"It wasn't even serious, not for me anyhow."

"But she took it as such, I gather. Did you sleep with her?"

"God no," he exclaimed. "That would have certainly led to marriage."

"And you didn't want that?"

"At the time, no."

At the time? Was he ready for marriage now?

"And not with her," he further clarified. "Once I was around her more, I found … Well, she can be …" His voice trailed away.

"Yeah, I get that."

"You have a strange way of talking sometimes."

"So do you."

He huffed a laugh and turned to face the fire.

She watched as he stared thoughtfully at the crackling flames. So strong, so handsome ... and so vulnerable. *I'm truly falling in love with him,* she thought, feeling her heart turn over. He *couldn't* die in six years. She mustn't let that happen.

Unfolding her legs, she stood up and went to him. He flinched, then relaxed as she sat down in his lap and curled her arms around his neck.

"Hey," she said. "Nothing's going to happen to you if I have anything to say about it. Okay?" She leaned in and pressed her forehead to his.

"Now how about a scone?" she suggested brightly, climbing back off. "And then I'll tell you some cool stuff."

She picked up the plate and held it out at him. He lifted an eyebrow, taking one.

"Listen," she said. "All I know, and I have no concrete proof ... some of it's just conjecture or instinct ... is that you need me somehow. And I think your friends might be right to worry. I suspect that Helena and this plan of hers is at the root of whatever is going to happen."

He shook his head and shifted around in his chair. "When Perry said he'd been there himself and they *had* initiated construction ..."

She waited for him to finish, then added the rest when he didn't. "It didn't ring true."

"No, it didn't. I've known Perry for a long time and something had him rattled."

"How long do you think this snow will last?"

"I have no idea," he answered wearily.

If she were back home she could pull out her phone and check the extended weather forecast, but here as it was now, they had no recourse but to wait it out.

"So, we'll just have to bide our time. I say we enjoy it. Now eat your scone and I'll tell you about when we went to the moon."

"You did *not.*"

"Yessiree Bob, we did. More than once. Of course that was over fifty years ago."

"You went to the moon over *fifty years ago*? I'm almost afraid to ask what you have accomplished since then."

You should be. But that was a discussion for another day.

She racked her brain for something harmless. "Let's see … um, we have many giant telescopes around the world, arrays of them, trained on the universe around us. And we've sent probes and spacecraft and robotic rovers with cameras and other instruments out into space and to the moon and some of the other planets and their moons."

He sprang up, dropping his mostly uneaten scone onto the plate, as if unable to contain his excitement. "My God." He walked over to the decanter of brandy on the side table and sloshed some into one of the glasses. "That's incredible." Bringing his drink with him, he came back over, took his seat again, and gulped at it.

"Oh, Augustus," she said. "I wish you could *see*. What they revealed … They programmed the Voyager 1 probe to pan around and take a picture of all the planets when it was at the edge of our solar system. And there it was, our Earth, a little blue-and-white marble floating in the darkness of space. A pale blue dot."

She realized how fevered she'd become and sat back.

"And … let's see," she said, grinning. "There's the pop-up toaster, electric of course. The electric can opener. The microwave oven …"

Twenty-four

The snow continued off and on throughout the night, only dwindling to the occasional flake as the first rays of the rising sun were brightening the eastern sky.

By the time Cheyenne awoke to a sparkling white countryside, it appeared to be over.

But as it turned out the winter storm hadn't spent itself yet. By mid-morning as everyone in the household quietly went about their business, taking peeks at the snowdrifts outside, thick clouds began covering the sky again, spitting snow and sending tearing winds across the land.

Gus had gotten up, taken one look at the unbroken blanket of white covering everything as far as you could see, and retired to his turret.

All of the fireplaces were ablaze. Even the carriage house and barn had plumes of smoke billowing up into the gray sky. The mustached groom had worked his way over earlier, spoken briefly with Myrna, then retreated again to the carriage house, where the stately driver remained burrowed inside.

There'd been no sign of Agnes. Nor had they seen Roy, the redheaded boy who occasionally helped out with the horses, or Eli, the burly man who so skillfully chopped wood. But that wasn't surprising given the state of the roads.

From what she'd overheard, they had plenty of coal due to a recent delivery, along with wood, staples, preserved meats, and canned vegetables and fruit on the shelves in the basement. If the storm persisted, there would be no elaborate multi-course meals but they wouldn't go hungry.

The girls, excited by the novelty of it all, were in good spirits, bustling about the house in between exclaiming over the deepening drifts outside. Some of their normal duties had been suspended for the day, as well, adding to their enjoyment.

Augustus managed to rally himself for the light lunch Myrna and the girls put together and came in just as the clouds parted and sent a shaft of sunlight streaming through the dining room windows.

Myrna, crossing the room, and Lydia, who had descended the staircase and joined them as they took their seats, visibly brightened.

"Looks like the wind's dying down," Myrna remarked, stepping over to peer out.

"Thank the stars," said Lydia, scooting her chair closer. "I'd like to get back into town soon. It's been too long."

This was the first time Gus's mother had been up and about for any length of time, and Cheyenne was glad to see she had recovered and some color had returned to her cheeks.

After a quick blessing insisted on by Lydia—"We may not go to service every Sunday but we can at least say the blessing"—Gus glanced up from spooning boiled potatoes onto his plate, and she knew he was thinking about how he'd like to get back to Helena's hotel site.

She took only some peas and a small piece of ham. She had learned to take advantage of it whenever food was offered, but she'd already had pancakes and bacon that morning.

Gus appeared to have even less of an appetite and merely picked at his food while his mother and sometimes Myrna on her way through chattered about this and that, with the occasional word thrown in by Cheyenne.

She wanted to ask about Celia—*I mean, they couldn't keep her away forever*—but Gus's brooding continence as well as Lydia's somewhat forced airiness seemed to discourage it.

They had just finished their small repast and were exiting the dining room, when from the direction of the road there came a muffled noise.

Gus, jerking around at the sound, quickly strode through the foyer and threw open the double doors.

Cheyenne ran out onto the verandah behind him, then jerked to a stop at the sight that greeted her as a great team of four horses came into view and surged up the driveway, straining to pull a large wooden roller turning behind it.

She had never seen anything like it. The men perched on the simple bench atop the large wooden roller were outfitted for the weather in heavy coats, hats with earflaps, gloves, and lap robes to cover their legs.

As they drew even with the house, they slowed long enough to raise a hand at Gus and call out a greeting before continuing on, leaving behind a wide, level track as they went around the curve and into the trees.

"What on earth?" she exclaimed when the noise had died away.

Gus laughed. "That, my dear lady, was one of the town's snow rollers. For packing down the snow. Have you never seen one before?"

She opened her mouth then closed it again and shook her head.

"Really?" He gazed at her quizzically as he moved over to push open the door. "You don't have them?"

"No ... we have snow plows. Motorized snow plows."

She followed him inside, the tan boots beneath the brown dress she wore thumping softly on the floor. Once all the roads were better, he would want to be on his way to check up on the hotel. Would she still be around then?

She pictured again the team of horses and their accompanying jangle as they burst into view and came around the drive, and the ghost of an idea began to take shape in the back of her mind.

I mean, why not? I'm here in this magical place in this precious moment in time, surrounded by a gorgeous, snow-covered landscape in the company of a man I'm beginning to love. And there was nothing, really, that they could do until the morning.

She could be yanked back at any second. These minutes, right now, might be all they ever had.

"Gus," she said, catching hold of his hand. "We can't do anything else tonight. And this time we have together ... it could be our last."

"No," he murmured. "Don't say that." He pulled her close, tightening his arms around her. "I need you here with me."

He loosened his grip and gazed down at her in concern. "Have you felt anything?"

"No. But sometimes it comes on all of a sudden. And if it does occur in phases then—"

"It might never happen again."

"Or I might go any second. So let's enjoy ourselves. Let's do something. Let's make a memory." *Something I can hold on to when I'm gone.*

"What would you suggest?"

"You know how there are certain things you wish you could try in my time?"

He inclined his head. "Yes."

"Like driving one of our cars or riding in an airplane?"

"Yeesss."

"Well, there's one thing I always wanted to do."

"I'm afraid to ask."

She playfully slapped at his chest. "It's nothing dangerous. I don't think." She rushed ahead at his look of alarm. "I want to go sleigh riding. I want to take a ride on a horse-drawn sleigh. With blankets and a flask of liquor for the occasional nip and sleigh bells jingling all the way."

"You have got to be kidding."

"Nope. Not kidding. I want the whole thing."

"The whole thing."

"I know you have a sleigh."

"Oh, you do?" He appeared both amused and unsettled at the same time.

She was pretty sure he had one because she'd seen the deteriorating remains of a sleigh in the corner of the carriage house over a hundred years from now when she'd first checked the place out.

"Come on, hitch it up. Or get Mustache to do it."

"Jasper, you mean."

"Yes, him. Let's go!"

He let her push him into the hallway, then twisted back around. "You realize it's going to be cold."

"The wind's died back. It'll be fine. Now get cracking."

"Get ... cracking."

"Yep, you get Musta—I mean Jasper moving, and I'll grab the liquor and assemble the girls."

"I'll take you if you want to go for a ride that badly but we don't need the girls, or even Mr. Gilbert, for that matter. I can have Jasper ready everything and I can—"

"I want Ruth and Clara to go with us."

He blinked at her, his mouth slightly open, as if nonplussed.

"What?" she said. "What's the problem? I know your mother or Myrna might not want to join us, but surely the girls would enjoy it."

"Fine. Why not?"

He started away from her, then quickly turned back. "Get the bourbon," he said.

Cheyenne smiled as she retraced her steps, envisioning what was about to come, and went into the library.

In the back of the cabinet, she found a bottle with a picture of a barrel on the front labeled "Straight Bourbon Whiskey." She went to take it with her, then paused. She put it back and hurried out of the room and up the stairs.

The flask she'd seen on Gus's bureau remained in the same spot. She crossed over, grabbed it, and hurried back out.

Downstairs again, she retrieved the bourbon, carried it to the kitchen, and holding the flask over the sink, carefully filled it.

Then, tucking it into the pocket of her dress, she returned the bottle to the library and went in search of Ruth and Clara.

IT WAS A glorious afternoon. The snowy Victorian landscape wasn't exactly as she'd always pictured it—there were no festive wreaths or groups of carolers yet (somehow she'd always imagined it being Christmastime), or even ice skaters on the pond they passed, which, to be fair, probably hadn't had time to freeze completely over yet—but there was the sheer exhilaration of being in Gus's company there in that still, hushed landscape, silent but for the soft clump of the horses hooves and the creak and whoosh of the sleigh and occasional sigh of the wind. Riding there beside Gus in that frosty winter wonderland experiencing those bittersweet moments from long ago filled her with an awe and a reverence that felt almost frightening in their intensity.

"Hey," Gus said, reaching over to take her hand as they accelerated along a straight, flat section left by the snow roller. "You all right?"

"Yes, I'm fine. This is great." But now that they were picking up speed, she was beginning to feel the low temperature despite the wool coat Myrna had found for her. She leaned over and grabbed one of the thick lap robes they had brought, tossed it over the seat to Ruth, who deftly caught it, then grabbed the other one and, sliding closer to Gus, draped it across them.

He smiled at her, his white teeth flashing, as she snuggled against him and reached into her pocket for the flask. She twisted the top off, turned it up—and fire swept down her throat.

"Smooth," she croaked, grimacing. And they had absolutely nothing to chase it with. She squinted at Gus and saw he was shaking with silent laughter. Gathering her courage, she turned it up again.

This time she barely managed to swallow it before breaking into a fit of coughing.

Outright laughing now, Gus slapped her on the back, the wind whipping through his dark hair as they sped toward the hill he seemed intent on. The girls had joined in the fun as well; she could hear giggling from the backseat, and not just from Ruth, she was heartened to hear.

"Here," she said, thrusting the flask at him. She glanced behind her as he took it and saw Ruth and Clara were munching on bon bons they had produced from somewhere, their dark eyes full of mirth.

Gus allowed himself two quick nips then turned his attention to getting them to the top of the rise. There was one moment when Cheyenne thought they weren't going to make it and might actually begin to slide back down.

Then they crested the steepest point—and nosedived off the other side.

Nearly coming out of her seat, Cheyenne screamed along with the girls, stomach dropping, as the sleigh underneath them came back to earth with a jar and they rocketed downward.

Oh no, they were going to overtake the horses!

But no, they were slewing to the side, runners kicking up ice and snow ... and then back over as they hurtled toward the bottom.

From the back Ruth and Clara yelled, "Have mercy!" and "Jesus almighty!" as the sleigh overshot, sweeping too far to the right, before swinging back across and finally settling into position behind the team.

Cheyenne managed to stop screaming now that they were slowing and breathlessly laughed at the madcap man beside her. The madcap man who was even more handsome when he was smiling broadly as he was now.

They navigated their way around a gradual curve, ascended a slight rise, and then accelerated again to a pretty good clip toward the entrance of the circular drive on this side. Funny, she had never gone farther down the old back road than the driveway. She'd always assumed it dead-ended or petered out after that.

The snow-laden trees on her left gave way to more open land, and she looked over and spotted a group of kids in the middle of a wide white expanse before a house set back off the road. Though not as big as Gus's, the home was still splendid. Did it remain standing in her time? The children, two older boys, a girl, and a smaller boy, were working on building a snowman in between pelting each other with snowballs.

She watched, smiling at the pail they'd used in place of a hat for the snowman, until they moved out of view.

The horses, knowing the way and no doubt anxious for some oats and a nice warm stall, eagerly turned in and took them up the drive and to the corner of the house, where Gus brought them to a stop.

He climbed down to assist her as Ruth and Clara clamored out.

"I'll take it, sir," Mr. Gilbert said, walking up.

Gus swiveled around. "Where's Jasper?"

"He's feeling a bit under the weather, I'm afraid." The older gentleman, dressed this time in comfortable looking trousers underneath the more formal coat he'd thrown on, took hold of the reins.

"Nothing serious, I hope?"

"Just a cold coming on, we think. Myrna had him bundle up by the wood stove."

He stepped up to drive the horses around, and Gus, offering his arm, accompanied her along the walkway to climb the steps.

At the double doors she paused before going in. "Thank you, Gus, for taking us."

He grinned at her slyly. "It was my pleasure."

She poked him in the ribs. "You wildman."

He threw back his head and laughed.

"Seriously, you zany wildman."

He only laughed harder and followed her into the relative warmth of the house, where Myrna, dear thoughtful Myrna, had cups of creamy hot cocoa and fresh, buttery shortbread cookies waiting in the front parlor by a roaring fire.

Everything had a celebratory air to it, though it wasn't yet the holidays. Myrna manned the fire and poured out ladlefuls of steaming cocoa while Cheyenne, Gus, and the girls got warm and snacked on the cookies.

Already pretty toasty from the nips of liquor she and Gus had been taking, Cheyenne soon had to move away from the fire.

She plopped down beside him on the sofa that would be gone over a century later and smiled at the girls standing over by Myrna, laughing and talking.

"Oooh, Mr. Gus," Ruth said, turning to face them, "can we play something?"

"Oh, can we?" asked Clara, adding her voice.

Gus threw his arm out, nearly flinging cocoa onto Cheyenne. "Why not?"

Shifting away from him some, Cheyenne suddenly remembered Lydia. "Hey, where's your mother?"

"Oh, I don't know," he said, attempting to sit up straighter. "Probably resting."

"Should we go get her?"

"She'll join us if she wishes." He gestured at Clara and Ruth conferring over by a table holding a larger wood-based phonograph with a brass horn. "If she doesn't already, she'll soon know we have returned."

A selection from the various cylindrical recordings, stored in small canisters, was finally agreed upon, and Ruth began cranking the wood-tipped handle.

Music drifted out of the horn, low at first and then stronger. As the slightly scratchy notes swelled and filled the room, Gus took the opportunity while Clara and Ruth were still occupied and Myrna had her back to them, to lean over and steal a quick kiss.

"Will you come visit me in my room tonight?" he murmured, his breath tickling her ear.

Would she? Yes, yes she would. She had just given him a nod, when Lydia walked in.

Cheyenne went to shift away, but Gus grabbed her arm and stayed her. "It's fine," he said.

A quick glance at Lydia confirmed it. Lydia was smiling cheerfully and didn't seem the least bit bothered by their intimacy as she crossed over to a side cabinet to pour herself a drink.

"My mother considers herself a free spirit and loves a good party no matter how small or impromptu."

Cheyenne watched in amusement as Lydia lifted her glass to them, took a large sip, and sashayed her way over to the now swirling and dipping girls (Myrna had taken over cranking the handle). This time Lydia was wearing a peach dress with fringe along the bottom, a precursor to the roaring twenties dresses to come, that shook and shimmied as she moved.

"I'm glad to see she's doing better."

He nodded his head in agreement. "As am I."

Across the room, Lydia raised her voice over the music. "Sing for us, Clara. I've heard you do it beautifully."

Clara stopped dancing, her hand flying up to her mouth. "Oh ... I don't ..." Her eyes darted in Gus's direction.

"Tell her to do it," Cheyenne murmured, thinking again of the old flyer she'd found.

"Um ..." He cleared his throat. "Yes, we would be delighted."

Clara turned to Ruth, who immediately stooped to consult the different canisters stored in the cabinet underneath.

"That one," Clara said, pointing.

Lydia, drink in hand, perched herself on the edge of a carved oak chair as Ruth switched out the cylinders.

A few seconds later, vaguely vaudeville notes rose up out of the horn and, growing louder, drifted—slow and melancholy— across the room.

Cheyenne's head jerked around as Clara, swaying faintly, began to sing.

"I get the down home blues in the winter when we gettt too colddd ... I get the down home blues in the winter when we geettt too colllddd ...

"I keep the railrooaad fare to take me where I waaannt to go.

"I like to see the sunshine beamiiinng, ooonn me everywheeerre ..." Her throbbing, moaning voice gained in

strength as she held the notes, and Cheyenne felt goosebumps break out on her arms.

"I like to see the sunshine beamiiinng ..." Effortlessly, the young woman sang, evoking something within Cheyenne, something powerful, full of darkness and of light at the same time. *"... ooonn me everywheeerre ..."*

Cheyenne sat there, transfixed, and listened as Clara, eyes nearly closed, poured out her heart and her soul, her voice filling the room and echoing faintly off the walls. She had a light but strong voice and a presence about her that Cheyenne could easily imagine capturing an audience and holding it enthralled.

Clara held the last note and then fell silent. She looked up shyly not at Gus, but at Cheyenne.

She could only stare back at her. She had the sense of witnessing something great, something that had been lost until then. Finally she swallowed and roused herself enough to speak. "That was amazing." She stood up, walked over to her, and grabbed her hands. "You have a talent."

"Only the words are mine," Clara said, "not the music."

Clara went to pull away, but Cheyenne held on tight and forced her to meet her gaze again. "I'm serious. If you really want it, you could be a star."

Clara yanked on her hands again, and this time Cheyenne let go.

Clara, appearing flustered but pleased, turned away, then turned back again. "You really think so?"

Cheyenne nodded solemnly. "I do."

"There's a theatre up in Spartanburg. They let you sing there sometimes."

"That would be a good place to start."

Where had the Blues movement begun? Who had captured those first early recordings? Columbia? "Hey, Clara?"

Clare, stepping over to join Ruth, looked back at her.

"When you feel you're ready, you'll want to get yourself to New York. And look for a recording company, because that's where the action's going to be in a few years. In recordings which they'll eventually make into viny discs."

Clara, whose eyes had grown wide, slowly nodded.

Twenty-five

It was not the next day but the day after that before Gus judged the roads were clear enough for them to attempt another trip to the hotel site. They met early that morning at the carriage house, forgoing any semblance of breakfast. Thankfully Cheyenne had been able to snatch a cup of coffee from Myrna, who had also pressed a parcel of thick sausage biscuits into her hands as she was leaving that she'd tucked away for later.

"Barring any difficulties," Gus said, tugging on a pair of gloves, "I am going to have Mr. Gilbert keep the horses at a good pace. If Helena or that husband of hers has gotten wind that I'm making inquiries, they may try to beat us there."

"But what will that gain them?" she asked.

"I don't know." He lifted his hat and then dropped it back down on his head. "I wouldn't have ever thought that Helena would do anything ... *untoward*, but now I'm not so sure. And Leonard, her remarkably convenient husband ... I wouldn't put anything past him. They might try to buy off or strongarm certain people. But if we can get there first, we'll have the advantage."

And if they didn't get there first? Would someone be waiting to stop them from learning the truth and blowing the whistle? But surely Helena and her husband had to know that sooner or later the investors and shareholders and bank officers and whoever else would figure out there was no hotel, if that was the case.

As Gus moved up to speak with Mr. Gilbert, she opened the door of the larger carriage Gus had chosen to take—*For my benefit?* she wondered—and used the footstep to climb in. She settled herself onto the cushioned rear seat. The interior had been lavishly decorated in blue-green button-tufted velvet with matching drapes and bronze trim.

Wait a minute. A memory of looking in through a grimy window at faded seats had just popped into her head, and it struck her as she looked around her that this was the very same carriage she'd found abandoned in the old carriage house.

Rubbing her arms against the chilly air of the interior, she turned her attention to the view outside the window. If the day was anything like the one before, it would rise above freezing and hover in the high forties. But for now, though the roads, such as they were, were clear of snow, ice still coated the fences and trees and a brisk wind blew fitfully.

Sooner or later, she thought again, *people will know.* If Helena and her husband Leonard, and perhaps Perry, were up to something, it made sense that they would want to be found out later rather than sooner if they did have some nefarious scheme going to steal money from unsuspecting investors.

But what then? Run off with the money? How much could it be? And for how long? For the rest of their lives? It didn't make sense. From what she'd picked up, Helena possessed deep ties to the community and an ancestral home she treasured.

Cheyenne was still ruminating on it, trying out different possible plots and scenarios, when Gus climbed in and took the seat across from her.

"So how did you get wind of a potential problem with the hotel?" she asked as he settled back and stretched his legs out. "I mean, there are always delays, right?"

"It was Henry." He twisted around to check the way ahead of them as they began moving down the drive. "He stopped at a barroom coming back from Pickens and ran across a man from one of the construction companies that lost out on the bid for the hotel. A bid that should have been sure-fire, as he put it to Henry."

"But doesn't that happen all the time?"

"The offer this other group made was so low as to be laughable. And by all accounts no one's ever heard of the outfit."

Cheyenne tried to recall what little she knew about building procedures and regulations. "Don't they have to solicit bids from everyone so it's fair?"

"Precisely," Gus replied, pointing a finger at her. "The man Henry spoke to seemed certain that something fishy was going on. Evidently the man is the chief engineer for his crew and would know. And he was utterly certain that you couldn't put up a hotel of that size for the price given even with inferior, broken-down horses and the shoddiest tools and materials."

"That doesn't sound good." Cheyenne tried to absorb this and think what it might mean. "Could Helena have been trying to—"

"There's more. This man claimed he had never seen anything like the drawings and specifications they had been provided with."

He continued at her questioning look. "He said they looked like they had been drawn by an architectural dilettante."

"A dilettante." She'd *seen* the word before, of course; she was a reader after all.

"Yes." He blinked at her. "Someone inexperienced. A dabbler ... or a novice at the very least."

"An amateur," she said, nodding.

He nodded back in agreement. Both of them went silent as they considered this.

"So," she said, trying to put it all together. "Construction bids were solicited based on inexpertly drawn blueprints ..."

"Yes, the man Henry spoke to said the incomplete plans were remarked upon but since he had enough experience to fill in the blanks and coordinate everything, they weren't too bothered by it."

"And then this engineer's company loses out after placing a sure-fire bid. To an outfit that has appeared out of the woodwork."

"Right. I think Henry and Daniel are on to something. I smell a rat. And so does everyone else I've spoken to recently."

"Except for Perry," she reminded him.

He shifted around like she'd made him uneasy. "Yes, well ... I've known Perry for a long time."

She waited for him to continue, then decided to let it go when he didn't. For Helena to pull off something as big as this she would need someone on the inside to help facilitate things and provide legitimacy to the whole endeavor. And who would ever suspect an upstanding lawyer like Perry, a friend of Gus's no less, of participating in anything fraudulent?

But why would Perry help Helena? She opened her mouth to ask how well Helena knew the lawyer, then closed it again. "So what exactly is the plan for today?" she asked instead.

"I want to see the site. By now there should be some groundwork completed, if not more, even with the supposed delays. And if we find it as untouched as I suspect we will, we're going to take a little detour to Pinnacle Mountain."

Her eyebrows rose. They were going up a mountain? In a horse and buggy? "How far is that?"

"It's on the other side of Pickens, where the hotel's proposed site is, at the base of the mountain."

"Oh, okay." She relaxed a little.

"No more than five or six hours, I would think."

Five or six hours! Each way? The dismay must have shown on her face, because he hastened to set her at ease.

"We'll be able to stretch our legs at the site and at the Sutherland."

"What's the Sutherland?"

"The allegedly greatly esteemed Mr. Ravenoff's purported previous place of employment."

"And who," she asked after deciphering this, "is Mr. Ravenoff?"

"The man who is to fill the role of hotel manager at Helena's Pinnacle Hotel."

She adjusted her position on the seat. "And what are you hoping to learn about this Mr. Ravenoff?"

"Everything I can."

IT WASN'T AN unpleasant ride. She got used to the rhythmic pace after a bit and they filled the time with conversation. The conditions which landed her there and the wonders of the future world from which she came were only alluded to once or twice before the subject was quickly changed, as if neither of them could stand the intrusion upon the reality they now shared. She found out he had been interested in photography since he was a child, had taken it up seriously in college and had begun by capturing the images of his friends and family. And she also learned that he hadn't been sure he was going to take over the mill and all that it entailed until his father—who she found out *was* the man with the mutton chop sideburns and his hand on a bottle in the photograph she'd seen—had unexpectedly died and it had been thrust upon him.

"But I don't mind, really," he said. "It's not so bad. And I'm excited about the direction we're heading in with us adding electricity, and soon, I hope, a telephone exchange system."

You have exactly six years left, she thought.

Without going into the particulars, she gave him a brief rundown of her life: graduation from high school, college, then work, marriage, followed by the loss of Ian and her subsequent separation.

She had experienced and witnessed so much in her world—things that would amaze him—but in a lot of ways her life seemed inferior. He was a man of the Gilded Age, an innovator who hobnobbed with prominent businessmen, bankers, and lawyers, all of whom were in the process of making history and ushering in the modern era.

What was she?

Nothing but a former wife and almost mother who had once held down a mediocre job that combined with Brent's paltry paycheck had barely sustained them.

Once again she found herself contemplating what it would be like to stay there in 1895. Things were so different—yet the same. It was still a man's world, whether it be the twenty-first century or the nineteenth. Back here with Gus, she wouldn't be the main breadwinner and she would most likely have a life of leisure, at least compared to her old one.

But it would be his, all his.

"Hey," Gus said, reaching out to touch her knee. "Why so quiet?"

"I was just thinking ... about how it might be if I stayed here."

He looked at her in consternation, and then turned his head to gaze out the window. "Would that be so bad?"

How to answer him? "It's just that ..."

"It's just that what?" he said, swiveling his head back around.

Oh, the hell with it. She took in a breath. "Women can't vote. Women can't hold political office. Or be a fully-fledged member of the military. Or sit on a jury."

Gus's eyebrows had risen so high they were nearly in his hairline.

In for a penny, in for a pound. With difficulty she held his gaze. "There is no real equality in marriage." *Because right now,* she left unsaid, *in the year 1895 a husband can still legally beat his wife or force himself on her.*

The seconds ticked by as they stared at each other silently.

Finally, he looked away. He appeared at a complete loss as to how to respond. Did he think she might be about to gather all the local women and form a suffrage society? Or worse? Though not quite at that point yet, it wouldn't be long before some female activist would tire of asking nicely and resort to violence or other extreme measures, like throwing themselves in front of a horse as suffragist Emily Davison had in 1913. Cheyenne had watched several videos of Emily after catching a documentary about the movement. Emily had stepped into the path of the King's horse at a derby, was trampled, and died four days later.

And still it had taken until 1920 for women to be granted the right to vote—and even later for all the barriers to be removed so African American women could.

"Don't worry," she said, taking pity on him. "I'm not a militant suffragette about to commit a terrorist act."

She knew immediately it had been the wrong thing to say when he blanched, eyes going wide and complexion darkening.

Had she completely misjudged him? So far except for the one time when he had been nearly out of his mind with worry for Celia, he had been unfailingly cordial ... kind even, and generous. But he was a man of his age. If pushed or defied, would he become a different person?

"I don't believe," he said slowly, "I entirely appreciate the manner in which you are regarding me."

Swallowing, she dropped her eyes to the floor of the carriage and held back a shiver.

The seconds and then the minutes ticked by, and she could think of absolutely nothing to say. She didn't know this man, really. And he didn't know her or the time she came from.

Abruptly, Augustus leaned across to peer out, and then banged on the side of the carriage. "Stop up there," he shouted to Mr. Gilbert.

Immediately the horses slowed, and they began moving over to a small pull-off area on the right.

"Come with me," he said when they came to a stop. He pushed the door open and climbed out.

She considered ignoring his high-handed manner and staying put, but something told her now was not the time to test him.

Besides, she badly needed to stretch her legs. Gus, who had moved off the road and was now standing facing away, made no effort to help, but Mr. Gilbert came around as she was emerging and took her hand to assist her down.

"Thank you, Mr. Gilbert," she said pointedly. She gathered up her skirt—the ground here hadn't dried completely from the recent winter storms—and walked across to Gus.

"Have you been mistreated in some way, Cheyenne," he asked before she had even reached him, still with his back to her, "in the time you've been a guest in my home?"

Damn, he was really pissed. "Uh ... no, I have not."

He turned around to face her. Though his expression was unreadable, the veins on his forehead pulsed an angry rhythm. "I don't know what you are accustomed to, but in my family we do not mistreat women. Neither I, nor my father that I am aware of, have ever locked up, force fed, beat, or made a woman do *anything!*"

Her eyes had grown wide at the mention of being locked up and force fed, and stayed that way as he continued.

"Why is it so hard for you women to understand that we simply care for you and want to see that no harm comes to you?"

"For our own good," she retorted flatly.

"Yes, for your own good. We are handed a great responsibility towards our women!"

"Love and protection in return for complete obedience, right?"

He inhaled sharply. "Do not twist my words, Cheyenne."

She thought she'd gone too far, but then he lifted his hat, dropped it back down again, and the moment passed.

"Walk with me," he said, gesturing at the faint path running up to the field beyond. He took a few steps, then paused when she hesitated. Pushing her shoulders back, she started forward to fall into step beside him.

She felt a tinge of uneasiness as they turned to follow the trees that blocked the field from the road. *Don't be ridiculous*, she told herself. *He's not taking you off to throttle you.*

They walked in silence, gazing out at the picturesque scene of round haybales dotting the golden field beyond.

"It is pretty here," she murmured after a bit.

He turned his head to look at her. "Is it not where you come from?"

"Oh, it is. It's just that ... the world's a much more crowded place now, I'm afraid."

"Is it that bad?"

She thought about it. "There are some who think it's going to be before it's over."

He nodded contemplatively, and they subsided into silence again. The day had indeed warmed up as she'd expected, and with the sun on them and the wind mostly blocked by the trees, it was fairly pleasant.

A little farther on, with no end to the seemingly endless field on their right, they both turned by unspoken agreement at a break in the trees and headed back the way they'd come.

Slightly ahead of her, Gus came to a stop before continuing on down to the carriage, and she halted with him.

"What you mentioned before," he said, gazing at her. "Do women do all of those things in your time?"

"What? Vote? Hold office? Yes, they do."

"But do they serve in the military?"

"If they want to."

"As nurses and the like." He said this like it was a given. "But not in battle."

"Yes, Augustus, in battle. In combat, as we say."

Something akin to horror filled his face, and he moved a step closer. "You mean they could send you ... and make you fight? Surely—"

"No, Augustus, it's okay. They won't force me. There's no draft for women in the United States yet."

"*Yet*?" He closed the remaining distance and pulled her to him, wrapping his arms around her. "I'm not sure I would like this world of yours."

She hugged him back, unexpected tears pricking her eyes. He did care. He was a good man. How could she have thought any different?

"Come on, now," she said, pulling back a little but keeping her arm around him. "Let's get to the carriage and have a bite to eat. Myrna slipped me some sausage biscuits, you know."

He threw back his head and laughed. "Oh, I don't doubt it. What would we do without our dear Myrna?"

Still smiling, they descended the small slope to where Mr. Gilbert stood waiting by the carriage.

"I have a flask of tea I believe is still warm," Mr. Gilbert said, opening the door, "if either of you fancy a bit before we resume our journey."

Gus hesitated, probably afraid to answer for her, the poor man.

Feeling a stab of affection for him, Cheyenne turned to the kind driver. "That would be lovely."

AND IT *WAS* lovely. The rest of the day took on the feel of an adventure as they determinedly made their way over to Pinnacle Mountain to investigate what might be one of the minor players in a fraudulent hotel scheme. She and Gus had found their footing again and they were out and about, on a *mission* no less, allowing her to see and experience more of life as it once was—something she never would have believed possible—and she found it exhilarating.

She hadn't been quite so excited about having to pee behind a clump of bushes back in the trees before getting under way again, but still.

"Thank you for bringing me," she told him impulsively as they travelled uphill to a crossroad ahead. She could see a closed carriage with only windows in the doors turning out onto the street ahead of them. "I'm enjoying myself."

"Are you, now?" he said. "Then you don't require much."

She looked at him, so handsome sitting there across from her. "Being with you is enough."

Smiling, he leaned forward and pressed his lips to hers. He had just begun to deepen the kiss, when the carriage slowed and Mr. Gilbert turned to address him through the front window.

"Piedmont ahead, sir! Shall I detour?"

"Yes," Gus called back, pulling away. "But just to ride through."

With a nod, Mr. Gilbert turned back to the horses and was soon expertly guiding them left at the intersection.

Just past an impressive structure with a double verandah and an awning up the hill to their left, which might have been a hotel or boarding house, and then a line of one-story homes on their right, the street sloped downward to a cluster of two- and three-story buildings, both wooden and brick that formed the town's main street by the river over here. Glimpsed between the gaps, she could see a low bridge spanning the water where the road they'd turned off of ran down and across before continuing upwards on the far side.

"That was this town's first mill," Gus said, tapping her leg and pointing over at one of the buildings across from them—a four-story brick and timber structure—as they slowly rounded the sharp curve by a large turreted building at the bottom of the street. "Opened in 1876, I believe, with a water wheel for power. Mill number two's on the other side. You probably can't see it, but there's a footbridge above the dam linking the two."

"Wow," she said, gazing at the conglomeration of buildings and accompanying structures positioned along the bank. "Impressive." Especially compared to how it looked in her time with many of the mills' buildings destroyed by fire and the street's establishments abandoned.

"Mill number one was the largest in the state."

Huh, she hadn't known that. She'd driven by what was left of it on her way through to other destinations many times, but hadn't thought much about the possible history of it. Pulling her attention back around, she gazed at the establishments on either side as Mr. Gilbert steered the horses onto a steep side street and relentlessly drove them up it.

At the top, just past a place with tall steps leading to the entrance, the way leveled out and met the main drag again between a café and a larger brick building.

After a short wait for a small buggy to pass, Mr. Gilbert guided the horses out and drove them back to the crossroad.

The intersection was empty and Mr. Gilbert was able to turn them without pause toward the river below.

Cheyenne looked out over the water on this side, admiring the natural beauty, as they made their way to the bottom and bumped up onto the bridge.

"Still enjoying yourself?" Gus asked when they were once again moving uphill on the other side.

"Yes, I am. But I'm a little worried about the horses."

He leaned across to look out. "We should probably rest them soon."

He waited until they had crested the slope and made it past the raised clapboard homes dotting the hillside here, before rapping on the glass and gesturing for Mr. Gilbert to pull over where the way widened ahead.

Mr. Gilbert got them over as far as he could and brought them to a stop by a hand pump and a smallish trough underneath a large tree now minus its leaves.

Both Cheyenne and Gus descended the step to the ground and walked around a bit to stretch their legs while Mr. Gilbert watered the horses and fed them some oats.

"How much longer till we get there?" she asked as they moved down a little and shuffled around, not wanting to go too far. The sun had gone behind a cloud and the wind had picked up again.

"Not much farther. A couple of hours."

Two hours. That wasn't so bad. She could do that.

Twenty-six

Gus relaxed back and fell asleep soon after, allowing her to lie over and rest as well. She must have slept at some point because in no time it seemed, she was opening her eyes to find them moving along a narrow, wooded track off the main road.

"Gus,' she said, kicking at him. "Gus!"

He jerked awake and pushed himself up. Blinking groggily, he leaned across to look through the window, then banged for them to stop.

Before they'd even ceased rolling completely, he was climbing out. "Have we passed the fork yet?" he called out.

The door banged shut, and Cheyenne straightened up and tried to shake off her exhaustion.

This wasn't even their last stop. They still had to visit The Sutherland before heading home.

When Gus still had not returned after a couple of minutes, she climbed out after him to find out what was going on.

The wind whipped into her, flapping the cloak she had fastened around her throat. She looked back at the road they'd come in on. You could tell there had been some recent traffic on it, but nothing like what you would expect for such a large project.

She checked the other way and spotted Mr. Gilbert and Gus up ahead, staring off to one side.

She started in their direction even though all she really wanted to do was stay in the nice warm—well, *warmish*—carriage until their final destination was reached.

"A few stakes and some ribbon," Gus spat as she reached them.

A token effort had been made to take down a few trees and thin out the vegetation in a small strip by the road and she could see a few markers, but that appeared to be the extent of it.

Frowning, Mr. Gilbert squinted across at the undeveloped land. "And you say Mr. Wells claims to have seen the ground broken? Wouldn't that entail the leveling of the site and dare I say, the laying of the foundation at a minimum?"

"I believe that would be a fair assumption." Gus looked over at Cheyenne, his eyes flashing with cold fury. "Nothing has been done since the last time I was here. Absolutely nothing." Abruptly he turned around with a huff of disgust and headed back to the carriage.

A second later, Cheyenne, and then Mr. Gilbert followed.

From that point on, it was a long silent ride out of there and along another road to The Sutherland at the edge of a strip of establishments not really large enough to be called a town.

Set back off the road with a circular drive, it was a simple affair with a low covered porch along the front and two more stories built up against the sloping ground behind it.

But though clean and simple in style, the place gave off an ambiance of quality with its well-maintained, gleaming white exterior, black trim, and wicker high-backed chairs and wrought-iron benches scattered about on the porch and lawn.

"Is this what Helena's hotel is supposedly going to be like?"

Gus snorted. "She might build a fancier hotel, but I don't believe she'll ever rival this one. History—roots—matter even more than wealth around here."

"Then why buy into it?" she asked as she unfastened the cloak to leave it in the carriage.

"People with new money also need lodging." He pushed the door open, climbed down, and held out a hand to assist her. "And we expected we'd make money either way."

He turned to Mr. Gilbert. "We'll wait if you'd like to join us inside where it's warm."

"Oh, no, thank you, Mr. Moore," replied the older man, sticking his head around the back of the carriage where he had just opened the traveling trunk strapped there. "I'll be just fine out here. I wouldn't be opposed, though, to a hot drink after I've tended to the horses."

"All right, I'll have something sent out to you," Gus said, and held out his arm for Cheyenne to take.

Gus considerately kept the pace slow as she worked to navigate the crushed gravel of the drive without turning an ankle in the new shoes Mrs. Davenport had picked out for her. The garments and accessories, held up by the weather, had finally arrived late in the afternoon the day before. Cheyenne had found the black cloak along with a few blouses, a skirt, some underthings, a gorgeous midnight blue frock with elbow-length sleeves, and some silk and lace peignoir sets boxed up with the rest, snuck in by Mrs. Davenport or one of the salesladies.

The made their way along, Gus holding her elbow, past a fancy carriage parked by the walkway leading up.

It was a spectacular contraption with multiple arched windows and not two, but four lanterns. The chocolate color of it shined, accented and made yellowish by the sun's rays hitting the gold trim and embellishments. She peeked inside as they moved past and caught a glimpse of a lavish interior done up in the same burnt orange and gold of the tapestry-like cloth hanging from the driver's seat and the coat of arms on the door. Gus's carriage was nice but this was something else entirely.

"Nice," she remarked.

"Pretentious," Gus responded, and she sputtered a laugh.

It was typical Gus, she was starting to realize. Though well-off himself, at least compared to some, he preferred things understated. Like the house he and his family lived in. It was decent-sized even for the period it was built in but somewhat small for the owners of such a large manufacturing company, who could surely afford loftier accommodations.

But it was their family home. And, as Gus had stated, history meant more than money.

The long porch was empty of visitors, but Cheyenne could hear activity and the murmur of voices within.

Laughter rang out from a dining area to their left as they entered and paused just inside.

She glanced over and met the eyes of a middle-aged lady coming out with a man about the same. The woman, wearing a champagne dress that did nothing to flatter her plump figure, looked down, taking in Cheyenne's outfit and embroidered purse, and Cheyenne was suddenly very glad she'd worn the strappy shoes and turquoise combination—and consented, at Lydia's insistence, to the hat with the bluish green plume now anchored firmly atop her head with hairpins.

The woman, eyes back up, smiled tightly in Cheyenne's direction—apparently she'd passed muster—and continued on across. The man, probably her husband, nodded at Gus and hastened to catch up with her.

Pleased she'd passed inspection and didn't stick out like a sore thumb, Cheyenne relaxed as she waited beside Gus until the other couple had moved away.

She stayed back, more than happy to let Gus take the lead, as he walked to the front desk and greeted the man waiting to receive them. He'd be called dapper, she thought, taking in the clerk's well-cut vest and trousers and hair carefully combed into a slight wave on top. Except for a mustache he was also clean shaven like Gus.

She listened with half an ear while slowly drifting in the direction of the staircase where a hallway branched off the lobby. Gus, after explaining who he was and his affiliation with the new hotel going up, made inquiries about meeting the current owner, and then when that failed, requested to speak with the manager on duty.

As, clearly, it is not you, Gus's glare seemed to say, and after a charged moment the young man hastened to do as bidden and disappeared through the recessed doorway behind him.

Was there a restroom over here? She stopped at the end of the carved wooden counter as Gus glanced over, spotting her. She flashed him a reassuring smile, then when he turned away, started forward again.

By golly, it did look like it was a restroom. Quickening her steps, she moved into the hallway and hurried over. She grasped the knob, found it mercifully unlocked, and pulled the door open.

Moving into the cool, quiet space, she crossed the black-and-white checkered floor, turned the corner, and found a line of stalls. She walked along them, checking each one, until she reached the end.

She was alone. Releasing her breath, she stepped over to a mirror over one of the sinks.

Once again she wished for a bit of makeup, some bronzer at a minimum, for her pale complexion. But at least her hair had withstood the wind, pinned up with the hat as it was. She reached up to tuck a wayward piece back in, then turned and entered the nearest stall, absurdly grateful for it.

A few minutes later, as she was coming across the lobby to rejoin Gus where he stood waiting slightly away from the counter, she remembered Mr. Gilbert's hot drink.

The dapper young man still hadn't reappeared, or else had disappeared again on another errand.

Holding out a hand, Gus took hold of hers when she reached him and led her over to where a group of leather armchairs were arranged around an oval table holding a vase of fresh flowers. Grown in a fancy glass-paneled greenhouse, she imagined as they sat down.

"What did you find out?" she asked in a low voice.

"Nothing yet. The owner is away at his residence and the manager, unfortunately, seems to have stepped out."

"So what are we going to do?"

He drummed his fingers on the arm of his chair. "I'd like to wait. At least for a bit."

They *had* come a long way. It would be a shame to leave with nothing. "I don't mind if we stay for a while."

He glanced at her gratefully. "Thank you, Cheyenne."

"Would you like for me to go and order refreshments for Mr. Gilbert while you wait here?"

"Oh, yes. I'd forgotten. I'm sure he would greatly appreciate that."

"No problem." She went to get up and then paused. "Um ... how shall I pay for it?"

"I suppose," he said, lifting an eyebrow, "they will present the bill to me and I will take care of it."

"Oh, okay." *Remember, this is a different world*, she told herself as she walked away from him. *You don't have to be the responsible one.* It was a strange sensation. In a way, it felt almost ... liberating.

At the entrance to the dining area, she hovered just inside, breathing in the mouthwatering aroma of roasted meats and accompanying dishes. She scanned the room for someone to help her amid the glittering sea of jewelry-laden, well-heeled patrons seated before white-clothed tables holding delicate crystal and china. Feeling self-conscious standing there by herself, basically on display, she was about to give up and retreat, when a male server with a luxurious mustache to rival Jasper's wearing a long white apron over his trousers appeared and wound his way over to her.

"Table for one?" he inquired, stopping before her.

"Oh, no. I just need to order something for our driver."

At "our driver" she received several quick glances and more than one set of ears cocked in her direction.

"And what would he like?" the server asked, flipping open a small silver-cased notepad.

She tried to keep her voice down while still making it audible to him. "Um … a club sandwich, I suppose? If you have that." The ones she and Gus had eaten had been delicious. "Chicken and bacon and so forth on toasted bread? And to drink maybe …" She paused as she tried to decide if Mr. Gilbert would prefer coffee or tea again.

"Our hot cocoa is especially popular," the server helpfully suggested. "The men often partake of it."

Hot chocolate on a cold day. According to the book on polar exploration she'd perused in Gus's office, some of the early expeditions had sworn by it. "Perfect. Hot cocoa and a club sandwich."

"And how will you be …?" His voice trailed away.

She took his meaning instantly. She motioned with her head toward Gus in the lobby where he waited. "Mr. Moore, Mr. Augustus Moore, will take care of it."

The man practically clicked his heels together. "Of course. I will see to everything myself if you would like to wait in here or perhaps—"

"I'll wait out there."

"Very good." He gave a slight bow and withdrew.

She escaped into the lobby, glad the hard part was over. She didn't want to go all the way back to Gus just yet, so she wandered over in the direction of the entrance. She thought about going outside, then discarded the idea. She didn't want to miss the server when he came back.

She wondered how Mr. Gilbert was faring. Had he climbed into the carriage to wait?

Unbidden, thoughts of her family and how they might be doing flickered across her mind. *No,* she thought, quickly shoving them away. *Not now.*

The front doors opened, emitting a nattily dressed man along with a burst of cool air. Right behind him, throwing a hand out to catch the door he'd failed to hold, came an equally mousy young woman. Cheyenne instantly pegged her as his date and also way out of her league. The woman had on a dress more suitable for warmer months that might have once been nice but now hung shapeless on her too thin frame. And her black shoes, probably chosen to match her handbag and wrap, looked more suitable for church, or maybe a funeral.

Cheyenne saw the woman's eyes dart nervously toward the dining room beyond and felt a twinge of sympathy for her. She knew what it was like to feel out of place.

Acting like he had all night and the world was his oyster, the slick-looking man—his hair appeared literally oiled—stuck his hands in his pockets, grinning cockily, and bounced on his heels as he gazed around him. Appearing entirely too pleased with himself, he continued to look around and ignore the lady's discomfort, even when she sidled closer and plucked at his sleeve.

Take her hand or give her your arm, Cheyenne thought at him. Why had he brought her there? Was he that thoughtless?

Cheyenne moved away while trying to keep a surreptitious eye on them and perched herself on the edge of a chair with a good view of the tables beyond.

Still disregarding the young lady, the man finally turned and sauntered over to the dining room. Stopping only briefly in the doorway to catch the attention of a female server Cheyenne hadn't seen yet, he continued on in, leaving the young woman to awkwardly follow behind him.

The waitress, or maybe she was the hostess, stopped and held out an arm to indicate a small table not far in. It looked like Slick was going to protest, but then he shrugged and sat down, leaving his poor date standing there.

Cheyenne could see the man's eyes roll even from where she was as he got to his feet again, waited for the young woman to sit down, and with mocking, exaggerated care, pushed her chair up.

Without seeing her face, Cheyenne knew she had to be mortified. She wanted to go over and smack him. Or her, for not getting up and walking out. But to be fair, maybe she was worried about how she would get home.

Cheyenne was so absorbed in the young woman's plight, imagining her disappointment after anticipating a magical night out with such a handsome catch, only to have him treat her so shabbily, that she didn't notice the server who'd taken her order until he was practically right in front of her.

"Here we go. Shall I carry it out for you?"

"No, thank you. I'll take it." It would give her a chance to stretch her legs some more.

She carefully accepted the tray laden with sandwich, cup, and carafe, and inclined her head at Gus, now pacing back and forth in front of the desk. "Mr. Moore. And thank you."

"Oh, it was my pleasure," he replied, giving her a cheeky grin, and pivoted away.

Well, well, it appeared Gus wasn't the only who could attract an admiring glance.

On her way by the dining area, she looked in and saw Slick finishing off his first drink and signaling for another. The pink cocktail by the young lady's elbow, however, had barely been touched.

She parked the refreshments on another oval table, this one holding a lamp, got the door open, retrieved the tray, and moved out onto the porch.

The door closed behind her as she crossed over, noticing how far the sun had traveled across the sky. Placing each foot carefully, she descended the steps. It was going to be dark by the time they made it back.

At the end of the walkway, she moved onto the circular drive and crunched her way down to the carriage. A smaller buggy and horse, most likely Slick's, now sat carelessly parked behind Gus's.

She had halfway expected Mr. Gilbert to be sacked out inside, but she found him in his usual spot, though he had taken the liberty of lying over with a bunched-up robe under his head. It didn't look very comfortable, but from the volume of the rumbling sounds he was making, he wasn't too bothered by his hunched position.

"Mr. Gilbert," she said, stopping below him.

He instantly awoke and pushed himself into a sitting position.

She held out the tray. "I have you some hot cocoa and a sandwich."

"Bless you, dear," he said, straightening his cap. "That will be very welcome indeed."

"I SUPPOSE WHILE we're here we should take advantage of the dining facilities."

Her eyes slid across the room to the entrance, where even now the male half of an older couple watched them curiously through the opening.

"If you don't mind, can we get going after you meet with him?" She'd come back in after spending a few minutes with Mr. Gilbert to find Gus still waiting for the manager, whom the clerk had reassured him would be back any minute.

Gus glanced over at the crowd of patrons eating and drinking and nodded. "Of course. Whatever you wish."

"You better believe it," she retorted.

He grinned in response, and she looked over, catching movement beyond him, and saw the gauche young lady who'd made the mistake of accepting an invitation from Mr. Slick—only she hadn't counted on being taken to a *hotel*—lurch through the doorway and start across the lobby.

Cheyenne, and Gus, who turned to see what she was gaping at, were so startled they could only stare as her male companion, surprisingly nimble considering the drinks he'd likely put down, came after her and caught her on the other side. He grabbed her shoulder and spun her around.

"Where do you think you're going?" he hissed, his voice clearly audible.

"I want to go home!" the young lady cried, sounding near tears.

He stepped closer. "Keep your voice down. You're making a scene!"

The young woman, hand over her mouth, shook her head back and forth.

"Christ," Slick said, then took hold of her arm and dragged her over to the side. "Listen," he said, lowering his voice, but not enough to keep them from hearing. "I brought you to a nice place here and Lord knows what I'm paying for that meal. Now get a hold of yourself and stop your sniveling!" He whipped out a handkerchief and thrust it at her.

Taking it, she dabbed at her tears and gave one last hiccup. "Thank you for dinner," she said in a heartbreakingly small voice. "But now I would like to go home."

Cheyenne gritted her teeth as she listened to the poor woman thank the jerk who so obviously felt the gift of his company and money for a fine dinner was something precious he'd bestowed upon her.

It was the oldest show on earth, and Cheyenne watched in growing disbelief as the man skillfully changed tactics.

"All right, come on now," he said, pulling her to him. He took the handkerchief from her and wiped at her face tenderly. "I think you and I could have something special. And we've got the whole rest of the night together. Let's not ruin it. All right?"

Mutely, the woman nodded, gazing at him with moist eyes. Cheyenne could *feel* her wanting to believe him.

Cheyenne stole a glance at Gus and knew he was taking in everything as well.

What Slick said next was lost as the dapper clerk appeared behind the counter and beckoned for Gus. "Mr. Chapman has returned and will see you now."

"... and we can order up some room service. Maybe some champagne ..." Cheyenne caught from Slick as Gus started forward. The young man had been steadily urging the woman backward and they were now nearly at the staircase.

"No!" the poor woman wailed. "I told you ..."

Cheyenne thought Gus was going to ignore what was happening right in front of them, but then at the last second before rounding the counter, he held a finger up at the clerk and veered away toward Slick and the young lady.

Oh shit, Cheyenne thought, heart leaping. She moved over to the counter and began following it as Gus came up behind the well-oiled man and his young captive.

"Sebastian!" Gus boomed in a loud voice. "Sebastian Crane, is that you?"

And indeed it must have been, because the young man whirled around, and upon seeing Gus, put himself in front of the woman as if to hide her. Cheyenne watched several emotions—irritation, consternation, and finally alarm—cross his features before he masked them.

"Augustus!" Only the faint tremor in his voice revealed his nervousness. He moved up to shake Gus's hand. "Fancy seeing you here."

"I thought that was you," Gus said. "How long has it been? Seven, eight years? The last time I saw you, you were, what, fifteen or sixteen?"

"Something like that." Sebastian kept his eyes forward and gave no reaction to the sound of the young lady turning and clacking her way unsteadily over to the restroom.

"I heard you were thinking of joining your father in his little mining venture in South America."

She began to sense Gus's aim as Sebastian answered him in the affirmative and they continued to chat back and forth. Gus made no mention of Cheyenne and asked Sebastian nothing about the young lady. It was all very casual. But he did mention Lydia and her impending excursion when she would certainly be paying a call on Sebastian's mother while she was out.

To which, Sebastian responded stiffly, "We shall look forward to it," his genial mask slipping a bit.

"And now I'm afraid I really must go," Gus told him. "And I believe you"—he smiled meaningfully—"have a young lady to drive home."

Without waiting for a reply, Gus touched the brim of his hat, bid him good night, and strode away.

Oh, he was good, she thought, admiring his skillful handling of the situation as he walked past, giving her a wink, and joined the waiting clerk.

Twenty-seven

After what felt like an interminable length of time but was probably no more than fifteen or twenty minutes, Augustus pulled open the door of the carriage, where she had gone to wait, and joined her inside. A grim-faced Sebastian and his unfortunate date had already passed by her, got into their buggy, and wrestled their way out from between Gus's and a trap that had pulled up behind them.

"What did he say?" she asked as Mr. Gilbert began maneuvering them out.

"Nothing, and everything," Gus replied enigmatically, sitting back in the seat across from her.

"It seems," he continued. "That although Helena's Mr. Ravenoff did indeed work here, it was not in the capacity of manager. Nor was it even as concierge. The only position he technically held was of night clerk, though I did get the impression that Mr. Ravenoff, possibly because he worked the evening shift almost solely alone—"

"Calling the shots," she inserted.

"Yes—had let his head be swelled by this, which led to a disagreement with a prominent guest, and he was subsequently let go. Mr. Chapman had quite a bit to say on the subject."

"So Mr. Ravenoff was fired. I wonder if Helena knows this. And that he was really only the desk clerk."

"That," Gus said, "is the question. Did the man merely embellish his past experience and Helena never checked and has no idea? Or does she and Leonard know who this character really is and just aren't concerned?"

Cheyenne nodded. "And why wouldn't they want the very best candidate for the job in order to give the whole endeavor the greatest chance of success?"

"Precisely. It doesn't look good."

"No, it doesn't. What else did you find out about our self-proclaimed manager?"

"Very little. Mr. Chapman said he took a chance when he hired him, and regretted it soon after. There was some kind of incident—he didn't really go into detail about it—involving a missing piece of jewelry. Anyway, Mr. Ravenoff listed a few schools and a previous address in San Francisco when he was hired and not much else. Nothing to help us."

"Unless we want to jump a"—she almost said plane—"train and travel a few thousand miles to check it out."

"Which not many people are going to be willing to do. And which I find a little too convenient."

She adjusted her position. Her right leg was already going to sleep. It was going to be a long ride home. "So what we know is ..." She began ticking things off on her fingers. "From the beginning, the whole thing was hinky. The plans were vague, the building contractor unknown, the bid too low. Second, construction was never started. Third, we've been told a lie about the background of the main candidate for the running of the operation, who is not actually qualified and might be a bit shady. And lastly ... What else?"

Gus let out a sigh. "It's just that when you look at all of it together ... At the time, it seemed like a sound enough investment, with someone I trusted. Someone I basically grew up in the same circles with. But Helena marrying this unknown Leonard out of the blue—it did seem odd."

"What do you know about him?"

"Not much. Only that she met him while staying with some friends of hers. Wealthy ones she was doubtlessly mooching off of."

"So he's not from around here?"

"Not that I'm aware of. No one's ever heard of him, which is bad enough. And then if you add in the fact that neither Helena, nor this husband of hers, seem to have any money of their own to speak of, though they have been pretty adroit at hiding it."

"Helena has no money?" This added a particularly compelling dimension to the whole thing.

"It's not well known but the house and property left to Helena are in danger of being seized for back taxes. I have a friend who has a contact at the county office who says she is nearly five years behind."

"Is this why you agreed to help her?"

"*No*. I wasn't aware of it then. It was to be an *investment* that would pay off in the future."

"Okay, so Helena is probably broke, as is her new husband, you suspect. So why not build the hotel?"

"It would take up to three years for the place to show a profit."

Ohhh. "Too long to save her ancestral home."

"Right." Mouth set in a grim line, Gus shook his head again in disgust.

Cheyenne tried to make sense of this, but the day had been a long one and she could feel herself sinking as a heavy weariness overtook her. "But if she uses the funds to keep her home, wouldn't she and her husband eventually be imprisoned for fraud?"

"Yes, I imagine they would. It really doesn't seem like a viable option."

No, it didn't. And ... Her thoughts drifted and whatever else was tugging at the back of her mind slipped away. She was simply too tired to complete the connection. But then she remembered how disingenuous Perry had seemed when confronted by Gus. "Wait, wouldn't she need help for all of this? With the legal stuff and the permits and the rest of the red tape? She had to have had help from someone to make it appear legitimate."

"You mean Perry."

"Yes. He must have helped if she *is* trying to pull something. What's going on with him? Anything rumored recently?"

Gus looked off to the side and gave a vague shake of his head. "I only know of one thing. But I can scarcely believe that he would be involved in anything like this. It's ludicrous. His wife is from a prominent family, he has a lucrative practice. Not to mention we have been friends for over twenty years."

"His *wife* is from a prominent family," Cheyenne pointed out. "Is he under her family's thumb perhaps and resents it?"

"It's true that his father-in-law is frequently a source of contention, but—"

"What else? What else were you alluding to? You said you only know of one thing."

"It's not anything I really know for certain. It's only what I've observed in the past."

"Which was?" she prompted, sensing this was important.

Gus drooped as if admitting defeat. "He has a penchant for the horses."

"For the horses?" she echoed.

"At the track. He likes to bet on them."

Ahhh. She nodded, contemplating this. "Has he lost big lately?"

"I have no idea. But I wonder."

AS ANTICIPATED, THE ride home was long and uncomfortable—her blasted leg kept going numb—and only broken up twice, once to rest the horses at the same pump and trough they'd used on their way up, and then for a quick supper at the café they'd ridden by on their way through Piedmont.

Cheyenne was so weary she felt nearly dizzy and had trouble keeping her eyes open as the thin older woman on duty—she'd been about to close up but seemed happy enough to accommodate them—set down their plates of roast beef with potatoes and carrots and crusty bread. Mr. Gilbert had followed them in this time and sat at his own table by the windows looking out onto the street.

It wasn't nearly as busy as it had been earlier that day, but there was still a fair amount of traffic moving by.

On the hill across from them sat the impressive structure with the double verandah she'd noticed on their way in. She watched as a large carriage, which had been moving steadily up the steep lane across from them, came to a stop in front of the grand structure and the distant figures of the driver and another man who'd come out began unloading trunks and bags from it.

While she ate, she mulled over everything they'd discussed, and what they hadn't. Her mind kept coming back to what Myrna had said that day in the cemetery. *He needs you.* And to the image of Gus's tombstone rising above it all.

He needs her for what? To help uncover Helena's scheme and stop her from embezzling the investment money?

She forked up a last bite of roast beef—her plate was still half full but she was already stuffed—and picked up her glass for a sip of the sweet tea she'd immediately ordered when she saw it was offered. Gus, deep in his own thoughts, continued to work on his food.

The feeling of dread concerning the fate of Gus and his family and what her role was in this mad situation she found herself in, temporarily dampened by the excitement of their journey to The Sutherland and what it might lead to, had returned with a vengeance. *But why?* They had found out in time to stop Helena, if she was up to something. So what was it?

It's not enough, she finally admitted to herself. Gus had said that the loss of the money he'd given to Helena wouldn't ruin him. He'd explained further that the latest banking panic, only two years before, had prompted him (though not Henry and Daniel) to keep his investment somewhat low. It *was* tied in, she sensed, to whatever happened to him, but there had to be more.

If she were there in her time right then would she look at Gus's tombstone and see that the date of his death had changed?

She couldn't be sure, of course—but somehow she doubted it.

A few minutes later after Gus, also not wanting to linger, quickly settled their bill, they were stepping out into the wind to get back on the road.

Her mood remained pensive as they rode along and the sun disappeared behind the trees and the light faded from the sky.

Inside the carriage the shadows grew until there was nothing but the diffuse glow of the lanterns shining in. Gus didn't seem any more inclined to talk than she did and lay against the side of the carriage with his eyes closed. He was forty-one years old here in this time, the same age as Brent, but in the dim light, he appeared younger.

For whatever reason, she was here, and unless she did something about it, in only six years' time he would die. And she would lose him, perhaps forever.

Eventually, she stretched out the best she could and lay over with one of the lap robes and tried to rest.

But this time sleep eluded her and she remained awake, exhausted but unable to turn off her turbulent thoughts.

What seemed like hours later when she finally heard and felt the crunch of rocks beneath them as they turned into the driveway, she nearly wept with relief.

They jerked to a stop, and she shoved the door open, dragged herself out, not waiting on Gus, and nearly fell stepping down. Stifling a cry, she caught herself and then lurched toward the steps. Her hat, askew now on her wilting hair, tilted precariously as she planted her foot on the bottom step and grasped the handrail.

Gus, not far behind, followed her up, across the verandah, and into the house while Mr. Gilbert drove the horses around the side.

"I'm going on up," she told him, heading straight for the staircase.

He murmured assent, sounding as exhausted as she was, and turned to speak to Myrna, who had come into the foyer upon hearing them.

As quickly as she was able, Cheyenne climbed the stairs and followed the hallway to her room. She grabbed one of the peignoir sets—white silk with pink lace—walked back down, and ducked into the blessedly empty bathroom.

A quarter of an hour later, after sticking her head out to make sure no one was approaching, she scurried back to her room and pushed the door most of the way to.

It had become her habit to join Augustus in his turret and then his room for most of the night before returning to the pink room sometime before dawn, but tonight she was so exhausted all she could think about was going straight to sleep.

She was climbing under the covers when he slipped into the room and approached the bed.

He stood over her, an indistinct shape in the dimness. "Goodnight," he said. He reached down and smoothed the hair out of her face, then leaned over and placed a kiss on her brow. "Sleep well."

"Goodnight. You too." She stifled a yawn. "Love you."

He went still for a moment, and then gently tugged the covers up. "I love you too, Cheyenne," he replied softly. And then he was gone.

Twenty-eight

Gus was already up and trying to place a call when Cheyenne came down the stairs the following morning.

From the sound of it he had successfully connected with Perry's office but was failing miserably at reaching the actual man himself.

"Explain to me, Madame," Gus barked into the mouthpiece in front of him as she glided silently past. "What exactly is the purpose of having a telephone if *no one can ever be reached on it!*"

On the other side of the opening to the largish space devoted to the household's laundry, empty for the moment, she paused and looked back at him standing before the boxy wooden instrument.

"Fine!" he shouted, and jammed the receiver he was holding to his ear down onto the hook.

He turned toward her, his face flushed with anger and eyes gone cold and flat, and for a brief instant before he registered her presence, she caught a glimpse of the tremendous emotions boiling beneath the surface.

As all six foot two masculine feet of him stood there gazing back at her without really seeing her, it struck her again that this was not a man to be messed with. This was a strong, powerful man from a harsh time in some regards that she barely knew.

A shiver of something very like fear as well as desire, rippled down her spine as she stood there rigidly.

And then she was crossing the floor to go to him.

He caught her as she threw herself against him, and fell back onto the wall with her.

Burying his hand in the hair at the back of her neck, he clamped his mouth onto hers, stifling the little cry she made, and kissed her hungrily, almost angrily, until she was gasping for breath.

She wrenched herself away and stepped back, shooting a look each way to make sure no one had seen their disgraceful display. Breathing raggedly, she attempted to tuck the hair he'd disturbed back in while Gus, with his right leg bent and boot propped behind him, grinned at her with the same slightly too self-satisfied smile she'd seen before.

"Oh, stop it," she snapped, swatting at him.

"What?" Laughing, he pushed away from the wall and straightened up. "I *was* thinking we might go out again, pay a few visits and make some inquiries, but if you have something else you would rather do, I assure you, I am more than willing."

He came toward her, smiling lecherously and waggling his eyebrows.

"Cut it out," she cried, snickering and trying to evade him as he reached out for her, making exaggerated "gimme" motions with his fingers.

Agnes picked that moment to step out into the hall, and both Cheyenne and Gus jumped to attention, going silent and wiping their face of expression. Which immediately struck them both as funny and caused them to crack up again.

"I'm glad to see someone has something to laugh about around here," Agnes announced in her lilting burr and, with a scowl, disappeared back into the kitchen.

Gus reached for her again and this time she let him pull her close. "Thank you, Cheyenne," he murmured against the top of her head.

"For what?"

"For being you." He released her and stepped back. "Oh, and," he said as she turned to move away, "you might want to"— he twirled a finger at her hair—"make some adjustments."

She attempted to tuck the strands in again, then gave it up. She was going to need the help of a mirror, and possibly one of the girls. "When I get back down I'm going to require some coffee."

He gestured at the library on the other end. "I've already had some brought in. Please help yourself. And then as soon as I try to reach Henry, I'd like to get going, if you don't mind."

"Of course." She went to walk away then turned back. "Don't leave without me."

DID SHE DETECT something even then that made her sense her time there was short? That this day might be the last one they had? Or was it merely her ever increasing obsession to figure out and stop whatever horrible thing she felt sure fate had in store for Augustus? For she didn't want to be away from him, not for a minute, if it meant there was a chance she might be able to stop what she could feel building over their heads like a thickening storm cloud. And she now knew she had fallen deeply and passionately in love with him. In some ways, he was a hard man full of depths and shadows, but he was also a loving man, capable of sweetness and laughter.

She hurriedly attended to her hair, gulped down a cup of coffee along with a delicious, jam-smeared sort of griddle cake that Agnes called a crumpet when she dared to ask, and was standing by the front doors when Gus came into the foyer.

"We'll get Henry first," he said, dropping his hat onto his head. "No need in all of us going separately. Then we can swing by Daniel's."

"What's the plan, then?" she asked, following him out and down the steps to where Mr. Gilbert waited with the carriage.

The plan was for them to grab Henry, which they did in short order (he lived fairly close by), and then to swing by Daniel's on the way into town where they hoped to catch Perry at his office.

Henry's family seemed a bit more well off than Daniel's and also had a telephone, which Cheyenne gathered was still somewhat rare even for fairly well-to-do people, and as a result was ready and watching for them when they arrived.

Daniel, on the other hand, did not have a phone and had to be waited on while he finished dressing, which took a good twenty minutes, according to the pocket watch Henry kept pulling out and checking. Despite his calm, relaxed manner, she could tell he was worried.

Henry, who up close didn't look a day over thirty, was expensively dressed it appeared to Cheyenne's critical eye but in a casual, offhand way which somehow, compared to Daniel's decidedly fussy suit and high white collar when he finally climbed in, still managed to convey a greater, more innate elegance.

The men's mindsets were in accordance about one thing, though, and that was their determination to get to the bottom of things and circumvent any mismanaging of funds which could prove disastrous for both of them.

Henry leaned over to retrieve his hat from the floor where it had fallen. "Oh, pardon me," he said when he bumped her knee, clad in one of Lydia's older dresses. Though quite flattering and not too ostentatious, which is why she'd worn it, the bodice of the dress was cut a bit low—with only sheer lace covering it to the neckline—and was borderline scandalous at this point in time when despite it being quite fashionable to show off one's cleavage in previous decades, it was now deemed inappropriate for women to flaunt their breasts or even show a bit of leg.

"Oh, you're good," she murmured without thinking, then had to remind herself once again to try and talk the way they did as Henry shot a glance at her. What should she have said? *Oh, that's quite all right*, maybe?

Daniel was a handsome man despite his somewhat prim manner and small rimless glasses he wore hanging from a chain, and despite the yellowish remnant of a fading bruise on one check. But Henry, now, he was almost on par with Gus with his tan skin that spoke of hours spent outdoors on some lawn or boat and wavy sun-bleached hair, cut short on the sides and left slighter longer on the top that he'd tried unsuccessfully to part down the center. But whereas Gus's confidence in his effect on the fairer sex held the capacity for a deeper, long-term connection, she sensed this might be lacking in Henry as of yet, whom she suspected left a trail of broken hearts wherever he went.

She shifted around so she could look out the window, taking in a deep breath, and in the reflection saw Daniel's eyes, which had strayed to her straining bosom, widen and quickly dart away.

A giggle bubbled up within her, and she had to clap a gloved hand over her mouth to cover it with a cough. She wondered what he would think if he could see some of the Real Housewives from the show she occasionally watched with their dresses cut to the navel and their tits bursting out.

She cut her eyes at Gus and caught him gazing sidelong at her, one side of his mouth quirked up.

Henry, who was smirking and must have also noticed the reason for her amusement, suddenly barked, "What's wrong with you?" and kicked her foot.

She let out a yelp, surprised at his audacity but also delighted. She knew it was only his deep friendship with Gus, which had now been extended to her, that had allowed such familiarity.

"Nothing's wrong with me." Grinning, she switched her attention to Daniel, who had turned a faint shade of pink. "How are you doing, Daniel?" she teased him.

Gus rumbled with laughter beside her.

Danial, rising to the occasion (no pun intended), looked over at her and grinned. "Oh, I'm doing just dandy," he drawled, and tipped her a wink.

They all laughed. It helped to loosen the tension in the carriage and everyone seemed to relax after that as they made their way toward town. *They've accepted me*, she thought. She felt like she'd been admitted into some exclusive club, and she found herself warming to both of the other men. She could see why Gus was such close friends with them. And why it would anger him so much that his two best friends were possibly going to be hurt by his recommendation to invest with Helena.

"Seriously," Henry said, not for the first time, as they bumped onto the bridge before the mill, "regardless of what Perry may or may not have to say, our investments need to be protected. What's another few weeks' delay while we reevaluate things? Any minute they could—"

"I know," Gus interrupted. "Let's see what he has to say for himself first, and what we can discover at the bank."

Daniel, quiet for the past few minutes, looked at Henry. "Have you spoken to Donovan?"

Donavan, Cheyenne had gathered, was Henry's friend and also a solicitor.

Henry hesitated, glancing at Gus across from him.

Gus narrowed his eyes. "Have you already spoken to him?"

"Yes, I have," Henry replied. "But only briefly. I gave him a rundown of the situation as it stands and voiced my concerns."

"And?"

"And he's going to be ready to move if I give the word. He's preparing to seek an injunction to freeze the funds. If necessary."

Gus let out a sigh and shook his head. "I hope it doesn't come to that. But I fear it might."

"As do I," Daniel agreed.

"ACCORDING TO THAT draconian receptionist out front," Henry informed them as he climbed back in after trying his luck. "He just stepped out for an early lunch."

Gus lifted up to bang on the roof of the carriage, then motioned for Mr. Gilbert to move up and turn down the side street ahead. "She may be covering for him."

"Or he's returned home for lunch," suggested Daniel.

Gus got Mr. Gilbert's attention again and pointed over to an empty lot down the lane running behind this block's buildings. "They usually keep the rear door open for the associates. I can get in that way."

"I'm going with you," Henry said.

"*We're* going with you," Daniel corrected. "You're not leaving me out."

"Well, I'm staying in the carriage," Cheyenne said. She wanted to know what was going on just as much as they did, but it seemed ridiculous, not to mention conspicuous, for all four of them to go waltzing in when they didn't even know if Perry was there or not. Plus, anything they learned they would share with her.

"Are you sure you'll be all right?" asked Gus before getting out once they'd come to a stop.

"I'll be fine," she reassured him, touched at his concern.

"I'll be right back," he said. "If you need anything, you have Mr. Gilbert." He leaned over, gave her a quick kiss, and then climbed out, letting the door swing shut behind him.

She watched as he strolled across the small lane to join Henry and Daniel where they waited. After a brief exchange, first Gus and then the other two stepped into an inset entryway between the arched windows and went in through a nondescript door, which was indeed unlocked.

The seconds and then the minutes ticked by. It was beginning to look like Perry *had* been hiding in his office. Had she made a mistake staying in the carriage? She imagined Gus and the other men bursting in and hotly accusing him, possibly getting physical, and Perry pulling a pistol out of the desk drawer and—

The carriage door opening jerked her out of her grim vision. It was Mr. Gilbert, checking on her.

"Anything I can do for you, Miss Tanner?" he asked. Mr. Gilbert, who did like to keep things proper, insisted on calling her by her last name, which Gus had provided to him after inquiring it of her. Out of habit she had given her legal name but she had no idea if anyone other than Gus knew she was technically married. Though, if you thought about it, since it would be over a hundred years from now before the ceremony actually took place, she could sort of be considered single. At this moment in time.

"No, thank you," she answered him with a smile. He was such a kind and capable gentleman—always flawlessly performing his duties, impeccably put together and with nary a complaint. She hoped Gus paid him a decent salary. "I'm fine right now. How are you?"

He appeared thrown by the question, as if unsure how to answer and slightly embarrassed. Finely he gruffly responded, "I'm doing well, thank you. Could be worse."

Yes, she thought, *it could,* picturing what was to come in future years as he moved away to check on the horses. World War I, then the Great Depression, followed by World War II.

She tried to recall what year the first world war had begun. 1914? 1915? Either way that was twenty years from now. Much too late for it to be what happened to Gus.

Six years from now, she thought. Six years and then he dies. But how? And why?

Twenty-nine

Cheyenne sat in one of the chairs by the hearth, luxuriating in the warmth of the fire. They were in the library having a drink before Gus drove the boys home.

"So there we were," Henry recounted, making it sound like a rollicking good time full of adventure. "I'm barely out of sight in a doorway, Gus is four steps up the stairs, and Daniel's—" He broke up at this and had to stop for a second. "Daniel's pressed up against a statue of Lady Justice." He looked over at Daniel. "I'm sure that was hard for you."

"Ha, ha," Daniel retorted.

All of them laughed.

"And we hear her coming." Henry pitched his voice higher to sound like a strident, older woman. "*Who's there! We do* not *allow unannounced visitors!*" He switched back to his normal voice. "And I'm looking at Daniel and positively convulsing trying not to laugh. Thank God we weren't in plain view because that battle-axe rounded the corner like a battering ram." He turned to Cheyenne. "It was a good thing you didn't come with us, because I don't know where you would have hidden."

"I've had a few experiences with the indomitable Mrs. Grigsby," inserted Gus. "Had she not been called back to the front, I shudder to think what kind of wrath might have been wrought upon us."

Unlike the back door to the law firm, Perry's personal office had not been left unlocked. The men had been hanging around, quietly arguing about whether or not to try and pick the lock, when they'd heard Mrs. Grigsby approaching. If she had continued on down the hall, they would have surely been discovered, but luckily someone had called out for her and she'd turned around, giving them time to flee back out the way they'd come in.

"It is suspicious, though," Daniel said, lifting his glass for a small sip of the whiskey he'd barely touched. "How hard to find Perry has suddenly become."

"Indeed it is," Gus agreed, a cloud settling over his face. "Very suspicious. And I think it's high time we took appropriate measures."

The rest of them exchanged nervous glances. Did he mean calling Donavan in or …?

"Henry," Gus said, rising from his chair. "You go ahead and contact your man and arrange for him to meet us at eight sharp in the morning."

He turned back to Daniel. "At least we've caught them in time if your acquaintance at the bank was right and there haven't been any recent withdrawals."

Daniel had been sent in when they'd approached and seen the young lady, who was supposedly sweet on him, behind one of the open windows.

"She's only a teller," Daniel protested, pushing his glasses up. "All she could say for certain was that to her knowledge no one has taken any large amounts out recently."

They had also checked all the eating establishments nearby and ridden by Perry's house on the other side of town, where the maid who answered the door claimed she had not seen him since that morning. And on the way back, desperate for the day to have not been a total waste, they'd even made their way up the narrow drive that wound through Helena's estate to the two-story, white-columned home she shared with her new husband. But that had been fruitless, as well. The housekeeper, curt to the point of rudeness according to Gus, had snapped that both Helena and Leonard were out and shut the door in his face.

"There's nothing more we can do right now," Gus said, and tossed back the last of his drink. "If you gentlemen are ready?"

Cheyenne got up and followed Gus into the foyer while they readied themselves to leave. "I shouldn't be too long," he said, sliding his arms into his coat.

She stepped in to give him a quick hug. "I'll see you when you get back."

WHEN IT HAPPENED, it happened fast. One second she was heading toward the kitchen to arrange for an early supper to be brought up to the turret after Gus returned, and the next she was staggering as the room tilted and the hair on her head lifted. *NO! Oh no, not yet!*

Throwing an arm out to catch herself, she tried to hold on, fighting against nausea as the floor underneath her feet grew dull, brightened, dulled, then brightened again.

Bringing her head up, she squinted at the spot of light ahead, but it was shrinking, going black until she was nearly in darkness. It had never happened quite like this before, and frightened, she closed her eyes.

No, don't give in to it! she thought, and ripped them back open. She frantically tried to put herself there in that time, with Lydia, Myrna, and the girls, waiting for Gus. *I'm here! I'm here in 1895, and he loves me! He needs me. I can't go back! Not now. Stay,* she willed herself. *Stay, stay.*

But it was no use. She could feel herself being pulled away. With a roar that swelled and threatened to deafen her, everything went blindingly white.

And then she was falling onto her knees.

For a long moment she remained where she was on the now old and worn floor, breathing in and out heavily.

She couldn't believe it. How fast it had happened. One minute she was there, she was *there.* And now ... It was all gone. They were all gone. Gus, Lydia, and Celia, Myrna, and the girls, Henry and Daniel, and everyone else. Gone. Long gone. And she was alone again in this cold, decaying ruin where he was lost to her. Perhaps forever.

She lifted her head. The eerily quiet, shadowy hallway stretched out before her, brighter on the end where the light streamed through.

She didn't even know if she had landed in her own time. How awful that would be if she'd ended up in the wrong decade and had lost not only Gus but everyone she knew and loved in her own world, as well.

She had failed him. Gus was dead and buried and would never look upon the world and smile and love and laugh again. With no one left to remember him. As if he had never existed.

A tear trickled down her cheek.

No, not as if he never existed. He might be gone but her love for him remained and would never be forgotten or taken away as long as she lived.

But it hadn't been enough.

An image floated into her mind of him smiling from ear to ear as they rocketed downward in the sleigh, and pain squeezed her heart.

She got to her feet, tears dripping down her cheeks, more exhausted than she'd ever been, and turned in a slow circle. The front doors were closed, the entire house silent around her. It seemed abandoned. But for how long? Wiping her eyes, she drifted forward. Did it even matter? Because of fate, providence, or just plain luck, she had been allowed to share Gus's life for a while, but it was over now and might never happen again.

And she was tired. She was so very tired.

She stopped before the front doors and looked over at the library and then across to the parlor.

Both appeared the way she remembered them. Dusty, nearly empty, curling wallpaper. She moved through the archway into the larger front room and approached the windows facing the walkway and drive. The curtains were all closed except for the gauzy panels in the center, which were parted precisely the way she'd left them.

Marginally encouraged, she turned and walked across the room, past the chaise lounge in the center, and through the far archway into the hallway beyond. If she had been dropped back into her own time, that would at least be something. She wouldn't be lost in an alien world with nothing familiar and no one to turn to.

Except for the faint echo of her footsteps, the house remained silent as she took the smaller passageway to the inner parlor.

After giving a cursory glance around and seeing nothing obviously amiss, she moved over to look behind the sofa.

And there sat her bigger bag and purse, with her keys on top. Right where she'd tossed them after coming back in from getting the pepper spray. Shoulders slumping in relief, she closed her eyes, bowing her head.

Then she grabbed the keys and stashed them in her purse in case she had to make a quick getaway. Her laptop and tablet were already in the other bag and anything else she could do without if she had to.

Where was her phone, though? She thought back to that morning, trying to remember where she'd left it. Leaning over the sofa again, she rooted around and found it in the side pocket of her purse.

She pressed the button to awaken it, but the screen remained dark. She pressed it again, this time holding it down to power it on. But again nothing happened. She'd expected as much. The battery would have surely died by now. Which made her think of the car again, left abandoned in the weeds behind the carriage house.

A chill went through her as she contemplated how long it had been since it had been driven.

Giving her head a shake—she wasn't thinking clearly—she reached behind the sofa once again for the keys she needed, and started out of the room. If she was indeed stranded, there was no point in putting it off; might as well get the bad news now.

She went through the sunroom but came to a halt before going out the door as an awful thought occurred to her.

All those years the house had been sitting there with no one vandalizing it or removing any of the remaining items. With no vagrants throwing down trash. No young people partying inside. No graffiti artists marking the walls. And hardly anyone stumbling upon it other than her and the lone patrolman who'd noticed the house when others hadn't. Like it had existed half in a different realm shrouded in mist and resisting discovery somehow when you weren't looking for it.

Feeling weighed down by dread, she forced herself to continue on out and down the steps.

At the bottom she stopped and gazed around her. Even now she could see a white wispiness low on the ground in the forest around her. Was it possible that it had been *years* since she'd been there? That her things, like everything else left in the house when that long-ago ancestor abandoned it, had miraculously remained untouched for who knew how long? It hadn't even occurred to her that this might be the case and with the light being so dim inside the little parlor, she'd failed to notice if there had been any dust or other signs of ageing.

She looked down at her set of keys. Were they dingier? She couldn't tell.

Plowing through the tall brown grass, she trekked uneasily across the yard. She thought she heard the sound of a vehicle in the distance but when she paused, it was gone.

Holding up the skirt of the dress she'd forgotten she was wearing to keep it from dragging in the dirt, she followed the still visible ruts down to the carriage house and veered behind it.

The car looked exactly as she'd left it, with no spots of rust or vines growing up around it or leaves covering it. It couldn't have been very long.

But that didn't tell her exactly how long or if the battery was still good.

Mentally bracing herself, she grabbed the handle and pulled hard on it, halfway expecting the door to stick and then come free with a loud *crack*, but it came open easily as always. She slid into the seat and inserted the key.

It didn't seem like it had been left sitting a long time. She couldn't smell any mold or mildew.

Here goes nothing, she thought, and tried it. The engine immediately turned over, but it didn't catch and died a second later. She tried it again, giving it more gas this time, but it still wouldn't catch. Not wanting to flood it or kill the battery completely, she let off, forced herself to wait a few seconds, and then turned the switch again and pumped the pedal.

She thought it wasn't going to work, but then it kicked over. She kept on the gas, not caring who heard it. Then when she was sure it was going to keep running, she let off and leaned her forehead against the steering wheel.

At least she'd have a way to go. She wouldn't be completely stranded.

Thirty

She waited in despair for two days for there to be some sign, some indication that it was starting again and she might be able to get back. But there was nothing. The house remained empty and mostly silent except for the normal groans and creaks of a structure sinking into oblivion. She heard no sound of footsteps, no faint echo of music. She perceived no current in the air, or rooms from years past seeping in. Only the cold hard concreteness of the scuffed boards, faded drapes, and stained ceilings above her.

Finally she could no longer ignore the missed calls and messages on her phone, and so on the third day, she got cleaned up and left the house.

It felt weird, and rather a letdown, to be wearing regular clothes again. *I could have been happy there*, she thought as she turned into the lot of the Hot Spot.

She would have missed her mother and her brother and Jill, of course, and maybe even Brent in time, and she would always think of her baby Ian. But back there with Gus in the house as it once was in its prime with his family and friends around her, she had felt almost at peace.

You knew you might not get to stay, her mind chided her. It had always been a possibility.

Even if she were somehow able to return to Gus's time, there was a chance she would continue to boomerang back whenever the phenomenon occurred. Or she could get back and it cease for good. There had been periods of rest in the past when there hadn't seemed to be any slippages.

Her luck, she would be jerked back and forth for years like the unfortunate husband in *The Time Traveler's Wife*. She climbed out and grabbed the bag of trash she'd accumulated out of the rear compartment, walked it over to the trash can, tossed it in, and turned to head inside the store.

She came back out a few minutes later armed with a large cappuccino in one hand and in the other, a bag containing a sub sandwich, a bag of chips, a hunk of banana bread probably soaked in preservatives, and a ginger ale.

She maneuvered her way into the car, hit the lock button, and lifted the top off the cappuccino. She had some calls to make and for that she needed fortification.

It wasn't actually as bad as she'd feared, she found out after she checked her missed calls and read and listened to all her messages. Jill had facebooked her to say she might be out of reach the following week because she and Ben were renting a cabin. There was nothing else after that from her, so that was all right.

Her mother had called because she had driven over to Cheyenne's old house when she was unable to reach her but had kept going when she didn't see her car. Which had precipitated a call from her brother wanting to know why she hadn't returned their mother's call and asking who drove the green car he'd seen parked out front when *he'd* driven by. It had been Serena's, of course.

The jig was up, as they say. She was going to have to tell them she'd left the house and that Brent lived there with Serena now. No need to go into all about the new baby necessarily. There'd be time enough for that later.

She waited on two teenage boys to finish crossing in front of her car where she was parked a few slots from the entrance, then broke off a chunk of the banana bread and ate it in between sips of the cappuccino.

She could tell them she had gone away on a spur of the moment girls' trip with Jill—on account of the stress from it all— to a cabin (like Jill and Ben had) where she hadn't been able to get a good signal.

But where was she going to tell them she was staying now? That was the conundrum.

For a brief moment she entertained the idea of saying she was staying in a long unoccupied old house inherited by Felicia, the co-worker she used to eat lunch and occasionally pal around with. But that would mean too many comings and goings if they insisted on visiting. *Just how long*, she thought distantly, *are you willing to remain in an abandoned house in the hope that you might see Gus again?* There was also the chance that her mother or brother might witness or even experience a slippage themselves while on the property, which was even more disturbing.

Eventually, with no better idea, she settled on being vague and telling them she was probably going to be staying with Jill for a while until she sorted things out.

She would have to keep away from their side of town and hope to not run into them. She could still talk to them on the phone without them knowing exactly where she was. And then once she went to work and saved enough money, she could quickly rent a place and act like she'd just returned.

She hated having to lie to them, but there was no other way. She picked up her phone to call her mother first.

OVER AN HOUR later, exhausted, she returned to the house. She bumped her way down to the carriage house, went to turn in, then changed her mind and kept going. She would put the car behind the magnolia. She could just imagine her mother's reaction to her being caught trespassing, *squatting*, in an abandoned house after everything she'd just told her about staying with Jill. They would be ready to cart her off to the loony bin. And that's without her even saying she'd actually been staying there in 1895.

Now that the shock of it all had passed and she had touched base with her mother and Caleb, assuring that neither of them put out a missing person's report—which could result in her keen-eyed deputy, if he did suspect someone had been staying there, putting two and two together—she was feeling less anxious and looking forward to piling up in her sleeping bag for some much-needed rest. Since she'd returned, though she'd felt exhausted much of the time, she'd only been able to sleep in snatches of an hour or two.

She waited until well after dark, keeping watch through the windows she could see out, and then built a small fire and settled herself on the sofa with only the smaller candelabra for light.

She opened her sandwich and took a bite, thinking about the photos of Gus in the attic. *I'll have to take those with me. And maybe the red dress.*

If she could bring herself to leave. *Could* she possibly buy the house? *And then, what, sit there slowly getting old while you wait year after year, growing more and more isolated until you're afraid to leave even for a moment and you're living off apples and pecans from the trees out back?*

Watching the flames, she continued eating as she turned her mind to how strange her return had been this time. Her move from one time to the next had felt more intense but also rougher, more turbulent, like an overheating boiler reaching its limit, and she feared that some peak in the cycle had been reached and had now subsided to a period of low activity.

Maybe it just wasn't meant to be. Maybe her landing back there with Gus had merely been a fluke and had no deeper meaning. For all she knew, the past couldn't be changed and it was pointless to try.

After she'd eaten her fill, she wrapped up the remains of the sandwich, ran upstairs to brush her teeth, then jumped back on the sofa and slid into the sleeping bag.

She turned on her side, tried to relax, and finally let her mind contemplate what might have happened after she disappeared. Did she ever get back? It didn't appear so. She let herself imagine it for a moment: six years going by while Gus waited and watched in vain. And then, somehow, his demise. Could she have been wrong about her showing up in 1895 and Helena's hotel scheme and Gus's death all being tied together? Had she been on the wrong track?

The candles had burned low and the fire turned to embers by the time she finally drifted off to sleep with this and other questions still swirling through her head.

IT HAD GOTTEN pretty cold the night before, though it was warming up fast, and the dew on the grass had turned to ice that was just beginning to melt. She stepped off the walkway and started across, heading for the trail leading to the cemetery. If Gus's headstone had changed it would prove that the past could be altered, although how her short visit, especially considering how ineffective it had been, could have produced such a marked divergence, she couldn't imagine.

She kept an ear out as she hiked over, alert for the sound of anyone approaching, staying to the slightly less overgrown, brighter areas where steam, along with the ever-present mist, rose from the sunlit ground. If she could make it onto the path and up into the trees, she'd be out of sight.

A couple of minutes later she stepped onto the trail, in shadow now where it was colder, and came to a halt. For a second she'd thought she felt something. She squinted around her at the brown and green tangle of pine trees and dormant vegetation. It hadn't felt like a slippage exactly; it had been more like a faint vibration through the ground beneath her.

All was quiet except for the sound of a far-off bird. *You're imagining things*, she told herself, and started forward again.

She hadn't gone more than ten or twelve paces when she felt it once more, and this time, the light around her dimmed and went grayish, as if the color had been leached out of everything, before flickering back to normal.

Her heart leapt. It was happening again! She spun around, desperately scanning for anything, a ripple, or a shimmer in the air to indicate her surroundings were changing.

She was beginning to think she had imagined it again, when like being hit by a gale-force wind, she was struck and sent reeling. She cried out silently as the world around her, the ground, the sky, the woods, revolved sickeningly and the sun and the stars and the moon took turns painting the heavens. It seemed to go on forever—ground, sky, woods, sun, stars, moon—until, swooning, she collapsed onto the path.

The air still felt strange, like the pressure was off—she could feel it in her ears as she lay in the dirt—but the spinning sensation had passed.

Then the weird thickness seemed to lessen, and ears popping, she was able to sit up and get to her feet.

She had to find Gus. Holding back hysterical laughter—she had really thought she'd never see him again—she speeded up until she was running.

Hitting the end of the trail, she burst out of the forest—and skidded to a stop at the sight that greeted her.

It should have been a welcome one. She could tell by the size of the trees around the home that she had landed roughly in Gus's time period. But everything was *wrong*.

The grass was too high. *Left like that since the previous summer?* The bushes hadn't been trimmed. A vine had been allowed to take over and now covered one of the windows. Even worse, only a single skinny trail of smoke rose from one of the chimneys. Normally on a cool morning like this, fires would be blazing in nearly all the rooms as well as the carriage house and barn.

And it was too quiet. She scanned the house and the land around it she could see as she stood there, rooted in place, breath rasping in and out—but she saw no one. Nobody outside, no horses, no buggies. No silhouettes in the windows. Which didn't mean anything necessarily, but it combined with the shocking state of the property filled her with alarm.

She stumbled forward. She had to be in time. She just had to be. Speeding up until she was running again, she pounded across the uncut yard, not slowing until she reached the walkway, and clambered up the steps.

Chest heaving, she paused to catch her breath before going in.

Please let me not be too late, she prayed silently, grasping and twisting the righthand knob—but it wouldn't budge. It was locked.

Dammit! She grabbed one of the knockers and used it to bang on the door.

Shifting back and forth, growing more and more agitated, she forced herself to wait a minute then grabbed the iron ring and banged again.

Finally, she couldn't take it any longer, descended the steps, and headed for the side of the house.

Even before she made it all the way around to the back, she could see there was no activity at the carriage house, either. Both the large doors were shut and there was no sign of Mr. Gilbert or Jasper.

She rounded the corner and came to a stop. Parked behind the house, where it must have come in from the other side, exactly where she had parked her first night there, sat what looked like a cross between an early automobile and a buggy with a folding hood. It had all the characteristics of a small carriage except it had a tiller for steering and was plainly not intended to ever be pulled by a horse.

A horseless carriage, she thought. She shifted her attention away from the disconcerting vehicle and looked over the unkempt yard, field, and track leading to the barn and found them as desolate as the front.

Truly frightened now, she forced herself to walk the rest of the way over to the rear door leading into the sunroom. *If I can't get in it, I can try the one off the kitchen*, she thought.

But she ended up not having to; the door opened right up.

Silently she moved through the sunroom into the dim house, past the kitchen and the dining room. Most of the curtains and drapes had been left drawn despite it being daytime.

What was going on here? Myrna or one of the girls always opened them to let in the warm sunlight.

She continued through the center of the home, beginning to get chilled. It was *cold* in a way it never had been when she'd been there before.

Wrapping her arms about herself, she took the ballroom hallway and passed through the front parlor entrance on this side. Something was off, she noticed partway across. She gazed around the room, and her eyes fell on the grandfather clock against the wall.

She wasn't hearing the tick of the pendulum, she realized. Someone had let it wind down.

Something was very wrong here. She hurried through the wider archway to climb the stairs, and nearly died of fright at the sight of a shadowy figure in the gloom above her. *"Gus?"* she gasped.

The figure started down the staircase, and she saw it was an older man dressed in dark clothing.

He came farther into the light, and her stomach dropped as she took in the black doctor's bag he carried.

Oh, no. Had it already happened?

Before she could utter a word, the man, obviously a physician, spoke. "Good, I'm glad you came. I'm afraid I'm in a terrible hurry and I must be off."

Dimly she remembered Celia mentioning a Dr. Carter as he swept past her. Was this him? And who did he imagine she was? Especially considering she had on nothing but a tunic dress, leggings, and the knee-high leather boots under a long cardigan.

Possibly only now noticing her distress, and what she was wearing, he paused before taking his leave and blinked, his eyes flicking downward. "It was a shame about Miss Myrna. She did her best to take care of him and keep things going."

Her heart sank. But wait … that made no sense. According to the date on her headstone, Myrna had passed away after Gus. "How did she die? I'm afraid I haven't heard."

"Oh, no, she's still in the land of the living, I'm happy to say. She's recovering, slowly, at her sister's I think, from what we believe was a mild case of apoplexy."

She tried to remember exactly what apoplexy was. "Her heart?"

"No." He touched his forehead. "In her brain."

She nodded. A stroke then, possibly. *Thank goodness it was a mild one.*

"But I'm afraid it won't be long for Mr. Moore now." He lifted his chin toward the stairs. "I've left some medication. All we can do is try and keep him comfortable."

Mute, she nodded.

"All right, I'll be waiting to hear word." He gave her a nod, and continued on around.

Swallowing, she managed to utter, "Thank you," to his departing back.

As soon as he'd moved out of sight, she whirled around and took the stairs as fast as she could to the second floor. Crossing the landing, she hurried down a hall that seemed to have gained in length—moving past cobwebs and through pools of darkness beneath unlit sconces—all the way to his room. She burst inside and bit back a scream at what she saw through the faintly smoky dimness. She had to grab hold of a nearby chairback to keep from falling as her legs nearly failed her.

Gus, no longer the handsome, viral man she'd known, lay on twisted sheets, his body wasted below a face pale and lined and hair sweat-dampened and shot with gray.

The man she'd grown to love, who at forty-one had still held the glow of youth, would never be called young again.

"Augustus?" she choked out, trying and failing to smooth the shock from her face.

Though it couldn't have been that long—*six years*, she thought—he looked a decade older than the forty-seven years he was.

"Augustus?" she said again as she crept closer.

His eyes, closed until now, flew open in the dimness.

"Gus, it's me."

With difficulty he turned his head and found her where she stood. With a suddenness that was all the more shocking, he lifted his head, still zeroed in on her, and croaked, "Cheyenne! You're here!"

She started forward as he broke into a fit of coughing.

"*No*," he gasped. "You have to go back!"

"What is it? What's wrong with you?"

"*Cheyenne*," he cried again hoarsely, weakly motioning her away. "You have to stay away. I have consum—" he broke off, coughing again. "Consumption," he finally got out, and fell back on the pillow.

Consumption! Which meant tuberculosis. What was easily cured in her time but was deadly in his. And he had to be in the final stages. "*How*?"

He stared up at the ceiling and made no reply.

"Gus?"

"On holiday," he finally answered, blinking slowly. "With Henry. To help *bring me out of it*. ... But it's no good, now. I'm just about done."

On holiday? she thought, shying away from the rest. Because of losing her? She could see it, though, Henry cajoling Gus into going away for a while to snap him out of it. Or was there something more? "Bring you out of what, Gus?"

A spasm of pain crossed his features. "Losing ... everyone." A dreamy, wistful quality entered his voice. "Gone all these years." His eyes began to flutter shut. "Everything," he murmured thickly. "The mill ... Mother, Cheyenne, and ..."

"I'm right here," she cried. Wait. The mill? Mother? Something had happened to Lydia?

"I thought I saw Cheyenne one day," he murmured, eyes half closed, as if talking to someone else. "In the window ... upstairs."

Unable to stop herself, she made to approach the bed again then stopped as Gus, regaining some of his senses, used what had to be his last bit of precious strength and cried, "No, Cheyenne, *please*!"

"I'm sorry," she said, halting and stretching out a hand. "What happened to your mother, Gus?"

She thought he wasn't going to answer, but then he did. "It was too much for her."

He lay there panting shallowly after that and she thought that was going to be it, but then he opened his eyes and shifted his head slightly to look at her again. "*Cheyyeennne*," he breathed, drawing her name out like he used to. "I have missed you."

A shiver crawled its way up her spine. It was wrong. It was all wrong.

As if he knew what she was thinking, he turned his head away after a second. "But I'm afraid ..." He paused to take in a few breaths. "I'm afraid the hour has grown late." His voice faded to a murmur and he seemed to forget she was there again. "All gone ... Mother ... and Cheyenne ... and ..."

She slowly backed away. He mumbled something she couldn't make out, then said clearly, "It was Leonard," before subsiding into silence again.

She had to get out of there.

She turned and fled the room.

In a daze, her mind reeling, she staggered her way back to the staircase and descended through the shadows alongside the somber faces of his ancestors into the amber light coming through the stained-glass window.

"Where *is* everyone?" she cried aloud, then cringed as her voice echoed back at her.

If not Lydia or Myrna, then Agnes, or at least the girls should be there. Had he sent them all away? Was there no one there for him now? It was possible. Even in 1901, consumption was highly contagious and had no cure. Her throat tightened at the thought of him lying there all alone trying to cope on his own except for the occasional visitor brave enough to venture out.

Blinking away tears, she moved through the house, flinching at every little creak. She took the first passageway, crossed through the also empty inner parlor, and turned left into the second passage.

Had it not been for the stroke, Myrna would have refused to leave, she thought as she reached the door at the end. Bracing herself, she pulled it open, then stood there as cold air wafted up over her. Shivering, she looked down the stairs leading into the basement. She could barely discern any light at all in the drafty space, only what was coming through the high windows.

"Ruth?" she called out. Her voice seemed to be swallowed by the darkness and was met by silence.

"Ruth?" she called out again, a little louder, and again heard nothing. She waited a few seconds, then closed the door against the frigid darkness.

Was there truly no one else around? She followed the passageway back up and crossed over to enter the kitchen. "Is anybody here? Hello?"

But there was no one there or in the laundry room or anywhere else. She felt panic welling up inside her as she walked through the sunroom and out the rear door.

I'll check the carriage house, she thought, hurrying down the steps. *And see if Mr. Gilbert or Jasper are still staying there.*

She had just stepped off onto the ground, nearly in a panic at the time she now found herself in and rushing too fast, when her foot came down on a slick spot and shot out from under her. Flying backwards with no time to react at all, the back of her head struck the step behind her—and everything went black.

Thirty-one

The sun was dropping behind the trees when she finally regained consciousness. She blinked her eyes at the orange-tinted clouds in the evening sky above her, her mind a blank. Then she registered where she was and shot up into a sitting position.

"Ow!" she cried as sharp pain stabbed through her head and down her neck. She reached a hand up and felt along her scalp, wincing as her fingers found a small gash. Carefully, she turned her head to look behind her. From the looks of the darker spot on the ground, it had bled a bit while she was out.

Oh, no, she thought, as it all came rushing back. *Gus!* He was upstairs all alone, either already dead or dying. She had to get to him.

She hauled herself to her feet, sending another bolt of pain through her head, and nearly passed out. She swayed in place, waited until the wooziness abated, and then dragged herself up the steps and into the sunroom.

Her head seemed to throb in unison with her footsteps as, eyes closed to nearly a slit, she continued on through the house to the back hallway. Had she suffered a concussion?

She reached up again to feel the laceration, hissing at the pain, as she entered the front parlor.

She jerked to a stop. She looked around in disbelief. Except for the lone chaise and a few side tables and chairs in the periphery, the room stood empty.

Sighing, she hung her head—she hadn't even noticed she'd returned to her time again—and then headed for the bathroom to clean the cut on her scalp.

THE NEXT MORNING, still in the twenty-first century, she felt a little better, especially with the codeine in her system from the pain pill she had dug out of her bag. She'd had to beg for them, she remembered, when her tooth had been too abscessed to work on.

She was sitting at the kitchen table she preferred with her first cup of coffee. After a bad night of picturing Gus as he lay dying over and over and mourning the young man he'd once been, she had finally been forced to shove the horror of his final moments out of her mind.

Now she was ready for some answers.

Before driving all the way to the library's main branch, she had decided to see what she could find out on her own.

She picked up her phone, grateful to Brent all over again for leaving it on (the least he could do) and did a few searches to see what she could access online. She was happily surprised to find that the main newspaper for the surrounding county, which would include Gus's mill, had an archive that included digitized replicas going all the way back to 1880.

She dug her credit card out and used it for the subscription fee—and then she was in.

In the fields provided, she entered "mill" and a range of 1895 – 1901, tapped Search, and got back over a thousand matches. She added the word "Pelzer," and told it to arrange them by the oldest dates first.

That got her 350 matches. She swiped up on the screen to scroll down. Most of the listings were for the year 1900 or later.

Swiping downward, she moved back up, examining the articles from before that, caught the words "Pelzer mill," and using her finger and thumb, pinched outward to zoom in.

Oh, Gus, she thought, reading the headline: TEN PERISH IN MILL FIRE. The mill had burned. Gus's pride and joy and his father's legacy, had burnt to the ground. On the very night she had returned to her time while Gus was taking Henry and Daniel home. She knew because she had seen the date on the wooden desk calendar in the library before she'd been whisked away.

According to the article, the fire had spread destroying everything with the exception of two outer buildings which had been badly damaged. The cause of the fire was unknown but was suspected to have originated from one of the recently installed fans.

The very same fans Gus had thought would improve things.

Shifting her eyes, she read on, and then sucked in a breath. She stood up, shoving her chair back. Staring down in shock, she read the paragraph again.

In addition to the eight employees working the night shift, Mrs. Helena Davenport, an acquaintance and business partner of the owner Mr. Augustus Moore, as well as his sister Miss Celia Moore were burned to death.

"*No*," she choked, spinning around. *Celia*. And Helena. Burned to death. Grabbing for the chair, she sat back down hard, face contorting in anguish. And what had Gus said about Lydia? *It was too much for her.*

Burned to death. Celia. Dear God. "*Nooo*." She put her face in her hands as sobs overtook her, and wept.

DETERMINED TO NOT break down again—she was so tired of crying—she tried to look dispassionately at what she knew. There had been a fire at the mill, resulting in the death of ten people, two of which had been Helena and Celia. Then Lydia had died. From grief? She could believe it. Celia, then Lydia. And eventually Gus. After losing his family and everything he and his father before him had worked so hard for, and after losing her. Lydia and Celia's marker must be out there in the cemetery—Lydia's probably in the back by Gus's dad's, and Celia's ... possibly near Gus, covered by grass and weeds.

Gus's headstone made a little more sense now. With Lydia and Celia gone, only Myrna had been left to help make decisions about the arrangements. And she had seen Cheyenne appearing and disappearing with her very own eyes and would have found that particular epitaph fitting. *Borne back into the river of time.*

She went back to the beginning. There had been a fire. And Helena had also died. The ghost of a suspicion began to hover in the back of her mind as she contemplated what she had previously taken for merely the ramblings of a dying man. *It was Leonard,* Gus had said. It was Leonard that what?

They had all suspected Leonard, and Helena, of planning to defraud Gus and others of their investment money. Was the mill fire related somehow? Helena *had* been there. Why? Looking for Gus? At that time of the evening? And why had Celia been there?

She took a sip of coffee, found it cold, and set it down again. What motive could Leonard have had to start the fire?

If he had been in cahoots with Helena, then possibly he'd wanted to get rid of her. Because she had known too much and maybe he hadn't wanted to share the money. But why do it that way? To shift suspicion away from himself? Because he thought that if she died at the mill instead of, say, "falling" down the stairs at her estate, then the authorities would be less likely to think he did it?

Hmm, she thought, picturing Leonard, a man she hadn't actually seen yet, as an aging but still suave Vincent Price giving an unsuspecting Helena a shove down the staircase. That was usually something men did when ...

When they wanted to collect life insurance money.

Had that been it? Had it all been so the bastard could cash in on Helena's death while throwing the blame off himself?

But what about the investment money? What had ever come of it? Exhaling heavily, she got up to heat more water for a fresh cup of coffee. She was obviously still missing a piece of the puzzle.

THE NEXT DAY after getting back from running out for some food and water and a few other things, paying again with her soon to be maxed credit card, she was sitting in the turret filled with Gus's things where she liked to go sometimes now, wrapped in a blanket and steadily working on a glass of chardonnay and speculating about Leonard again, when she finally thought to do a search on the man himself.

At first she didn't find anything. Then she tapped Videos, scrolled down, and one of them jumped out at her. *The Dastardly Case of Leonard Davenport*, it was titled. There were two other videos of a similar nature, as well, from other YouTube broadcasters.

With mounting excitement, she brought up the episode—from a Victorian true crime show called *I'll Be Damned*—and started it playing.

A thin young woman with straight brown hair seated at a desk in a shadowy room with her hands clasped before her came on and, getting right into it, began speaking.

"Leonard Davenport, born Tobias Fletcher, was the son of Jude Fletcher, a sawmill worker, and Hattie Davies, a seamstress who sometimes brought in work to help make ends meet." A picture of a man in overalls standing by a sawhorse and then a woman seated before an old-fashioned sewing machine were briefly shown. *"At the age of only nine years old, his mother died of cholera."* A blurred photo of a child in ragged clothes with no shoes and a dirty face was shown next. *"And seven years later when he was sixteen, the family home caught fire and burned to the ground, killing his father. Tobias, as he was known then, managed to survive the blaze and because there were rumors of strife between he and his father, was interrogated briefly.*

"But with no real evidence to positively link him with setting the fire, he was not charged and soon disappeared for parts unknown.

"Not much else is known about him after that until around 1895 when he resurfaced as Leonard Davenport, a name he would insist on going by for the rest of his days." A photo of a youngish man that had to be Leonard flashed up on the screen.

He looked both like and unlike the mental picture she had created of him. He had the same thin mustache and outward elegance, but underneath it lurked a smirk in the disdainful expression on his face.

"Eventually he would meet and befriend Miss Helena Joan Wright, last remaining heiress to a candy company fortune." Leonard's picture was replaced by a photograph of Helena. Cheyenne recognized her instantly though she'd never seen it before.

Instead of a full-length shot, it was a portrait of her face and shoulders with her hair piled up similar to the way it had been in the one with the faux pillars.

Cheyenne paused the documentary and looked away, blinking her eyes. It was really them. Helena and her husband. *What had they done? What had* he *done?* He had already been suspected of arson once before. *Had* he started the mill fire?

She started the video playing again.

"... unfortunately, all of the money had been depleted by this point, leaving Helena virtually broke and in danger of losing her family home. It was at this opportune moment that Leonard set his sights on Helena with her impoverished circumstances and proposed. Dollar signs were no doubt running through his head. Why, you might ask, since Helena was reputed to be all but penniless? Because he could then cash in on the one hundred thousand dollar insurance policy—quite a substantial amount back then—he planned to take out on her after making her his wife. A policy he did indeed start shortly after he and Helena made it official."

A copy of said policy complete with a scrawled approximation of Helena's signature across the bottom was shown next.

"In a later, rare interview with Leonard while incarcerated at the South Carolina State Penitentiary—where he would serve thirty years of the life sentence he was given in lieu of the death penalty for confessing to setting the fire that killed ten people, including his wife Helena, as well as the murder of Perry Wells before passing away of cancer—he would also admit to forging Helena's signature on the policy."

Cheyenne sat back in the chair, stunned. *Perry ... murdered.*

A black-and-white, slightly jerky clip came on of Leonard seated before a long table, facing the camera and gesturing while talking to someone.

"But this is where it gets a bit complicated," the brunette host continued. *"And to make sense of it, we have to go back to the beginning and understand why Helena agreed to marry him in the first place. After all, she might have been essentially destitute, but she was from good stock and he had neither money nor pedigree—nor it was said, did he possess an irresistible charm or devastatingly good looks."*

A landscape photo of Helena's home, similar to the one she'd found of this house in the attic, was shown next.

"It was her love of her family estate and her place in the only society she had ever known that convinced her to marry Leonard, if his story is to be believed. According to him, he convinced her to marry him by concocting a plan to scam investors in a fraudulent hotel scheme in order to garner money to save her home."

A portrait of a man with a receding hairline came up next that she was pretty sure was Perry.

The host's next words confirmed it. *"Perry Wells, lawyer and friend to textile mill owner Augustus Moore, was approached by Helena and Leonard shortly after they learned of his serious gambling debts. And thanks in part to Helena's womanly wiles, or so Leonard claimed, Perry soon found himself drawn into a plot that was to benefit all three of them. Helena would have the money she needed to save her home, Perry could pay off his debts before he was ruined or worse, and Leonard, which wasn't even his real name, would take his share and disappear into the sunset. But how the plan was supposed to go and how it actually did, turned out to be two different things."*

The video cut away to a series of ads. Cheyenne let them play while she absorbed everything and finished the last of her wine. Helena, Leonard, and Perry had all been in on it together to steal what they could of the hotel money. Which she already basically knew. What she couldn't figure out was how Helena had thought they would get away with it. By blaming "Leonard," who had conned poor little ol' her and run off with the money? But how would she explain her influx of cash?

It turned out she was only partially right she found out when the documentary came back on and the pleasant young woman continued. *"The plan as told to Perry and Helena was for Helena to leave with Perry as if he were Leonard (who would then quietly melt into the crowd with his part of the money) to go abroad on a little trip, whereupon she would claim Leonard, whom she would insist had conned her like all the rest, had taken off with the money.*

"And lawyer Perry Wells—a friend of Mr. Moore's, who was a longtime associate of Helena's and principal investor in the hotel—was to leave his wife a note telling her he had gone away on a possible business venture. In reality he would be keeping a low profile with Helena while they waited in some tropical paradise."

A cartoon drawing of a small island surrounded by water popped up on the screen.

"Then when enough time had passed, Perry would go home, claim he won big gambling at some other location while he was away, and pay the men he owed. And after a brief period, Helena

could return with or without some potential new husband and a sizable sum she would claim came from him or some other friend or suitor she met after Leonard left her—that she could use to pay the back taxes and other arrears on her estate.

"*And* Leonard," said the host, making quote marks with her fingers, "*who didn't really exist and would have since disappeared, would assume the blame for the missing money.*"

The brunette paused for theatrical effect. "*Only that's not quite what Leonard actually had in mind.*

"*His initial goal had been to come up with some way to get Helena to marry him so he could kill her for the insurance money, but then he became greedy and wanted the investment money as well when his scheme worked better than he expected.*"

Another photo of Leonard came up, looking younger this time. His last school photo, maybe?

"*All of this was revealed to the investigators when Leonard eventually made his full confession to avoid the death penalty after the body of Perry Wells was found.*"

Leonard's image was replaced with what looked like a college photo of Perry with more hair.

Barely breathing, she listened in horrified amazement as the young brunette recounted how a sharp-eyed detective recently transferred in from another county and already assigned to investigate the fire had thought he recognized the husband of one of the women killed in the blaze—a prominent woman who didn't even work at the mill and just so happened to be there—as none other than the boy suspected of arson and the murder of his father years before.

Following this lead and finding the missing investment money (which he'd learned of in the course of his investigation) and Perry's continued absence a little too out of character as well as convenient, despite the note, and because the reason Leonard had given for why Helena had been at the mill in the first place— which was supposedly to inform Augustus Moore, a business partner in her hotel venture, of an impending spur of the moment trip—had sounded contrived to his equally keen ears, the suspicious detective had taken a little ride out to the old homestead, where the unmistakable scent of decay led him behind the ruins of Tobias's childhood home.

And there at the bottom of the old well, Perry's body was discovered.

Cheyenne listened raptly, her mind whirling, as the host revealed the details of exactly what Leonard had done, some of it direct quotes straight from the man himself. She then gave a quick recap and began wrapping things up, declaring how greed had been Leonard's downfall, how if he had followed his previous MO and took the money and run, as it was suspected he'd done on at least one other occasion when he had been working under his birth name and he and the money from the petty cash fund had gone missing, he might have managed it. He might have gotten away with one, either staging Helena's accidental death and receiving the life insurance payout and possibly her home—*or* taking his part of the investment money and starting over again someplace else under a new alias, but not both. Despite the detective being suspicious of him, if he had not found Perry's body, Leonard might have gotten away with setting the fire that killed Helena. And had Leonard not killed Helena, he might have escaped with his share while leaving everyone to believe that "Leonard," the conman, the imposter, had disappeared with the money.

But he had wanted both the insurance payout and the investment money. And the only way for him to remain in the home and appear the grieving husband while collecting the insurance payout *and* pocketing the investment money was to make Perry permanently disappear, leading everyone to believe that in desperation, fearing for his life because of unpaid gambling debts, he had fled with the money and then possibly met with foul play or else was hiding out living in secrecy somewhere.

Cheyenne couldn't believe the audacity and evilness of it. Leonard had gone with Perry to pull the money out of the bank late in the afternoon, only hours after Daniel had gone in to elicit information from the infatuated counter girl—what exactly they had indicated it was for, wasn't said—and then had penned a note supposedly from Gus summoning Helena to the mill just after quitting time. After that it had been merely a matter of following her, and Celia, inside. Celia, according to her uncle's driver who had brought Celia and watched her accompany Helena in before settling back and falling asleep, had come to show Gus an old tintype photograph of their grandfather she thought he would like (and to beg him to let her come home, Cheyenne bet).

On his way out after dropping Helena, Leonard had halted the buggy, snuck back, and slipped inside unnoticed. Celia's fate, as well as Helena's, had been sealed the moment they'd gone inside the mill. Despite having undoubtedly retrieved and disposed of the note, Leonard wouldn't have been able to call a halt to his plans, even if he'd wanted to, not with Helena, and now possibly Celia too if Helena had mentioned it to her, being under the impression that Gus had summoned her there—something Gus would have then disputed. So he'd made sure the women were ensconced in Gus's office, then proceeded to set fire to several piles of excess cotton fluff, kicking some of it into the corridor and affectively trapping Helena and Celia, using matches he dropped strategically, moving rapidly from the end of the weave room by Gus's office to the bales stacked in the card room and then out another door. "You wouldn't believe how quickly those mills go up," Leonard later stated. "The floors are soaked in machine oil. One little spark and all that lint and cotton dust just ignites."

After setting the fire, he had driven into town and made sure he was seen in one of the stores purportedly for last minute items, before returning to Perry's office now that everyone else had gone home. Once he'd verified that Perry had gotten the note ready for his wife, Leonard had struck him over the head, strangled him, then wrapped his body in a rug and dragged him out to his carriage waiting by the rear entrance.

Next he had retrieved the bags Perry had brought with him in anticipation of receiving his share and leaving with Helena, then drove his team hard to his old childhood home, where he dumped them and Perry's body down the well.

Finally, he had raced back to the mill, where of course he had been met by an ungodly conflagration as the structure burned to the ground.

Cheyenne got up to refill her glass. And just like that Gus had lost the mill, as well as Celia, then Lydia, and finally his health and his life.

All so Leonard could have his damn cake and eat it too. *The son of a bitch*, she thought. If only she could get back and stop him now that she knew what he had really been planning.

This time she took her wine out onto the second-floor balcony outside Gus's room. She set down the single candle she'd brought with her and stood there taking sips and letting the slight breeze sweep over her.

What was Gus doing right now in 1895? she wondered. Was he worrying about her? Her heart ached to think of what he was going through all alone.

The mill would have burnt down. Celia and Helena and eight of his employees would be dead. Was Lydia already gone? Or did she still linger?

And what could be done about it? Nothing. Even if she were to be pulled back—and she'd had zero indications that the phenomenon was about to occur—she might very well end up getting there too late again.

You might be able to save him *at least*, she thought. How long would it be before Henry took him off to some far-away location where he would contract tuberculosis?

The moon, a perfect golden Man in the Moon crescent— glowed behind wispy clouds in the night sky above her.

There were so many things she didn't understand. So many things she still yearned for. So many questions about her place in the universe and what her purpose was now.

She stood there a little while longer, listening to the lonely sound of the wind chimes on the verandah below tinkling softly in the night breeze, and then picked up the candle and went back inside.

Thirty-two

She had been thinking a lot about Richard Matheson's *Bid Time Return*, which she'd read and loved after watching *Somewhere in Time*, the movie based on it. In it, the main character immerses himself in the past in every possible way. He ensconces himself in authentic surroundings, outfitted with appropriately cut hair, vintage clothing, and personal items, down to the antique coins in his pocket. He then spends several feverish days trying to put everything else out of his mind and hypnotize himself into believing he's traveled back to 1896. Only to fail. Until he sees his name in an old guest book and realizes he does succeed. And it is this absolute faith in his success that finally allows him back.

Should she be trying harder? She had already seen the effect she could have on the anomaly. And she had already journeyed back, more than once, and knew it could be done. Should she put on the dress she'd been wearing when she'd returned, pin up her hair, remove all modern items from her sight, and try to will herself into the year 1895?

Maybe if the time was ripe when the timelines were drawing near and close to intersecting, it would be possible for her to bring an occurrence about, but as it was …

Even if she could travel back to before the fire happened, it was very possible she might not be able to remain. And meanwhile her life here would be falling apart and getting more out of control as the days passed.

She should just leave. Before someone caught her there. *Trespassing. Squatting.*

The thought brought her up short where she was coming out from returning the rest of a juice and bag of popcorn she'd been snacking on to the wine cellar.

She shut the basement door. She had been way too lax lately. She pictured the deputy coming in and catching her unawares. *That's all I need.*

She went back through the house. She could not let that happen. If she couldn't bring herself to leave just yet, then she could at least try to keep from being arrested for it.

She began putting everything away she'd left lying about—the kettle for heating water, her cup with the remains of the hot chocolate she'd mixed up earlier, the water bottle by the sofa. Then she went to work sweeping up and trying to make the fireplace look the way it had before.

She took a walk through the house afterwards, still feeling uneasy. In the inner parlor, she paused and glanced over at the sofa. All the deputy had to do was look behind it and she would be discovered.

No, you dummy, her mind mocked. *All he has to do is look at you lying on the sofa when he catches you sleeping there.*

But ... most likely it would be in the daytime if he did show up. And she could be ready to dash outside if he made an appearance.

She walked over, shoved the sofa farther out from the wall, and arranged her bag and purse together, folded up the sleeping bag, laid it across the top, then covered everything with the darker blankets to better hide them. Then she pushed the sofa back as far as she could. *There,* she thought. That might work.

What else? She looked around, thinking idly about riding over to Walgreens when she was finished to look for something to read and maybe one of those booklights if they had any, before it got too late. If she ran into her mother or Caleb she could say she'd returned to get some of her things. Without Wi-Fi readily accessible on her tablet, she'd been left with only what was already downloaded and her reading material was getting low.

The food in the wine cellar, she thought. She needed to do something about that. None of it was concealed all that well if anyone made an effort to look. She needed to hide it better, maybe stick everything behind the oddly shaped, bluish-green Ball jars of unidentifiable, deadly-looking produce she'd seen on a bottom shelf. She pulled her phone out and checked to make sure it was completely silenced out of habit, then tucked it into her pocket and headed for the basement.

IN THE SMALLER parlor a few minutes later, she had just retrieved her purse and slid her phone into the side compartment, when she thought she heard something.

Reaching across, she stuck it back under the blanket behind the sofa and walked over to look through the windows on the far end of the library. But all she could see was the curve of the overgrown drive beyond.

It was probably nothing. Still ... She followed the passageway and turned toward the front of the house. She really needed to leave this place. But could she bear to go so soon? She would be severing her last possible tie to Gus. If a slippage ever did happen again ...

Letting herself imagine it, she lost herself in a vision of the floors and walls and ceilings around her pulsing in and out with flashes of color as her surroundings switched back and forth until, amazingly, she found herself back in the house as it once was when it was grand, with Gus right outside waiting for her by the carriage.

Pulling open the front doors, she moved out onto the verandah, dreamily crossed it, and descended the steps.

Abruptly like a slap in the face, she was jerked out of her daydream as she realized two things: she had walked outside without checking first, and there was a familiar patrol car parked to her left, the glow of its headlights hazy in the dusky twilight.

Paralyzed, she got a glimpse of movement behind the windshield, and then the door was flying open. But something was happening. The ground beneath her feet was vibrating and the air around her buzzing and crackling. Suddenly, as if the oxygen was being sucked out of her lungs, she couldn't breathe. Frightened, she could only watch as the deputy emerged from the car.

And then she was yanked away.

THE NIGHT WAS silent, the hazy beam of headlights gone. She roamed her eyes around what she could see of her dim surroundings. Here, wherever, whenever it was, the moon was waxing toward complete fullness, bringing the thick vegetation that had crept up close into sharp relief.

Beginning to tremble, she twisted around to look behind her.

The vacant, skeletal remains of the house loomed above her, only partially erect with one side leaning toward the middle below a caved-in roof. Both the second-story balconies and the verandah had fallen away, and the windows that weren't empty black holes contained only broken glass.

My God, how long must it have been for it to have fallen completely into ruin? A hundred years? Two hundred?

Gradually, as she stood there aghast, she became aware of a sound.

A faint thrumming was coming across the night sky.

Shaking and breath coming in small gasps, she slowly shifted around, dread crawling up her spine. Abruptly the sound changed to a harsher continuous roar. *Like massive jet engines, or some kind of thrusters*, she thought, the hair rising on the back of her neck.

As she stared toward the highway where the eerie sound seemed to be coming from, the roar cut out, and for a couple of seconds there was complete silence. Then it started again, even louder.

It was moving closer. Silence descended again, and she frantically scanned the night sky. *Where?*

There. Her blood seemed to freeze in her veins as she caught sight of the ominous dark shape slowly gliding into view over the tree line, blotting out the stars behind it.

Suddenly a deafening, trumpet-like blast rent the air, and Cheyenne screamed, her voice lost in the blood-curdling alien noise reverberating across the landscape. Nearly undone, she clapped her hands over her ears and turned to flee. But where? She lurched instinctively toward the house then caught herself and angled away and ran along the front, horribly exposed if anyone— or *anything*—was looking. This couldn't be happening!

She made it to the corner and flew around it and flattened herself against the side, trying to blend into it, as the monstrous object slowly moved across the sky. *Oh shit, oh shit, oh shit.* She realized she was making gibbering noises and made herself stop. Still pressed against the old boards, she inched her way down to the rear of the house.

Her breath rasped in and out. Terrified nearly out of her mind, she desperately tried to think. *Hide!* her mind was screaming at her, but *where?*

The huge alien shadow floating across the moonlit sky continued on, noiseless now, and slowly slid out of sight.

From farther back near the edge of the field that had once been the garden, there came a zapping sound. She snapped her head around. In the ghostly light of the moon, the trees shifted and swayed as something moved between them.

Staring hard, she began to discern a strangely diffuse green glow, followed by bright flashes of white light as something long and tentacle-like lashed down into the underbrush. She could hear it, too—an inhuman sort of rattling hiss.

This is it, she thought. Then her instinct to survive kicked in as a roundish body emerged and propelled itself on whip-thin legs hellishly fast through the brush.

Now! The carriage house! Springing forward, she flew through the dead grass and weeds, twigs and thorns slapping and tugging at her. Out of the corner of her eye, she could see the thing's progress, glimpsed by flashes of green and white, as it closed in on the house. It hadn't seen her!

No sooner had she thought this than she risked a look over her shoulder and saw it rear up and change direction.

No, not the carriage house, she thought as the thing let out a high-pitched screech. It was too easy and it was almost upon her. Speeding past it, she swerved over and felt the ground change under her feet as she amazingly hit the less overgrown section where the track had once been. She began searching for the turnoff to the barn. There wasn't as much moonlight here under the trees and so much undergrowth she was afraid she was going to miss it.

She almost did miss it, but then she spied the brighter patch of ground there and fought her way over, shoving through the heavy vegetation.

Finally, when she'd just about given up and decided to burrow down where she was, she emerged from the thicket and nearly ran into the barn. Or what was left of it. It had collapsed years ago and now nothing remained but a pile of splintery gray lumber and part of the roof slowly being taken over.

Her skin crawled. It was too quiet. She dropped into a squat, scanning the shadows behind her. Then as silently as possible, she crept over and squeezed under the raised corner of the roof, now on the ground, that remained intact.

Keeping low and to the side where it sloped down, she slithered across and through the pile of timber to get away from the more open front, wiggled around to get behind the outer planks—and went still.

And it was a good thing. Out by the track something whipped through the forest with a crackling sound and then went quiet.

It knew she was here somewhere, and it was listening for her.

Staying motionless, she took breaths in and out shallowly and tried not to think about what other critters she might be sharing her space with.

An eternity later it seemed, there still hadn't been any sound or movement.

But she wasn't fooled. The damn thing was somewhere close by, trying to wait her out. *Well, fuck you. You'll have to come in here and drag me out.* Immediately she had to suppress a shudder at the thought.

Was it possible it didn't see the remnants of the barn? Maybe; it was in a heap and mostly covered by vines and leaves.

On and on the hours dragged. She could hear other creatures like it moving about in the distance, but the one she was sure was lurking nearby remained stationary.

She thought it had to be after midnight, though she couldn't be sure, when, as her muscles were screaming in protest and she felt like she might lose her mind if she couldn't change position soon, she caught a haze of green and then a bright flicker through the cracks between the boards and knew the thing had passed within yards of her.

Only when she heard it again a little farther out and knew it was still moving away did she finally shift herself around in tiny, slow increments.

SHE AWOKE IN foggy, dim daylight to the rustle of leaves and the sound of a bird calling out. For a moment she thought she was still in the dream she'd been having of military trucks and other vehicles rolling in a line up the driveway under the yellow rays of the rising sun.

Then it hit her. She'd been sleeping!

Wincing, she pulled herself up and out from under the old gray boards and crossed her arms against the cold. All she had on over her clothes was the sweater she'd been wearing the night before, and it was freezing. She sat there a minute listening and wishing desperately for something to drink. Then, hearing nothing alarming, she crept forward to look out.

It was hard to believe in the morning light with only the normal sounds of the birds and squirrels that just the night before she had been facing sure death from something she could hardly fathom.

Was humanity about to face a fight for its very survival? Or had it been an isolated threat that would swiftly be dispatched by their military, the way it had been in her dream, that they'd never see the likes of again?

She would have to hope so.

Well, here goes nothing. She moved out from under the section of roof and straightened into a half-crouch and scanned the forest around her.

When nothing happened, she tentatively began picking her way out to the approximate area of the track, moving as quietly as she could. Finding it easily, she looked down, frowning. The parallel grooves in the dirt were clearly visible.

She looked up ahead of her, eyes going wide. Starting forward again, she increased her pace until she was jogging, daring to hope.

The carriage house wavered back and forth from decaying wreck to well-kept outbuilding until finally, as she came abreast, it settled into the derelict structure of her time.

She came to a stop and bent forward, bracing her hands on her knees, breathing hard.

After a moment she straightened up, got going again, and quickly made it to the edge of the wild back lawn. The house looked as she remembered it. Old and abandoned but standing strong, not falling in and rotting.

I guess ending up with Gus when he was still young and we were in love was too much to ask. Unexpected tears stung her eyes as a vision of his smiling face filled her mind.

Stop it, she told herself, and began pushing through the dead grass.

Everything felt strangely surreal in the gray light, and she ached all over as though she'd suffered a trauma. Which, she guessed she had. You couldn't get much more traumatic than what she'd faced the night before.

She had one foot on the bottom step to the sunroom when she remembered the deputy.

Gasping, she jerked away, and quickly moved up against the back of the house. Wondering what fresh hell she might have to face now, she followed it over and slipped around the side.

How could she have forgotten? He had *seen* her.

But only briefly before she'd disappeared. Her thoughts raced. Had the cops swarmed the place? Had they found her things? Was her car even still parked behind the magnolia? It had been nearly dark. The deputy had merely caught a glimpse of her before he climbed out and she had disappeared. Maybe he thought it had been a trick of the light. We see what we expect to see, not necessarily the evidence gathered by our eyes.

She reached the front and cautiously leaned out. The driveway stood empty. Releasing her breath, she sagged against the side of the house. At least she would be spared that.

After a moment, she straightened up to head back around so she could go in through the sunroom.

THE ONLY THING she felt confident of now was that she could be sure about nothing. She had thought the anomaly had peaked and was now entering a dormant stage. Now she didn't know what to expect. And what had felt almost magical in the beginning as if she were flying on the winds of fate where nothing bad could happen, had now become very real. She could quite possibly end up sliding back again. If not to Gus, then to some other time—and maybe not being able to return if she remained on this property.

She didn't want to give up on Gus, but she feared she might not ever be able to change his destiny. And this last excursion had frightened her badly. Never, ever in her life had she been so scared. She trembled just thinking about it.

It was make or break time. Because she couldn't keep going through this. And sooner or later she was bound to get caught staying there. When she'd walked through with a critical eye after returning, she'd spotted evidence her deputy had come inside. In the foyer, she had found a partial shoeprint, larger and obviously not hers. Which meant he'd discovered the double doors open again. And this time he would have taken a better look. Though presumably he hadn't located her food stash or the stuff behind the sofa. Nothing appeared to be moved, and when she opened the cabinets in the wine cellar, the old Ball jars she'd lined up across the front looked undisturbed. Fortunately it had been nighttime or he might have noticed more or seen *her* prints somewhere in the house.

But he'll be back, she thought. He'll be intrigued now, wondering if he *had* seen someone—or if he'd seen something else. She gave a mirthless laugh, imagining him believing he'd seen a ghost. One that unlocked doors. (Though that was exactly what she had thought for a minute her first time there when the door had come open.) And yet she couldn't bring herself to give up on Gus and leave, either.

Her mind was telling her to hightail it out of there, but her heart wouldn't let her. *Just a little longer*, she promised herself. *I'll sit and do nothing but think of him*. If there was the slightest chance she might make it back ...

But did she want to chance it? Did she have it in her to go through something like what happened the previous night again?

She honestly didn't know. But just in case ... She turned away from the windows she'd been pacing back and forth in front of. There were some things she needed to take care of.

She couldn't go visit her mother and brother in person, unless she wanted to answer a bunch of questions and add more lies to the ones she'd already told, but she was able to send them quick messages on Facebook. Nothing that would seem too odd in case another occurrence never happened and she eventually left the house, just reassurances that everything was fine and that she loved them, along with a quick selfie she took under a tree that could have been at Jill's. That way if there was another slippage, she had at least been able to tell them she loved them one last time.

But she hated to leave it that way, with no one having a clue what happened to her. After thinking long and hard about it, she decided to do something different with Jill.

In a Kay's Jewelers eleven miles away—the closest decent store—she found what seemed like a sign: a 14K gold crescent moon on a thin, delicate chain.

She paid the man helping her extra to gift-wrap it, and then left to drive over to Target.

There she bought a mailer, a giftbox, tissue paper, and a birthday card—along with a Mr. Goodbar and a Coke. Then it was on to the UPS store.

In the parking lot she got things ready while she guzzled Coke and ate part of the candy, careful not to smear chocolate on anything.

She placed what she'd brought with her to go with Jill's present between two layers of tissue paper then lay it flat in the bottom of the giftbox, put the card—a midnight blue one with a gold crescent moon surrounded by shooting stars and HAPPY BIRTHDAY trailing down the tail of one—on top of it, and then added the wrapped box containing the necklace. To keep it from sliding around, she packed some of the tissue paper around it, then put the lid on the giftbox, wrote *"Don't open till your birthday!"* across it, and placed it down in the mailer. There was a little space left on top, so she added some wadded-up tissue, then closed it up and climbed out to head inside.

A few minutes later with the package on its way to Jill, she climbed back in, happy to be finished with what could be a fool's errand, started the car, and pulled out to drive to the library over there.

She caught them at a busy time and ended up having to wait. But eventually an older man stood up to leave and she was able to get a computer.

Keeping an eye on the clock, she began searching for the episode on Leonard. She'd never done a still image from video and had been forced to look up how to do it before coming in. *There.* She started it playing, fast forwarded to something she needed to check, and then moved to the frame she wanted and paused it.

The library was starting to clear out now as people headed home to start dinner. She glanced at the instructions she'd written down and then looked over at the lady behind the circulation desk. Maybe it would be better if she got some help.

A half hour later after enlisting the friendly, adept woman's assistance in printing most of what she wanted—the last item proved impossible—Cheyenne was going through the doors with two printouts: a copy of Leonard's younger photo, which she'd been thrilled to see showed the name Tobias Fletcher listed underneath it; and a copy of the insurance policy he had taken out on Helena. It wasn't the best quality but you could read most of the pertinent information and make out the scrawl that was supposed to be her signature across the bottom.

She had also searched for any newspaper articles on the fire that had killed Leonard's father, but she'd known that was a long shot and as expected hadn't found anything back that far.

What she had would have to be enough.

Thirty-three

A storm was definitely brewing. It had been growing darker as the day went on, and heavy clouds had converged across the sky as far as she could see through the parlor windows.

At least maybe the deputy wouldn't come out in such nasty weather. *Dangerous* weather.

Around four o'clock it began to rain and she was forced to light a lantern. She was afraid to use candles. If the deputy did show up and she had to blow them out, he might smell it.

Usually she got pretty good reception there in the inner parlor where she was now, but possibly because of the storm, she was currently down to one bar. She checked it again. And now not even that. Giving up, she reached over the sofa and tucked it away, then wandered out of the room.

Through the glass panes in the foyer, lightning flashed in the distance. A few seconds later as she entered the library, the rumble of thunder came. She walked over and leaned across to look out again. A thick mass of dark, foreboding clouds covered the entire right side of the sky all the way to the horizon.

Shivering, she pulled back as the wind gusted and sent what sounded like sleet spattering across the glass.

I hope a limb doesn't land on my car, she thought as the wind picked up even further and began to howl. It would be tough to explain why the hell her car was parked back there.

An hour later she was huddled in the inner parlor as rain came down in sheets, listening to the shriek of the wind as it buffeted the house. Every so often in between the sharp cracks of lightning and booms of thunder she could hear the snap and thud of trees falling and breaking in the woods all around.

She didn't know if it would be better to be in the basement, or the attic. She didn't want the house to fall down onto her, but she didn't want to be carried off by the wind, either. Better to stay where she was.

At least she was in her time and not in some horrifying future filled with—*No!* she thought. *Don't think about that.*

Jumping slightly at a particularly bright flash and loud bang of thunder, she let her mind drift to how it had been with Gus.

They had been good together. She could have fit in there … as long as she was with him. She thought of Gus as he was then. Handsome, young, with years ahead of him still. *Ah, Jesus.* Springing to her feet, she grabbed the cup she'd been drinking from, and with a cry, hurled it across the room, smashing it against the wall.

As if a switch had been thrown, the rain abruptly stopped and the wind fell away.

She waited for the sound of a bolt popping or thunder rolling across, but heard nothing. Except for the drip of water somewhere and the small creaks of the house settling, it had gone strangely quiet.

She looked over at the coffee dripping down the brittle wallpaper and felt something underneath her feet. Stumbling forward, she staggered across the room. The faint vibration grew until it felt like the floor was bucking beneath her. Outside the library windows, the sky flashed back and forth from pitch black to blinding bright over and over, faster and faster. She ripped her gaze away as something gave a tremendous *clap* like the world's biggest lightning strike.

And all at once she could hear them, though the rooms remained the same around her, faceless, formless voices floating in through the dimness. Myrna's … and then one of the girls. Cheyenne held perfectly still, listening to their ghostly murmuring. Was Gus there?

She was so close.

Finally she crept over, retrieved the lantern, and walked back over with it.

The phantom voices fell silent.

She could hear the wind again, only distantly but she sensed it growing. Switching the lantern to the other hand, she reached into the pocket of the hooded flannel she had on to make sure she still had the folded printouts, then left the room, heading toward the voices she'd heard.

"Myrna?" she called out. "Are you here?"

She reached the entrance to the kitchen and looked inside, shadows fleeing from the light of the lantern, and then continued on.

The wind had stopped again. Was Gus somewhere close? She'd never been so near yet so far before. Was the effect losing its strength?

"Gus!" she cried, unable to stop herself. "I'm here!"

She moved past a dark library and through the doorway into the front parlor and came to a stop. The room in front of her had a strange luminosity around it, like the edges and corners of the walls and ceiling and the remaining furniture were glowing. She blinked her eyes, but the shimmery outline around the fireplace and the chaise and—

She gasped. There were other things in the room now, radiant and blazing with color. "Oh please," she whispered, moving on in and gazing around in awe.

She could feel herself there, on the precipice. "Gus!" she cried. "Myrna! Where are you?"

"I'm right here," came Myrna's voice, and Cheyenne whirled around, homing in on her face, indistinct but there in the air before her.

"Myrna! You have to help me." She reached out a hand and, incredibly, felt it collide with a warm arm.

"What is it?" She heard dimly as she clutched at it.

"I want to stay."

"Of course you can stay," Myrna said in a clear voice. "Why don't you come on over here and sit down."

Keeping her eyes focused straight ahead, afraid to look at anything too closely, she let Myrna lead her over and deposit her into one of the chairs. She halfway expected to fall through it and land on the floor, but it remained solid and took her weight.

Flames wavered in the fireplace and warm circles of light from the oil lamps dotted the room.

She swung her head around, the bright rugs and drapes sliding by, and tried to focus in on Myrna's faintly alarmed face. "Myrna?" she said. "Where is Gus?"

Myrna seemed to take forever before she answered. "Hasn't he gone to take Mr. Henry and Mr. Daniel home?"

Cheyenne pushed herself up. There was still time. She reached down to touch the hard wood of the chair arm again, then looked around her. She was really here.

She gave her head a shake. She felt like she'd just awakened from a dream. She turned back to Myrna. "I need to get to Helena's."

"You need to get to Helena's?" Myrna began worriedly bunching up the ends of her apron.

"I don't have time to explain, but it's imperative. Who can drive me?"

"Maybe you should wait for Mr. Gu—"

"No! I have to go *now*. It's literally a matter of life and death."

Myrna's eyes went even wider. "The trap's here, but you'll have to use Jasper because Mr. Gilbert, he—"

"Never mind, Jasper's fine," she said, already striding out of the room.

Myrna's tentative voice stopped her. "Miss Cheyenne?"

She halted in the doorway. "Yes?"

"Don't you think you should put something else on?"

She glanced down at herself. Shit. She'd forgotten she was wearing her normal clothes. "What time is it?"

Myrna looked across at the grandfather clock. "It's coming up on a quarter past five."

She took a second to consider changing. But the mill closed at 6:00 and sometime after that when there was only a skeleton crew on hand was when the fire started. "I don't have time." She turned to continue on, then paused again. "I do need a jacket, though," she said as it occurred to her.

"Here, I'll get you one. I believe Miz Lydia left something on the hall rack."

She hastened out of the room, and Cheyenne tried to prepare herself for what was to come. If, *if*, she made it in time, it would only be half the battle. But it was the main battle. The one that could turn the tide and save not only Helena, if she could convince her not to go, but Celia, eight workers, Lydia, and Gus as well six years hence.

Myrna bustled back in with a jet-black cape of Lydia's, and Cheyenne quickly donned it. She felt a little ridiculous in the intricately beaded, lacy thing, although it was beautiful, but it would help keep her warm.

She rushed through the house, practically running by the time she reached the sunroom. She encountered no one. Agatha would have already gone home for the day, and possibly Lydia was in her room and the girls in their respective spaces.

Yanking the door open, she hurried out and down the steps, careful not to slip at the bottom, and sped across the shadowy backyard toward the carriage house.

It didn't look like anyone was around, but Myrna had said Jasper was there. Or maybe they were both there but it was Mr. Gilbert's day off?

"Hello," she called out, pushing open the door. "Jasper? Are you here?" She moved on in to the center of the room. Someone had built up the fire in the wood stove recently, and she could feel the warmth radiating from it. She turned to start down the hall then paused at the sound of a door closing and then footsteps.

"Oh, hello," said Jasper, walking in. His hair and mustache were both wet like he'd recently washed. Had he used the hand pump out back, she wondered distantly, or the tub in the outside bath?

"I need you to run me over to Helena's," she began, aware of the minutes ticking away. "I'm sorry to barge in on you like this, but it's vital ..." She came to a stop at the expression on his face as his eyes swept from her loose, uncovered hair past the cape to the jeans and moccasins she wore.

Reaching out a hand to forestall him, she said, "It's a long and quite possibly unbelievable story," which only made him look even more confounded. "But I need you to take me to Helena's. I don't have time to explain all of it to you, but it's crucial I get over there as quickly as possible. For Gus's sake." *For the entire family's*, she thought. "Please. People's lives could be at risk."

When he still didn't immediately move and merely shuffled his feet, she gave up and walked around him in exasperation, heading for the door she knew led to the cavernous area where the trap would be. She'd drive her damn self. Somehow. Or ride one of the horses. She had to catch Helena in time. If she never reached the mill then Leonard would have no reason to set the fire that would ultimately claim Celia and eight others along with Helena.

"Wait," said Jasper, catching up with her as she stepped through and started across to where the little buggy sat. "I'd be more than happy to take you." He stayed beside her, keeping pace. "If you'll wait here, I can go get a horse."

As she paused by the trap it abruptly occurred to her to wonder how well he had recovered from his illness. "You have recovered from your illness, I trust?" she asked.

"Oh yes, Miss. It was merely a chill I caught. I'm over it now."

"All right. Good. Now, Jasper, I need you to get me over to Helena's right now."

"Yes, ma'am," he said, and trotted over to push open the doors.

"And be quick!" she urged him, then turned and hauled herself up onto the seat.

It seemed forever before he made it back with a large horse in tow. What time was it? Had Leonard already given Helena the fake note summoning her to meet Gus?

For heaven's sake, hurry up! she shouted mentally at Jasper as he worked to get the lamps lit and then the horse harnessed and hitched and hot coals transferred to the footwarmer.

Finally, he took the reins, climbed up, and they were off. "I suppose you know the way?" she asked him.

He nodded, shooting her a sidelong glance. He still didn't know what to think, but he had enough sense to understand that Gus would want him to help.

The rest of the ride was mostly spent in tense silence. He asked the whereabouts of Gus, which she answered, and then fell quiet, leaving her to her thoughts.

She was aching to see Gus, the Gus she knew, but that would have to wait. The fate of everyone involved depended on her catching Helena and ousting Leonard for the murderous conman he was.

"Listen," she said when they were close, turning to Jasper in the half-light. "When we get there, I need you to park down away from the house a bit. I don't want to alert them that I'm coming."

Abruptly, Jasper slowed the horse. "I'm sorry, but I'm afraid I'm going to need to know what's going on." He stared across at her, his features implacable. "It would be remiss of me to—"

"Okay," she said, seeing where he was going. What harm would it do at this point to explain, anyway? She couldn't tell him *all* of it, obviously, but maybe just enough. "I can't afford to spend a lot of time trying to convince you, so you'll just have to trust me.

Because believe me, people's lives are at stake." She gazed back at him earnestly, hoping he would see the truth in her eyes.

"Helena and Leonard," she continued carefully, "are in the midst of committing fraud. They are planning on taking all of the investors' money and keeping it for themselves." Leonard and Perry would have already gone to the bank and Perry didn't have long to live if she had the timeline right.

"And I have come into possession of certain information that points to Leonard planning to do much more than steal the money." She paused to think how to word it so he would be satisfied and get moving again. Just spell it out, she decided. "Leonard has a life insurance policy on Helena."

Jasper faced forward again, lifting the reins, as the horse shifted impatiently. "*Whoa.*" They were the only ones on the road now, though they'd passed two other carriages before turning onto the smaller lane that led to Helena's drive.

"And that wouldn't necessarily be a problem," she added, "but you see, Helena doesn't know about the policy."

He gazed downward as he absorbed this. "She doesn't know about the policy," he murmured as if to himself.

"That's right. She's not the one who signed it. It was Leonard. He forged her signature."

He huffed out a breath as the implications of this sunk in. "And you think he's going to do something to her?"

"*Yes.* And if he is successful at what I believe, what I *know* he's planning to do tonight, Celia could be hurt as well. I don't have time to explain it all—" she broke off as Jasper shouted at the horse, slapping the reins, and they lurched forward.

He'd heard enough, and he drove them hard down the narrow lane and up the first part of Helena's drive. There he slowed the horse and, at a snail's pace, had it turn onto a small offshoot to their left.

Not far down it, but far enough to put them in the trees, they came upon a weathered gazebo. Above it the sky had turned the color of blue sapphires against the darker ground and trees. There was enough space for Jasper to guide them around the gloomy structure, and she checked it out as they moved alongside it.

It must have been charming in its time, but now weeds had taken hold, pushing up through the lower latticework and around the simple bench seats inside, and the graying cedar shingles on the peaked, two-tier roof were beginning to curl.

Jasper continued on around so they were pointing out, and brought the trap to a stop.

"They don't use this much anymore," he said, climbing down.

He came around and held out an arm to help steady her as she stepped down to the ground.

"Okay, I'm going," she told him, feeling again in her pocket for the folded printouts. She just prayed she was in time. "I have to keep Helena from leaving with Leonard. It's crucial that I stop her."

"I don't like this," Jasper murmured in the semidarkness.

Of course he didn't. If anything happened to her, Gus could hold him responsible. "Don't worry. I don't plan on confronting Leonard. I just need to catch Helena alone."

She could tell he still didn't like it, but he said nothing more.

"I'll be back as soon as I can," she said, and started away from him, back up the little offshoot.

Thirty-four

The undergrowth and trees had begun to thin out on each side of her. She was making quicker time now that she was on the driveway but felt uneasy being so out in the open as she moved along the interlocking stones the surface was paved with. A few weeds were beginning to poke through around the edges, betraying Helena's currently impoverished state which wouldn't include such meticulous maintenance.

Where the drive looped around at the end, she headed to the left, following the small shrubs that skirted the circular area until she was past the marble bird bath in the center, and then cut back across.

She had just reached the square stone pillars on the other side of the double-sided carriage steps she'd noticed the first time she was there, when she picked up the unmistakable clatter in the distance of someone approaching. She could see the shape of the tall trees lining the walkway ahead of her but they weren't thick enough to provide any coverage. Passing between the pillars, she moved onto the lawn and jogged toward the woods beyond where she could get out of sight, trying to listen and judge how far away they were.

She wasn't going to make it. Quickly changing direction, she angled back toward the low rock wall along the front, increased her speed until her shoes were pounding on the grass and her breath was rasping in her throat, and flung herself down in front of the higher part on this side of the opening. She would have to time it just right, but it was her only option.

The clatter coming up the drive increased and light glimmered in the darkness as whoever it was drew near, and then began to fade as they continued on. Rolling onto her hands and knees, she scrabbled over, hoping no one was looking out from the house, and peeked around the pillar beside her just in time to see the side of a carriage pulled by two horses as it swung to the right. She couldn't be sure but she thought it looked like Leonard driving it.

Quickly, she slipped around to the other side and stayed low until she was sure he had disappeared from sight. Had he already penned the fake note? If he had, then it might already be too late. But if he stopped for a moment inside to do it, she might still have time.

As night settled around her, she rethought her original plan to head for the columned entrance under a balcony with a scrolled railing, hoping to slip inside if it was open. Instead, she quickly shot across the gap and slipped back around to the inside, and began following the rock wall until she had made it past the large portico and the section extending over here came into view.

Though the home was of an earlier style she thought might be Greek Revival or some approximation of it, this outer addition from what she could tell appeared very similar to the sunroom at Gus's. Going for broke—she didn't have time for anything else— she veered toward the glow of the white steps leading to the door.

Please let it be unlocked. Or she didn't know what she was going to do.

She bounded up the steps, shooting a glance at the nearest window, reached a shaky hand out, and grasped the handle to try it.

It moved easily, and she pulled the door open and stepped inside. Had someone walked outside for some air and then neglected to secure it on their way in? The estate was situated off by itself; it was possible they weren't as careful about locking up here.

In the faint light, she could make out wicker furniture with flowered cushions and throw pillows grouped in the immediate area by the glass sections above the lower bricks that made up the outer walls, leaving an open space before a single step to the inner door.

Trying to still her quivering limbs, she took a second to gather herself, then darted past the narrow window of the adjoining room, stepped up, and tried the knob.

It turned in her hand and she slowly pushed the door open, trying to peek through the crack as she did so. She had no idea where Leornard, or Helena for that matter, was and she could just imagine how they might react to her intrusion into their home. She pictured Leonard discovering her, pulling out some antique-looking gun, and shooting her dead. Shuddering, she tried to bring back her earlier resolve as she moved on in.

She was in a dining room with a closed door to her right, a fireplace to her left by a large, formal table, and on the other side of it, a wide opening leading out to what looked like the entrance hall.

Gus's home was certainly nice but this was on a whole different level. She tiptoed across and peered out. There was a lot of white—white walls, white marble, white columns—lit by softly burning lamps and wall sconces, which had been offset by dark furnishings, tasteful rugs, and drapes. Where there weren't rugs, there was gleaming wood floors. Chandeliers and gilt also reined heavily here but there were more open areas and high, wide archways. In design and décor, it had more of an airy, classic feel to it.

Going straight through the entrance hall and into the main part of the home seemed like a bad idea, so she opted for the closed door in there instead.

On the other side of it, she found a smaller, round version of the formal table with four matching chairs between a sofa and another fireplace. She quickly crossed the room and stuck her head around. She looked up and down the hallway and saw no one.

Silently, she crept out and moved toward the staircase she could see the curve of ahead.

Something thumped above her and she paused, listening. Someone was moving around upstairs. Was it Helena, or Leonard?

The question was answered when she approached a doorway to her right and picked up movement within. A second later she heard the sound of a man clearing his throat, which she assumed was Leonard and not some butler they'd somehow managed to retain.

She continued creeping closer, hugging the wall, and saw that unless Leonard came out while she was in the process, she might be able to slip by and ascend the staircase without him seeing.

Tiptoeing as fast as she could, she hurried the rest of the way, shifted to the other side, and rounded the bottom stairstep.

Grasping hold of the banister, she started up, desperately praying he didn't emerge while she was in full view.

Halfway to the top, one of the risers gave a *pop* beneath her foot. She froze in place—and then started up again. She had to get higher.

She made it three more steps without any noise and forced herself to go still again. Sure enough, she could hear Leonard moving out into the entrance hall.

She could sense him standing there, looking up the staircase where she hovered unseen.

The seconds ticked by while she remained in place.

Finally, she heard his footsteps as he retreated. Silently releasing her breath and sagging in relief, she waited a few seconds more and then began ascending the stairs again.

Not stopping this time even when there was another *pop* at the top, she looked left and then headed right to get out of sight.

She glanced into each space she passed as she moved along. *Where was Helena?*

"Leonard, is that you?" came Helena's voice from a room ahead of her.

Zeroing in on it, Cheyenne speeded up, desperate to catch her before she came out and alerted Leonard. She had to stop her even if it meant tackling her.

Helena, in the process of packing clothes into a large trunk, gave a small yelp and spun around as she burst inside and immediately shut the door behind her.

"Shh ... shh, it's okay," she told her, approaching with her finger to her lips. "I just have to talk to you."

"What are you doing?" Helena cried. "Who let you in?"

"No one. I snuck in. I have to talk to you. I have to tell you something and I don't want Leonard to hear."

"You're crazy!" Helena, looking lovely as usual in a cream traveling suit with her chestnut hair done up, backed away to get on the other side of the bed. "Get out of here before I scream for help!"

"Helena, *listen* to me. There are things you need to know. I swear to you it is a matter of life and death." She moved a couple of steps closer. "Five minutes," she implored, holding her hands out.

"Wait!" she said as Helena, grabbing onto the bedpost, opened her mouth. "I can prove it. I can prove it right now.

"Gus knows, Helena. But that's not exactly why I'm here."

At the mention of Gus, all expression dropped from Helena's face.

Cheyenne hurriedly continued now that she had her attention. "I'll explain everything, I promise. But right now you need to hear me and do what I say. Any minute your husband *Leonard* is going to come into this room with a note supposedly from Augustus summoning you to his office at the mill. But it's not from Gus, I assure you."

She paused, thinking she heard something, then focused back on Helena. "I don't have time to explain everything, but I found out some stuff about him that not even Gus knows. Your husband is not who you think he is." She held up her hand as Helena went to say something. "I know you believe you know the truth about him, but you don't." She thought she heard something again and cast her eyes about the room for a place to hide.

There was no closet but there was a tall wardrobe that might work. "Listen," she said, turning back to Helena, who had nearly climbed onto the bed in an effort to keep away from her. She hadn't yelled for help yet, though, which told her that Helena might have already begun to harbor her own suspicions about her husband. She waited until Helena met her eyes again and then came out with it. "He has an insurance policy on you."

She said it quietly but the effect was like she'd shouted it at the woman. Jerking, Helena blanched, then went pink and blinked at her in shock. "What do you mean? I don't know of any policy."

"Exactly." Cheyenne felt around in her pocket for the printouts, but before she could pull them out, she caught the sound of someone—*Leonard*—whistling to himself as he moved down the hall.

"Helena, listen. You can't act like you know anything." She stepped over and grabbed hold of her arm. "*Okay?* He's dangerous." She could hear him right outside now. "Please don't let on I'm here." She let go of her and backed away. "Go along with it and get rid of him and I'll explain everything."

She heard the rattle of the knob and a creak as she ripped open the wardrobe and, stepping all over whatever was in the bottom, jammed herself in and hauled the doors closed. One of them didn't shut completely, and she peered through the crack as Leonard entered the room.

She waited in an agony of anticipation to see if Helena would give her away and then let Leonard murder her to hide his schemes.

It was really happening. In his hand, Leonard had a slip of paper he was holding out to Helena.

"What's that?" Helena asked, moving around to take it.

"It was just dropped off. It's from Augustus. He wants to discuss something *important* with you." He said this with sickening disdain.

"I didn't hear anyone," Helena snapped, unfolding the note.

"Just *go,* my dear, and pat his hand and say whatever you need to say so we can get on with our travel plans."

He tried to put his arm around her waist but she pulled away. She held the note up as if she needed to read it again, but Cheyenne thought she was stalling for time. Had she seen Gus's handwriting before? Did she recognize that it wasn't his?

If they had once been as close as she suspected they'd been, then it was very possible that Gus had written to her in some form or another. Unexpectedly she felt a stab of jealousy at the thought of them together. *It doesn't matter*, she told herself. Gus would never consider being with Helena, especially once he found out what she was capable of.

"All right," Helena said, folding the note and turning toward the vanity table beside her. When Leonard remained standing there, she turned back to him. "I'll be right down," she said, a hint of annoyance entering her voice. "I'm assuming you're going to run me over there?"

Leonard, who had finally started out of the room, paused in the doorway. "Yes, you know there are a few last-minute things I wanted to get. I can take care of that then swing back to pick you up."

Helena made one last protest before he disappeared into the hallway. "Surely we don't have time for this."

Leonard stopped and swiveled around to face her. "We have plenty of time before the train leaves." He stared stonily back at her. "Unless you want to add to his suspicions and risk him trying to prevent us from going?"

"No." She gave an irritated sigh. "I'll be right down. I'll do my best with Gus, but we're going to have to hurry. I don't want to be rushing around at the last minute."

Oh, Helena, you could have been an actress in another life. If she were going to give Cheyenne away, she would have already done it. Now if Leonard would just get out of there so she could convince Helena to leave with her. And then she would finally be able to see Gus again.

Leonard's footsteps faded as he moved away and then there was silence. Helena remained over by the vanity a little longer, fiddling with some bottles grouped on a mirrored tray, then said, "You can come out now."

Cheyenne needed no more prompting. Her legs were beginning to cramp and she could barely breathe. Letting the doors fall open, she leaned forward and clumsily climbed out. "We need to go."

Helena whirled around. "Not until you give me some answers."

"I'll tell you everything, but we need to get out of here. We can talk on the way."

"What does Gus know?" Helena asked, unperturbed. She clearly wasn't budging until she learned more.

"He only suspects that you and Leonard, and poor Perry, might be scheming to take the remaining investment money. He doesn't know the extent of it, though. Now let's get going. Jasper's waiting at the gazebo."

Helena narrowed her eyes. "Why *poor* Perry?"

That threw Cheyenne. "Never mind." She certainly couldn't tell her that in an alternate future Leonard strangled Perry and stuffed him down a well while she and the others burned with the mill.

"What doesn't he know, then?" Helena moved closer to the door, cocking her head, then walked back to Cheyenne.

"He doesn't know about the life insurance policy." She reached into her pocket and brought out the crumpled printouts. "I have a copy of it right here with your supposed signature."

"It's not mine. There must be some mistake." Helena stepped closer and leaned in to look at the paper Cheyenne smoothed out.

"Leonard forged your signature."

Helena sucked in a breath. "Where did you get this?"

"It doesn't matter. What matters is you now know what he is planning." Cheyenne paused for a second as a faint sound reached her ears, and lowered her voice. "His name is not Leonard."

"I know."

"Did he tell you his real name is Tobias Fletcher," she said, "suspected of arson and the murder of his father, among other things, twenty years ago?"

Helena's brows drew together. "Tobias? He never told me that name."

Cheyenne shifted the other printout to the top and held it out. "Him when he was a kid."

Helena looked down at the photo of Leonard as a child with his birth name written underneath, and a change came over her expression. Shock was still there, but the disbelief had transformed into anger and something else. Embarrassment possibly, that he had almost conned her too?

Cheyenne contemplated telling her the full extent of what Leonard had been prepared to do. But then she would have to try and explain how she knew.

Helena took the papers from her so she could flip back to the copy of the life insurance policy. "One hundred thousand dollars." She gave a disgusted laugh then thrust them back at her. "How do you think he was going to do it?"

Cheyenne stared back at her, thinking *You don't want to know.*

"What? Tell me!"

Cheyenne slowly shook her head. "That's what the note was about. He was trying to lure you away." To your death, she thought. After setting the fire that would ultimately kill twelve people if you included Lydia and Gus. "He wants the investment money *and* the insurance payout. And probably your estate here as well."

"The bastard! He will *never* have it!" She made as if to stalk angrily away, and Cheyenne quickly caught her arm to stop her. "Wait! Use your head. We need to leave. He's dangerous I tell you! You don't know what he may do."

"No, she doesn't," Leonard said, stepping out of the shadows into the room.

Helena and Cheyenne both jumped then gasped at the shiny gun in his hand, pointed right at them. *How much had he heard?*

Instead of a sleek little derringer like she'd imagined, the gun looked more like something out of the old west with a big sturdy frame and enough shots to easily kill both of them.

"What are you doing?" Helena cried.

"What has to be done, my dear." He motioned the gun at them. "Now both of you, get over here. I mean it, let's go. Move it!"

Cheyenne lurched forward then glanced back to make sure Helena was following and saw she was still standing there staring in disbelief at Leonard. "We better do what he says, Helena."

What the woman had been planning to do was bad but she had never meant for anyone to die, and Cheyenne couldn't help but feel a tiny scrap of sympathy for her. Of course she wanted to save her home, but the path she had taken only led to ruin, as she was now seeing.

Just when Cheyenne was about to prompt her again, Helena stiffly started toward her.

"That's right," Leonard said, motioning again at another doorway leading out. "Let's go."

Helena, in front of her now, suddenly shouted, "What are you going to do, Leonard?"

"I'm going to escort you to the dressing room. Now shut up and keep moving."

"Leonard, you can't do this!"

"Yes, I can. Just like you can be the tight-fisted, frigid shrew you've become. Now hurry up."

Together, they moved across the room with Leonard training the revolver on them the entire way. Cheyenne wanted to do something, but he was leaving her no chance.

"What are you planning to do with us?" Helena asked in a shrill voice, then stumbled when Leonard hit her between the shoulder blades, knocking her forward.

"I'm going to lock you in while I make my escape, you sill cow." He went to push her again then didn't have to when Helena lurched into motion.

You liar, Cheyenne thought. He wasn't going to run off anywhere and leave them there alive to tell everyone what he'd done and had been planning. Disappearing into the sunset might not be so easy this time. And if they caught him ...

No, he was going to push them into this room, kill them, and then—

Her train of thought stuttered to a halt as she perceived the flaw in her logic. Shoot them, and then what? Go on the run? The authorities were bound to figure out that he did it. So what …? Her tired, addled brain finally made the connection and instantly, with a sick feeling, she knew what his game was. It was why he hadn't already shot them.

It needed to look like an accident.

"That's right, through there," Leonard said. "Maybe she'll show you the precious family jewels she refuses to part with."

If she was going to do something, it had to be now, especially if he was reluctant to fire the gun for fear that someone would hear it or find the bullets later. Hold on. Had he overheard her say Jasper was at the gazebo? Apprehension filled her at the thought of the unsuspecting groom waiting for her by the trap with no idea of the danger.

She waited until Helena had opened and then walked through the door at the end of the short hallway, then swiftly spun around, intending to knock against him and catch him by surprise and get around him. But he must have been expecting it and before she'd made it halfway, he struck her hard across the temple with the gun, instantly stunning her—and she felt herself falling as the floor rose up to meet her.

Thirty-five

It was the pulsing pain that brought Cheyenne back to awareness. Groaning, she attempted to sit up but only made it partway before a sickening wave of dizziness swept over her. This was the second time she'd been knocked out. How many blows to the head could she take? She held still until the wooziness passed and then pushed herself backwards to prop against the door behind her. "Helena."

Pacing back and forth across the shadowy space, the other woman gave no indication she'd heard.

"Helena!"

"What!" Helena spun around, ceasing her pacing.

Cheyenne tried to bring her into focus, pressing a hand to her forehead. "We need to get out of here."

"There's no way out of here!" Strands of Helena's hair had worked themselves loose and now clung to her forehead in short wisps. "He's locked us in. We're here for the evening. Paulette won't get here until—"

"Helena!"

The urgency and tone of her voice finally got through to her and Helena fell silent.

"He's not going to leave us here to be found."

Helena made a sound of irritation. "What are you talking about? Here we are ... for the duration."

The woman couldn't be that dense. "He's not going to let us ruin it for him, is what I'm saying."

Helena stared fixedly at her. "You mean ...?"

"I'm betting he sticks with what he planned." *A variation of what he'd originally intended.*

"Killing me? Now killing both of us? How?"

Cheyenne shrugged. "An overturned lamp or dropped candle, would be my guess. That'll be the prevailing theory, anyhow."

"But you said he wanted the estate!"

"If things go the way he wants them to"—would they, she wondered, now that everything had changed?—"he'll still get the land and the insurance money. And at least this way he won't go to prison." And he would still kill Perry. Because the lawyer was a loose end and because he needed someone to frame for the missing investment money. And Jasper … A chill ran through her again at the thought.

"He'll never get away with it! They'll question why we didn't just run out."

"People get caught unawares in fires and pass out from smoke inhalation all the time. They won't be able to prove he did it."

"But we've been locked in!"

Cheyenne shook her head. "Maybe he believes the fire will destroy any evidence of that. Maybe he's counting on them believing we were trapped before we understood what was happening and then were overcome."

"But what about Perry? You mentioned him before."

"Leonard wants to keep the investment money, too. He's planning to murder Perry so he can blame the missing funds on him." She could worry about explaining how she knew this later. "He was going to do it tonight after he called you out to the mill and set fire to it. But things have changed, so now he's gone to plan B." Would he still put Perry in the well? *I hope he does*, she thought angrily. That way he might still get caught if the same keen-eyed detective got put on the case.

Helena's hand went to her throat. "Dear God, the son of a bitch just might get away with it."

Cheyenne exhaled a soft laugh. "He just might. And I can't begin to tell you how hard I've tried and what I've gone through to stop all of this."

At least Celia and the others and Lydia, and hopefully *Gus*, would be safe, and he'd still have the mill. He would lose her and always wonder what really happened, but at least maybe he wouldn't go off and contract tuberculosis now.

Sighing, she looked listlessly around the smallish space. What could they possibly use to help get them out of there? To her left there was a chair in the corner the same walnut wood as the dressing table beside her, and on her other side, only cabinets and sections of tall shelving. Directly across from her where Helena stood, the entire wall was taken up from top to bottom with nothing but storage cubbies above and below garments hanging on rods.

With difficultly she got to her feet and, catching a glint of silver, stepped over to the dressing table to look behind a porcelain trinket dish and a dark, almost medieval-looking box she assumed held the jewelry Leonard had mentioned. And why was there so much light? She turned away from the one low-burning lamp and raised her eyes.

Up high against the outside wall, there was a line of narrow rectangular windows, allowing the rising moon's light to stream in. "What about one of those?"

Helena turned to squint up at them. "They're kind of small. And high."

"It's better than the alternative," she countered drily.

"And I believe there are bars," Helena said, turning away.

Which brought Cheyenne's attention back to what she'd spied before. Reaching around, she picked up the larger, flatter of the two matching silver objects lying there. "Maybe we can do something with these."

Helena walked around to see. "A shoe horn and a nail file?" She looked at them doubtfully. "I don't know."

"It's all we've got." Setting the file down, she looked back up at the windows again. It would be tight, but if they laid flat they might fit. *If* they could loosen the bars. "I need to get up there."

There was a pair of low cabinets about waist high between the tall shelving, but even standing on them she wasn't sure she'd be high enough.

She looked around for something to stand on. "I have to get higher."

Spying the chair in the corner again, she walked over and lifted it to bring it over.

"And there's this," Helena said, pulling a small ivory-cushioned stool out from under the dressing table.

"Okay, bring that too."

Cheyenne looked from the stool and chair to the cabinet top to the rectangular windows. Even standing on the chair it wouldn't be easy.

Unfastening the cape, she swept it off and tossed it into the corner. *Sorry, Lydia.* But she couldn't risk it getting in the way. She raised the chair and heaved it up onto the cabinet, then turned it to position the legs. They fit, with a little room left to spare.

"Okay," she told Helena. "I'm going to try and climb up."

Helena nodded silently, her eyes glassy and unblinking.

Using the stool, Cheyenne awkwardly climbed onto the cabinet beside the chair, then got her feet under her and straightened up. "Here goes."

With Helena keeping the chair steady, Cheyenne grabbed hold of the back, lifted one leg and pulled herself up onto it in a crouch. Carefully, she stood up.

It wasn't as bad as she'd feared. She could reach the window, but it would be even better if she could get higher so she could work on the—

She'd forgotten the nail file. Not that it or a shoe horn was going to do much.

Wait a minute. She struggled to decipher what she was seeing. What had appeared to be bars across the rectangular windows looked to actually be pieces of wood between the panes, forming a diamond grid. She stretched an arm out to touch one of the thin segments.

Thank God. It wasn't metal. Maybe they had a chance. "Helena," she called down to her. "They're not bars! Give me the stool so I can bust through."

"But how will I get up there?" Helena asked, making no move to get it.

Cheyenne eyed the distance to the floor. "You can do it. You have to."

After a second, Helena grabbed the stool and held it up to her.

She got her first inkling that what she'd feared was on its way to coming true as she took it from her, leaned in to peer at the nearest strip of wood dividing the panes, and picked up the unmistakable scent of smoke.

Almost immediately Helena shrieked, "I smell smoke!"

"Shit!" He'd really done it. He'd set fire to the goddam house. And she didn't know a lot about the fire departments of this day and age, but considering how far away from town they were, she doubted they would get there in time to save it. Or them.

"Hurry up!" cried Helena. Smoke was now seeping in through the gaps around the door.

"Okay! I don't want to fall." Gripping the shelving behind her, she looked down as Helena, waving a hand in front of her face, began to cough. "You need to block the smoke!" What had merely been thin tendrils had already grown to a steady stream pouring in. "Get something. Pile it up and block the space at the bottom!"

Helena grabbed a bunch of scarves and flung them down in front of the door and then went for some dresses she ripped down from their hangers. She dropped them and kicked them across the space. "It's not working! It's still getting in!"

"Keep trying," Cheyenne yelled, which immediately set her to coughing, and she had to fight to keep from toppling over.

Twisting back around to the window, she hovered in indecision. Now that she was on the brink and her time had run out, she found herself frightened by the scope of what she had to do. She would have to not only break the glass out but also knock away the wood pieces running across. What if she wasn't strong enough? And then she'd have to get both Helena and herself across the roof and down to the ground safely.

You have to, or you'll both die! With a snarling roar, she turned her head away and swung the stool up and into the window and was rewarded with the crash of glass breaking and wood splintering.

Below her, Helena had given up and retreated to the other corner, where she had her skirt pulled up over her mouth and nose.

"Helena! Move over here and get ready!"

Dropping her skirt, Helena started over, then had to stop as she was bent double by a fit of coughing.

"Keep moving!" Cheyenne shouted at her. "Before you pass out!"

Helena managed a deep, wheezing breath, stumbled forward, and fell into the cabinets to prop against them.

Turning back, Cheyenne swung the stool hard into the window, then swung it again. And again. And again. Then she spun the stool around and began using the curved legs to knock out the remaining pieces of wood and glass. Ramming hard into a stubborn section, she lost her grip when it suddenly gave way, and the stool slipped out of her hand and soared through the opening.

Throwing her arm across the sill, grateful she had sleeves, she grabbed the other side, and got her knee up. Also thankful she had on pants, she hung there for a second before pushing off hard with the leg stretched out beneath her, and heaved her upper body up and across with her head hanging out into the night air.

Barely keeping balanced as she was overcome again, tiny flashes of light had begun to dance across her vision by the time she could get control of herself and turn her body to check on Helena.

Down below her, Helena had slid to the floor and now sat there motionless with her eyes closed.

"Helena!" she shouted, and began to wriggle the rest of the way around until she was balanced across with her legs hanging out.

"Helena!" she yelled again, and amazingly saw her stir. "That's right, get up! Get *up*!"

Helena, hair half ripped down and looking wretched, sat up, gagging, got turned around, and pushed herself to a standing position.

Cheyenne, breathing raggedly, suddenly comprehended that she wasn't sweating merely from exertion. It was getting hot in there.

"I can't do it," Helena wailed, holding on to the precariously perched chair.

"You can! You have to! It's easy." She paused as a heavenly breeze wafted across her, then shifted back a little as Helena finally managed to get her body up far enough to raise her leg and use the shelving beside her to get herself on top of the cabinet.

"That's it! Now get up on the chair."

"There's no one to hold it steady," Helena cried, looking up at her.

"It'll be fine if you're careful! Stand on the chair and climb up onto the sill and turn around so you can drop down. Okay?"

Without waiting for her reply—she was starting to feel faint— she wriggled backwards until she was hanging by her hands, said a silent prayer, and let herself fall.

She hit the roof below her, throwing out a hand to keep from pitching forward and smacking her head, and tried not to roll off the mildly sloping surface.

"All right," she yelled after she'd gotten her balance. "Come on!"

"I can't," came her faint reply.

"You can!" If Helena couldn't do it, she was doomed. Cheyenne scooted back some, then hollered, "Just go for it! Don't let the bastard win!"

A moment later, Helena's head and shoulders appeared and then she was twisting around, fighting her skirt.

Yelping, Cheyenne threw herself forward as Helena dropped straight down without hanging, caught hold of her and, taking Helena with her, flung herself backwards. Falling onto her back, she might have flipped and tumbled all the way down if not for Helena's body landing on her and pinning her against the raised seam of the roof.

Like being on the top of the world with one foot in Tibet and one in Nepal, she thought as they lay there with the wooden shingles falling away on each side of them.

"We've got to stop meeting like this," she murmured as Helena caught her breath.

"Pardon?"

"Nothing. Let's go." Cheyenne pushed against her and Helena sat up, got onto her hands and knees, and shakily rose to her feet.

"Out of the pan and into the fire," Helena whispered, gazing across.

Carefully standing up, Cheyenne stretched her neck and peered over. Flames were rising from the second story. From about the center point on, the home was now engulfed in a raging orange-red inferno. She could feel the heat of it too, as it rippled intermittently over them. If the townspeople hadn't known about the fire before, they surely did now. Huge dark plumes of smoke were billowing into the air, reflecting the growing fury of it and setting the dark sky aglow.

Something made a popping sound. She looked over and spotted a burning ember bouncing across the thin pieces of wood they stood on as the blaze crept toward the area above the window they'd climbed out. "Come on, we have to get down."

"But *how?*"

"We'll jump if we have to."

They could both be hurt or killed if they fell wrong, but there was no other way. At least they'd have a chance.

Staying low and taking small side steps, Helena started downward on the opposite side of where Cheyenne thought she remembered some bushes. "Hey, we need to try over here," she called across to her.

Helena responded over her shoulder, "There's a tree."

Even better. "In that case."

And just in time, too; she could feel the fire like a wall of heat growing closer and closer behind her, the roar of it gaining in volume as the black smoke spewed out and settled around them.

She began sidestepping her way after Helena. She was quaking inside. How many feet could a person safely fall and still live?

Near the edge, they slowed and began inching their way forward.

"I'll go first this time," cried Helena unexpectedly after looking back, never a good idea, at the ungodly inferno heading their way, her face shaded orange from the fire. Then before Cheyenne could do anything, Helena stepped forward, jumped out, and fell downward.

She leaped to the edge as the sound of branches breaking then a sharp cry rang out and looked over just as Helena hit the ground on her back.

Cheyenne's hand crept up to her mouth as she waited for Helena to move.

Oh, no. Not after everything.

She hesitated a moment longer, tears filling her eyes, pondering in an abstract way the possibility of her ending up dead beside her, then gathered herself, eyeing the tree, a spindly, decorative specimen, searching for a likely branch. Because she couldn't wait any longer. The heat felt like it was baking her alive and any minute the sunroom was going to collapse beneath her.

Helena had taken out the nearest branches when she'd crashed into it, but there were still some halfway decent limbs. Just not in front of her.

She sucked in a deep breath of hot air that felt like it scorched her throat, then took two running steps and launched herself with a guttural cry over the edge. Spreading her arms wide, she flew out and then down and thought she was going to miss it entirely and smack into the ground to lie beside Helena, but then her sleeve caught and jerked her inward and she managed to seize a smaller branch long enough to break her fall when it gave way. Throwing her arms around her head to protect it, she tried to roll when she hit and came to a stop on her back.

She lay there wondering if she'd done internal damage and didn't know it, and then remembered Helena lying a few feet from her. That plus the sight of the growing flames rolling across the spot she'd jumped from got her moving.

She cautiously raised then turned her head, and when she found nothing obviously wrong, lifted herself up, feeling a jolt of pain in her lower back—but luckily it didn't feel like it was her spine—and got to her feet, wincing at a twinge in one of her knees.

She stumbled over to where Helena lay and dropped down beside her as the flames licked skyward, sparks flying out and igniting the closest trees, their tops flaring like matchsticks. She bent over her, about to call her name—and then didn't bother at the sight of Helena's blank, unseeing eyes. It was no use. She was gone.

She grabbed hold of Helena's arm, thinking to drag her away, when without warning a section of the roof over the sunroom collapsed, and flames burst through with a roar.

Leaving her, she staggered away from the burning home. *I'm still alive*, she thought. And Gus was out there, somewhere. *Her Gus.*

She realized she was heading the wrong way and moving into the surrounding woods instead of around to the front where at the very least Jasper would be waiting, if he hadn't gone for help. *Unless Leonard took him out*, she thought with a tremor of anxiety. Drunkenly swerving to the right, she kept going until she was well past the blazing house, then cut across the lawn.

In the light of the roaring flames, the shape of a small buggy materialized out of the smoky gloom in front of her. Whose ...? *Was that the trap?* She jerked her attention around to the burning home and stopped, fear spiking through her. A dark figure, lit from behind by the red-orange flames consuming the structure, was coming down the steps with someone draped across his back.

"Gus!" she tried to shout, but it came out as only a croak. *No!* she thought as the other person, Jasper it looked like, was placed on the ground and Gus, she was sure of it, turned and sprinted for the house again.

She tried again and screamed as loud as she could though it hurt her throat. "Guussss!"

Faltering, Gus whipped around, stiffening in surprise, and then lunged forward and broke into a run straight for her.

"Gus!" She started across to meet him. It was him. Her Gus from before the mill burned and Helena and all those workers and Celia and Lydia had died and he'd contracted TB and then wasted away and grew old before his time.

It was really him, her still young, handsome Gus with the rest of his life ahead of him. Crying now, she threw herself into his arms, breaking down completely in relief and joy at seeing him alive and well. "Oh Gus, I'm so happy to see you."

"*Cheyenne*. I thought I'd lost you!" He kissed the top of her head over and over, hugging her hard.

"I'm so glad you're okay," she said through her tears. "I was afraid I'd never make it in time."

Pulling back slightly, she drank in the sight of him, hardly daring to believe it, never more thankful for anything in her life. "I thought I'd failed you."

"How? In what way?"

Wordless, she shook her head. So much had happened. And now so much hadn't happened.

"Later," she told him, wiping her eyes and letting him lead her away from the fire to the larger carriage she could now see a little farther down. "Wait," she said, remembering the groom. "We need to help Jasper!"

"Cheyenne ..."

Oh no. "What? Is he ...?"

"I don't know. It doesn't look good." He glanced back as part of the second floor collapsed down onto the first one with a mighty crash. "The fire crew should be here soon. There's no way they've missed that. Though I don't know what they'll be able to do."

He took her hand to assist her into the carriage. "I'll get you home and send for a doctor as soon as I can. But right now, I need to see to Jasper."

"Gus, wait." She peered out at him before sitting back. "About Helena. I'm sorry, but ... she's dead. I had to leave her lying behind the house. I didn't know what else to do."

"Dammit." Her turned away and then after a second, turned back again. "It's okay, you don't have to worry about that. I'll inform them so they can recover her as soon as they can."

"How did you know something was wrong?" she asked as he went to move away.

"When I got back and Myrna told me where you'd gone and how agitated you'd seemed, I drove straight over. I found Jasper inside and I was going back for you when I heard you holler across."

"You could have been killed."

"Living without you is no kind of life."

She gazed at him, looking so vibrant and handsome, and struggled to reconcile her intense relief and gratitude that he was safe with thoughts of that other lost Gus in another time who had suffered so much.

She gave him a tremulous smile, which he returned, and happiness glowed within her. "We have a lot to talk about," she said.

"Yes," he agreed. "Whenever you're ready."

Thirty-six

"Come on," said Celia, tugging on her arm to pull her faster toward the staircase. "He's got the camera ready."

Laughing, Cheyenne let her lead her down the stairs, where Gus waited at the foot. It wasn't the way she had envisioned it would be when she wore the crimson gown. There was no big party and group of admirers at the bottom while music played in the background and she gracefully descended to gasps of delight at the vision she made. But there was darling Celia and her beloved Augustus, and her infectious giggle and his dark eyes shining with love and obvious pride were better than anything she could have imagined.

Helena was dead, her house burnt to the ground, and Leonard had been taken into custody. He had been sure his ruse would work and he'd be able to claim the fire and their deaths had been an accident. "I wasn't even at the estate when it happened!" he'd protested later when they'd apprehended him on the way to Perry's office after wandering around the general store in town. It seemed he had planned to claim there had been no fire when he left to go get some items for their upcoming trip abroad and that Cheyenne must have arrived after he left but before the fire started. Apparently he had heard enough of her and Helena's conversation (the sneaky bastard must have caught on to something and snuck back to listen after delivering the fake note) to know that Jasper was waiting at the gazebo. Taking a trail he knew about through the forest, he had crept up behind Jasper and at gunpoint forced him to drive the trap up to the house. Once there he had marched him inside, grabbed a vase, and when Jasper turned around, cracked him over the head with it. He must have figured the injury would be attributed to a fallen beam.

But he hadn't counted on anyone making it out alive. Not only had Cheyenne made it, Jasper had as well. After being rushed to the hospital, he had languished unconscious for several days but then had finally awakened and was currently under observation but expected to make a full recovery. With Jasper and Cheyenne to tell the police what happened, corroborated by Helena's body and the life insurance policy, which they'd managed to verify with the company that issued it, and Leonard's true identity, which was also quickly confirmed—by the very same detective who'd recognized him before in an alternate reality—Leonard's fate had been sealed and he had soon confessed. And he had done it all for greed. But this time, only one person had lost their life.

The only difficulty had occurred when she'd had to explain how she knew about the life insurance policy and Leonard's real name. But Gus, sticking to the story they had fabricated for just such questions, had stepped in and told them he'd received a tip about Leonard from an anonymous source which had led to her doing some digging on her own and uncovering the policy on Helena. When asked what the tip was, Gus had replied that some unknown person had sent a messenger with a note simply stating that Leonard was not who they thought he was and was also known as Tobias Fletcher and that none of them, especially his wife, should trust him.

And when they were asked to speculate on who might have sent it, Cheyenne had contributed, "Who knows?" shrugging her shoulders. "Maybe someone who knew him as Tobias years ago and knew what he was capable of. Or someone else he conned, or blackmailed, or unwittingly roped into his plot. The man he used to draw up the hotel plans, perhaps?"

When they questioned her about her knowledge of the policy, she had told them she'd got to thinking about the part of the warning that was specific to Helena, intuitively began to harbor certain suspicions, and as a result had placed a series of calls to some of the major insurance companies who had telephone exchanges, including one based in San Francisco, where Mr. Ravenoff reportedly hailed from. "They basically had the impression that I was Helena," was how she'd worded it, not wanting to outright say she had impersonated her, "calling about her policy." This of course, she'd added, had also led to her having to exclaim, "Oh, dear me, I must have called the wrong number. I do apologize," numerous times when they were unable to find said policy, until she finally lucked up on the right office.

She wasn't sure the police completely bought their story, but they chose not to pursue it further and had let it go. The printout, she had burned in the fireplace after showing it to Gus. It was too obvious that it hadn't been produced on an ordinary printing press and would have been hard to account for.

Perry, never knowing how close he'd come to a gruesome end, had escaped death but not disgrace and was now also behind bars, awaiting trial for his part in the fraudulent hotel scheme. She knew Perry's situation bothered Gus, but there was no going back from what Perry had done, how he had planned to swindle so many good people, friends of his, and what it would have led to. Gus had quietly listened, his face ashen, when Cheyenne described to him the acts that Leonard, along with the hapless help of the other two, had orchestrated and committed before she'd intervened. She had glossed over the part where she'd found him dying, but he had gotten the picture, and his hand had been shaking when he took the glass of brandy she poured him.

Against all odds Gus, taking her hand now and smiling as Celia scampered ahead of them, had survived, along with Celia and Lydia (and Perry and the workers at the mill).

She paused just inside and gazed over at the others spread out loosely by the piano across from Mr. Gilbert and the camera on its tripod. Everyone was there: she and Gus, Agnes hovering in the periphery, Ruth and Clara, both of them smiling, Celia, and Lydia chatting with Myrna.

Gus moved over to help Mr. Gilbert, who had agreed to take the picture so Gus could be included at Cheyenne's insistence.

"Here," called Celia. "By me, Cheyenne!"

She obliged and walked over to stand by her, leaving a space for Gus.

"Okay everyone," Gus said as he bent over and twisted a knob. "You need to squeeze in." He straightened up and pointed. "Drag those chairs over. Some of us will have to sit in the front."

He spoke some more with Mr. Gilbert, then dashed over to where they had arranged the chairs, grinning at Cheyenne, and plopped into the one between her and Lydia. Celia was on her other side.

"Okay," called out Mr. Gilbert. "Say whiskey!"

"Whiskey!" they all obediently yelled back, smiling broadly.

Cheyenne stuck her hand up behind Celia, wondering if she would notice.

"Hold it!" Mr. Gilbert shouted. Then after a few seconds, there came a click, and it was done.

They stood up, and Gus slid his arm around her waist. "I love you," he said, gazing down at her as the others dispersed to help themselves to the punch and hors d'oeuvres Lydia had arranged for this little party of theirs. Henry and Daniel, who had both managed to get back their part of the money recovered from Leonard, were due over any minute.

"I love you, too," she murmured back, knowing it was true, and though she would miss her mother and brother and Jill until her dying day, she never wanted to be away from him.

The time slips had ceased after her last rough crossing, and now that it had been weeks and there had been no sign of the phenomenon, Celia, who hadn't let up in her insistence to return home, had finally, reluctantly, been allowed back.

Maybe another episode would occur tomorrow, or maybe never again. But the violence of the last few times along with the continuing stillness made her think it was at rest now and would remain inactive for a long time to come.

Gus, handsome as ever in dark evening wear with a lock of hair falling onto his forehead, came back over with two glasses of champagne and handed one of them to her.

"Cheers," he said, holding his out.

"Cheers," she echoed, and tapped her glass to his.

Epilogue

Dammit, Jill thought as the aging supermarket came into view again. She was going to have to call Caleb. She pulled off the road onto the section of asphalt over here, brought the SUV to a stop, and fished out her phone. If not for the gentleman inside who had recognized Cheyenne's photo, they might not have even found the house.

"Hey, it's Jill," she said when Caleb picked up. "Where did you say that old back road was? I've been up and down twice and I can't find it."

On the other end, Caleb, still despondent but functioning at least, described once more where the last turnoff was supposed to be.

"Are you sure?"

Yes, he told her, explaining again that it was hard to see, and then offered to drive down and show her if she needed him to.

"No, that's okay. Let me look some more before I give up."

She promised to send him a text with an update on how she fared, ended the call, and pulled back onto the road. At least she knew she was close and heading in the right direction.

She was moving slow, almost at the four-way ahead where she was going to be forced to turn around again, when a squirrel hovering at the edge of the road suddenly ran out in front of her. Slamming on the brakes, she jerked to a stop, barely missing the creature.

And there it was right beside her, a badly overgrown strip of pavement nearly obscured by the grass and weeds and overhanging trees and vines.

Shooting at look into the rearview, she jammed the gearshift into reverse, backed up, and cranked the wheel to turn in.

It was rough going at first, and once this was over she was going to have to do some explaining to Ben about the scratches she was sure were now marring the SUV. But she didn't care. She hadn't come this far to quit now.

Speeding up minutely, she continued on, even though she doubted she'd learn anything more than what they had already been told. All the detectives and investigators had been able to say with any degree of certainty was that Cheyenne appeared to have been staying there before she disappeared. Some of her things had been found in the home and her car had eventually been located behind a tree at the back of the property.

Unlike the turn onto the old back road, she had no difficulty identifying the beginning of the drive leading to the house. She got on the gas to get over a root sticking out of the ground and turned into it. The trees had grown up overhead like a canopy, and she could hear them scraping against the top as she proceeded.

The house, with yellow tape still wrapped around the posts flapping in the breeze, came into view, and she slowed the SUV, taking it in. Without the police tape and restored to its former glory, it would be a magnificent specimen of that lost Victorian time. She could see Cheyenne being drawn to it.

Speeding back up, she continued on, past a faint trail branching off to the right she thought might go to the family cemetery Caleb had told her about, and rolled to a stop before the steps. Probably she wasn't supposed to be there, but she hadn't been able to quit dwelling on everything and going over and over their last conversations, and she had to try and understand what had happened. Why hadn't she as Cheyenne's best friend not delved deeper and made sure she was really okay, despite the fact that she had downplayed her breakup with Brent? He had called Jill after it hit the news, full of regret and wracked with guilt for leaving Cheyenne in such financial distress. *As well you should be,* she'd thought angrily. But he had honestly seemed to be suffering, so she had held her tongue.

She couldn't stop thinking about that one night when she'd had the strange feeling that something was wrong and had tried to call her. And there was also what she had found with her birthday present.

She reached up and touched the gold crescent moon on the chain around her neck. Out of some weird sense of obligation because that was what her friend had wanted, she had kept quiet about the gift (except to Ben) and had refrained from opening the box. But then a few days ago, out of frustration, she had finally broken down and ripped it open. And there in the bottom she had found the photo. Nestled in tissue paper like some precious artifact. That's how it had seemed, too—faded and fragile in her hands when she'd lifted it out.

But there had been no mistaking it was Cheyenne. Especially considering Cheyenne herself had sent it to her. *Was it some kind of message?* she'd wondered, picking up the photo again and again and staring hard at it until she couldn't take it anymore. Finally, against Ben's wishes but with his eventual support, she had thrown a few things into a bag in case she stayed overnight—which was looking more and more likely as tired as she was—and had hit the road to see for herself the place where her oldest and best friend had spent her final days.

Shutting off the engine, she opened the door, climbed out, and clicked it shut. Except for the rush of the wind in the trees and the faint tinkle of some rusting wind chimes, it was utterly silent. *Desolate,* she thought with a shiver.

Pulling her jacket tighter around her, she moved around the car and up the weedy, leaf-covered walkway, and climbed the steps to the verandah. Ducking under the yellow tape, she crossed over to the double doors.

They were probably locked. And there was no way she was busting in. She reached out and tried the knob, and as expected found it unmoving. She gave it another try and then turned and walked across to the old swing on the end, glancing into the nearest window. But it was too dim inside for her to see much.

She gave the swing a push and listened to the creak of it as it swayed back and forth and tried to picture Cheyenne there.

After a moment she went back across, descended the steps, and walked along the front to make her way around the side. She'd come this far.

A light mist had formed and seemed to float above the ground in the woods around the neglected property slowly being taken over by nature.

She had almost made it to the back when from around the corner came the strangely muffled whicker of a horse. She jerked to a stop. A horse?

After a few seconds when she heard nothing else, she moved up, peeked around the corner, and then walked all the way around.

There was no horse. Anywhere. Not in the grossly overgrown yard where she stood, nor in the fallow field beyond, nor on the track leading down to an outbuilding on her left. Could it have gotten out of sight that quickly?

It must have. Or else she was hearing things. *Get ahold of yourself*, she thought and began picking her way over to the pitted back steps.

She carefully climbed them and, fully expecting this door to be locked as well, halfheartedly twisted the knob while pushing against it and was so surprised when it came open that she reared back and immediately let it fall shut.

Glancing around uneasily, she pushed it open again, and tentatively stepped inside. Goosebumps broke out on her arms as she walked on in to a time capsule of years past.

Moving slowly across faded, rumpled rugs and dull boards, she gazed into each space, especially the one in the center she believed Cheyenne had been sleeping in from what one of the detectives had told Caleb, and tried to imagine how it must have been for her, and how it would have been back in the day.

Working her way around, she crossed through a foyer bathed in amber from a stained-glass window under the white globes of an opulent chandelier, peered into a large room containing only a few pieces of furniture, then returned to the grand wooden staircase.

She grasped the banister and started up. Had Cheyenne noticed the same rose wallpaper on the wall between those old portraits? How many times had she gone up and down these stairs?

Emerging onto the second-floor landing, she turned left, her disquiet warring with a sense of marvel at the home and the glimpses of a bygone era it gave.

She looked at the turret rooms in particular with interest, especially the one still containing moldering belongings. And the balconies ... She could definitely see Cheyenne out there, with wine or maybe coffee, gazing at the forest and countryside beyond.

For about the hundredth time she found herself speculating about what could have happened to her friend. One day she had apparently been staying there, still connected and following leads on jobs, then she had sent her mother and Caleb one last message, mailed her a birthday necklace with a strange antique-looking photo—and fell off the face of the Earth.

She was about to head back down, feeling more confused than ever, when as an afterthought, she pulled open a door and found a narrow flight of stairs leading up into darkness.

She went to shut the door back, and paused. After everything she'd gone through, she couldn't leave one space unexplored. Heaving a sigh, she returned to the turret room where she had seen the small nub of a dusty candle.

Digging the lighter out of her pocket—after years of being quit she'd picked up smoking again, something Ben would *not* ultimately be supportive of—and held the tiny flame to the wick until it flared to life.

Carrying the tarnished sliver holder and its flickering passenger with her, she retraced her steps to the attic door and, holding onto the railing for dear life with her other hand, forced herself to move upwards through the darkness.

You're doing this for Cheyenne, she told herself. *For Cheyenne.*

At the top, she nearly bumped into the door. "Okay," she whispered, pulling back, and twisted the knob and pushed against it. But it only moved a few inches and scraped to a stop. Shifting around, she set the candle down on a lower step, and then in almost complete darkness, hit the door hard with her shoulder and knocked it open.

Cold air swept over her and she fumbled for the candle to block it before the flame could be extinguished.

Cupping her hand around it, she steadied herself, then climbed the rest of the way up and into the space beyond.

Raising the candle, she saw it was high enough for her to stand and straightened up after making sure there were no cobwebs above her.

She looked around, her eyes beginning to adjust. There was also light coming in through two triangular windows on each side of the open space.

Picking her way through the collapsing cartons, crates, lamps, splintery chairs, and other items stacked in the center, she wove her way over, stooping as the ceiling grew lower, to the clearer spot where the light was brighter.

Several framed portraits and a mirror had been left stacked against the rough boards.

Would someone be back to take this stuff? Who would end up with all of it?

For the first time, she thought about how long her car had been sitting out front. She quickly flipped through the old photos of long-dead people, then stood back up as much as she could. What did she think she was going to learn?

But since she was already there ... She moved across to a trunk with leather straps and lifted the lid. She leaned away from the smell of mold and decay that drifted out. It was filled with discolored, moth-eaten gowns. She dropped the lid back down.

As she turned to get out of there before she was discovered and arrested—Ben would *love* that—her attention was snagged by something propped against the back of the trunk.

She leaned over and tilted it out.

It was a picture. A largish framed portrait of a group of people. Had it been taken in this house?

Curiosity piqued, she slid it out, lifted it to balance it atop a metal milk can, and bent over it for a better look.

A line of people, servants she thought by the way they were dressed, who seemed happy enough, were standing close together in what did indeed look like the larger room downstairs. And in front of them were four people seated on chairs.

Her mouth turned up into an answering smile as she gazed one by one at the cheerful faces across the back and then moved down to the more formally dressed ones in the chairs along the front.

The lady on the far left, also smiling, appeared to be in her late fifties or early sixties. Beside her a handsome dark-haired younger man beamed at the camera. On the other side of him, a pretty woman dressed in a fancy evening gown with her hair ... her hair ...

Nearly screaming, she jerked back from the photograph as if she'd been burned. *It can't be,* she thought, pivoting away from an image that was unmistakably there and yet completely impossible.

It's the photo she sent, she tried to tell herself, *making you see things that aren't there.* Her mind was simply playing tricks on her. It couldn't be Cheyenne.

But she knew it was, exactly like in the inexplicable old photo she'd received.

She felt almost dizzy as she forced herself to step back over, but then it passed and she was able to look down at the framed portrait again. It was obviously old. It was that or believe that someone went to a lot of trouble to get everyone in period clothes, somehow transform the front parlor into new again, take the picture, put it through some kind of process to make it appear aged, then place it in a vintage frame so it would look antique before stashing it away up here. Which was ludicrous.

She had to bite back a scream again as she shifted her eyes over and saw what was above the head of the girl beside Cheyenne.

The photo atop the milk can and the walls and the floor and the very air she breathed seemed to shift, everything going off kilter for a second as her vision of reality shifted and stretched to include new, previously unthought of possibilities.

Above the girl, unbeknownst to her, two fingers had been raised behind her head to form a set of bunny ears.

In a daze, Jill turned and stumbled across the attic, descended the narrow staircase, and moved back through the house along the dim hallway and out the rear door between the tall windows.

It was when she hit the ground at the bottom and started across to go around the side that she finally registered what she was hearing.

There was a vehicle running in front of the house.

She wasn't inside, though. *I'm glad I got out when I did,* she thought. What was the worst they could do to her? Run her off? Well, let them. She was ready to get out of there so she could go somewhere and try and get her mind around what she'd seen.

Even as she tried to push them away and direct her attention to facing whoever waited for her, her thoughts kept coming back to certain facts. The photo Cheyenne had sent was of her, for sure. This was the house she had been staying in. And it was irrefutably her in the group photo making the same stupid bunny ears she'd been ruining pictures with for twenty years.

Impossible. And yet ... She rounded the side of the house and as she'd feared, a gray sheriff's car sat behind her Equinox.

As she came around in front of it, the male figure behind the wheel jerked into action, shoving the door open to climb out.

"Sorry," she called over. "I was only looking around."

"You're not supposed to be here, ma'am," the deputy said, coming toward her with his hand on his weapon.

"I know. I'm sorry. But it was my best friend that disappeared from here." A gust of wind swept across, blowing a strand of hair across her mouth, and she had to stop to peel it off as the deputy continued across the overgrown lawn to meet her.

He had taken his hand away from his gun, at least.

He stopped a few feet from her. "You say you knew the woman that went missing?"

"Yes, since we were kids." He was fairly young she saw. "I'm Jill and that lady, Cheyenne, she was my best friend. I had to come. I just drove down here from Virginia." Why was she telling him all this? Any second he was going to order her to move along.

But he didn't. He continued to stand there regarding her silently. And then he said something unexpected.

"I thought I saw her one time." He shifted around. "I suspected somebody had been staying here, but hey, no harm no foul, and because I had never seen any direct evidence of it ..."

"You saw her?"

He nodded. "I'm going to deny this if you tell anyone."

"Understood." She wasn't sure she wanted to hear this, but that was why she was here, to learn everything she could, and Cheyenne had sent her that picture for a reason.

"I came out later than I usually do," he said, gazing off to the side. "In the early evening just before sundown. And while I was sitting here, down the steps and into the yard comes this woman. I only saw her for a brief moment, kind of spotlighted in my headlights, you know? But going by the photos of your friend, it was her."

Jill nodded. Where was he going with this and why wouldn't he want anyone to know?

"But when I jerked open the door and stepped out, she just ... *poof* ... disappeared. One second she was there and the next she was gone."

This was a man of the law; he couldn't possibly be making this up. She struggled to understand. "But where did she go?"

He shrugged. "You tell me. She wasn't there in front of me, and she wasn't around or in the house. I checked."

Shaking her head, she tried to absorb this new information. "So what do you think—"

"I don't know. After a while I convinced myself that it was raining and getting dark and maybe ..."

"You didn't see what you thought you did," she finished for him.

He nodded. "Well," he said in the quiet, possibly regretting saying so much. "You're not actually allowed out here so you're going to have to take off. Sorry. And I wish I had more to tell you about your friend."

"Thank you anyway," she responded automatically, thinking about the faint path into the trees she'd seen on her way in. "If you don't mind, though," she said as he hitched up his pants and turned to head back to his vehicle. "I would like to walk out to the cemetery before I leave. It is a cemetery, isn't it?"

"It is. From the Moore family that once lived here."

"I won't stay too long, I promise. And then I'll be gone."

"I guess that will be all right." He started walking and she fell into step to the right of him.

"You have a good evening," he told her when he reached his door.

"You too," she replied. "And take care."

She followed the old driveway as far as she could, then cut through the tall grass to get to the path. She paused and looked over her shoulder. The young deputy was still sitting there in his car. Waiting on her? Worried for her?

Turning back, she pushed through the undergrowth and stepped onto the trail that had been worn into the ground by generations of feet as they buried and then visited their loved ones.

Most of the vegetation had died or gone dormant this late in the winter, making the way relatively easy to navigate. As she moved along, theories and possible explanations for the framed photo she'd found went off like flashbulbs in her mind before instantly being rejected.

She could see the cemetery now, tall stones rising above wrought-iron pickets covered in vines. She sensed that Cheyenne had been there as she approached, leaves crunching underneath her boots. If Cheyenne knew about it, she definitely would have checked it out.

Feeling a sense of quiet reverence, she passed between the iron posts and entered the old burial ground.

Stepping through the tallish grass between the plots, she moved inward and started along the first row.

And there she found her.

CHEYENNE TANNER MOORE. BELOVED WIFE AND MOTHER. DIED MARCH 15, 1944. With no birth date given.

Any lingering doubt she might have had after this was dispelled by the headstone just past it.

The name on it was JILLIAN IANA PALMER.

Jillian for her, which Cheyenne knew Jill was short for, and Iana for Cheyenne's lost little boy, Ian, who hadn't survived. Tears filled her eyes as she stared down at the grave of Cheyenne's daughter, who had died at the age of eighty-eight, four years after her husband going by the inscription on the other side of the headstone.

She stayed there by little Jill Iana, as she pictured her, and then by Cheyenne's final resting place again for a bit. Then she stepped over to read the engraving on the stone beside her. AUGUSTUS MOORE. BORN MARCH 3, 1854 and DIED MAY 1, 1945. *The grave of the handsome, beaming man in the photograph,* she thought.

She did some calculations in her head. Augustus would have been ninety-one when he died the year after Cheyenne. And in the photo he had looked fairly young. Even if he had been as old as forty then, that would mean it had been taken somewhere around the year ... 1894, 1895? Which would mean Cheyenne had died at around the age of 85. After nearly a half a century with him.

Eventually, she turned and wove her way back through the cemetery. Sometime between passing between the iron posts again and starting down the path, she began to notice a strange sensation. A few paces on, she recognized what it was.

She was feeling a sense of relief. And peace.

Smiling softly, she thought of the photo again as she reached the end of the path:

Each of them grinning broadly, and there in the front row, Cheyenne in a decadent gown looking the merriest of them all.

Author's Note

In taking full advantage of a novelist's prerogative to embellish and tweak certain facts to suit a story, I did loosely base the character Clara on an actual person I discovered while researching the origins of Blues music. The real Clara Smith, billed as the "Queen of the Moaners," was born in 1894 and lived in the city of Spartanburg, not too far from my hometown, and did strike out on the vaudeville circuit. She wasn't as well known as some of her contemporaries such as Bessie Smith, who was no relation, but still managed to achieve great success across the Southern states, performing and then headlining at major theatres before beginning to record with Columbia Records. If you've never heard her, give her a listen.

Sharon Mikeworth
Piedmont, SC